"Move to intercept!"

As swiftly as they had formed up, the pixies ran off in all different directions, mostly eluding the disorganized mob that swung at them. In the confusion, they mainly hit one another. Lasset dipped under meaty arms and around thick backs, making toward the werewolf.

Picket and Nonni, his shield-sister, intercepted the beast on the garden walk, ten yards from the door. They brandished silver salad forks. The cutlery had been extracted at great personal risk from Trehinnick's parlor by a foraging party of pixies as soon as they knew the nature of the threat. The old man hadn't touched it since his wife had died, ten years before. He never knew any of the set was missing, but it had been necessary to remove it to make weapons to save his life. Picket stabbed up at the wolf's throat. The tines brushed its cheek. The fur crackled and burned.

Angrily, the werewolf snapped at Picket. While it was distracted, Nonni feinted with her fork. She was quicker than the moon-touched wolf. She actually managed to get the tines tangled in the fur on the back of his paw before he snatched it away. Picket was more successful on his second try. He jabbed the wolf in the shoulder. The wolf howled in pain. Lasset was grimly satisfied. By then, he and six more pixies had caught up.

They stabbed at the beast's suddenly exposed right side, jabbing him with butter knives. No mortal steel or iron could penetrate the cursed hide, but sacred silver laid open gaping black wounds in the hairy hide. The wolf howled again. He rose to his hind legs. Unlike a true wolf, he could fight on two legs as readily as on four. The pain inflicted by the silver distracted him. . . .

—from the "The Battle for Trehinnick's Garden"
by Jody Lynn Nye

Also Available from DAW Books:

Mystery Date, **edited by Denise Little**
First dates—the worst possible times in your life or the opening steps on the path to a wonderful new future? What happens when someone you have never met before turns out not to be who or what he or she claims to be? It's just a date, what could go wrong? Here are seventeen encounters, from authors such as Kristine Katherine Rusch, Nancy Springer, Laura Resnick, and Jody Lynn Nye that answer these questions. From a childhood board game called "Blind Date" that seems to come shockingly true . . . to a mythological answer to Internet predators . . . to a woman cursed to see the truth about her dates when she imbibes a little wine . . . to an enchanting translator bent on avenging victims of war crimes . . . to a young man hearing a very special voice from an unplugged stereo system . . . these are just some of the tales that may lead to happily ever after—or no ever after at all. . . .

Fellowship Fantastic, **edited by**
Martin H. Greenberg and Kerrie Hughes
The true strength of a story lies in its characters and in both the ties that bind them together and the events that drive them apart. Perhaps the most famous example of this in fantasy is *The Fellowship of The Ring.* But such fellowships are key to many fantasy and science fiction stories.
  Now thirteen top tale-spinners—Nina Kiriki Hoffmann, Alan Dean Foster, Russell Davis, and Alexander Potter, among others—offer their own unique looks at fellowships from: a girl who finds her best friend through a portal to another world . . . to four special families linked by blood and magical talent . . . to two youths ripped away from all they know and faced with a terrifying fate that they can only survive together . . . to a man who must pay the price for leaving his childhood comrade to face death alone. . . .

The Future We Wish We Had, **edited by**
Martin H. Greenberg and Rebecca Lickiss
In the opening decade of the twenty-first century, many things which were predicted in the science fiction stories of the twentieth century have become an accepted part of everyday life. Many other possibilities have not yet been realized but hopefully will be one day. For everyone who thought that by now they'd be motoring along the skyways in a personal jet car, or who assumed we'd have established bases on the Moon and Mars, or that we would have conquered disease, slowed the aging process to a crawl, eliminated war, social injustice, and economic inequity, here are sixteen stories of futures that might someday be ours or our children's, from Esther Friesner, Sarah Hoyt, Kevin J. Anderson, Irene Radord, Dave Freer, and Dean Wesley Smith.

FRONT LINES

EDITED BY
DENISE LITTLE

DAW BOOKS, INC.
DONALD A. WOLLHEIM, FOUNDER
375 Hudson Street, New York, NY 10014

ELIZABETH R. WOLLHEIM
SHEILA E. GILBERT
PUBLISHERS
http://www.dawbooks.com

First Printing, May 2008
1 2 3 4 5 6 7 8 9

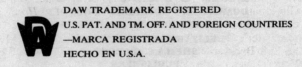

ACKNOWLEDGMENTS

ACKNOWLEDGMENTS

Introduction copyright © 2008 by Denise Little.

"The Observer" copyright © 2008 by Kristine Kathryn Rusch.

"Mr. Wel, Phi, I" Million Dollars and a Slipper" copyright © 2008 by Ray Street.

"Whatever" copyright © 2008 by Charles P. York.

"Same Bottle" copyright © 2008 by K. D. Wentworth.

"Fairy-tale Endings in Unmarketable Seasons" copyright © 2008 by Donna A. S. Sinclair.

"Manufacturing Miracles" copyright © 2008 by Louise Marley.

"The First Casualty" copyright © 2008 by Kristin Ward.

"Bloody Footprints in the Snow" copyright © 2008 by Jean Rabe.

"Cull of War" copyright © 2008 by Josepha Sherman.

"Home" copyright © 2008 by Donald J. Bingle.

"The Battle for Technimous Oaks II" copyright © 2008 by Fran Lavad Atur.

"Will, Open Hand" copyright © 2008 by Michelle Simmons.

"Pomander Small" copyright © 2008 by Jim Fiscus.

"Honor in a Thin Season" copyright © 2008 by Dean Wesley Smith.

"Shake" copyright © 2008 by M. Turville Heitz.

"Autumn at the Apothecary" copyright © 2008 by Lisa Silverthorne.

"In Thought" copyright © 2008 by Peter Orullian.

"Theodora Carson" copyright © 2008 by Melissa Mia Hall.

"Free at the Falcon" copyright © 2008 by Jean Bangor.

Certain characters depicted in "Temptation from The Wizard of " reused by permission of their copyrights © 1970.

"In Denial-Undoing" copyright © 2008 by Nina Kiriki Hoffman.

"The Last Backyard Defender" copyright © 2008 by J. Steven York.

CONTENTS

INTRODUCTION

Denise Little

THIS book is a tiny glimpse into what it means to be in the front lines of a battle zone—in all kinds of battle zones, whether human, alien, pixie, or toy. The title and the idea for the book came to me when I was watching CNN. The story was being told by a reporter embedded on the front lines with a group of soldiers in the thick of a nasty battle in Fallujah. I thought about how surreal it was for me to be sitting comfortably in my living room in America, while my mind and heart were with that bunch of guys getting shot at on the screen. What I felt for them had absolutely nothing to do with my opinions about the big political picture, or what was going in Washington and Iraq's Green Zone. It was something much more powerful. I wanted those boys, so brave and stalwart in the face of enemy fire, to survive and to get back to safety. I wondered if I could ever understand what it would be like to live the way they do, in the thick of battle where even the simplest of actions, from a drive down the road to a visit to the mess hall, might mean confronting death head-on. And if I understood, would it change the way I lived my life?

I had no answer to that question. I just knew I wanted the guys on the front lines to make it. And I knew all too well that there was nothing I could do on my living room couch to protect them.

My family has a long history of military service, complete with scars and missing body parts. Most recently, my brother spent over a decade as an officer in the Marines, including two years on the ground as a Forward Air Commander, or FAC, working alongside the grunts to call in strikes from close air support (he's a pilot). His summation of the experience: I love the Marines, even when I'm getting shot at. Getting shot at wasn't all he faced. In the course of his service he was also nearly drowned, frozen, lamed, and starved, depending on where he was stationed and what the military situation was there. He doesn't talk much about the rough times, but he saw plenty of them.

At one point he was in Albania for months. The country had essentially fallen apart and had been looted after the collapse of what amounted to a national pyramid scheme. My brother frequently got shot at while defending landing zones, but that wasn't the worst of it, according to him and the guys stationed with him. The guys in his MEU (Marine Expeditionary Unit) were living on MREs (Meals-Ready-To-Eat) for MONTHS (no acronym—just an emphasized time measure). What little food there was in the country was being air-dropped in by the UN and international charities until the situation stabilized. Meanwhile, the military was taking care of its own. Which meant MREs—lots of them. And nothing else.

I've eaten MREs. They have a number of things going for them, especially if you need indestructible food and are short on plumbing facilities. The military has spent billions on making them the best that they can be. But after a few days, they get very, very hard to stomach. So I got worried about my brother and his friends.

I'm nothing if not hands-on when I tackle something I'm worried about, so I started sending care packages once a week. Not just a few homemade cookies, but every kind of taste-of-home food that I could think of that could endure container shipping. Nacho kits, Jordan almonds, dried fruits, Tang, Rice Krispie treats, mixed nuts, you name it. If it would survive a sea voyage, and it was tasty, I sent it. I figured that the mail wouldn't be a problem, given that Albania was in Europe, and the situation, while tense, wasn't an out-and-out war.

I was wrong.

Unbeknownst to me, this backlog of food was clogging up military shipping in the European theater. Things were more than tense in Albania, and it was a *big deal* to get the mail to the troops—it took multiple birds in the air to provide cover for the cargo planes and choppers, armed forces to secure and hold the landing zone, and so on. So the packages sat. And sat. For months. The pile just kept getting bigger as new boxes arrived once a week. And that's how matters stayed until a general inspecting the mail facility noticed the massive pile of cartons I'd sent and asked what they were. Mail to some Marine, he was told. He instructed the mail guys to get off their duffs and get those boxes to the troops. About two month's worth of food for a family of four was loaded up on a helicopter (by that time I'd mailed enough food to completely fill it) and dropped into a war zone at a probable cost to taxpayers that I don't even want to contemplate. (My brother estimates a quarter million bucks. My reply: Ooops.)

Mail call the day those boxes arrived in Tirana became a Marine legend. Like Christmas, only more so. My brother shared, of course. He said opening the boxes and passing out the goods was like watching clouds of locusts descend, although, this being the Marines, they were organized locusts. Distribution was handled with military efficiency. Every American soldier on the front lines in Albania ate real food from home that day, after months of MREs. The guys who could got together and had a feast. (The nacho kits were a particular hit. But I pity the guys who ended up with the organic veggie crisps.)

I got heartfelt thank you notes from all kinds of folks. They made me cry. (It was such a little thing in comparison. I sent food. They put their lives on the line.) The notes weren't all I got—the MEU took up a collection to send me a "thank you" present in return. Given that

Albania was a looted no-man's land at the time, shopping opportunities were limited. I ended up with a red sweat suit that proudly proclaimed "American Embassy, Tirana, Albania." I guarantee I'm the only person in Green Bay who has one of those.

Military types abound in my family tree, which means there are always interesting stories to tell when the family gets together, though there are also some equally interesting side effects displayed by the people who've been on the front lines. A cousin who did two tours in Vietnam still dives under the nearest table when he hears firecrackers. I've got an uncle who describes gardening as "terrain readjustment." He says he learned his earth-moving skills on a larger scale during WWII, and he has the medals to prove it.

When I learned about war in school, it was always from the top view down. How Washington led the troops at Bunker Hill. How Eisenhower and the Allies fought WWII. How the Napoleonic Wars changed Europe. But the stuff I learned in school seemed to have little to do with the things I heard from the soldiers I knew. The tales they told about being in battle had nothing to do with the big picture and everything to do with the guys they served with. Those stories gave me a tiny taste of what it's like to be in a war zone on the front lines.

That disconnect from the larger picture of warfare, the way a general sees a war versus the way a person with boots on the ground sees it, struck me as something worth exploring. One is political, the other is personal. A first-hand view of battle is chaotic, intense, emotional, and seems to have little to do with strategic goals and everything to do with simple survival.

So this book isn't about the big picture, or what it means as a society to fight a war. Instead, it's all about the life of the people on the front lines of battle, in every kind of scenario imaginable. The stories in this collection range from epic intergalactic struggles for the future of man to the microcosm of a single abandoned toy soldier in some boy's back yard. Some are funny, some touching, some tragic.

Front lines are present in the most amazing places. I learned a lot putting this anthology together. I hope you enjoy the voyage as well.

THE OBSERVER

Kristine Kathryn Rusch

A<small>ND SO</small> we went in.

Combat formation, all five of us, me first, face masks on so tight that the edges of our eyes pulled, suits like a second skin. Weapons in both hands, backups attached to the wrists and forearms, flashbangs on our hips.

No shielding, no vehicles, no nothing. Just us, dosed, altered, ready to go.

I wanted to rip something's head off, and I did, the fury burning in me like lust. The weapons became tools—I wanted up close, and I got it, fingers in eyes, fists around tentacles, poking, pulling, yanking—

They bled brown, like soda. Like coffee. Like weak tea.

And they screamed—or at least I think they did.

Or maybe that was just me.

The commanders pulled us out before we could turn on each other, gave us calming drugs, put us back in our chambers for sleep. But we couldn't sleep.

The adrenaline didn't stop.

Neither did the fury.

Monica banged her head against the wall until she crushed her own skull.

LaTrice shot up her entire chamber with a backup she'd hidden between her legs. She took out two MPs and both team members in the chambers beside her be-

6

fore the commander filled the air with some kind of narcotic to wipe her out.

And me. I kept ripping and gouging and pulling and yanking until my fingertips were bone. By then, I hit the circuits inside the door and fried myself.

And woke up here, strapped down against a cold metal bed with no bedclothes. The walls are some kind of brushed steel. I can see my own reflection, blurry, pale skinned, wild eyed.

I don't look like a woman, and I certainly don't look like me.

And you well know, Doc, that if you unstrap me, I'll kill the thing reflected in that brushed metal wall.

After I finish with you.

You ask how it feels, and you know you'll get an answer because of that chip you put in my head.

I can feel it, you know, itching. If I close my eyes, I can picture it, like a gnat, floating in gray matter.

Free my hands, and I'll get it out myself.

Free my hands, and I'll get us all out of here.

How does it feel?

By it, I assume you mean me. I assume you mean whatever's left of me.

Here's how it feels:

There are three parts to me now. The old, remembered part, which doesn't have a voice. It stands back and watches, appalled, at everything that happens, everything I do.

I can see her too—that remembered part—gangly young woman with athletic prowess and no money. She stands behind the rest of us, wearing the same clothes she wore to the recruiter's that day—pants with a permanent crease, her best blouse, long hair pulled away from her horsy face.

There are dreams in her eyes—or there were then. Now they're cloudy, disillusioned, lost.

If you'd just given her the money, let her get her education first, she'd be an officer or an engineer or a goddamn tech soldier.

But you gave her that test—biological predisposition, aggression, sensitivity to certain hormones. You gave her the test and found it wasn't just the physical that had made her a good athlete.

It wasn't just the physical.

It was the aggression and the way that minute alterations enhanced it.

Aggression, a strong predisposition, and extreme sensitivity.

Which, after injections and genetic manipulation, turned her into us.

I'm the articulate one. I'm an observer too, someone who stores information and can process it faster than the fastest computer. I'm supposed to govern the reflexes, but they gave me a blocker for that the minute I arrived back on ship, then made it permanent when they got me to base.

I can see, Doc; I can hear; I can even tell you what's going on, and why.

I just can't stop it, any more than you can.

I know I said three, and yet I didn't mention the third. I couldn't think of her, not and think of the Remembered One at the same time.

I'm not supposed to feel, Doc, yet the Remembered One, she makes me sad.

The third. Oh, yeah. The third.

She's got control of the physical, but you know that. You see her every day. She's the one who raises the arms, who clenches the bandaged and useless fingers, who kicks at the restraints holding the feet.

She's the one who growls and makes it impossible for me to talk to you.

You know that, or you wouldn't have used the chip.

An animal?

She's not an animal. Animals create small societies. They have customs and instinctual habits. They live in prides or pods or tribes.

She's a thing. Inarticulate. Violent. Useless.

And by giving her control of the physical, you made the rest of us useless, trapped inside, destined to watch until she works herself free.

If she decides to bash her head against the wall until she crushes her own skull or to rip through the steel, breaking every single bone she has, if she decides to impale herself on the bedframe, I'll cheer her on.

Not just for me.

But for the Remembered One, the one with hopes and dreams and a future she squandered when she reached for the stars.

The one who got us here but who can't ever get us out.

So, you say I'm unusual. How nice for me. The ones who separate usually kill themselves before the MPs ever get into the chamber. The others, the ones who integrate with their thing, get reused.

You think that the women I trained with—the ones not in my unit, the ones who didn't die when we got back—you think they're still out there, fighting an enemy we don't entirely understand.

I think you're naïve.

But you're preparing a study, something for the government so that they'll know this experiment is failing. Not the chip-in-the-brain thing that allows you to communicate with me, but the girl soldiers, the footsoldiers, the grunts on the ground.

And if they listen (ha!), they'll listen because of people like me.

Okay. I'll buy into your pipe dreams.

Here's what everyone on Earth believes:

We don't even know their names. We call them The Others, but that's only for clarity purposes. There are names—Squids, ETs—but none of them seem to stick.

They have ships in much of the solar system, so we're told, but we're going to prevent them from getting the Moon. The Moon is the last bastion before they reach Earth.

That's about it. No one cares unless they have a kid up there, and even then, they don't really care unless the kid is a grunt, like I was.

Only they don't know the kid's a grunt. Not until the kid comes home from a tour, if the kid comes home.

Here's what I learned in our ship: most of the guys never came home. That's when the commanders started the hormonal/genetic thing, the thing that tapped into the maternal instinct. Apparently the female of the species has a ferocious need to protect her young.

It can be—it is—tapped, and in some of us, it's powerful, and we become strong.

Mostly, though, no one gets near the ground. The battle is engaged in the blackness of space. It's like the video games our grandparents played, which some say— and I never believed until now—were used to train the kids for some kind of future war.

The kind we're fighting now.

What I learned after a few tours, before I ever had to go to ground, was that ground troops, foot soldiers, rarely returned. They have specific missions, mostly clearing an area, and they do it, and they mostly die.

A lot of us died that day—what I can remember of it.

Mostly I remember the fingers and the eyes and the tentacles (yes, they're real) and the pull of the face mask against my skin.

What I suspect is this: the troops the Others have on the ground aren't the enemy. They're some kind of captured race, foot soldiers just like us, fodder for the war machine. I think, if I concentrate real hard, I remember them working, putting chips in places, implanting stuff in the ground—growing things?—I'm not entirely clear.

And I wonder if the talk of an invasion force is just that, talk, and if this isn't something else, some kind of experiment in case we get into a real situation, something that'll become bigger.

Because I don't ever remember the Others fighting back.

If Squids can look surprised, these did.

All of them.

*   *   *

So that's my theory for what good it'll do.

There're still girls dying up there. Women, I guess, creatures, foot soldiers, whatever they want to create.

Then we come back, and we become *this*: Things.

Because we can't ever be the Remembered Ones. Not again.

But you know that.

You're studying as many of us as you can. That's clear too.

I'm not even sure you are a doc. Maybe you're a machine, getting these thoughts, processing them, using some modulated voice to ask the right questions, the ones that provoke these memories.

Since I've never seen you.

I never see anyone.

Except the ghosts of myself.

So what are you going to do with me? Reintegration isn't possible; that's been tried. (You think I don't remember? How do you think the Remembered One and I split off in the first place? Once there was just her and the thing. Now there's three of us, trapped in here—well, two trapped and one growling, but you know what I mean.)

Sending us back won't work. We might turn on our comrades. Or ourselves. (Probably ourselves.)

Sending us home is out of the question, even if we had a home. The Remembered One does, but she's so far away, she'll never reintegrate.

Let me tell you what I think you should do. I think you should remove the chip. Move me to a new location. Pretend you've never interviewed me.

Then you'd just be faced with the Thing.

And the Thing should be put out of its misery.

We should be put out of its misery.

Monica and LaTrice weren't wrong, Doc. They were just crude. They used what methods they had at their disposal.

They were proactive.

I can't be. You've got all three of us bound up here.
Let us go.
Send us back, all by ourselves. No team, no combat
formation. Hell, not even any weapons.
Let us die.
It's the only humane thing to do.

THE WAR, ME,
17 MILLION DOLLARS
AND A STRIPPER

Dave Freer

"My father said I should ask you for advice, sir."
I looked at the green kid that had just been
sent up to replace Johnson. If they conscripted them any
younger boot camp was going to need diaper changing
tables. I kept hoping they'd run out of men and send
women. But apparently the colonial authorities were
deeply worried about what that would do to discipline
and that it would cause heroics. Likely! And they fussed
about separate bathroom facilities. That part was good
for a bloody laugh anyway. Pronger reckoned that the
Governor-General owned shares in the cathouses in Colorado City, and had to protect his profits somehow.

"First piece of advice," I said. "Sir is for Orificers,
sonny. It's Corporal."

"Second piece of advice," said Lance-Corporal Pronger O'Grady, looking at the cards on the makeshift
table, also known as a piece of broken plank. "Don't
play one-up with this bastard." He looked at his watch.
Folded his cards, gathered them up and put them in his
waterproof tin. "I'm due on watch at oh seventeen hundred. Anyway, I want to get out while I'm losing." He
stood up, and nearly knocked his brains out on the roof
of the Casino Royale. You'd think that by now he'd have
learned how high the bunker roof was. But then he
hasn't learned not to play cards with me either.

"I meant about fighting the Slimach, S . . . uh, Corporal." said the kid. "I've heard lots of war stories . . ."

I looked at him. Tall, gawky kid, too young to really need to shave. Big Adam's apple. Skinny, suntanned face, battledress without mud and with, mark you, ironed creases. About a ten-second survival time when the Slimeballs hit us again. He stood to attention in front of me, that's how bad it was. I sighed. "Got any chocolate?" I asked.

He nodded. "Yes, Corporal. My mother . . ."

"Second piece of advice," I said, sticking out my hand. "Don't ever admit that you've got food, smokes or alcohol. I'll have a piece, for teaching you that."

Pronger laughed. "Bet that wasn't in your war stories, Private Tarvin."

The kid fished a bar of Strudberg out of his ammo pouch. He wasn't quite that green. I saw that he had a book in there too. And Strudberg wasn't issue cardboard chocolate either. Mummy must love him a lot. "No, Corporal," he said offering the entire bar to Pronger.

Pronger shook his head. Sighed. Broke off two squares and handed it back to him. "Under no circumstances do you play cards with Corporal Kenso, Tarvin. You're too trusting and I don't want you to die owing him millions. You break off a piece and give it to him. Never give him the whole bar. And that wasn't in your war stories either."

The kid could learn. He carefully broke off a square and offered it to me. "No, Corporal it wasn't," he admitted. "I met a man who killed five of the Slimach with his bare hands, though."

We both laughed at that. You can't even shoot the damn Slimeballs dead, unless you get lucky. Their chitin-fullerine hides are just too tough. You ever hear some guy sounding off about the fighting and the glory, how he personally killed sixteen Slimeballs with his bare hands, and you know the bastard's a clerk that's never been closer to combat than a hundred miles from the front. That he's never been face down in the mud in a trench while the Slimeball's artillery softens up the hillside . . .

and prayed it would end . . . and prayed that it wouldn't.
No real soldier really wants to talk about it much. Or
even think about it. Maybe that's why I never remember
it too well. I savored the chocolate. It didn't come my
way too often. "Of course war stories leave out quite a
lot, Private."

"Yeah," said Pronger. "The good bits. You know: the
mud. The rats. The trots from the grub. The boredom."

I nodded, although the kid didn't understand yet. He
would if he was still alive in a few weeks time. He'd get
used to us too. Being scared half shitless most of the
time tends to make us a bit strange here on the front
lines. Pronger was right as usual. Being scared half shitless and bored is great compared to being scared totally
shitless and not bored. "Bored is good. You can learn
to play cards. It beats fighting Slimies."

Pronger took a quick look outside the piece of rotten
blanket that makes the Casino Royale's door. He smiled.
"Looks like rain."

The kid nodded. "There is a cold front coming
through."

Pronger beamed beatifically. "That's another good bit
I'll bet they didn't tell you about. Keeping watch in the
dark in the pissing rain with sleet going down your neck.
It's the best."

The kid looked at Pronger as if he were tearing up his
superman posters.

I sighed. I'd eaten the boy's chocolate, and maybe I
owed his mum something. "The freezing rain is pretty
good because the Slimies don't like fighting in the rain.
The other good thing is the seventeen million dollars I've
won from Corporal O'Grady here. We play a lot between
assaults. If it rains, he stays alive to lose more to me.
You never volunteer for anything except guard duty in
the rain."

It was too much for the kid, straight out of the gung-
ho they force-feed them in boot camp. "Don't you want
to fight the Slimach, Corporal? They're coming to destroy our homes, our families. Our colony! There is glory
to be won!" There was just a faint sneer in his voice.

Pronger and I just looked at him. After a minute or so Pronger shrugged. "Tell me about it once you've seen your buddies die in the next assault," he said quietly. "Son," and Pronger must have been at least, oh . . . two earth-years older than the boy, "Forget all that crap you've been told about glory and honor and killing lots of Slimes. Forget what you've seen on the newscasts or maybe heard from some loudmouth in the bar. Your daddy told you to talk to the NCOs, right? To learn from us?"

The kid nodded. "I thought you'd tell me the best ways to kill Slimach . . . uh, Slimes. Not how to be a coward," he added defiantly.

"Your daddy is a wise man, so I'll ignore that," I said putting a block of fuel into the burner. "Tea before you go, Prong?"

He looked at his watch. Nodded. "As you're offering, Smash." He looked at the kid again. "They drilled you good in boot," he said. "There are no easy secret recipes to fighting Slimes. What they don't tell you is that the bastard things just don't stop, and they don't die either. And you can't run away from them because they're faster than us. And Corporal Kenso here is an eighteen-month vet. There are damn few of those. You treat him with respect."

That was true enough too. Other than the survivors of the first Slimeball war, thirty years back, it kind of made me an old man around here. Sometimes I forget I'd be nearly twenty-two years old if Deneth's World didn't have a thirty-three year rotation. The kids make me feel old. And I still don't know exactly why I've survived. Maybe I'm faster or stronger than the average conscript. I'm sure as hell not as dumb, but that ain't hard. I don't do discipline too well, which is why I'm a corporal—for the third time. Prong is on his way up for the second time. He got to sergeant last time before he put a captain from the Signal Corps in hospital after a fight over some girl. The way I heard it was that the captain wasn't too impressed that the fluff preferred some NCO to him. I put a pannikin of water on the burner. Chasing women between tours might just kill Pronger, if the Slimes didn't first. Pronger's brains stopped working when he saw the opposite sex.

The new kid was looking at me with big eyes. Even he realized that eighteen months on the front was a long time. The last war only lasted three years, and this one was getting close to that. I knew that unless we hit a miracle like last time, this one wasn't going to end in our winning. I sighed. "Look, kid. All I can tell you is to keep down when we've got incoming and to stick with the concentrated fire drills. You can't hit the joints as easily as they tell you."

Pronger nodded. "And they still don't die, even if you knock all the legs off. They take a long time to bleed to death." He tossed some of my tea in the pannikin. We both like it to stew a bit. "So did they get you straight out of school, kid? Or did you get a life first?"

"I had a job for a few months," said the kid.

"So what did you do?" I said. He was suntanned. Looked like he worked outside.

"I was a stripper."

His reply nearly made Pronger drop the pannikin. I could see the stupid half-grin on the kid's face, but he'd kept his voice pretty even. Prong turned around and gaped at the kid, who was trying to keep a straight face again. Even in a gay bar for the blind the kid wouldn't cut it, never mind at Prong's favorite hangouts. "Ah, go on!"

"It's true!" said the kid. "I spent three months stripping."

"Yeah? Where?" said Prong.

"South East Aquaculture, Corporal," said the kid, nearly falling apart. "Stripping the eggs out of fish." I guess no one explained to him that you don't take the piss out of your NCOs, but lucky for him Pronger thought it was pretty funny too. "My dad's a reproductive biologist there. We breed sea trout."

"I guess everyone's dad's a reproductive biologist," I said, rescuing the tea, impressed despite myself. I hadn't had much to do with the sea, other than a holiday at the coast once. They'd kept a quarter acre strip of beach free of sandlice, and me and seven hundred other kids played on it. The sea here on Deneth's World had nothing much in the way of stuff we humans could eat, just little water-roachy critters, most of which was either tiny or didn't taste too good. I'd eaten some farmed fish though, before the war. It was pretty pricy stuff.

The bit about his pa being a reproductive biologist was a shock to the kid though. Maybe he never thought about it before, but his ears went red. I'd bet, stripper or not, his knowledge of girls was probably theoretical. If he lived till we got to R&R I'd have to see that he went off with Pronger for some education.

And just then it all became academic, because the Slimes hit us with everything they had and then some extra. They must have been building up to it for months. Nobody knows quite what makes the Slimeballs tick—heck, the first settlers didn't even know that they were there for twenty-five years. They came up from underground in the central desert and started moving in on the farmland. When the farmers and then the police tried to do something about it . . . it kind of escalated pretty damn quick. The farmers thought they were dumb animals at first. But it seems as if they just liked to kill things and eat everything themselves, because they had artillary and explosives to blow obstructions to pieces. The first war the Slimes pretty well pushed humans off the continent and into the sea. They overran nearly everything but Colorado City. And then they started dropping dead along the edge of the ocean. Some of them died retreating. My old man said the stink was something incredible. Nobody knows exactly why, but maybe eating human livestock and human crops did them in. Just after the war the colonists had been too damn busy surviving to worry about why. I guess we should have. But it was not something I did a lot of thinking about for the next hour. Somewhere in that madness we lost the bunker roof. Slime long-range artillery leaves ours cold. Any decent size target is toast. Tanks proved a disaster. And they cooked what air force we'd managed to build. Hey, we're an ag colony world. My history teacher said they had more manufacturing capability in 1850 on Earth than we do now. The experts talk about explosive shells for our hand weapons, but we're still using pump-action shotguns. It's not much against a Slime, but they work better than rifles. Anyway, they talk a lot of shite. We never captured a Slime. They don't even let us hang onto the bodies. The damn things eat them.

When the barrage stopped, I knew that they were coming. And the incredible thing was that the three of us were alive. Me and Pronger pulled the kid upright. Picked up our weapons and staggered out into the trench.

Or we would have, if there'd been a trench. It must have copped a few direct hits. Green's head looked out me from a pile of rubble. It wasn't attached to the rest of him.

"Hole up in the bunker!" I yelled. They were coming. Glistening bodies in the late afternoon sun—rank upon rank of them. The minefields had been pretty much nullified by the pounding we'd taken. The Slimies came scurrying forward. One of them found a mine that had somehow made it through the bombardment. The kid loosed off a shot.

"Hold you fire until they're right on top of us," snapped Pronger. Not that it was going to make any difference . . . but that was what we'd been trained to do. When they were just short of us, a heavy machine gun began hosing them from further up the line. Three-four hundred yards. Most of the Slimes are about the size of a bull—and that's if you don't include the legs. Four legs with claws and four with hooks for walking on. Their shells can take a direct hit from about twenty yards without cracking, and even if you knock a few limbs off, they just keep coming on what's left. It usually takes at least ten men with pump-action shotguns to take out one of them. And usually not all of the ten make it through the experience, because they have to be close.

When the Gatling gun cut loose, it gave us an odd sort of break. There had been at least twenty of the Slimes heading for us. Now they all headed for the Gatling nest. Except for the one that was having trouble keeping up with its buddies. It might have been the one that hit the mine earlier. It was short a couple of legs and was leaking ichor. But it made up for being slow by being goddamn big. It was a giant among Slimeballs. And it had our number.

I heard tell that in the first war someone shot a Slime with an antique Holland and Holland fifty-caliber elephant gun, and it still killed him. The jury is still out on dumdum solids and buck shot. Enough dumdums in the body and they do die. But "enough'" is a lot, and they keep killing while they die. Buckshot into the joints and you can knock the bastard things down. Enough men with cool heads can stop them most of the time. Our regiment mixes the two. If a private can hit a barn door from inside, he has buckshot. Otherwise, they figure no one can miss a Slime's body with a solid slug. Not once they're close enough to shoot at. One thing about the Stripper: Either he was so frightened that he took orders, or maybe he just took orders. He waited until Pronger and I started shooting before he fired again. Prong or the kid must have got the joint because it fell over sideways. It only had one leg on that side, anyway, after its brush with the mine. Not that that stopped a Slimeball. I got a claw. And took aim at the legs with my third or fourth shot. I lose count, and it always happens so fast.

It still kept coming, dragging itself over the torn earth.

It was down to one leg and two claws now, but it was expanding out of its ball shape so it could drop on us. We just kept shooting. I saw a claw fall and spear Pronger's foot, slicing his leg as it fell past. He screamed. And I was out of ammo. . . . I had gotten through twelve shots, and there was no time to reload. It fell onto us, the remaining claw spearing down . . . It must have been half dead, because somehow either it missed me or I got out the way. Fell over. Which is why I didn't get hit on the head by a falling Slime.

I was stuck in the dark under a Slimeball in what was left of the Casino Royale. It was leaking ichor onto me. I could hear Pronger moan and swear. No sound from the kid. He'd probably bought it. And there was a horrible noise—something scraping and digging. The damned thing had one leg left, and it was still trying to kill us. I'd seen someone gutted by one of those hooks . . . A bayonet was the stupidest goddamned thing that they issued us with, but it was all I had right now. My weapon was somewhere in the darkness. Empty. I felt along the slick greasy body. My mind wasn't quite with the rest of my head, because I was thinking how weird it was that the critters got named from remains that the colonial surveyor xenobiologist found on the beach. Dr Slimach thought that the damn things were extinct. So they were called Slimies because of him. Not because they were.

I found the joint. The scrabble-scrabble was closer now. Prong moaned as I felt and thrust up. Got nowhere. I sawed at it. I might as well have tried to cut down a tree with nail scissors. But the Slimeball felt it. The joint twitched and damn near took my hand off at the wrist with one hard edge. Only the bayonet saved my hand. And the Slimeball did what I could not. It forced the blade in through the joint with its own twitch. Ichor ran down my arm as it pulled away. I found the butt of the bayonet and pushed with all the strength I had and wiggled the blade as much as I could. I nearly lost my hand again as it thrashed about, and part of the leg must have knocked me out.

Next thing I remember, I had arrived in hell. I'd kind of figured that I had fair chance of going there, but I thought it would have more than one flame and wouldn't stink of Slimeball ichor. And I didn't think that the kid deserved to be there even if he was a stripper. "Corp," he whispered, "are you still alive?" He nearly set fire to my hair with that lighter.

"What kind of answer would you get out of a corpse?" I asked, rubbing the bump on my head. There was no sound of a scrabbling clawfoot.

"You've got to help me with the other corporal. Quickly!"

We crawled over to Pronger. He didn't look so good. His face was whiter than I had ever seen it. I took the fancy lighter the kid's papa must have bought him and had a look at my buddy. He groaned. "What hurts, Prong?"

"My foot, my leg, oh fu. . . . Arh . . ."

If we hadn't been dead—well as good as—and Prong in real pain and shock, I would have laughed. That claw must have missed the famous Prong by a ball-hair width. And he was bleeding like a stuck pig—but not one that had been hit in the femoral artery. It wasn't just women he was lucky with. His foot and ankle hadn't been quite so lucky. The claw had pinned his foot through boot, and then he'd fallen over.

He only screamed once when I pulled it out. It was the only way I could see to straighten the ankle. "Gimme your bayonet," I said to the kid, fishing in my spare ammo pouch and pulling out a candle stub. Why the hell I hadn't thought of it earlier I don't know. "I'm going to have to cut that boot off, and stop the bleeding. You see what you can do about some pressure on the cut."

He nodded. "Sure, Corp. Where is your bayonet?"

"Stuck inside the Slimeball's last leg joint," I said, taking his nice shiny, new-issue one, that hadn't been used to open tin cans.

I had cut half of Pronger's boot off before the kid stopped staring at me and started on some pressure bandaging.

Five minutes later we had old Pronger so that he was just in pain, not agony, and so that his blood wasn't polluting that nice Slimeball ichor that was half an inch deep on the floor. "What do we do now, Corporal?" asked the kid.

It wasn't an easy a question to answer. This much we've figured about our enemy—Slimies hunt by heat. They can see, but they also see body heat. And they move faster than we do, although when it comes to stamina, we have them licked. It made getting back to our own lines a big risk, especially as Pronger wasn't going to be running anywhere. I shrugged. "We dig out of here and make for the lines." It would depend on how far this push had taken them. Still, if we waited, the Slimies would dig in and find us. Now, in the chaos, was our only chance.

The reality of the situation had plainly gotten through to Pronger, too. He shook his head. "I'm never going to get out of here. Leave me, Smash. You and the kid go."

I had to hand to the kid. He said: "No way, Corporal," even before I got my mouth open.

I shook my head right back at Pronger. "You owe me seventeen million dollars, Prong. You're not going to get out of it so easily. Me and the Stripper will get you home. And don't you call him "kid" anymore. He's a man now."

That actually got a weak laugh out of Pronger. "I want a rematch. You mark the cards."

"I just use your marks," I said grinning at him. "Come on, Stripper. We'll leave my retirement money here while we go and look for a way out of the Casino."

Stripper and I took the candle and crawled away. He looked at the huge body above us. I mean the Casino Royale had been a pretty small hole, but even so this was a big corpse. A few tons.

"This is the first Slimer I've actually seen," he admitted. "I didn't know they unrolled."

"It doesn't happen that often. But I've seen it a couple of times," I said, pushing through some small round rocks. "But not this close up."

"They look like big sandlice," said the Stripper.

I hadn't thought of it, but unrolled like this they did. "Yeah. Where the hell did all these round stones come from? There are millions of the damned things."

There was a silence from my companion. Then he said in an odd voice—odd even for a seventeen-year-old trapped under the corpse of a Slimeball: "They're not stones, Corp. They're eggs."

"Eggs?" The eggs I knew came with bacon.

"Yeah," he said looking at one carefully. "I've stripped a couple of million out of fish. These are more like sandlouse eggs. We use those to feed the trout at swim-up. These are just like them, but a thousand times bigger."

"There are sure as hell enough." I grumbled as we pushed through them.

"Sure. The whole body cavity of a sandlouse is just solid eggs before they go to spawn. Might explain why shooting the Slimers in the body doesn't do much. You're just breaking eggs."

"Can't make a Slimy omelette without it. Come on. Let's go and dig out closer to Pronger. I'm not so keen on climbing out from under a Slimeball's ass."

We found an entrenching tool and got busy digging. I told Prong about the eggs. "I guess we stopped one of the bastard things breeding, eh?"

"Tch! " he clicked his tongue. "And they're not so proud about having women in the military. No wonder they fight better than us. They get a shag occasionally."

"Hey. They might only have women in the army," I said. Even talking rubbish was better than thinking about the trouble we were in.

"Explains why they're so desperate to get at me," grinned Pronger. "We finally got the reason for the war, boys. Us."

"That's how the sandlice work," said the Stripper.

"You mean that's why they bite you on the beach? Love bites?" I said. They'd been known to kill people, just by sheer numbers.

"They're only like that just before breeding," said the Stripper. "They spend months down in the sand, and noone even knows that they're there. What I mean is that you only have females in the sand. The males live in the sea. The trout love them."

"Someone has to, as the girls are on the beach. Ah. We're out." I pushed and pulled a few lumps of rubble and scrabbled some earth aside, and there was a hole we could squeeze through. It was dark up there.

We had some fun getting Pronger out, but we managed. We could see next to bugger all. But we knew where we were going. We just had to head for the explosions and hope that we didn't walk into any Slimeballs. I knew that we had not a snowflake's hope in hell, but we walked either side of Pronger anyway, helping him hop. In the dark the Slimeballs would see our heat before we saw them. After a while, we took it in turns to carry Pronger. We were getting closer to the fighting.

It was a long way. Thank goodness that the Stripper was a strong lad, and a good one. Too good to be going to die here, with me and Pronger. We shared his chocolate. And Prong's brandy, although he needed it more than both of us.

And then . . . it began to rain.

Not just rain but an icy solid downpour, the way it does at this season. The downside of a thirty-three year orbit is that we have a long, wet winter. About three earth years of it.

"Oh, shit. Like we needed this,"said the Stripper.

I grinned at him in the dark. Reached out and squeezed his arm. "Oh, yeah, boyo. We do. Almost as badly as we need this trench I nearly fell into."

"You found a trench?"

"Yeah. It'll be the one that leads back to the second line. And if we're in it, and good and cold and wet . . . well, we might just get home."

"Corp. My God," said the boy with a sob. "Really?"

"Maybe. But at least we get to stop walking through the minefield," I said, helping him down with his load. "I'll take Pronger for a bit."

We walked on in the cold and dark. "I have to get back to my father," he said, after a while.

"Tell him he gave you good advice." Pronger said, obviously between clenched teeth.

"I need to tell him why the Slimeballs are trying to get to the sea. He'll be able to tell someone. He's got contacts. He was in the first war . . ."

"Who's that!" A light stabbed out of the darkness.

"Corporals Kenso and O'Grady and Private Tarvin From line one. We could use a medic and some help," I sang out. I didn't care if my voice shook.

Three men piled over the sandbags and pushed through the tanglewire to us. One of them took Pronger. The second picked up the Stripper. The boy just folded up on us. Turned out he'd lost a fair amount of blood too, from a cut across his chest and bits of shrapnel he'd absorbed, but he hadn't said anything.

The third man—a lieutenant—looked at me. I guess I probably wasn't too pretty, covered in blood, mud and reeking of ichor. "Do you need some help, Corporal?"

I shook my head and looked at my companions, alive and being carried to safety. "No, sir. I got me a Stripper and seventeen million dollars. What else does a man need?"

And that is how a Stripper and my seventeen million dollars—that I've yet to see—won the war. Or at least gave us a solution. We let the Slimeballs through to the sea. Every thirty-three years they're gonna screw up everything in the corridors we channel them into. But standing between them and sea . . . well, like Pronger, they don't think of anything else when they want to get there, and they won't let anything stand in their way. Even losing half his foot hasn't changed O'Grady. The trout are eating lots of little Slimers, but that doesn't seem to worry them. The female Slimeball larvae swim upstream in the rivers and eat trout on their way to the desert, so maybe it is about quits.

Pronger knows lots of real strippers he keeps trying to introduce the two of us to. Me, I'm seeing the Stripper's older sister. She's decided we're getting married and having kids.

I guess the two species aren't that different, except cosmetically

But thank goodness for cosmetics.

TOUCHED

Christina F. York

MOLLIE gritted her teeth, and fought back tears. Around her men were dead and dying, life seeping out through their jagged wounds.

Worse, the battle still raged as she struggled to control her fear and concentrate on healing as many as she could reach. The acrid smoke of cannon choked her, and the clashing of swords and battle-axes rang in her head like the bells of a thousand churches.

She carried no weapons, only her healing potions, strung around her body in bags and pouches, like a peddler toting his wares. But her potions and powders were props that labeled her as a healer. Her power required no assistance.

She knelt beside Albert, a young man from her own village. Only a few weeks earlier, she had helped his wife through the birth of their first son. Now, pressed into service as a soldier by the village elders, by order of Lord Radulf, he was crumpled on the ground, his right leg bent at an impossible angle. Blood pulsed from a wide slash across his chest in time with the faltering beat of his heart.

Mollie placed her hands on his chest and closed her eyes, shutting out the sight of the other wounded men. She choked back her fear and focused her power on the man beside her.

His heart beat stronger, and she sensed the growing strength of the blood flowing in his veins. Beneath her hands, the wide gash narrowed, flesh growing together to contain muscle and sinew and blood. His leg slowly straightened as the bones aligned themselves and reunited.

She pulled her hands away. He would live. He would go home to his wife and baby son, who waited anxiously for his return.

Moving among the wounded, Mollie fought the growing tide of panic that threatened to engulf her as she mended rent flesh and healed shattered bones.

The horror that confronted her at every turn was overwhelming, the stench of burned flesh and spilled blood mixing with the dust and smoke into a gagging, nauseating cloud. An arrow flew past, inches from her chest. She stifled a scream of terror and focused on the next casualty.

This was her calling: to heal the sick and wounded, to mend bodies, ease suffering, and relieve pain. It was her gift, a gift that had revealed itself when she entered her teens, setting her apart from the other young men and women.

But nothing in her young life had prepared her for the tumult and agony of battle. She approached another mangled body but turned away. Even her power, strong as it was, could not raise the dead.

The battle raged through the heat of the day, until sundown obscured the field, and the armies withdrew into the darkness.

Those still able to walk helped their comrades back toward camp, leaving Mollie to move among the bodies, searching for survivors, for one more victim to heal.

She wandered across the field for hours in the dark. Her ears still ringing from the clashing of swords and roar of cannon, she strained to hear the faint cries of men too weak to do more than moan in their agony.

Her power was strong, and as she placed her hands on each of them, their wounds healed, their pain ebbed, and they were able to walk from the battlefield. Eventually, she was alone in the dark, surrounded by the bodies of those she had been too late to save.

Exhausted, her soul battered by the carnage she had witnessed, she dragged herself back toward the fires of the camp, searching for food and water and a few hours of fitful sleep. She knew the battle would resume with the dawn.

As she huddled beside a dying fire, a messenger approached. "Lord Radulf requests your presence in his tent," he said.

Mollie struggled wearily to her feet. The summons was a demand, not a request, and no amount of polite words would make it any less so.

She trudged behind the boy, following him through the flickering shadows cast by guttering campfires, until they reached the tent of Lord Radulf. The boy gestured toward the guard at the opening and melted into the darkness.

Silently, the guard drew aside the door and gestured for Mollie to enter.

Radulf sat on a simple stool, studying maps spread across a low table. Torches burned on either side of him, their wavering light casting grotesque shadows of the seated man and his advisors on the tent walls.

When Mollie approached, he glanced up from his maps, and nodded curtly. He waved a hand to indicate the half-circle of men who stood behind him. "I am told you served us well today. Many of our men live, thanks to you. For that, you deserve our gratitude."

She did not know the lord well; he was a distant and powerful figure among the villagers, a man who ruled many villages and demanded their fealty but lived in none of them.

"I do what I am called to do, my lord," she replied. Not knowing what else to say, she held her tongue, and waited.

Radulf returned to the study of his maps. "Your skills will be needed on the morrow, healer. Can we place our trust in you?" he asked, without looking up.

Mollie looked around the circle of faces and then back

at the top of the leader's head, still bent over his papers, before she answered. "The battlefield is a frightening place. But I will do all I can."

"I have seen her power, my lord," one of the advisors said. He was an elder in Mollie's village and knew first-hard of her healing abilities. "It will be enough." He looked at Mollie, "Your healing saved many lives today and will save many tomorrow. You do a great service to your people."

Mollie dipped her head. "Thank you, Elder Bok."

The old man nodded, and all the men returned their attention to the maps. Her dismissal was clear.

The ground was hard beneath her, and the cold seeped into her bones despite the heavy woolen cloak she wrapped around herself. Sleep came only in brief moments, interrupted by nightmares of the battle.

Still, she reminded herself as she woke from yet another image of choking and blood, her suffering was nothing compared to that of those around her or the men who had died. She consoled herself with the knowledge that she had saved many men, who would return to their families safe and whole.

Dawn was no more than a suggestion of rose and gold on the horizon when the camp began to stir. Mollie heard the rattle of swords in scabbards, the grunts of men as they rose from the hard ground. She smelled the stale beer and hard bread that served as breakfast and the stink of the latrines, carried on the cool morning wind.

Her stomach grumbled with hunger, then clenched into a tight ball when the bread reached it. She bit back the bile that rose in her throat and ignored her protesting stomach.

Mollie hurried along behind the men as they advanced on the enemy's position.

During the night, the smoke had cleared away, and she could see the ranks of opposing forces. Helmets glinted in the early morning light, and the heavy tramp of booted feet echoed across the still morning. As she watched, the two forces launched themselves at one another, meeting with a thunderous clash that shook the ground on which she stood.

The din rose into the air, startling birds from the surrounding trees. Cannons roared, and smoke once again filled the air, blanketing the field in an impenetrable gray cloud.

The battle raged for three days. By day, Mollie fought back her fear and healed every man she could reach, sending them back to camp mended and whole. By night, she wrestled with the cold and the nightmares that brought her awake with cries of terror dying in her throat. Through it all, she knew that her gift, her power, would see the soldiers safely home.

On the third day, Mollie ducked beneath a swinging ax-blade to reach a wounded man. The ax missed her by inches, but she barely noticed it. Her attention was riveted by the man who lay before her.

Albert.

She had thought him safe at home by now, regaining his strength alongside his beloved wife and infant son. Instead, he lay bleeding at her feet, his breath rattling in his chest as he struggled to draw air into a lung pierced by a sword.

Mollie threw herself down next to Albert and pressed her hands against the wounds. She concentrated, feeling the lung bind itself together and begin to hold the precious air.

Within minutes, Albert was healed, and Mollie moved to the next man. And the next. And the next.

But no matter how many men she healed, she could not forget the image of Albert. Was this all she had saved him for? What if she hadn't reached him in time?

Questions buzzed in her head like so many angry bees. She pushed them away. Elder Bok had told her she served her people, and she believed him. It wasn't her place to question the ways of the leaders.

She staggered back to camp, her heart heavy, leaving behind more bodies beyond her healing power. She walked slowly among the knots of weary men, her gaze sliding over their faces. How many of them had she saved? She couldn't be sure. After three long days, all the faces looked the same.

The men recognized the bags and pouches that signified her calling, some of them calling out their thanks. But most simply stared into the fire, too exhausted to even speak.

At last she passed a group of men from her village, with Albert sitting among them. They called out to her, and she joined the circle, warming her hands at their small campfire.

Albert smiled at her, but his eyes remained troubled. "Thank you, Mollie," he whispered, so softly she might have imagined it.

"Are you well?" she asked, concern lacing her voice.

"Yes, thanks to you. Only tired," he answered.

"Why haven't you gone home?" She clapped a hand over her mouth, but the words were out before she could stop them.

Albert looked at her solemnly. "I serve Lord Radulf. As long as I can fight, he needs me here, until the battle is over."

Mollie couldn't miss the sadness and the fear in Albert's eyes. She knew he was thinking the same thing she was. She had saved him twice. How many more times would there be before she was too late?

She bade the men good-bye and continued on her journey. Though it was not her place, she felt a growing need to talk with Radulf, to assure herself that what she was doing in his service was right and worthwhile.

Determination built within her, as she circled the camp, each circuit bringing her closer to Lord Radulf's tent. Finally, she found herself standing in front of the tent, facing the same guard who had held the door for her three nights before.

But when she asked to be admitted, the guard hesitated, and Mollie began to turn away. Perhaps this was not the time.

Elder Bok approached at that moment.

"Greetings, healer," he said.

Although he had known her since she was a child, he

addressed her by her formal title. It was a reminder that she was no longer "little Mollie" but that she carried a much greater responsibility. A responsibility that she must face.

"Greetings, Elder Bok."

"Has Lord Radulf summoned you here?" The elder stopped beside her, looking down at her quizzically.

"No. I wished to speak with Lord Radulf, but he is occupied with more important matters." She shrugged, feeling her resolve fading as she stepped back. "It can wait until a better time."

"There will be no better time, I am afraid," Elder Bok replied. He took her by the arm and led her past the guard, into the lord's tent.

The scene inside the tent was much the same as it had been a few nights earlier. Radulf was poring over his maps and charts, his advisors assembled around him, offering suggestions.

The conversation stopped when she entered the room, and the lord looked up from the papers spread across his table.

"The healer wishes to speak with you, my lord." Elder Bok released Mollie's arm and moved around the table to assume his place among the advisors.

She was alone, facing the rank of old men. Their stony faces gave no hint of comfort, no clue to the content of their hearts. They waited in silence.

Her mouth was dry as Mollie struggled to swallow the huge lump that had lodged in her throat. Whatever had possessed her to approach Lord Radulf?

"My lord," she began. Her voice broke, and no more words came. She swallowed once more, and began again.

"My lord." Her voice didn't crack this time, and she continued. "I have healed many men during the days of battle and seen them safely off the battlefield. Their bodies are mended, but their spirits are not restored. That is beyond my power.

"When I came here," she said, "I thought I was helping my people. But they are not being sent home. They are returned to the battle, to be injured again and again.

"I cannot raise the dead, lord, and I cannot reach everyone in time. There are too many—"

Radulf had turned away from her, and her voice trailed off.

"It is no concern of yours, healer," he snapped, without looking at her. "The battle takes time, and we need every man until our victory is assured.

"These wise men, these leaders, provide me with advice and counsel. That is their job. Your job is to heal. I advise you to stick to what you know best and leave other matters in more experienced hands."

He looked at each of the men in turn, as though seeking their approval, then finally turned his gaze upon Mollie. "Trust me," he implored, his voice dropping to a soft entreaty. "We know what is best."

The sincerity in his voice and the regret in his expression opened a wellspring of guilt in the young woman. How could she have doubted the leaders? She was only a simple village girl, even with her healing powers. Who was she to judge the actions of her betters?

Tears welled in her eyes, and a blush of shame rose in her cheeks. The rebuke was mild in light of her transgression, and she silently backed away until she could bolt from the tent.

The guard paid her no heed as she crept around the tent, and Mollie was grateful that the darkness hid her shame.

But as she moved away, she heard Elder Bok's voice inside the lord's tent. "Truly, my lord, she is just a girl, with no understanding of the world outside her village. Her powers, though, are greater than any I have seen."

Mollie stopped, her veins running cold with the realization that the advisors were talking about *her*. She didn't dare to move, to alert them to her presence only a few feet away. She froze in place, her breath shallow, as she waited for some noise to cover her retreat.

Lord Radulf's voice rumbled in reply to Elder Bok. "The girl has her uses."

Before he could say more, a sentry called a greeting to the guard at the door, bringing the latest report. While the guard was announcing his arrival, Mollie sped away, fear pushing her into the night.

Morning came, and with it the battle resumed. Exhausted men, many of them wearing garments that bore the stains of earlier injuries, dragged themselves into the field.

And Mollie followed them.

She had her uses.

But with each man she healed, her heart grew heavier. Instead of a feeling of triumph, grief and despair rose in her. No matter how many she healed, no matter how often she saved each man, he would return to the battlefield, until the time when she would be too late.

Her powers were strong. She could heal any injury, ease any physical pain. But she couldn't heal the fear and hopelessness that she saw in the faces of the victims. She could save their lives, at least temporarily, but she couldn't mend their souls.

She couldn't send them home.

Not as long as they could fight.

She knelt beside another man, one who reminded her of her long-dead father. Somewhere, she was sure, he had a wife and children—a family who wanted him to come home.

She stroked his arm, feeling the shattered bones gather themselves together. "Do you have a wife?" she asked. "Children?"

"Two daughters and a son." He winced as the bones began to knit, shooting needles of pain through his arm. "My wife died two years ago."

Mollie ran a fingertip along his wrist and saw the relief in his face, as the pain subsided. "Are they young?"

"My son is nearly grown," he replied. "And my elder daughter will make me a grandfather soon. But the baby," his face softened, and his eyes grew moist. "My wife died in childbirth. She left me little Kate."

His arm still bent at an odd angle, and Mollie felt bone and sinew straining, pulling the limb closer to whole.

And she knew what she had to do.

She pulled her hands away, severing his connection to her healing power. She moved away, leaving him with a damaged arm, one without the strength to wield a sword or ax.

If he could no longer fight, the elders would be forced to remove him from the battle. They would have to send him home.

Mollie moved swiftly through the raging fight.

She ignored arrows and swords, and the boom of the cannon.

She breathed in the acrid smoke and choking dust, and she didn't notice her lungs aching for clean air. An ax caught one of her pouches, tearing it from her body, but she was unharmed.

At every turn, there was another injured soldier. And she healed each of them.

Or nearly so. As she took her hands from each man and moved to the next, she left him with a souvenir of the battle: a severed foot, the stump already scarred over; a misshapen arm; a blind eye; deep lines on limbs and trunks and faces, the scar tissue drawing the flesh around it into ugly contortions.

On each body, she left a visible warning of the true price of war. A vivid sign for anyone willing to see, of what the battle had cost. A reminder for every man who might send a son to war.

She moved faster, touching as many men as she could reach. She eased their pain and saved their lives, but none of them would leave the field whole enough to return.

She did, as she had told Lord Radulf, all she could.

SAME, SAME

K.D. Wentworth

THE second night after we'd infiltrated the stone-ridden Rur Valley, the lieutenant brought us our very own real live Spink. I was plenty riled when the hulking native entered the lantern light, two-meters-plus of pink, spongy skin. It stood there, looming over us, with wattles and jowls like someone's old granny back on Earth.

"Don't saddle us with that goddamn thing," I said. "We can't be watching it all the time. Harjo Company's got enough to do with the big push coming up tomorrow." Up to that moment, I had been eating something anonymously glutinous out of a plastic packet. The congealed gravy smelled like dog food, but it was guaranteed nutritious by our superiors. Weren't none of us getting fat on it, though. I dumped the rest of it in the dirt.

"Brass say otherwise, Sergeant Watson." Lieutenant Cleary stood to one side. "Say hello to Paf, your new translator." A grin spread across his face that had nothing to do with humor. The lieutenant'd had it in for us for days, something about making him look bad at the last big inspection, like it was our fault we hadn't connected with Resupply in over ten weeks.

"Y'all make him welcome, you hear?" Without waiting for an answer, he sauntered away, letting the darkness swallow him.

"Yeah," I said to his back, "we'll do that." I glanced

37

at the Spink. They were so sure that this one was tame that they'd even armed it with a pistol, just a stunner, to be sure, but—

A shudder ran down my spine. I never understood why Spinks would take arms against their own kind. They must have rules, "codes of conduct" the brass call them. Every sentient culture we've ever encountered does, but, on this world, we just couldn't figure out what they were. So, for some reason that makes sense to them, a small percentage of the natives abandon their own troops and join ours, by all accounts, fighting alongside us.

Before he got killed two of these skinny valleys ago, my buddy Wes was always saying don't trust them. Any species that warred against its own kind in an interplanetary conflict was nuts. Hell, though, all aliens are nuts, when judged by human motives.

The brass liked the idea of getting something for practically nothing, and Spinks have a gift for picking up new languages. It seems that part of their brain doesn't switch off after childhood like a human's. They weren't great with syntax, but they understood us a helluva lot better than we understood them. So, numbers permitting, we were assigned one Spink per unit, "translators" they called them, or sometimes "cultural envoys."

Freaking traitors was more like it.

Our unit had bedded down in a fall of boulders for cover, apparently the site of an old avalanche. On both sides of the valley, granite peaks loomed against the star-crazed sky, and down at the far end the tiny amber lights of a settlement gleamed, surrounding a small landing field that we had to take. Three ships were already in port when we first slipped into the valley. Then another Spink ship had landed about an hour ago, this one big enough to be a troop transport.

Mo McCready was hunched under a tree, or the purple-leafed excuse that passed for one in those parts, mumbling to himself. He hadn't been the same since we'd taken out that native compound last week, and when we searched the rubble, we learned those particular Spinks hadn't been armed. Stuff like that happens,

Pritchard and I tried to tell him. By the time you figure out if they're holding a weapon or hoe, it's too damned late.

Red and green targeting lasers were lighting up the night sky on the other side of the mountains. I hauled McCready to his feet. He was shivering. "This here is Paf," I said, "our new translator."

Spinks smell like garlic laced with sulphur. Pritchard exhaled loudly, then edged away. I felt like retreating myself. Took a bit of getting used to.

"Goddamn, Sarge, they gave it a weapon," McCready said. As a matter of fact, McCready smelled pretty rank himself.

"Yeah," I said. "That Cleary is all heart."

"Heart," the Spink said and edged forward, regarding us with tiny black eyes buried in folds of mushy pink flesh. Its nostril slits flared. "Is inner organ?"

"Shut up, Spink," I said. "Don't want to hear nothing out of you right now." I turned away. "Pritchard, you take first watch."

The next morning, just as dawn crept along the eastern horizon, we moved out, taking the Spink. It was cold enough to see your breath. In the thin morning light, the native was hulking, a head taller than the tallest of humans. Its chin bobbed forward with every step as though a string connected its head with its feet. Someone had tricked it out in tattered cast-off bits of Earth Force uniforms, but no one would ever have mistaken it for one of us.

"Jeeze." Pritchard flinched it passed him. "Looks even worse in the light."

Our new Spink lumbered along, bare headed. Its skull was too massive to wear one of our helmets. I thought about telling it to keep its head down but then didn't bother. If it got killed, we'd just be rid of it that much sooner. Better all the way around. After serving with us, no one on the other side was going to welcome it home anyway.

A squadron of single-man fighters poured in from the

west soaring over the mountains to lay down covering fire. Lieutenant Cleary trotted up, his face slick with sweat despite the chill. "Take Harjo Company south," he said. "Carlisle and Minerva Companies will sweep in on the north. Recon says the Spinks have been refueling the ship that landed yesterday. Two of the others have been off-loading supplies. Use your hot-grenades, and don't let any of the damn things take off again."

Incendiary grenades were highly prized because they burned so hot that matter for a hundred yards radius pretty much vaporized. They weren't dirty, like a mini-nuke, but they worked great for making holes in things you wanted to get rid of. So great, in fact, that we had only two left. Guess Lieutenant Cleary didn't know that, or maybe he did and didn't care. No use complaining. Resupply was at least three hundred klicks behind us.

I nodded, then doubled the pace. Harjo Company slipped through the grayness, passing dark conical com pounds build low to the ground. Not a single native came out to offer resistance. We cut through fields of some kind, trampling a purple-leafed root crop. Several times we spooked a herd of some kind of domesticated animals. I could see lights up ahead, wheeled vehicles rolling in, lots of movement. Engines were whining.

Paf touched my shoulder. I jerked away, stumbling in the soft plowed dirt. "Goddammit, don't do that!"

The Spink stared down at me, its tiny eyes reflecting the dawn. "Power protects landing field," it said. "Much power if you touch. Not being alive, it is bad?"

Pritchard stopped, rifle clutched in both hands. His skin seemed ashen in the dimness. "What's it babbling about, Sarge?"

I rubbed chill nervous sweat from my face. "Beats me."

Something exploded to the west of the landing field. We hit the soft ground and pushed our faces into the dirt. The earth shook beneath us. I had that familiar sick surge of adrenaline zinging through my veins that does absolutely no good.

Dirt rained down on our backs, and I crawled forward to Pritchard, who was checking his handheld scan, the only working one left in our unit. Earth Force fighters soared past overhead and came around for another strafing run. It was all noise and confusion. "Can you see anything?" I said.

"They've generated forcefields around their ships." His face was tight with fear. "Nothing's getting through from above."

The com in my helmet clicked. *"Cleary, here,"* the tinny voice said. *"Intelligence thinks the forcefield generator is in that small bunker on your end. Take it out!"*

"Sure, right away—*sir,*" I said grimly, "since we're not doing anything important at the moment." Another explosion rocked the valley and this time rock shards rained down on us along with the dirt. I rose in a half-crouch. "Come on, you lazy bastards!"

Pritchard just lay there, so I grabbed his pack and rolled him over. A shard had pierced his neck like a dagger, just beneath his helmet. Dark blood soaked into his canvas pack. His eyes stared up sightlessly. I stood over the body, hands clenched. He'd enlisted with me, back on Earth. We'd known each other for three years, a lifetime out here.

Our tame Spink loomed up beside me. "Being not alive?"

Cleary's voice crackled in my com. *"Where the hell is Harjo Company?"*

"On our way!" I replied, then picked up Pritchard's handheld and ducked around the Spink. "On our freaking way."

Arthurs joined up with McCready, then Broam, Peterson, and the rest of the company closed ranks. Out of the corner of my eye, I saw that the Spink, Paf, had grabbed Pritchard's rifle. I snatched the weapon out of its hands. "Give me that!"

It released the stock without a struggle. "Much fighting now," it said as though in explanation.

"Yeah," I said, looping the extra rifle over my shoulder. "You'd better go first."

Without another word, it surged ahead of us with that peculiar head-bobbing gait.

I could see the closest Spink ship now, round and ugly, bloated like a tick and bathed in a bluish light. Our sleek fighters broke off and headed back toward the mountains. No point in wasting firepower. I supposed they'd return if we took out the generator. Then again, maybe not.

We caught up with the Spink just where the tarmac began. It was down on one knee, gazing at wheeled vehicles off on the other side, brimming with natives and dashing in many directions. The landing field looked like an anthill someone had kicked over.

I spotted a low building on our end, no bigger than a shed, all curves, no straight edges. The generator? I headed for the tarmac, but Paf took my arm and pulled me back.

"Not going there," it said.

"The hell I'm not!" I wrenched my arm free. Its garlic-sulphur stench washed over me.

"Going there," it said stolidly, "then not being alive." Its nostril slits flared, then it picked up a clod of dirt and tossed it at the tarmac. *Blue* flared, and the dirt—sizzled.

"That's more than just a damn forcefield," McCready said, his dirt-streaked face ashen.

"Harjo Company!" Cleary's voice demanded in my ear. *"What's the holdup?"*

I switched the com off and, heart pounding, tried to think as the last of our air support droned back over the western peaks. If their ordinance hadn't been able to penetrate the forcefield, a hot-grenade was only going to blast a large hole in the ground. It wouldn't touch that ship.

A burst of laser fire came from the south. Spink projectile weapons chattered back. We hit the dirt again, all of us, except for Paf. Instead, the big Spink calmly took aim and fired its stunner with careful precision as projectiles chewed up the ground around us. Ten meters away, two Spinks crumpled, then a third just stood

there, staring at Paf. Our "cultural envoy" took that
one out, too.

"Jesus!" McCready popped back onto his feet. "I
wouldn't have believed that, if I hadn't seen it for myself!
How can you be so damn cold?"

Paf lowered its pistol. A thread of pinkish fluid dripped
from its arm where it'd been grazed. "This one is—you
would say—priest."

"So you sent your own kind to heaven to save us?"
McCready shuddered. "Man, that's sick."

"Heaven?" Paf said. Its nose flaps twitched. "One not
knowing that designation. Explain."

"Don't matter why he did it," I said, easing off the
ground myself. My ears were ringing from all the explosions, and I felt dizzy. There was still lots of activity
on the landing field outside the blue force bubbles that
protected the Spink ships. "Saved your ass. That's all
you need to know."

"Just so he can send us to heaven, too, more than
likely." McCready shook the dirt off his rifle. "Stay away
from me!"

The Spink obediently edged back.

The forcefield generator sat a hundred meters away
inside a faint blue shimmer. "We can't go through," I
said grimly, "so it will have to be under."

Peterson tapped his helmet. "The lieutenant is on my
com, wants to know what's wrong with yours?"

"Nothing that an off switch can't cure," I said. "Tell
him to shut the hell up! We're busy!"

He mumbled a more politic answer to Cleary while I
primed the hot-grenade, then started scraping out a hole
under the edge of the tarmac with my knife. The surface
went down a good half meter. Out on the landing field,
one of the transports kicked on its engines and the
ground rumbled.

McCready was on his knees, helping with the hole.
"Won't they have to turn off the forcefield to take off?
We could get in then."

"We'd fry from the backwash before we got anywhere

near it " I said grimly as I hacked at the compacted dirt. "Keep digging!"

Peterson bent over me. "Cleary says this is a supply depot. We've got to keep these ships from taking off!"

Sweat dripped into my eyes as I dug, burned like a son of a gun, but I couldn't stop to wipe it away. "Yeah, I'll just trot out there and stop them with my bare hands!"

Shouting went up over by one of the peculiar wheeled vehicles as we were spotted. Spinks poured out of its segmented chassis and, skirting the blue shimmers around the ships, headed our way. Peterson and the rest took up defensive positions. "Hurry, Sarge!" he said over his shoulder.

The hole was almost deep enough. If my calculations were right, the hot-grenade would vaporize a crater *beneath* the forcefield-protected tarmac, so we could tunnel under and come up inside the perimeter, getting to the generator that way. I wedged the device in place and punched in the demolition code. "Run!"

We sprinted east for the plowed fields. Spink weapons fired as we ran, cutting down Arthurs and Broam. Off to the right, I could hear screaming, then something hot creased my leg. Without warning, I was down in the soft dirt, hands clenched around my bloody thigh. Without missing a stride, Paf seized my pack and dragged me as though I weighed no more than a sack of potatoes.

I'd lost count of the seconds, but the incendiary would be going off any time now. "Keep—running!" I said to the Spink through a red-hot haze. "We're not—far—far enough—"

In the distance, something whumped. The Spink threw its ungainly carcass over me, driving the air from my lungs. The ground shook as heat flared. I tried to make my lungs work.

Finally, I thought to click my com back on. *"—in there!"* Cleary was shouting. *"Take that damn ship out!"*

Paf rolled to one side and then pulled me up. "Being

hurt?" Its black eyes glittered like black ice in its ugly
face.

I tried to tear a strip from my shirt for a bandage, but
my hands shook too much. The Spink understood and
ripped a length of material from its own tattered shirt.

Over by the landing field, our soldiers poured down
through the steaming hole we'd made. Weapons whined
and chattered. I couldn't tell which side had the advantage, and I was pretty much close to not caring.

Paf stayed with me like it didn't care either. "I—don't
get it," I said as the Spink bandaged my bloody leg.
"Why do you take our side? Those—" I gestured
weakly—"are your people."

Its nostrils flapped. "They die, not die, all same,
same," it said. "Humans die, very bad."

The pain ate at me. I shrugged out of my pack.
"Why?"

"Humans not—" It hesitated. Out on the landing field,
one of the Spink ships took off, blasting toward the rap-
idly brightening morning sky. "Not—being ready."

"To die?" I blinked. "Jesus, no one is ready for that!"

"Spinks ready," it said. "All Spinks, all the time. Live,
die, same, same."

"You're not afraid to die?" I tried to make sense of
that, but the pain had hold of me, and it just wouldn't
come together.

"Not having that word, 'afraid,' " it said. "Explain?"

A chill ran through me. Everything felt fear, even goddamn oysters and cockroaches. Life couldn't evolve without it.

"You let that freighter get away!" Cleary was shouting
into the com. *"I'll have your—"*

I clicked it off again. Nothing I could do about any of
it at this point anyway. Either we'd take the landing field
and medics would be around to collect me afterward, or
they'd drive our guys off and I'd die here, bleeding into
the alien dirt.

"Why do you work for us?" I said wearily, trying to
push myself back onto my good leg, using my rifle as a

crutch. "It can't be the money." Twenty meters away, several bodies sprawled across the furrows, the broken remnants of what was left of my men. Dying certainly wasn't "same, same" to them.

"Humans needing us," Paf said. Its brutish face contorted. "Those who are being priests help. Is—you would say—'duty?'"

"If you care about us, then why do Spinks attack our shipping lanes?" The world tilted crazily and I sank back to the ground. Hot blood trickled down my leg. "Why start all of *this*?"

"Same, same," it said. "Attack, not attack, same, same."

"It's not the same, goddammit!" Black spots ate away at my vision. I tasted iron on the back of my throat. Something exploded over on the landing field, not as big this time, but I could feel the heat even this far away. Screams echoed back through the valley. "You brought all this down upon yourselves!"

Its black eyes regarded me with no more commonality between our frames of reference than I'd have with a traffic light, in fact, probably less. "One not understanding," it said solemnly.

"Yeah," I said, hunched against the ache in my thigh. "You got that right."

Black shapes loomed to the south, but I couldn't make out the uniforms. Could be either side. I struggled up again and readied my rifle. The injured leg wouldn't hold me, and I balanced on one foot. My heart pounded. I was drenched with cold sweat. "Go home," I said. "We don't need you."

"Being ready to die?" Paf said, hands twitching at its sides.

"No!" I hopped toward the landing field and almost fell. "And you shouldn't be either!" More black shapes appeared, jogging toward us in the paleness, but the light was behind them. I still couldn't make their forms out. Did they have that peculiar Spink bobbing motion?

"Then this one must staying." It pulled its stun pistol. "One said—words that—made promise."

"An oath?" I edged forward. "That was goddamn stupid!"

The black shapes resolved themselves into Spinks, at least a dozen. The ones in the lead took aim and projectiles pinged into the soft dirt less than a meter away. Paf moved in front of me and fired back, using a wide beam. They wilted at its touch. I felt sick, watching it fire on its own kind. The pistol's charge faltered, and Paf threw it aside. The Spink wrenched my rifle out of my hands and fired on them with that too. Several projectiles struck its spongy body. It jerked, but kept firing.

"Stop it!" I shouted, then fished in the dirt for Pritchard's rifle which had fallen off my shoulder. Shots zinged past my ear and I dropped flat.

Over on the landing field, another ship exploded. Fiery debris rained down, peppering the planted fields, the quaint little conical houses, the bawling domesticated animals, the Spink soldiers, and the attacking humans. Everyone was in equal danger. "Same, goddamn same," I muttered, covering my head with my arms.

Paf crawled to my side, bringing its garlic-sulphur stench. "Being yes!" it said. "Same, same!" It leaned in close, pulled the knife from my belt, and reached to cut my throat.

I raised Pritchard's rifle and shot it point-blank between its black-ice eyes.

Our forces overran the valley that afternoon, then abandoned it three days later. It was empty by then, sterile, worthless, the Spink supply ships in rubble, the landing field cratered, farms ruined, civilians dead. Medics evacuated me to a hospital ship at the edge of the Spink system along with the rest of our wounded, far too few in number. Whether fighting for us or themselves, Spinks are ruthlessly efficient.

My leg was salvageable, so the brass will assign me to another unit once it's healed. For now, the battle for the Spink world and our goddamn shipping lanes goes on without me. I lie here in my bunk on clean sheets, breathe in cool conditioned ship air that somehow smells like garlic laced with sulphur, and try to understand why they do it, the Spinks, what they could possibly see in humans that's worth gunning down their own kind, why they would ever trade even one of their lives for ours.

Hell if I know.

THIRTY-TWO BULLETS IN TWENTY-THREE SECONDS

Diane A.S. Stuckart

He wasn't supposed to be here . . . not today. Halfway to town, he'd stopped and wheeled his horse around, telling himself he should forget trying to interfere and go back to the ranch. He'd even ridden a few lengths back in that direction before he pulled up the bay gelding a second time and resumed his original direction. Tomorrow he might regret what he was doing, but something inside him insisted that he had no choice. Now here he was, crouched atop the splintered porch behind Fly's Boarding House, watching and waiting for something that might not even happen.

Jack Allister frowned and tugged his stained gray Stetson lower on his brow. From his vantage point on the roof, he could see a portion of dusty Fremont Street beyond and the usual bustle of townspeople milling past the open lot. As always, it was a varied procession—weary cowboys in stained chaps and broad-brimmed hats, natty gamblers in crisp white shirts beneath black vested suits, respectable ladies bonneted and in bustled gowns, sober shopowners in gartered shirtsleeves and pressed trousers. They had no idea they were being watched, that he was privy to these few careless seconds of their lives spent crossing that gap from one building to the next.

And, if all went well, they'd never have to know.

He gave a grim nod of approval. The more potential

witnesses on the streets this cloudy day, the less likely it was that this brewing fight would finally explode into full-blown battle. Then he could go back to the ranch, back to his chores and dawn-to-dark days, back to the hard cot where he unrolled his bedroll each night . . . at least, until the next time the trouble threatened.

He eased from his crouch down onto his belly. Stretched to his full length, he crawled snakelike toward the back of the sign that rose over the building's front edge. That wooden façade offered a bit more cover while allowing a better view of the street below. Pausing, he surreptitiously tugged his kerchief from around his neck and mopped his flushed cheeks. It was a cold afternoon for October in Cochise County, but he had already sweated right through his Sunday-best blue chambray shirt with its double line of wooden buttons down the front.

How long he would have to stay on his rooftop perch, he didn't want to guess. Unfortunately, this was the only plan he'd been able to conjure up during his frantic ride from the ranch this morning. But if the boys caught sight of him, if they found out he'd disobeyed orders and come here trying to play peacemaker, there'd be hell to pay.

"Not your fight," Frank and Tom had insisted whenever the subject of their dispute with the town's vigilante lawmen had come up.

They and the others, Billy and Ike, had all agreed that Jack wasn't to be dragged into the feud that had been brewing between the two groups for months. After all, he wasn't truly one of them, wasn't a brother or even a cousin. He was only a hired hand, paid to do chores and keep his mouth shut around anyone from town who was considered the law. He had no business mixing in their affairs.

Ike, in particular, had taken a hard line. "I find out you came into town, I'll nail your lily-white hide to the barn wall!" had been his parting words to Jack the previous morning. So saying, he had buckled on his six-shooter and grabbed up his Winchester before riding out with Tom to spend the day wandering the various saloons.

Normally, Jack would have done as ordered and stayed behind. He'd been a bit afraid of the wild-eyed Ike from the first time he'd met him . . . hell, he was pretty much in awe of all the boys, though they'd treated him right enough these past weeks. Tom and Frank had fed him, given him a place to sleep, and some work to do. "Nobody goes hungry when they stop by our ranch," had been their response when he'd tried to thank them.

But rumors that more than words would be exchanged this day had reached the outlying spreads. The news had come fast enough that he knew he must ride into town and take a stand on his employers' behalf. He owed them that much.

When Jack was certain he'd not been seen crawling along the boarding house roof, he raised up a bit and reached beneath his shirt. Carefully, he pulled out a cloth-wrapped revolver and balanced the unwieldy bundle on the rooftop before him. He felt like a schoolboy sneaking a drink of whiskey behind the barn, the way he'd been forced to hide the hog leg under his fancy shirt. Only recently, the marshal had posted a new law saying that a man couldn't carry a gun in town. The penalty was a $25 fine and, if the marshal or one of his deputies was in a particularly bad mood, a buffaloing—a blow upside the head with that lawman's six-shooter.

A damn stupid law. Hell, in this part of the world, a man needed a gun to keep himself alive. His pa had been shot down a few years back in another town like this one, by another marshal who made it his business to strip men of their pride and their guns. If Roy Allister had kept his revolver with him that day, he might have outdrawn the man who'd killed him for no greater offense than taking part in a drunken brawl with another cowboy.

Jack had been there when it happened. He had seen the entire event unfold from much the same sort of vantage point as the one from which he now watched. That particular day, he'd not had a weapon, had not possessed any means of stopping the inevitable. He could do nothing more than witness his father's ignominious death, a swift gasping end in a puddle of piss and blood on that faraway dusty street.

He'd not let the same thing happen again on this day.

With cool deliberation, Jack untied the knotted cord around the bundle and unwrapped the oiled cloth cradling his father's pistol. A stray beam of sunlight hit its dull finish, giving the weapon the gleam that no amount of polishing had ever managed to reveal. He turned it over in his hands, running his fingers along its familiar edges.

The revolver was the sole thing of value his pa had left him. It was a heavy piece that shot wide and had a kick that would take your arm off if you weren't careful. The wooden grip was scarred and worn smooth from years of handling. Pa had carried the pistol with him all through the war, had kept it afterward mostly to bring down the occasional rabbit for supper. Jack had fired it but once, during an afternoon spent blasting old bottles off rocks with his father. A professional shootist would never consider carrying such a bulky piece.

But Jack wasn't a shootist, so it didn't matter what gun he used.

He unbuttoned one shirt pocket and pulled out a handful of bullets, letting them roll around his palm for a moment. Six shots. That was all the ammunition he had. Still, it should be enough . . . one for each man and a couple of spares. He loaded each bullet into its chamber and gave the cylinder a spin, just for luck. Satisfied, he plucked off his hat and set it beside him, then transferred the pistol to his right hand, his gun hand. He stretched his arm so the barrel lay propped across a raised bit of timber, its dark mouth open to the street below.

The wind had picked up a bit. Despite the chill, his lips were dry, and he wished he dared climb off the roof long enough to grab a mouthful of water from the nearby trough. No one seeing him could possibly guess his plan, his reason for being in town this day, even if someone caught him in midclimb. But word of a fellow acting strange could get back to the marshal, who might have cause for suspicion. For already there'd been trouble today beyond the rumors.

The stories had been swirling about like a sharp desert breeze by the time he'd reached town. Word was that both Ike and Tom had had run-ins with the marshal and his brothers a short time earlier on account of guns—Ike for carrying a pistol and Tom simply for being suspected of packing one. The accounts pointed blame in every direction, but all agreed Ike and Tom had gotten the worst of it. Both men had ended up buffaloed, and a bloodied Ike had gone to jail. Knowing the local judge, Ike would likely be free by now and on his way to meet up with Tom and the other boys.

Jack tried to find a more comfortable position, blinking away the dark spots that had suddenly begun dancing before his eyes. No, not nerves. It had to be the cold that was starting to get to him, but he wouldn't abandon his post. He didn't know where the boys had left their horses, so he'd chosen a lookout close to several stables. From here, he'd likely see them pass by no matter where they were headed. More importantly, he would be able to spy trouble if it was following them . . . and warn them if it was.

His pistol grew leaden in his grasp despite the way he had it propped. He set the heavy weapon down a moment to flex his fingers, careful not to shift about too much. Apart from attracting attention, any sudden movement on the wooden structure was liable to send a splinter sharp as a cactus needle through his clothes and into his flesh.

He wished he had a pocketwatch to check the hour. It had been after one o'clock when he had scrambled onto the roof. He squinted up at the sun next time it peeked through the clouds and tried to judge the time.

Perhaps an hour had passed, but surely no more than two. Simply watching and waiting could wear a fellow down, it seemed.

He must have drifted off for several minutes, for suddenly he was jerking to attention at the sound of a familiar rough voice below.

Ike.

"I have got them on the hip, and I'm going to throw them good." Ike's rankled voice drifted upward, and Jack eased himself closer to the building's edge for a better look. Even from this removed vantage point, he could tell the man had been drinking again. But it seemed that ire rather than alcohol was fueling this particular tirade.

Ike was flailing his arms as he talked to the other Billy—young Billy Claibourne—standing next to him. Billy looked both mad and scared, a dangerous combination of emotions. As for Ike, Jack saw the older man's high forehead was half hidden by the bloody bandage wrapping what must be his injury from his earlier altercation with the marshal. His stylish suit looked slept in, and Jack recalled how Ike supposedly had been up all night playing cards with Tom and the marshal. Strange, Jack thought, that the two enemies would have sat down at poker together.

The lawmen versus the cowboys. That's what it had been all about the past weeks . . . hell, it had been going on for longer than Jack had been in these parts. Why the two groups had taken such a dislike to each other, he didn't know, but a cowboy mixing with a lawman was like tossing a bobcat and a coyote into a hole together. A fight was sure to commence, and it wouldn't end up pretty.

Jack shook his head. He didn't understand how respectable ranchers like Frank and Tom could be caught up in such bad business. Ike was another matter. Though a smart enough fellow when he was sober, he had a tendency to drink too much and fall in with bad sorts, dragging his brother Billy along with him. Still, the worst that Jack knew could be proved against Ike was a time or two he'd rustled cattle across the border down in Mexico. But as for the lawmen, that was a different story.

He sneered a little. Calling those fellows "lawmen" was like polishing up a pisspot. Hell, everyone in town knew the marshal's brothers were nothing more than gamblers and pimps. The fact they pinned on a star every so often didn't make them upright citizens, any more than slapping a pair of trousers on a mule made him a man. He'd heard Ike talk about a recent stage robbery, and how some of those so-called lawmen had been the ones to do the crime. They'd even tried to bribe Ike not to tell what he knew about it. Maybe that's when the worst of the trouble had started.

He strained to hear more of the conversation, but the voices below had dropped to murmurs. Ike kept glancing about as if expecting to be set upon by someone, his expression beneath his sandy beard looking like he was spoiling for a fight. *Maybe Billy will talk some sense into him.* Unfortunately, Jack had little real hope of that happening. Ike listened to no one, especially when he'd been bending an elbow.

He heard the jingle of spurs and saw Billy Clanton and Tom McLaury, dressed in their town best, joining the pair in the middle of the horse lot. Jack breathed a silent sigh of relief. They had brought their horses with them, which surely meant they were preparing to head out for the ranch, rather than linger here on the streets. Then he noticed one of the group was missing. They couldn't leave yet, not without Frank.

He scanned the street beyond and promptly saw the elder McLaury. He was headed toward the corral, leading his horse and accompanied by Sheriff Behan. A smooth-talking man with a penchant for tailored suits, bowler hats, and fancy canes, the sheriff appeared to be lecturing Frank in a genteel fashion about the rifle strapped to his saddle.

Jack frowned, not liking this. Politics had allowed the town both a marshal and a sheriff, each backed by a different faction of the citizenry. From what he'd seen of Behan, the man did little law enforcement but simply sided with whoever best served his own end. Most recently, that had been Ike and the boys, though that could change with the next switch in the weather. He doubted the man had ever been in a gunfight . . . wondered if he'd ever even skinned his revolver.

Jack grabbed up his own pistol again, assessing the situation. Frank was shaking his head at whatever Behan was saying. For his part, the sheriff had not lost his smooth manner, though he'd acquired a nervous expression. Certain he was sufficiently hidden by the sign and the pitch of the boarding house roof, Jack trained his weapon on the sheriff, just in case.

"Boys, you have got to give up your arms," he heard Behan urge as he drew even with the other men. His tone sounded more conciliatory than threatening. "There's bound to be trouble with the marshal and his brothers if you don't."

"I ain't going to do it," Frank countered, "not unless they disarm first. I've got business to do in town before I leave, and I ain't chancing it."

Jack could see that Billy Clanton had a rifle tied on his mount, as well. All legal, according to the marshal's regulation, if they were in process of leaving town. The sheriff must have realized the same thing, for he let Frank's protest pass. "What about the rest of you boys?"

"You know I ain't heeled," Ike insisted, assuming an aggrieved look and putting a hand to his bandaged head. He spread his arms wide. "See for yourself."

Behan looked uncomfortable as he patted down the other man, though when he stepped back his expression was one of satisfaction. "I believe you, Ike. Tom, are you packing?"

"Johnny, I have nothing." The younger McLaury readily opened his tan duster to reveal he had no hidden weapons beneath its folds.

Billy Claibourne, meanwhile, shook his head in protest. "No need to ask me, Sheriff. I'm on my way out of town. I'm not with these fellows."

Behan smoothed his flamboyant mustaches and nodded. "Very well, but I sure wish you all would stop by my office, just to make things look proper. I told the marshal I'd disarm you. It might go better if everyone leaves here with me."

Ike gave a harsh laugh. "You need not be afraid of us, Johnny. We will not make any trouble. Right, boys?"

They nodded all around, and Behan spread his hands in a combined gesture of surrender and dismissal. "I'll go tell the marshal and the others I went to disarm you, but you're on your own getting past them. I have done all I can do."

Jack remained unmoving upon the roof, his pistol still at the ready as he watched the departing sheriff. Even Behan apparently thought there was a chance the lawmen might be waiting somewhere in town, planning to ambush the boys. Time for a new plan.

He turned his attention to the boys and heard sounds of an argument. A few words drifted up to him . . . *trouble . . . guns . . . law* . . . but it looked as though they were ready to head out. Should he join them on their trek out of town, adding his revolver to theirs in case trouble happened? Or should he wait until he was certain they were halfway home to the ranch before he followed?

Jack glanced toward the street again, and the decision was abruptly made for him. Walking down Fremont Street toward that very horse lot was the marshal, Virgil Earp, and his brothers, Wyatt and Morgan. The trio was accompanied by the same lunger dentist, Doc Holliday, whom Jack had seen with them on occasion. Sheriff Behan stood some distance beyond them, his expression wary.

Jack tightened his grip on his pistol, unnerved despite himself at the lawmen's sudden appearance. The Earps were dressed in their usual gambler's black, unrelieved except for the starched white of their shirts. The marshal carried a cane, though he gripped it like a club. Holliday, the hot-tempered dentist turned gunman, wore a long gray duster that opened with his every step, revealing a glimpse of the shotgun concealed beneath Fleetingly, Jack wondered why Holliday was allow to pack a gun in town, when honest men were not.

The four men halted a few steps from where Ike stood, guns drawn and looking like Hell's avenging angels as they blocked the way to the street.

"Throw up your hands!" the lawman he recognized as Wyatt demanded.

The marshal echoed, "Throw up your hands," and waved the cane he held for emphasis, adding, "we have come to disarm you!"

Ike stepped toward the man, arm aloft and demeanor abruptly sober. "We ain't looking for any trouble, Virgil. Let us pass."

For a moment, silence held. Jack allowed himself to hope Ike's peacemaking attempt might prove a success. Every man stood but a few feet from the others . . . close enough to see the outrage in their enemies' eyes, near enough to watch the sweat beading on their brows. Surely men within arm's reach of each other could not shoot one another down in cold blood!

And then he heard it with the rest of them, a soft sharp metallic click that was a pistol hammer being drawn back.

They were going to do it! The Earps were going to shoot down the cowboys, no matter most of the boys were empty handed. He swallowed hard, unwillingly pulled back to those few fatal seconds when he'd seen his father face a similar threat. That day, he'd been a frightened bystander, unable to help.

But this time, he had a gun.

Smoke erupted from his pistol as Jack squeezed the trigger six times in rapid succession. One corner of his mind watched him firing, relieved to see he was not trying to hit anyone, was not trying to kill. All he wanted to do was draw the lawmen's attention away long enough for the boys to grab their own weapons and defend themselves.

Answering gunfire abruptly thundered through the lot,

smoke and dust billowing as bullet after bullet roared past the shouting men below.

His ammunition long since spent, Jack dropped his pistol and flattened himself against the roof. A shot or two fired in his direction, whizzing past him to lodge in the building beyond. Reflexively, he tried to count the shots, but quickly lost track amid the echoes and shouts. The high-pitched scream of the saddled horses caught up in the onslaught added to the confusion, while the action became a mere blur with the gunsmoke hanging cloudlike over the scene. He saw shadowy men fall, heard a cry, "They have murdered me," but whose lament it was, he could not tell.

Then, just as suddenly, silence fell.

The stillness lasted perhaps as long as the gunbattle had, maybe half a minute, before sound rushed in again. Mortally wounded men were moaning, those less injured were cussing, while shouting townspeople poured into the lot from Fremont Street and behind through the OK Corral. Who was dead and who still breathed among the lawmen and cowboys, Jack could not tell for sure.

Not caring now if he were seen, he grabbed up his hat and scrambled back along the topside of the boarding house toward its edge. He shimmied down the same porch rail he'd climbed up, half jumping and half falling before he was close to the ground. He was taking a risk— what if someone guessed he and not one of the nine men in the lot had initiated the shooting?—but he had to know if his friends were safe. A fence separated him from Fremont Street, so he quickly scaled it and circled back around to blend with the citizens who'd rushed to the corral to help or to gawk.

Frantically, he scanned the crowd. Where were they, Tom and Frank and the rest? He glimpsed the gray-garbed Holliday leaning up against a nearby stall, his pale face tinged blue as he coughed into a stained handkerchief. The tubercular dentist was the sole gunfighter that Jack spotted among the townsfolk.

A cold knot, as if he'd swallowed down a river rock,

settled in his stomach. What if everyone else was dead? It would all be his fault, for firing first. No matter his only motive had been to try to avert a slaughter.

A rough hand abruptly grabbed him by the collar and dragged him upward, so he was balancing on his toes. "What in holy hell are you doing here, boy!" Ike Clanton yelled down at him, giving him a shake that made his head snap back.

Jack stared back up at him, fear and relief rushing through him like a bitter tonic. Save for his earlier injury, the man appeared unhurt. He should have know that Ike, at least, would have made it through the gunfight unscathed.

"What in the hell?"

The second voice belonged to Billy Clanton. Revolver gripped in one hand and one leg wrapped in a blood-soaked rag, he stumbled toward them. His furious gaze was fixed on Jack.

"Kid, what in blue blazes are you doing here? Everyone told you that you had no business here in town."

"I-I'm sorry, Billy . . . Ike," he managed. "I thought you might need help."

"Help," Billy snorted, tucking his pistol into his waistband. "Things went bad enough today. Who knows what in hell might have happened if you'd been been there shooting it out with the rest of us."

"Maybe them Earps would have kept their pieces in their holsters," Ike retorted, "if they had seen he was just a young'un."

He let loose of Jack's collar and gave him a shove that sent him to his knees. "You're damn lucky you come out on the good side of this, boy. Now, you're gonna do what your elders tell you to do next time, right? No more sneaking into town without permission?"

"No, sir," Jack gasped out as he got to his feet and dusted himself off. "But, Ike, what about Tom, and Frank, and Billy Claibourne? Are they . . . all right?"

"Right enough," Ike replied. "Better'n those Earp boys. Now, go git them horses and wait over in the corral. I suspect Sheriff Behan is going to want to chat with us a bit."

"Y-yes, sir."

Jack had turned to obey, when Ike's calloused fingers clamped down on his shoulder again. The older man stuck his bearded face close to Jack, his florid features grim and breath still sharp with whiskey. Glancing about as if to make sure no one among the onlookers was listening, he whispered, "You was up on that roof shooting, wasn't you, boy? Right before all hell broke loose."

Jack hesitated. He could lie, say he'd been down at the saloon looking for them when the shooting started, but he knew the wily Ike would see right through the tale. Slowly, he nodded. What would Ike do, turn him over to the sheriff?

To his surprise, Ike merely grunted and muttered, "Good thing you was there, boy. Things might have gone different for us Clantons and McLaurys iff'n you'd stayed back at the ranch like you was supposed to. Now, don't worry . . . I don't think none of them others saw you."

He gave Jack a final shove and started toward where Frank sat propped against the outer wall of Mr. Fly's photography studio, cursing weakly over his bloody shoulder. Jack could see Tom standing next to him, and Billy Claibourne, as well. Both those men looked dirty and shaken but relatively unharmed. But what about the lawmen whom they had battled?

The crowd parted briefly, and he could see the three Earps lying sprawled in dust, surrounded by townspeople and wailing womenfolk who he guessed were their wives. He couldn't tell if they were alive or not. Something in the women's cries made him fear the worst.

Jack scrubbed a dirty hand across his eyes before his own tears could leak down his cheeks. Twelve years old was too damn old to be crying, he told himself. He did what he had to do to save Frank and Tom and the others. Still, he would always wonder if he'd done the right thing. Maybe things would have settled themselves out if he hadn't started shooting . . . but maybe, like Ike said, things would have gone worse.

He glanced up at the roof of the boarding house where he'd spent the past couple of hours keeping watch. In his haste to reach the ground, he had left behind his father's pistol, likely fallen into a corner behind the sign. He could come back later and find it, if he wanted.

He abruptly realized that he wouldn't do it . . . not tomorrow, or ever. Let someone else stumble across the pistol someday and wonder whose it was, and why it was left behind. Let them take it. He didn't want it now, didn't need it.

Besides, he didn't have any more bullets left.

By the next day, word had reached the outlying towns about the brutal gun battle between the cowboys and the lawmen just off Fremont street, not far from the OK Corral. The fight had lasted no more than half a minute, as reported in the town's aptly named newspaper, the *Epitaph*. Numerous citizens had stepped forward to give their accounts, most blaming the Earps for the tragedy. One was quoted as opining how the fight took twenty-three seconds, and someone else said more than thirty shots were fired, most at point blank range. Why more of the combatants hadn't been killed was perhaps the greatest surprise of all.

By the next day, too, the undertaker had finished his work. Jack made himself come into town one final time to see it. In the front window of the funeral parlor, the dead men lay in their open coffins, displayed like the finest of drygoods. They were dressed in their Sunday best, looking quite lifelike though their waxy features hinted at the anguish of their final moments. The coffins had been situated so everyone who passed by could get a good look at the outcome of that battle and view its victims.

A banner painted by one of the family hung above the three men, the length of cloth an angry accusation against the gunfight's victors. For the second time in as many days, Jack blinked back tears as he pressed closer to read the stark words, knowing in his heart they were meant for him.

> *Morgan Earp*
> *Virgil Earp*
> *Wyatt Earp*
> *Murdered on the*
> *Streets of Tombstone*
> *1881*

PEACEKEEPING MISSION

Laura Resnick

THE war between Canada and the United States had dragged on for more than twenty years by the time peacekeepers parachuted into Ohio—though sending troops to keep the "peace" in a crazy hellhole like North America was like sending forces to the South Pacific to keep the ocean dry.

Much of the world had already forgotten (or, in fact, never knew) the origins of this costly war. All that most people knew was that those crazy Canadians and Americans hated each other with a rabid passion that defied all reason. Most of the international community had given up believing there would ever be anything friendlier between them than the occasional brief ceasefire. And, as all the world knew after two decades of watching this insane conflict, all a ceasefire really accomplished was to give those nutty North Americans a chance to rest up enough to begin another round of all-out fighting. War and chaos just seemed to be their default setting.

We in the Middle East couldn't understand it.

As an intelligence officer, my mission was to liaise with local militia leaders in an attempt to end the latest round of senseless strikes and retaliations. So on June 6, I parachuted into Ohio with the Mohammed-Moses Brigade a.k.a. the Perilous Prophets, an elite unit of the best-trained peacekeepers in the Israeli-Palestinian Army.

The original company had been formed forty years ago, shortly after Israel and Palestine realized how silly it was to have *two* countries crammed in such a tiny place and decided to unite as one nation and share the land fairly, in peace and brotherhood.

Why couldn't those crazy North Americans, who had something like five hundred times as much land, do the same?

"That's just how Americans and Canadians are," said the Druze military intelligence colonel who had prepared me for my first mission here three years ago. "Incapable of reason."

On that occasion, I had been assigned to infiltrate the embattled district of Hollywood, in the decimated wasteland of southern California, in an attempt to help the underground movement there, Filmmakers For Freedom, reestablish communications with their comrades in New York, known as the Thespian Peaceniks. My predecessor on this assignment, a much decorated intelligence officer from Ramallah, had stepped down a few weeks earlier, reporting that the powerbrokers of the Hollywood community would be more receptive to a Jewish liaison officer. I was sickened by that kind of intolerance, but I put my feelings aside for the sake of the mission and accepted the assignment.

The Middle East League hoped that the combined pressure of (what little remained of) the coastal American entertainment communities could convince Washington to sit down at the negotiating table. My job was to do whatever it took to bring this about.

Thousands of miles away, my colleague Khalil Bouhabib was trying to convince the now impoverished TV community in Toronto to pressure Ottawa to do the same.

Those goddamn Canadians. They sent Khalil back to Jerusalem in twelve different boxes. Each one with a maple leaf stamped on it. Bastards.

No one is meaner than a Canadian.

Except maybe an American. It turned out that the Hollywood community was just using me to get locations on the hideouts of Canadian actors who'd been longtime US residents and were still living there secretly, unwilling to go back to their native land. Thanks to the war, there was no film work in Canada. Also, any Canadian who'd ever worked in American films, TV, or theater was a "traitor" in Canada by then. Hence the notorious Stratford (Ontario) Festival massacres, a few years ago—a whole generation of classically trained actors wiped out in a single season. What a goddamn waste. According to our intel, there are still several thousand Canadian actors living in hiding or under false identities in the US—although the paranoid Actors Equity Association wildly inflates the likely numbers.

Anyhow, what can I say? I'd spent most of my life in Gaza before being sent to America. So, despite my training, I was naïve. I had no idea how depraved people can be. When the Hollywood underground asked for my help, I agreed to put them in touch with William Shatner.

I'll never forgive myself for what they did to him. His acting wasn't *that* bad.

It was a cruel lesson in the ways of North Americans, and I never forgot it.

A lot of people believe the war began with a bloody incident twenty-one years ago, known as the Puck Riot, when Montreal attacked Syracuse over the disputed outcome of a hockey game. But the conflict's true origin goes back even further.

A few years ago, Iraqi human rights workers came across a cache of documents hidden in an old sushi joint in Detroit. Suspecting these were important, they turned them over to Lebanese intelligence, a longtime ally who, in turn, shared them with us. (International cooperation like this has been the bedrock of the Middle East's ongoing economic growth, scientific progress, and social-welfare advances. If only those squabbling Europeans and bloodthirsty North Americans could understand this and put down their swords.)

Anyhow, the newly discovered documents turned out

to be top-secret correspondence that told the whole story of how the war *really* began.

Twenty-two years ago, a geographer in Moose Jaw, Saskatchewan, discovered that the US border, unbeknownst to anyone until then, illegally extended into Canadian territory by 217 meters.

Representatives from both countries met in Bismarck, North Dakota, to discuss the situation.

Rather than move the official border, the US State Department proposed that the Canadians cede the disputed land to the United States. Canada's Minister of International Cooperation refused to agree to this. The Governor of North Dakota remarked that, with this refusal, the Minister was failing to live up to her all-too-Canadian title.

According to reports relayed to Washington at the time, the Canadian minister replied, "What do you mean by that, you rube?"

(However, some historians think that since Minister Michelle Bouvier was a francophone Canadian, she may actually have called the Governor a *rue*, which is French for "street." But it remains unclear to this day why she would have called Governor Williams a street, so this theory has never gained significant support.)

The subsequent exchange of insults between the two parties is too culturally specific to make much sense, but the upshot was that the American governor shot the Canadian minister. (Governor Williams was killed four years later by a direct missile strike. His personal journal was recently found by Pakistani peacekeepers patrolling house-to-house in what's left of Bismarck. In his private writings, his longstanding bigotry against Canadians is detailed in shockingly specific language. Among other things, he firmly believed you could detect any Canadian, no matter how cleverly disguised, by smell.)

In an attempt at damage control after this disastrous summit, the Americans bribed the Canadians to hush up the minister's murder by giving them Detroit. We think a key piece of documentation must have been destroyed, because no one can figure out why Canada agreed to such a bad exchange. Meanwhile, the Americans kept their North Dakota border right where it was. And more than a few Canadians went home fuming with wounded pride and a burning sense of injustice—a dangerous combination in the frozen north.

Indeed, many staffers on *both* sides resented the infamous Bismarck Capitulation, as it came to be known in the cache of secret documents that were uncovered in Detroit decades later. Some Americans believed their government should never have ceded an inch of territory to "those smelly moose-huggers" from across the border. Meanwhile, a number of Canadians were bitterly disappointed in their Prime Minister, who they thought should have held out for Silicon Valley or the Big Apple rather than settling for the Motor City.

These malcontents on both sides of the secret Bismarck agreement began sowing discontent among the masses of both nations. Canadians grew to resent America's economic imperialism and bad daytime television. Americans began to hate being the butt of so many Canadian jokes. So, next thing you know, rebel movements intent on destabilizing both governments turned a rather dull hockey game between Montreal and Syracuse into the war's first battlefield.

After that, things just kept escalating. The Pentagon ordered missile strikes in Quebec. Ottawa retaliated by invading Washington state and pushing all the way south to Oregon. North Dakota invaded Saskatchewan, but it was years before anyone noticed. Montana went up in flames as brother fought brother.

There was a brief period of hope after the Negev Peace Agreement, when the Israel-Palestine government forced the North Americans to sit down and negotiate a ceasefire. But the IP diplomats really had no idea what they were dealing with. They walked away from the Bedouin tent where the accords had been signed and celebrated a job well done. Within days, though, there were riots in Calgary, Vancouver, Orlando, and Kansas City protesting the terms of the agreement. And within weeks,

Des Moines, Savannah, San Diego, Toronto, Victoria, and Whitehorse were rioting, too.

The Middle East tried to ignore these violent, isolated outbursts as the usual saber-rattling of the rabid citizens of those two famously infantile nations. We all hoped that if we just pretended not to see their tantrums, they'd get tired of throwing them. And for almost a full year, the tense ceasefire still held.

But then a splinter rebel faction of lunatic Canadians slipped into New York and burned down Yankee stadium. Then the so-called Tea Party Martyrs, a motley but massive underground militia of Americans, retaliated by dumping seventeen tons of Mercury into Lake Ontario, as close to the Canadian shoreline as they could. (Were they too ignorant to understand the toxic water would damage their own ecosystem, too? Or were they just too bloodthirsty to care? In North America, you never really know.)

That was when Israel-Palestine, Lebanon, Iran, Iraq, Egypt, Jordan, and Syria created a joint task force, The Middle East League, to try to prevent all-out war from breaking out again in North America. (Oman, Yemen, and Saudi Arabia would have joined the League, too, but they were too busy trying to establish a lasting peace between England, Wales, and Scotland.) Our diplomats hastened to Washington and Ottawa to see what could be accomplished. (I hear that talking to the US president was like trying to reason with the sea. And some of our diplomats confided upon their return home that they believed the Canadian Prime Minister was suffering some form of psychosis. Consequently, some of the Middle East's best psychiatrists joined the next few peace missions to Canada, disguised as junior diplomatic aids. Unfortunately, no diagnosis was ever reached. Doctors thought the PM's condition could be anything from syphilis to schizophrenia to just being a power-hungry jackass.)

However, the League's hope of negotiating a renewed ceasefire, never mind real peace in the region, was shattered when a gang of radical senior citizens in Miami, armed with light artillery, began attacking Canadian cruise ships that docked there under the terms of the Negev agreement. In response, the Maple Leaf Brigade began firing homemade missiles across the border at Maine, Vermont, and New Hampshire. When his boyhood home was destroyed in one of these strikes, the US president ordered carpet bombing in Nova Scotia.

And so the war was back on again.

Maybe it's the climate that drives men mad here?

By the time I dropped into Ohio with the Perilous Prophets, I was well into my second tour in Nam, as we called North America, and the senseless rage of this continent was eating away at me. I needed to get out. Get out *soon*.

My initial recon of the volatile southern Ohio Valley revealed that the inhabitants had burned down every maple tree in their region. This senseless destruction of life was just another way, in their view, of attacking Canada symbolically. Some of the younger Prophets were disturbed by such wanton waste.

In this bastion of hyperpatriotism, Ohioans had renamed Canadian bacon as "freedom bacon." Canada's maple syrup products had been banned here for years; they weren't even available on the black market in Ohio, as they were in New York and New Jersey. Clothing merchants had to show proof that their wares contained no Canadian wool. No one bought furniture anymore made of maple wood, and people burned their old maple furniture by night in communal bonfires.

In northern Ohio, various factions were lobbing a deadly assortment of homemade rockets, expired Soviet ordinance, and heat-seeking missiles across the border into Ontario. Most of their artillery couldn't clear Lake Erie, though, and wound up in the drink. The environmental consequences were increasingly dire, but neither the Middle East League nor the Peace In Our Time triumvirate on the Saudi peninsula could get permission for our experts to assess the damage to the lake's marine life.

My mission here was to facilitate a key step in a multistage process designed to get Canada and the US to withdraw to their original prewar borders and come back to the negotiating table. The Middle East League knew better than even to *mention* the subject of the North Dakota-Saskatchewan border that had, as top-level officials inside both North American governments knew, led to the start of the war in the first place. That dispute was so sensitive, so volatile, so seemingly irresolvable, the first parameter established for a new wave of proposed peace talks was that the subject wouldn't even be put on the table. It would be postponed until a later, indefinite set of talks.

I thought this was a doomed strategy. How could we *ever* get these two nations to stop fighting if we didn't force them to discuss and resolve the issue that had led to twenty-one years of war in the first place?

This strategy was the idea of the Mexicans, who were desperate. Their once-thriving economy was in trouble because of the flood of American refugees pouring across their border after most of California was occupied four years ago. Canada had vowed to bomb Mexico if they didn't turn over American refugees involved in cross-border raids against Canadian occupiers; and the US had vowed to blockade all Mexico's Gulf ports if they complied with the Canadians.

So Mexico had begged the Middle East League to try once again to end the war. And I had been sent to Ohio, one of the hottest fronts in the war these days. My assignment was to establish contact with the chiefs of the most active fighting forces here—whether official military, rebel, splinter, or counterrevolutionary—and convince them to cooperate with a call from Washington for a ceasefire. The federal government was by now so weak and ineffectual that it would topple altogether if it tried to end the war *without* the full political support of the country's various militias.

"But we're not *at* war," said Herb Neiheisel, leader of the Battling Ohioans, soon after I located his base camp near the lakefront town of Sandusky.

"You're kidding me," I said to Neiheisel. "You and

Ontario exchange heavy artillery fire almost every day. Civilians in both countries—women and children—are killed by direct strikes, as well as by enemy raids, on a weekly basis. It's illegal for Canadians to travel to the US, and vice versa. It's illegal for an American to marry a Canadian, and vice versa. American forces are occupying Saskatchewan—"

"They are?" said Neiheisel in surprise.

"—and Canadians have occupied Washington, Oregon, and California. So tell me . . ." I spread my hands as I asked, "In what way are you *not* at war?"

"We *won* the war," Neiheisel said smugly. "Those goddamn Canadians just don't accept it yet."

After three years in this place, I should have known better than to ask a logical question.

"Okay, fine, you won the war," I said, "but since the Canadians don't accept that yet, and your life would be easier if they *would* acc—"

"I ain't interested in no *Canadian* making my life no easier."

Trying to untangle the double negatives, I said, "But what about your children?"

"They fight Canadians with pride, just like their daddy."

Neiheisel looked about thirty-five, surely not old enough to have kids of military age. "How old are they?"

"My son is twelve and carries light ammunition to combat units under fire. My daughter'll be fifteen in October. She can already take apart and reassemble an AK-47 in the dark."

"But don't you want them to be able to finish school?" I asked, searching for an argument that might open this man's mind to the possibility of a ceasefire. "Go to college? Get married and have kids of their own?"

"I want them to *kill Canadians*!"

Since this was the most important combat leader in northwestern Ohio, I tried once more. If there was any possible way Neiheisel might consider peace, I had to find that crack in his stony exterior.

So I said, "Are you sure you're taking the best position?"

"Of course I am!"

"Because I've talked with 'General' Joe Johnson of the Columbus Defense Forces, and he—"

"You've talked with the General?" Neiheisel's eyes brightened. "Now *there's* a patriot! A great leader! A true soldier of the people!"

In fact, Johnson was an opportunistic thug who used a totally fictitious military title and had probably killed his first wife. But he was the single most powerful man in Ohio. Even the governor—no, *especially* the corrupt, spineless governor—took orders from Joe Johnson, the so-called General of Ohio.

"Yes, I've been in talks with him," I told Neiheisel. "And General Joe favors peace."

Neiheisel's eyes bulged. "*What?*"

"General Joe says twenty-one years of war are enough, it's time to end the fighting, start rebuilding the country, and raise American children in peace and prosperity."

Neiheisel frowned thoughtfully. "General Joe said that?"

"Yes," I lied. "The General favors peace talks."

In fact, General Joe had threatened to cut out my tongue just for suggesting a ceasefire. But maybe I could go back to Columbus and work on him some more after I gathered support elsewhere for the idea. And, as per my training and my instructions, I would do whatever it took to *get* that support, if it was at all possible.

I suddenly heard the high-pitched scream of a missile approaching its target, and I was on the ground with my arms covering my head even before Neiheisel shouted, "Incoming!"

The missile exploded about two hundred yards from us.

As I got up and started brushing myself off, I said to Neiheisel, "General Joe knows that ongoing hostilities could jeopardize peace talks. The president needs a ceasefire. This can only work if Ohio will cooperate."

I heard another whining missile coming toward us. But Neiheisel, also rising from the ground, shook his head. "No, that one won't make it this far." He listened a moment longer, then nodded as the noise disappeared. "Went down in the lake."

"So what do you think?" I prodded. "Will the Battling Ohioans cooperate in a ceasefire?"

"What I think is, those two missiles are the start of a full-scale barrage, and you'd better get the hell out of here if you don't want to violate your status as a peacekeeper and help us kill some Canadians today."

"But—"

"I have to think about it, and today's not a good day for thinking," Neiheisel said, as another missile flew overhead, confirming that this was indeed the start of a battle. "Where can I get a message to you?"

"The Israeli-Palestinian peacekeeper base at Columbus."

"Expect to hear from me soon," Neiheisel said.

Well, he wasn't kidding. Two days after I slipped out of Neiheisel's embattled base camp and returned to Columbus to report my findings to date, I got his message. He sent me General Joe's severed head in a box. The enclosed note said, "Death to all traitors."

This goddamn continent.

I decided I'd had enough of this insane war. The next morning, I applied for a transfer.

After taking a mental-health leave back in Gaza, I'll be headed for the peacekeeping mission in Liechtenstein. Maybe I can do some good there. At any rate, after three years in North America, I'm just sure I can't do any good *that* crazy hellhole.

THE FIRST CASUALTY

Cynthia Ward

> Truth is the first casualty of war.
> —Aeschylus

For two days, Count Bellinor and one hundred knights of Westshore rode north across barren moors; and Sir Lucius rode always at the count's side. When the count's company entered the hill country of Adriana, an army rode forth to meet them. Emrys, Duke of Adriana, greeted his vassal Bellinor with the warm courtesy of long friendship and bade the count and his champion sit with him at the high table for the celebratory banquet that would precede the duke's wedding day.

Sir Lucius sat at the right hand of his liege, Count Bellinor, who sat at the right hand of his liege, Duke Emrys. Emrys and Bellinor were age-mates, thirty years old; they were strong, brave knights and high-born, handsome men, pursued by ambitious ladies and amorous maidservants since their beards were but downy wisps. Yet beside Sir Lucius their splendor faded, for the young man was surpassingly handsome, with a lean-muscled build, fine fair features, sharp green eyes, and short dark hair as sleek as a seal's pelt. Any woman looking upon the eighteen-year-old knight would consider him a very paragon of virile beauty, unless she chanced to look upon his hands and saw that his fingers were webbed.

Not all women found this a flaw. In the few hours since his arrival at Duke Emrys's great castle, young Lucius had made assignations with two maidservants and a lady.

Sitting quietly at the high table while his lord chatted about old loves with the duke, Lucius sipped good Burdigalian wine and looked out over the great hall of Duke Emrys's castle. Though the hall was vast, it was crowded with a thousand armored knights in silk surcoats blazoned with their lords' devices. Amid the bright flash of burnished steel armor, gold plate gleamed. Lucius's eyes widened. Rare indeed was the knight who could afford gilded armor; yet a score wore it here.

The features of the men in gold would not come into focus; Lucius closed his left eye and saw the bluff florid faces of robust men in their cups. Lucius opened his left eye and the faces blurred again. He closed his right eye. The blurs resolved into pale, fine, almost delicate faces of extraordinary handsomeness. Lucius's heart began to beat fast as a war drum.

He leaned close to Count Bellinor. "My lord," he murmured, "I believe that among Duke Emrys' guests are knights of the Fair Folk—"

"What is this you are saying?" Count Bellinor asked, looking at Lucius askance. "I see only true men, Lucius. My good friend Duke Emrys would never treat with Faerie demons. Your origin gives you strange fancies—"

"My lord, the Fair Folk are not demons," Lucius said, trembling to correct his liege but driven to speak. "They are soulless, save those who are baptised, like my mother, or those who take service with the Devil. It may be the duke does not know what creatures lurk among his guests—" Lucius returned to his point "—and so we should alert him. Elfin kingdoms lie under the hills of Britannia—"

"My lords!" Duke Emrys cried, rising to his feet and raising his goblet. "Dear guests, I would have you meet my lady fair, who tomorrow shall be my wife! *You!*" He gestured at a stumpy servant bowed under a platter of roast boar. Lucius closed his right eye, and the short ugly man became even shorter and uglier, a squat, rag-clad, humpbacked figure with brown-slippered feet that pointed backward. "Servant, send word to my lady Andraste to join us for a cup!"

The lords and knights cheered—all save Lucius, who, now that the duke was standing, got his first clear glimpse of the man seated on the duke's left. The man was a tall, handsome, unknown lord in golden armor. Lucius closed his right eye. In his infancy, his mother had anointed his left eye with a powerful ointment. Now his left eye showed him a figure of such perfect male beauty that Lucius knew he must look upon an elf lord.

"My lord," he whispered to Bellinor, "the man seated upon His Grace's left is no man—"

"Boy, you begin to annoy me," said the Count. "That is the Duke's ally, Prince Greidal, lord of a distant land. Hold your foolish tongue, Webfoot."

"Yes, my lord," Lucius said, bowing his head contritely. He had never seen a foreign lord before, and he had never seen a fairy save his mother, who had disappeared long ago; he must be mistaken. He would bedevil his liege no more with rash speculations. While he was a knight's son, he was but half human, and lucky to have been taken into Bellinor's service. He appreciated what the Count had done for him.

He saw again the squat ugly servant whose backward-pointing feet were visible only to his left eye. The little man was naught but some brownie who had settled in Duke Emrys' castle. Even the humblest household might have a hobgoblin sweeping its hearth; this boggart was merely uncommon bold, to assume chores in a lord's busy hall.

The cheers died away, and with elf-keen ears Lucius heard Count Bellinor whispering to his liege: "Your Grace, is this wise? It is accounted bad luck for the groom to see his bride on the night before the wedding—"

"A man who has Andraste as his bride has won Fortuna herself," Duke Emrys answered without looking at his friend. His face changed suddenly, brightening like steel under the sun, and with a gesture that spilled wine from his goblet, he cried, "Behold my bride! My betrothed, my beloved, my ally Prince Greidal's sister, the Princess Andraste!"

Lucius followed the Duke's gaze, and met green-gold eyes. They held his gaze; yet he saw the whole of Andraste's form. He stopped breathing. He had more experience with women than most men twice his age; yet the first sight of the Duke's betrothed made his body ache like that of a stripling falling in love for the first time. He could not look away.

Over the thunder of his heart, Lucius heard his liege's soft moan: "I must have her!"

"My lord!" Lucius said, quiet but intense. "These are not fit words for guest or friend, and you are both to the duke!"

Bellinor seized Lucius's arm, tearing him away from the compelling green-gold gaze. Bellinor's pale eyes blazed like white fire as he replied in a low but frighteningly passionate voice: "I *will* have her. Tonight."

When he retired to his guest chamber, Lucius could hardly remember the banquet, for fear of what his liege might do, and for the terrible strength of his longing. In his turmoil he could not settle on chair or bed; he paced the room, stumbling on the uneven floorstones, lost in the haze of love.

It was well that Duke Emrys' betrothed had remained in the hall not five minutes. Had she tarried longer, Count Bellinor would clearly have flung himself upon her. Had she tarried longer, Lucius might have expired from the force he exerted upon himself so he would not throw himself down at Andraste's tiny feet or smother her breath with his kisses.

A knock set Lucius's heart to pounding. Fired by visions of impossible beauty and green-gold eyes, he flung open the door. A maidservant hurried into the room. Closing the door, she wrapped her arms about him and fastened her lips on his.

Lucius pushed her away.

"What is this?" she cried, and her voice was uglier than a crow's croak. "You said you wanted me more than a thirsting man wants water!" She was uglier than the misshapen brownie he'd seen in the hall, though when she'd approached him before the feast, he'd been happy—indeed, eager—to make a more intimate acquaintance. "You ask me to come to your chamber, only to spurn me? Hellspawn!" she shrieked, and slapped him.

"I've naught to do with Hell!" Lucius exclaimed, rubbing his stinging cheek.

"You are more false than the Prince of Lies, Webhand!" the maidservant replied, and she fled weeping from his room.

Lucius closed the door and leaned against it.

She is as beautiful as a fairy, Lucius thought, his mind returned instantly to Andraste. *These outlanders are all fearfully fair. May I never journey to Prince Greidal's land!*

He crossed his arms. His hands tightened on his upper arms until he thought his bare fingers must crush the steel plates.

How can I live without her?

Another knock on the door increased Lucius's unease even as it filled him with foolish hope. He said, "Who is there?"

"Your lord," came the voice of Count Bellinor. "Admit me."

Lucius opened the door and Bellinor strode in. His face was taut and white with deadly determination and terrible strain. He seized the front of Lucius's surcoat in his sinewy hand.

"We have tonight, for Emrys will not go near her again until the wedding tomorrow," Bellinor said roughly. "I have roused my company to prepare for departure. Come with me, Webfoot, and bring a cloak to cover her when we bear her away."

Lucius began to shake. But the shaking stopped when he and his liege confronted the honor guard of four knights standing watch over Princess Andraste's door; and in only seconds they had slain the Duke's hand-picked men.

Lucius followed his liege into the apartment of the Duke's betrothed. Screaming wrathfully, Princess Andraste's ladies-in-waiting ranged themselves protectively before her. Count Bellinor raised his sword to cut them down. With a startled cry, Lucius knocked his lord's blade aside; then with his fist and sword-pommel, he laid the four women out senseless on the floor.

He raised his head and looked up the princess. Her green-gold eyes met his, level, fearless, oddly calm. Lucius stood transfixed, his blood roaring in his ears. By God, she was more beautiful than all the angels of Heaven!

Bellinor lunged forward, closing steel-gloved fingers on her silk-clad arms. She writhed in his grip, half-turning away from the two men. Lucius, no longer confronted with the full force of her beauty, plucked off his cloak and threw it over her. The count flung her across his armored shoulder as easily as a bolt of linen.

"We must go!" Lucius whispered. "Someone may have heard the screams, the fighting—"

He thought suddenly of his mother, who had disappeared when he was a boy. She had been a fairy damsel, a seal maiden, whom Lucius's father had won by stealing her shape-shifter's pelt. Had it been like this for his mother? A terrifying capture?

"Keep silent, woman!" Bellinor commanded, laying his sword edge against an exposed patch of white neck. At the contact, Andraste went limp on his shoulder.

Fairies fear iron, Lucius thought, and then he shook his head. *Even a halfwit fears a sword at the throat.*

He closed his eyes. *We have shared bread and salt with Duke Emrys. We have broken every rule of hospitality known to man, and surely we have brought war upon our land.*

"Do not tarry, Lucius!" said his liege.

Now they must make their way all across Duke Emrys's great castle to the stables.

*   *   *

"A message has come, and I must be gone!" cried Count Bellinor. "Ivernian raiders have fallen upon Westshore!"

Duke Emrys's gate guards raised the portcullis, and Count Bellinor's company rode into the night. Lucius rode in their midst, the limp burden across his thighs hidden by the press of horse bodies.

By a miracle of God, Lucius and Count Bellinor had gained the stables unseen. Now they all rode for their lives, a hundred and one men in flight.

Though Lucius was in full plate armor and Andraste was wrapped in cloak and ropes, he seemed to feel her. The heat of her scalded his thighs. Thoughts of her beauty made him reel in his saddle like an exhausted man.

Which he was soon enough, with all the other men. They had feasted and drunk late into the night and had gotten little or no sleep before riding 'til the dawn, and into the heat of a sun-scorched midsummer day.

When the count called a halt at midday, it seemed to Lucius that they had been upon the empty moors for a hundred years.

The count took the burden from Lucius's thighs, and he dismounted, suppressing a groan as stiff muscles shrieked. He was astonished when Bellinor placed the motionless captive in his arms. He wondered if the count feared that he would behave shamefully before his men if he kept the beautiful woman, however carefully covered, in his arms.

"Let no one look upon her, Lucius," Count Bellinor said harshly, and turned away. "Men, we ride again in moments!"

Did the men know what had occurred at Duke Emrys's castle? Did they wonder about the cloak-hid captive?

Lucius carried the woman behind a hillock, away from curious eyes. He set her on the heather with a supportive arm about her shoulders and visions of her flawless beauty in his mind, but he did not pull aside the veiling cloak.

"Are you thirsty? Do you wish to eat? Do you—" he blushed "—need a moment's privacy?"

She did not respond. She did not move.

Though only half human, Lucius had a mortal's needs. He moved several steps away from the cloak-wrapped woman and, raising mail skirt and unlacing trousers, he pissed in the furze, oddly abashed by the thought that she could hear him.

Fastening his laces, he turned to see the count crouching beside the woman. He took a step toward them, and Bellinor moved away. Lucius's shoulders bowed under the weight of this confirmation that the count had made Lucius his conscience. Bellinor was a Christian knight as surely as Lucius; why did he not put his trust in God's strength?

Lucius strode to the nearby bourn to wash his hands and refill his waterskin. Then he knelt beside the cloak-wrapped woman and drew bannocks and dried fish from his belt-pouch.

"Are you sure you need nothing, my lady?" he asked.

The woman did not reply.

Lucius devoured the dry oatcakes and salty fish as though it were mana from Heaven. He was so dazed with hunger and the hours of riding that he fancied he heard music, a faint wild air.

Count Bellinor's voice roared: "Where are they? Where are Michael and Rhys and Flavian? Where are—"

"Silence!" Lucius cried, leaping to his feet. Bellinor and his knights stared at Lucius. Ignoring them, the young man turned his head in every direction, then started up a hillside. Bellinor and a few knights began to follow. Lucius said, "Keep back!"

The soft wild tune grew louder, and still louder, and Lucius found himself on the broad hilltop, at the edge of a circle of flattened grass. He put one foot in the ring.

The music surged suddenly loud as fairies great and small, beautiful and hideous, danced past him in a swift merry round, circling a band of pipers and drummers wildly playing. The desire to dance came upon Lucius, as fiercely compulsive as the desire to make love to Andraste.

"Lucius!" Count Bellinor cried. "Half your body has *vanished!*"

The tiny fairies were dressed in leaves and flowers, the high elves in silks and gold, the monstrous goblins in furs or rags or moss. Most of the Little Folk were in the air, gamboling on butterfly pinions or dragonfly gauze. Among the tall, beautiful elves and the gnarled, gruesome goblins danced men in plate armor, who spun and leaped as if they did not wear over seventy pounds of steel and who laughed as if infected by all the joy of the world.

Lucius seized Michael's wrist and pulled him out of the fairy ring.

"You plucked him out of thin air!" the Count exclaimed in astonishment and fright.

"What are you doing?" Michael screamed. "Let me go!" He lunged toward the fairy ring.

Lucius struck him in the face. He staggered back.

"Stay out of the fairy ring, lest you be trapped 'til the world ends!" Lucius shouted at Michael. "Or you may escape, only to turn to dust from the passage of centuries!"

Lucius put his face back into the ring and drew out Flavian. And Rhys, and three other men.

His head spinning with the beautiful, terrible music, Lucius removed his foot from the circle. The fairies disappeared, but the music did not. The six men he had saved from the fairy ring fell upon him, striking with steel-sheathed fists. Lucius raised his arms to protect his face and fell upon the ground, curled in a ball. Fists and feet rang on his armor. His face throbbed, bruised and torn by the first quick blows.

The steely clangor ceased, and the music filled his mind again. Cautiously, he lowered his hands. The six men were gone, and more knights were advancing upon the fairy ring, their eyes intent yet blank.

"Mount up and ride!" Lucius cried, rising as quickly

as pain and heavy armor allowed. "Ride for your lives! Ride for your *souls!*"

The count and the knights clambered into their saddles, and Lucius ran to the captive. Bearing her limp weight, he struggled into his saddle and rode after the fleeing knights. It was a good while before Lucius realized that, despite his grim warning, the count had lost more than six men.

Count Bellinor's hundred were now eighty-five.

Lucius shivered. He'd had an even narrower escape than he'd thought from the Fair Folk.

Were they the vanguard of an elfin army?

"My lord!" Lucius cried, spurring his horse to the Count's side. He leaned toward Bellinor and nearly overbalanced from weariness. But he kept his seat and spoke just loud enough for the Count and no other man to hear him over the thundering hoofbeats: "My lord, this woman is surely a lady of the Good People! Let us leave her here, lest their uncanny pursuit grow more terrible—"

"Are you afraid?" the Count roared in scornful anger.

"*No*, my lord!"

"Are you not my faithful and obedient champion?"

"*Always*, my lord!"

Bellinor said, "We shall all *die* ere I surrender the woman."

Lucius was horrified. And yet, thinking on what he had suggested, he realized he had spoken foolishly: He could not leave the woman. Better that the count keep Andraste no matter the cost, so Lucius might still look upon her perfect face.

Better that Lucius should die than never see her again.

Why had her beauty not affected every man in the duke's hall as it did them? Had she enchanted Lucius and his liege?

No! Lucius shook his head violently. He would surely have seen the enchantment. There was no spell. He *loved* Andraste.

She leaned against his breastplate as limply as if she were boneless. Why was she so dreadfully still? Was it the patience of the Faerie, who live a century for every day of a man's life? Or was she dazed by the proximity of so much steel?

Andraste looked nothing like his mother, yet Lucius found himself thinking of her, for she had often been this quiet. One morning he had awakened to find her gone, and his father, attempting to console the weeping child, had said that she had found her shape-shifter's pelt and so had returned to the sea. He'd made it sound as if by her very nature the seal-fairy *had* to leave once she found her pelt; but now Lucius wondered if his mother had left for the same reason a man leaves the dungeon if he finds a secret passage out of his cell.

The sun was sinking in the west when Lucius saw the smudge of forest on the southern horizon: the border of the County of Westshore.

He cried, "Home is near!"

Horses had died from the grueling ride. But with spare saddle horses and the lost men's steeds, the count and his knights had not been hindered in their flight. Now the knights spurred their weary mounts to fresh effort and cheered as at a tournament.

From the forest emerged a great host.

Lucius cried, "An army, my lord!"

"What? *Halt!*" Count Bellinor rose in his stirrups and shadowed his eyes with his hand. "That gilded force is not my army, come to greet me!"

Lucius said, "They are the golden knights of Prince Greidal, your captive's brother."

"*How* have they preceded us to our border?" the Count cried. He swept his motionless knights with his gaze. "Men, set your lances and form two battle lines!" He turned to his champion. "You have the best eyes of us all, Sir Lucius. Tell us what you see!"

Lucius's eyes narrowed. Hundreds of warriors in gilded plate rode toward them in ordered lines. How could so many men and horses be so richly caparisoned? Lucius closed his right eye and saw a much smaller force, with only a score of knights in gold. The remainder of the advancing army was a rabble of warriors without armor, or mounts, or even the semblance of human appearance. Lucius saw hideous cyclopean faces and fanged mouths; bodies overgrown with scales or fur; raven and bear and tusked boar heads on misshapen men's torsos; skins of unnatural hue, the white of snow, the brown of loam, the gray of stone, the green of leaves. He saw a lofty, gnarled *thing* with oak-bark face and tree-branch limbs. He saw strange creatures of every size, from the tiny sprites flitting above the horses to a gray giant at the center of that monstrous army, looming above the tall gold knights on their tall white destriers like a child above tin soldiers. And he saw horses with no riders that advanced like destriers; and every one of these bare-backed gray horses had eyes like red coals and teeth like ivory daggers.

Lucius answered his liege: "I see the Host of Fairie."

At his words, it seemed the elf-maid stirred in his arms.

The count's battle-hardened knights cried out in astonishment and fear.

Beneath the cover of their shouts, Lucius said to his liege: "You kidnapped a Faerie princess in very truth, my lord, and her people are come to win her back."

"I shall not give her up!" Count Bellinor declared. He turned in his saddle, sweeping his men with a fierce glare. "What is this fearful babble? You are good Christian knights, and you wear and bear steel, which no fairy may stand against! And do you not wear the cross?" he demanded, drawing his own gold cross out of his breastplate. "The fay cannot bear its sight!"

"If they are of the Seelie Court, my lord," Lucius murmured, "the cross will mean naught to them." He raised his voice so all would hear. "Our steel armor shall repel their elf-shot like dust motes, our steel blades shall slaughter them like cattle. Our steel would dispel the fairy glamor when we are among them—but if you wear your surcoat inside-out, you shall gain the ability to see through their glamor *now!* And so you will be forewarned of their true shapes, and will know which of their number are real and which illusion!"

The knights shoved lances in saddle-sheaths and tore

silk surcoats over helmed heads. They swiftly inverted the garments and drew them on again, blazons hidden and seams jutting. They cried out in horror at the true sight of the Host of Fairie, and some turned their horses to flee.

Then Count Bellinor cried, "There are at most a hundred fairies in that rabble! Our number are near even. And we are knights of Christendom! The fairies are no match for us!"

At his words, the knights rallied, cheering bloodthirstily, and set their lances for the Host.

"Two battle lines!" Bellinor called. "Straight and true!"

"My lord," Lucius murmured, "better we should form the lines at angles, like the edges of an arrow, to pierce and sunder that dangerous mob."

Wrathfully Bellinor asked, "Do you question my battle wisdom, Webfoot, who are little more than a stripling?"

"No, my lord." Lucius reached for his lance.

The count seized his arm. "You shall stay behind the lines, Sir Lucius, and hold my woman fast! I will not have her slipping away in the confusion of combat, and I trust no one else to keep watch over her."

"My lord, I am your *champion!*" Lucius exclaimed. "I am the first knight of Westshore! I must fight!"

"If the elves break our defense, you will have a surfeit of fighting. My greatest warrior must defend my prize!"

"The fairy knights are charging!" called Sir Perrin, and other knights shouted in eagerness to close with the enemy.

"Stay behind the lines, Sir Lucius, as you value your position!" Count Bellinor said, and he spurred his destrier forward, to the center of the front line. He lowered his visor and set his shield. "Front line," he cried, "*charge!*"

"Westshore! Bellinor and Westshore!" The first line charged, forty-two blooded knights and their fierce lord. The second line, forty-two equally battle skilled, followed more slowly. Behind them, frustration eating his warrior heart, Lucius waited. He pulled on the steel gauntlets forged for his webbed fingers, then drew his sword with his right hand. His left arm pinned the captive against his breastplate so she would not fall or leap from his horse.

The score of knights in gold armor—gold doubtless enchanted to steely toughness—also advanced in a line. The rest of the Faerie Host showed no organization nor any concept of military discipline. The gray horses— kelpies—ran in and out of the mob, foam flying from their flanks and their fangs. Many of the goblins struck at each other or at dwarfs and boggarts instead of advancing toward their enemy. A goat-eared elf-archer pausing to draw bow was nearly crushed by the gray giant's broad foot.

Elf-shot rained upon the advancing men; the stone-tipped arrows bounced off their steel armor, but they felled many horses.

The front lines, human and elf, met in a deafening crash, and the earth shook with the impact. A few gilded lances snapped on steel plate—and every iron-shod lance that struck gold plate shattered like a rotted stick.

God defend! thought Lucius, his hand clenching on his crosshilt. *Their gold armor is enchanted against iron! Is our steel equally useless?*

Not all the men in the front line met gold-armored opponents, for they outnumbered the score of elf-knights; several iron lance blades impaled dwarves and boggarts, who screeched as harshly as rusted metal twisting.

Some of the men who met the elf-knights were unseated by the gilded lances—but every elf-knight remained in the saddle. The gold-armored fairies drew swords and struck at the unhorsed men; not one dismounted to continue the fight honorably. Several unhorsed men were felled immediately by slim gold blades thrust through their visor slits. But most of the unhorsed men drew their swords in time, and steel met gold with a sound like sweet-throated bells. Surprised by the musical tones, two human knights hesitated and were killed. Other men, unheeding, struck heavy blows; a gold sword was broken, a gold breastplate crushed.

"Praise be to God!" Lucius cried. "The enchanted elf-armor does not affect steel."

The second line of men now reached the battle. And for Lucius, isolated from the combat by his lord's order, yet heated with battle fever, the fighting dissolved into a strange, chaotic smear of images, of discontinuous sights and sounds:

The gray giant's club, vast as an oak, crushed dozens of men in one sweeping blow. But even as he struck, lances pierced his legs, and a sword sliced the back of his knee; the giant howled and fell, his tendons severed. His great body crushed a dozen goblins and even more human knights. A man spurred forward, sinking his lance in the giant's shield-broad eye; the giant fell silent, and his remaining eye glazed. A goblin with a wildcat's snarling head swung a branch and swept the giant-killer off his horse, and a burly dwarf crushed the giant-killer's helm with a stone mallet. Blood poured from the eye slits.

An unhorsed man swung his sword so hard the elf-knight was knocked from his saddle, but before the man could land his killing blow, a swarm of tiny bat-winged fairies surrounded his helmet in such a close-packed mass that Lucius knew he was blinded. He slashed at the obstruction; the little bodies exploded in bursts of red, like winesacks, and the reek of blood grew stronger. Then he screamed shrilly as the unhorsed elf-knight drove the gold sword up under his mail skirt, sinking the long blade deep.

A human knight rode slashing among the elf-archers, and one of the stone-tipped bolts loosed at him entered a hole in his visor. He fell off his horse and did not rise, and Lucius knew that if the man still lived, he was paralyzed by the elf-shot.

A warhorse reared to trade blows with a screaming kelpie, and the kelpie's fangs sank into the horse's throat. Its rider drove his lance into the kelpie's belly. The gray horse-monster shrieked as terribly as the Ivernian banshee is said to and closed its fangs heedlessly on the man's steel-sheathed leg. It dragged the man out of his saddle and trampled him, thick black smoke rising from its steel-scorched hooves.

Everywhere, steel swords pierced gold armor, elf flesh, goblin flesh; the human knights fought valiantly and well. But the giant's great blow and deadly collapse had felled too many men, putting the count's already outnumbered knights at a disadvantage from which, for all their skill and will, they could not recover. One by one, the human knights were killed.

Lucius held the unmoving woman against his breast-plate and braced himself for his last battle.

Suddenly his liege was before him. Count Bellinor's visor was raised, his face twisted. His left arm spouted blood; he had lost his hand. With his right hand he raised his sword above his head, crying, "If I can't have her, no one will!"

"Don't kill her!" Lucius yelled, horrified by his lord's intent to break all the rules of chivalry and Church. "Let her go safe to her brother!"

"Her brother will kill us no matter what we do to her!" Count Bellinor screamed. "She must *die!*"

Lucius's mother had been compelled by his father to leave the sea and marry him. She had had no choice. As the woman in Lucius's arms had no choice.

Bellinor swung at her head.

Lucius's sword deflected Bellinor's, and sank into Bellinor's eye. The point grated on bone.

Bellinor fell backwards off his horse.

Lucius raised his visor and stared dully down at the count's motionless body. He could not believe he had slain his own liege lord. He closed his eyes. He was damned to Hell for his betrayal. Yet he had not been able to allow Count Bellinor to slay the woman, soulless fairy though she be.

Blades clinked lightly on his cuirass. He opened his eyes. He saw gold helms stained red with blood and sun-set, and gold swords pointed at his bare face, and the gorgeous, wrath-twisted face of Prince Greidal.

The tall elf-knights stood in a circle about Lucius's horse. The prince took his sister from Lucius's lax arm;

the elf-knights pulled Lucius from the saddle. He struck stony earth with a crash, and the breath rushed out of his body.

"You are a dead man, you useless piece of mortal trash," Prince Greidal said as he cut the ropes binding his sister's cloaked body. "If you or your worthless brethren have done Andraste any harm, your death will be a slow one."

"She is yet innocent," Lucius said, though he knew they would not heed. Torture to end his life, and the tortures of Hell to follow. Liege-slayer.

He laid his head back on the earth and closed his eyes.

"Because of this knight I am unharmed," said a woman's beautiful voice, strange and familiar. Lucius looked up in astonishment, and met green-gold eyes. "This knight protected me from the mortal who stole me," said Princess Andraste to her brother. "And I know this knight would never have harmed me."

Prince Greidal's hate-wracked expression did not alter. "You lean helpless against me! I say they harmed you, sister, and he shall pay for their deed!"

Andraste pushed free of her brother's arms. "I am but weak with iron-sickness, and you know it," she said fiercely, and Lucius loved her helplessly. "And this is no common mortal, brother, but a son of Faerie!"

Greidal snorted. "Why then did he ride with a mortal host?"

"Such contempt you show for a halfblood, Greidal ap Auberon, when you were so mad to make alliance with a mortal lord that you betrothed me to a man I loathe!"

"Hold your tongue, hot-tempered sprite!" Greidal said. "I pledged you to the mortal duke because you wanted him!"

"Aye, I did—until he proved a tedious lover."

"Sister, why did you not tell me of your change of heart?"

"I did," Andraste said. "Many times. You would not hear. But you seem now to be listening, and so I say, let this man go!"

"No."

"His father was mortal," Andraste said, "but I've seen his webbed fingers. He is a selkie's son. He is one of us."

Greidal's eyes narrowed. He did not look away from his sister as he said, "*Go*, half-fay boy. Ride away, and warn your mortal kin never to offend an elf, or no word of my dear sister's shall be enough to stay my vengeance on you."

Lucius forced his gaze away from the impossibly beautiful woman. He mounted his horse and rode away from the Faerie Host and his dead comrades.

At dawn he rode into the ancestral hold of the Counts of Westshore, high on a crag above the coast of the Ivernian Sea, and he told what had happened in Adriana and upon the heath. A servant brought him food and drink, but he did not eat. He was ravenously hungry, yet hardly aware of it; he was surrounded by men and women, yet hardly aware of them. He wandered out of the castle, ignoring cries for him to stay, shoving aside the men who tried to hold him. He walked through the border forest, heedless of the dangers of bear and wolf, and came eventually to the moor.

By day and night he wandered the barren waste, sipping from the bourns when driven by thirst but ignoring hunger, ignoring exhaustion. He knew the tales of men who glimpsed a fairy maiden and fell so deeply in love that they wasted away; he knew why.

Nothing compared to her. No mortal woman, no mortal experience. Better to die than live without her.

Finally he sank down and could not rise. He lay still, though he knew he was dying, and Hell-bound for betraying his liege. Hell could be no worse than the torture of living without her.

"What a faithful lover you are, halfblood!"

He hallucinated her voice in a death-delirium, he knew, but still he forced his eyes open. He gazed into green-gold eyes. She knelt beside him, the fair Andraste. The impossibly beautiful Andraste. Far more lovely than his dull mortal mind had been capable of remembering. She was no hallucination.

"I had no need to put a glamor on *you*," she whispered, gathering him in her arms, and kissed him. Vitality rushed through his veins like wine, and he stood to embrace her, returning her kiss with all the strength of his love.

They vanished from the moor.

BLOODY FOOTPRINTS
IN THE SNOW

Jean Rabe

DERMOT was George.

He was in the lead boat of our flotilla, standing with his hand cupped over his eyes, staring at something that I certainly couldn't see. I was barely able to make him out, me being one boat back and trying to peer through a blizzard while at the same time trying to row. I did my best, but I wasn't quite in sync with the other soldiers. To be fair, I'd never rowed anything before, and my arms and shoulders protested mightily with each pull.

No, I'd never rowed, and I'd never been in such frigid weather.

Damnable war to put us in this icy muck on Christmas night.

We had a lantern on each of our boats, which would have made things a lot easier if we could have used them. But Dermot . . . George . . . we were supposed to call him George . . . told us not to light them. The enemy might have scouts along the bank, he said, and we couldn't risk someone seeing us. That's why we couldn't talk either. Bad enough that these old flat-bottomed Durham boats creaked every few minutes when one of us adjusted ourselves on the hard bench seats. The ferries the horses and artillery were on weren't so silent either. At least the howling wind helped cover the noise.

Surprise was everything, George had told the twenty-four hundred of us before we pushed off. If we lost that crucial element, we'd all die painfully. Some of us would be dying regardless, I knew. Every generation had at least one war, and every war had casualties. I just prayed I wasn't going to be one of those casualties this time around. I had a wife and twin girls at home, probably sitting around the tree now, contemplating their presents. They'd never felt cold like I was feeling; my family had never seen snow.

I don't think this snowstorm was bothering George. I didn't see him shiver even once while he briefed us, and I never heard him complain.

Easy to respect the man.

Though he was in charge, his navy blue coat wasn't any thicker than ours—those of us who had coats—and his boots weren't any better. He had the same weapons, a smoothbore single-shot musket, hatchet, and a knife, a bit more braid on his sleeve, maybe, and a half-moon of beaten metal that hung on a cord around his neck—his badge of office. He'd given himself no edge over us and took not a single favor, though regulations would have granted him a few. I think we all admired him because he stayed on our level and because he led from the front, where it wasn't safe. We followed him with increased fervor, our sergeant-turned-general. I think we'd follow him to hell.

He'd not had a real command before this war, not on this scale with this number of men, and so I suspected he was either relishing it or worrying over it—or perhaps both. In any event, I don't think he had either the time or the inclination to let the cold and the snow bother him. But it bothered the proverbial hell out of me, bothered me all the way down to my bones.

I could see my breath puffing away like I was smoking, and I could scarcely feel my fingers. I had to look down to make sure they were still wrapped around the oar handle. My knuckles were as white as the snow that seemed to be coming at us sideways now. Ice was mixed with it, and little pellets stung my face and made me wince.

As far as I was concerned, this river and this weather were as much the enemy as the men we closed on. I looked over the side, seeing chunks of ice bump against the boat, stark against the blackest-black river. The current was swift, which made rowing onerous, and it made soft shushing and burbling sounds that I would have found pleasant were I here under other circumstances. I might have appreciated the air, too, clean and crisp and so easy to suck all the way in to the bottom of my lungs. No trace of pollution.

I heard some night bird make a skreeing sound, and I guessed that it was perched in one of the tall trees along the riverbank. It skreed again, then I heard the faint flutter of its wings. I wondered what it looked like and what it was hunting . . . nothing so dangerous as what we were after.

This trip was taking too long, I knew, as George told us we needed to reach our objective while it was still dark. It had to be past midnight, us out on this river for more than an hour already, heading across and up several miles. Another regiment was supposed to have already crossed and was supposed to have put a few artillery batteries on the cliffs above Trenton.

That's where we were headed, Trenton, New Jersey, on the Delaware River. Spies reported that the enemy was entrenched there. I found myself looking forward to the confrontation . . . it would get me out of this uncomfortable boat.

Perhaps it was an hour later, or two, I really couldn't tell how much time had passed before George's boat touched against the bank, and I saw him climb out. Our boat was next, and I was thankful to be off the water. I thought it would be warmer away from the river, but as I followed George, I discovered that was a foolish notion.

We started marching, not waiting for all of the boats to unload. I heard George say we couldn't wait, couldn't assemble more than two thousand soldiers on this bank. There wasn't room, as thick as the trees were. Two and three across we went, the snow still coming down hard and the wind whipping around us.

I know I mentioned earlier that George didn't have any better boots than the rest of us. But not all of us had boots. Two of the men directly behind me had socks with holes worn in them. They'd taken a spare shirt and ripped it into strips and wrapped them around their feet. I was thankful I had boots. I was shivering, and I didn't want to turn around to see how they were faring.

So I pictured the red-coated enemy and kept marching, squaring my shoulders and looking between the gaps in the men in front of me and seeing George. Leading from the front, he'd be an easy mark. I found myself hoping he'd fall back and stay safe. We needed George, and if he went down, I wasn't sure who this detail would fall to.

We'd traveled maybe two or three miles before word filtered up that not all the boats had made it to the bank. George had ordered us to cross at three points, and another commander, this one called Cadwallader, had a regiment, some militia men, a couple of big guns, crossing the river above Trenton. We were down five to seven hundred men, they guessed, which made me worry if Cadwallader's force likewise suffered. We passed the word up to George, who motioned for us to keep going. I wondered if those men—probably some of them my friends—were lost, their boats tipped over and they drowned. Maybe they were still out on the river somewhere and had simply fallen behind. Word came up, too, that two barges with horses and artillery had landed and that they drew up the end of our irregular column.

Another mile and the snow slacked off, making it easier to see. The brightness of the snow made the trees to the west and the north look like slashes of charcoal on a dark gray canvas. The brightness also let me see bloody footprints in the snow in front of me. I knew then that there were men in the line ahead without boots, and I cursed the people who put us in this position, forcing a war on us and forcing us to fight it in near-unbearable circumstances. So we lacked proper clothing and shelter. We hadn't a single blanket and no medicine. And though we had ammunition, we didn't have a plethora of it. Food . . . I had a piece of bread so hard I'd chipped a tooth on it. But that was two days ago. We'd had nothing to eat since.

If we had any ammunition left after the battle, maybe George would let us go hunting. How hard could it be to shoot a rabbit or a deer?

I saw more blood turning the snow pink. I shuddered and fixed my gaze on the back of the man I marched behind. I'd not heard a word of complaint from the bootless men in the ranks behind me, and I knew those in front weren't complaining either.

It wasn't in the makeup of any of these men to complain—out loud—about our pitiful army. It wasn't in me, either. We all would follow George without reproach and without question. Follow him to hell, then hopefully to home—to home if we won this battle and this damnable war.

We'd had supplies when this started, when we'd moved along the river to a place called Swedes Ford and then farther the next night, December 12th. The following morning, the 13th, we marched to Gulf Mills. We were going to a winter encampment at Norristown . . . because we were exhausted and were exhausting our terribly meager provisions, because many of the men needed a doctor to look at them and maybe cut off a frostbitten leg. Gulf Mills was a good spot, high and affording a strategic vantage stretching from the Schuylkill River at Matson's Ford for miles inward. It formed a barrier that would keep the enemy anchored in their camps and from coming out to get us.

But the higher-ups weren't content to keep us there. George got orders on the 17th that we had to move, retreat to the hills of Valley Forge, where we were to establish a more permanent quarters and begin our next campaign. George and a dozen men guarded the pass between Valley Forge and Gulf Mills, though sometimes George went back to check on the rest of his troops, and a lieutenant took over in his absence.

In the three years I'd spent in the military, I'd never been through such dark, desperate times. One night, as I stood beneath the Overhanging Rock, seeking respite

from the cold and snow and waiting for the next orders,
I wished to be wounded and sent home.

These orders that set us on our current march, the one
that put us across the Delaware and in such horridly cold
conditions, could well signal the end to our stint here.
Walking skeletons, that's what a good number of us
were. George's rag-tag, half-starved, half-naked, half-
frozen loyal men, all following him to hell and leaving
bloody footprints in the snow to mark our passage.

The sky was lightening when we were signaled to a
stop, and whispers from ahead relayed that the objective
was just over the next rise. We checked our guns, and
some of us prayed. Between gaps in the bodies, I saw
George cross himself. I hadn't known he was Catholic.
Something we had in common.

Did the enemy we were after have a god?

In 1776, during the American Revolution, George
Washington's men were after England's garrison, which
consisted of Hessian jagers and mercenaries and a troop
of the British 16th Light Dragoons, all entrenched in
Trenton. We'd all studied it in history classes, and the
battle during our military training . . . we studied a lot
of battles at the academy. But this particular one was so
many centuries ago, close to a thousand years, that
we'd . . . me at least . . . had glossed over it. Because
the real crossing of the Delaware had taken place on
Christmas, we'd been pulled away from our families at
the holidays to keep things historically accurate.

I only knew a little bit about the original battle because I'd been listening to Dermot . . . George. Perhaps
that's precisely why we'd been thrust into a war recreating the battle at Trenton—it was so long ago we wouldn't
know the particulars and wouldn't have an advantage
over our enemy.

However, I suspect George . . . Dermot . . . knew
everything about the American Revolution that there
was for a modern-day man to know. It wasn't that Dermot was bookish, though he was, Dermot was just into
American history. He had an incredible, enviable passion
for it and could recite all the names of the presidents

and the vice presidents up until the time more than three centuries past when the Dayle Forces invaded from Andromeda and turned the entire planet into once country they called Dayleland. Dermot studied up on the Dayles, too, what we could find out about them.

They looked a lot like us, though were slightly taller and with bone-white skin, lived twice as long, and had three times the appetite for violence we did. They liked that we fought back; in the beginning, when they landed, we were able to stand up to their initial wave of troops. And they liked that from time to time pockets of resistance would form to drive them out of our cities, sort of like the disenfranchised Brits who looked for independence back in 1776 America—the fellows we were portraying. But when our freedom fighters back home stopped fighting because the odds were just too overwhelming, and the Dayles got bored, they came up with a new way to amuse their warring interstellar selves.

They gathered groups of men from different continents, formed armies, instructed us in the "art of war," and sent us off to fight each other so they could watch and have a grand time. Somewhere along the line I guess they figured they were depleting the population a bit too much. So they started pitting our armies against the armies on other worlds they'd conquered on planets like this one that they'd terraformed with harsh terrain that would task the combatants.

When this particular war was over, and provided I was among the living, I'd have to ask George how close the Dayles got to what New England and the Delaware River really looked like. I'd never been to that part of our world, coming from what was once New Mexico and never traveling farther east than what was once Texas . . . until the Dayles plucked my unit.

As I said, every generation had its war, the Dayles saw to that. If you were unlucky, you got treated to two. Recreating old Earth, which we were leaving our bloody footprints on now, was a relatively new wrinkle, and I'd heard only a handful of battles had been fought here— Napoleon's Waterloo, the Huns' sweep, Pancho Villa's whatever. I would have preferred recreating Pancho Villa. I would have handled the temperature better.

I suspected that the conditions my distant ancestors faced in the real Valley Forge were as tough as these . . . the Dayles were sticklers for authenticity, down to giving us threadbare clothes and not enough provisions or boots.

George was a stickler, too. When he learned where the Dayles were sending us and what battle we were to recreate, he combed the records for some of the real George's letters and memorized several passages. "By a spirited continuance of the measures necessary for our defense, we shall finally obtain the end of our warfare, Independence, Liberty and Peace," he told us before we crossed the river. And he vowed he would "share in the hardships and partake of every inconvenience" that his soldiers would be forced to endure. George . . . Dermot . . . would have shared the hardships regardless of any letter from a moldering Founding Father.

If I'd studied history better, I might have known what our enemy in Trenton was equipped with and just how many there were. Hmmm . . . bet George didn't even know that or he would've shared those tidbits. And if I'd not been so caught up in my musings, I'd have heard the first part of what George was saying.

". . . from the north should have moved in by now. But I don't hear gunfire. Cadwallader might have already taken the town. We can't operate on that assumption, however, and so we move in now. Spread out along the south perimeter of the town, and on my order crest the rise and fire on any Red Coats you see."

I cleared my throat and risked a question as George strode by. "The enemy, General . . . I might have missed something earlier. But do we know anything about the enemy?"

George set his jaw firm and his posture rigid, but there was no familiar light in his eyes—they looked flat like a dead pond. "British 16th Light Dragoons, Hessian jagers, and mercenaries. I do not know their mettle."

"Nor their home planet, it seems," a soldier behind me whispered.

George obviously, thankfully, hadn't heard that. "I do know they will be in traditional red coats and will be armed no better than us. That they likely know nothing of the real Valley Forge and the Delaware River, and might never have heard of the planet Earth-called-Dayleland." George drew his lips into a thin line. "But I know they will fight as hard as us and that they will bleed and die like us. And I pray that the day is ours."

Several minutes later we were quietly moving into position. Whispers from the east brought sad news that two of ours had fallen, succumbed to the cold. The Dayles were probably rethinking their authenticity angle; I knew they liked bloodshed and might consider death to the weather a waste.

A dozen more steps and we were at the top of the rise and looking down on a town that was shoddily made but terribly inviting. No matter how rickety the buildings appeared, I suspected they'd cut the cold, and I wanted desperately to be inside of one. We were lined up the length of the town and wrapping around the eastern edge and three-men deep. This wasn't the best way to fight a war, standing out in the open, standing to shoot, presenting prime targets. But it was the way the first Americans fought, and so it was the way we would fight. The Dayles were known to punish soldiers who did not conform to their forced reenactments.

But were they watching this particular battle, the Dayles? There could be other battles going on at the same time on other parts of this planet—and elsewhere in this terra-formed version of New England, too. Maybe they were watching Cadwallader . . . wherever he and his men were.

The shot of a musket shattered my musings. It was followed by another and another. I sighted a Red Coat, too, and took aim.

They were as ugly as the galaxy is wide.

I figured they'd look human, or close to it. But they were saurians, a race I hadn't seen before, not even in the vids at the academy. They were seven feet tall, some of them close to eight, and they were covered with a mix of brown and yellow scales that must have been metallic, as they glimmered in the light of the lanterns hanging from posts and buildings in town. Their faces were horselike, with barbels hanging from their lower jaws and high ridges above their wide-set eyes.

To see them in the historical uniforms of the British—red coats and leather crested helmets—would have been laughable, especially with their yard-long tails hanging out holes in the back of their pants. But their rifles made the scene sobering. Some of them were dressed in bright blue coats with Prussian style grenadier mitres showing a brass or bronze front plate. Some of them carried small-caliber rifled weapons, probably stolen from a Pennsylvania regiment they'd slaughtered.

I fired, then ducked so that the man behind me could fire while I reloaded. One shot, that's all these blasted muzzle-loading muskets allowed. Fifteen to eighteen seconds, that's the speed some of us had been clocked at reloading during practice. We hadn't practiced much, though, not wanting to waste our precious ammunition. I was closer to twenty seconds on a reload, listening for the man in the third rank to fire, then jumping up and firing again.

Aiming didn't help much, as these flintlock muskets were not precise. Luck and God's will had more to do with it than skill. I don't know if I hit something, but the British lizards were dropping. So were some of us, as they returned fire. The man to my right fell, clutching at a hole in his chest. Another man a few yards away dropped to his knees, then rolled down the rise. A moment later, we were following him, charging down the rise at George's direction.

Leading from the front, he was ahead of all of us, angling toward what probably was the town's church. George had told us in the briefing that spies were privy to some of the Hessian commander's plans. Those included constructing some sort of defense around the town . . . a ditch or spikes, posts to slow us down. But the commander had not bothered with any of that, it seemed. And they had to know that we were coming. They had spies, too.

The Hessians among the lizards were shouting in a language we couldn't understand. The Dayles hadn't allowed us any translators, as they didn't exist in 1776, and so we could only guess at what our enemy was saying. They continued to yell, a string of sibilant hisses that sounded like a hundred tea kettles left too long on the fire. And they formed up in the center of town.

It looked as though they might put up a frightening defense, as they started shooting and more of us started dropping. We returned fire, pausing in our down-the-slope run, then tried to reload as we kept going.

I watched George as I went, my admiration for the man growing. He fired his musket and struck one of the Red Coats, drew his hatchet from his belt and threw it, cleaving into the leather helmet of another British lizard and dropping it. The soldiers around George fought better. Hell, I was reloading my musket faster, moving down the slope quicker, not flinching or looking when the soldier a few steps ahead of me—one of the shoeless ones—screamed when a musket ball slammed into his stomach. I darted around him and continued toward the gathering lizards.

I jumped when the sound of fire from a big artillery gun punctuated the battle. It came from the east, and so we knew the horses and artillery pieces had made it into position. Another blast came from the north, across from us. We had them boxed in, and the only way out for the lizards was cutting through our line.

A series of high-pitched whinnies came next, followed by thundering hooves. Two dozen soldiers on horseback charged down the main street, slashing the lizards with hatchets and knives. I took a knee at the edge of town and fired again. Someone behind me fired over my head. We'd both missed, but as I worked to reload—I figured I was up to three shots a minute—I vowed I wasn't going to miss the next one.

The noise was incredible, which surprised me. I'd not thought these primitive weapons could produce so much volume. Coupled with the artillery fire and the horses, the shushing of steel, and the screams of the victorious and the dying, this was as loud as any of the vids I'd seen on World War IV and V. My head pounded from the cacophony, and I found it difficult to think.

It was getting difficult to see, too, as it had started seriously snowing again. The air was white and gray—the smoke from musket fire. Sprays of blood were everywhere. I could see blurs of red and bright blue, the jackets of the lizards, and these were what I tried to aim at. I looked for George, but I couldn't see or hear him, so I concentrated on shooting the enemy and praying I wouldn't get shot in return.

I don't know how long the battle dragged on. It seemed like forever, the noise and the cold wrapping around me and making my head spin. But I suspected the time was actually short, and if I'd paid attention, I could have marked its passing in the number of shots I fired.

Three a minute.

But how many shots had I taken? And how many minutes had passed?

We moved into the houses—oh, blessed relief from the cold and snow. We weren't there for shelter, though we couldn't help but appreciate that. We were there for cover, firing out the windows and through cracked doorways, the enemy's shots hitting the wood instead of us. I reloaded and propped my musket on the window frame, finding it easier to sight without the snow coming into my eyes. I saw a lizard in Hessian garb, his pants ripped and legs showing black underneath. At first I thought he was wearing long socks, then I thought the aliens just had legs the color of charcoal.

It wasn't until after I'd killed him that I realized the black was from the cold. Before we'd started this arduous trek, I'd been with George in a camp hospital, and we saw men with frostbite so bad their legs had turned black. The men were scheduled for amputations, and thankfully George and I left before seeing the aftermath of the surgeries.

George? I took a shot, and seeing the path before my window clear, I craned my head out, looking for our general. I still couldn't see him, nor could I hear him . . . the air was still filled with the sounds of gunfire, horses, and screams.

"Move out," I told the other men in the building with me. The lizards had moved away, and we needed to follow. Too, I wanted to see where George was. I could use a little more inspiration right now. Out on the street, I caught a glimpse of a Red Coat lizard. He was running past a white saltbox, darting around the corner. Two more raced after him. "Follow them!" I tried to sound impressive. Maybe a part of me thought if I saw another war in my lifetime, I might have a chance to play George.

The sun was coming up, the sky was warming, and the snow was mixed with sleet now. It made the street slippery, and I imagined the gravel was painful to the soldiers without boots. We hurried after the lizards, sloppily reloading as we went, glancing left and right to make sure none of them were hunkered between buildings. There were at least a dozen dead within easy eyesight. I'd counted at least a dozen more on the street we'd taken to get here. The casualties would have been higher had the weapons been better. Inaccurate one-shot guns did not make for a high body count. There was some consolation in that . . . it also meant that we weren't losing too terribly many men.

Around the corner, there was George. Blood was streaming down his trousers, a nasty leg wound from the looks of it. But he was standing, barking orders to the line of soldiers to his right and waving his knife at the lizards, who had retreated to the orchard on the southeast side of town. There were ten more dead lizards at the edge of the orchard, including one that had more braid and buttons than the rest. Some sort of officer, I could tell. I raised my musket to take aim at one of the lizards in the trees, then stopped when I heard George hollering at me.

They'd surrendered, he called.

Indeed, squinting through the rain and snow, I could tell none of them had weapons raised. Rifles lay at their feet. It looked so unreal . . . lizards in ancient Earth military uniforms standing in an orchard in the dead of winter on a planet that had been terraformed for war. Many of them had blackened fingers and arms from the intense cold. Clearly they were a tropical race. Had the Dayles brought them here to see how they would fare in Valley Forge climes? Had it been random, plucking a military unit from one of their conquered worlds, paying no attention to climate?

The real George Washington had easily routed the enemy from Trenton. Our George had told us all about it, that the German garrisons with its Rahl, Knyphausen, and Lossberg regiments, and its Hessian jagers, had been forced to surrender . . . the British 16th Light Dragoons, too. That about two dozen of the enemy were killed, a hundred wounded, and a thousand captured. The numbers were different in our Trenton, however. Easily seven or eight dozen of the lizards sprawled dead in the snow, and of the several hundred in this orchard, about half had wounds.

The real George wasn't wounded that day. Ours was bleeding buckets on the street and was now leaning on a soldier for support. The real George's troops only had four wounded casualties . . . plus however many froze to death before getting to Trenton. We'd lost . . . I didn't know how many. Close to two dozen at least. I'd seen that many fall to lizard rifle fire, and certainly more had to have died farther down along the town border.

So while we weren't wholly accurate in our reenactment, we won—we got that part of our history right for the damnable Dayles.

I was among the soldiers collecting the knives, hatchets, and rifles the lizards had dropped. We patted them down and took their powder and shot. Then we marched as many into the stables as would fit—seeing how there were no horses in terraformed Trenton, save the ones we brought in. We crowded the rest of the lizards in the livestock pens outside. We laid the wounded in the parlor, kitchen, and bedrooms of the big salt box and got a fire going in the fireplace to warm them. George was seated just inside the front door, back propped up against the wall and being tended to by the closest thing we had to a doctor. The Dayles hadn't bothered to put furniture in any of the buildings, just made them look good on the outside, so we couldn't make George very comfortable.

But the wind was cut in this building, and that helped all of us. The prognosis on George was good, though he was still bleeding like the proverbial stuck pig. The shot had gone all the way through his leg, and the medic was cleaning the wound with melted snow and wrapping it tight with strips from a shirt that probably had come off a dead man. George didn't complain, and the only evidence of his pain was his occasionally gritted teeth. He kept giving orders, directing the men to take the boots off any dead men—our soldiers and the lizards—and give them to our men without boots. To take coats from the dead and pass them around, any ammunition and weapons, too. He sent fourteen men out hunting, as one of Cadwallader's men said they'd spotted deer in the woods just north of town.

Why hadn't the Dayles made Trenton truly authentic and given it food stores and cattle and whiskey bottles in the cupboards of the brick homes? While I helped look after the wounded lizards, giving up on trying to understand their hissing language, I saw another of Cadwallader's men come in waving a folded piece of parchment.

"Found it in their dead commander's coat pocket." He presented it to George, who held it up to the window so he could better read it.

A spy had detailed information about our approach across the Delaware and our intention to invade Trenton to keep them from pushing on to Philadelphia. It was written in our language, though the grammar was inaccurate and some of the words incongruous. George suspected the lizard commander couldn't read it and so hadn't thought to construct any sort of a defense around Trenton.

"Helluva war, this." It was the first time I'd heard George sound . . . defeated. "Helluva war, this so-called revolution." He got one of the men to help him up, wincing when he put some weight on the bandaged leg. He adjusted his coat and rubbed at the buttons, made sure the half-moon was hanging properly around his neck, then he bowed to the injured lizards.

"I do not believe you can understand me." He searched their eyes for some spark that might tell him otherwise. "But we will find a way to communicate, you and I. And together, we will find a way to win this war."

Then he was out the door, and I was following him, a dozen questions churning in my mind. I had the good sense only to think them and to wait for George to explain himself.

Win this war?

I thought we'd already won with the taking of terraformed Trenton. Was there another battle? I knew there was more to the Revolutionary War than this one fight, but I had hoped other units were handling the other skirmishes. George hadn't mentioned there being orders beyond Valley Forge. And George had said nothing about including the enemy.

He hobbled to the stables, refusing any aid and using his musket for a cane. He struggled opening the big door, then went inside and regarded the Hessian and Red Coat lizards. It stank in this overlarge barn, from the blood and the musket powder clinging to clothes, and from the lizards themselves who carried the pong of rotting plants. There were gaps in the wood, so it was almost as cold in here as it was outside.

Again, George tried to find one of them that could understand him. And finally he was successful—sort of successful. It looked as though the lizard picked up parts of George's speech, nodding once in a while and hissing to his fellows, maybe translating. Me? I wished I hadn't been able to understand a single word.

"We are not your enemy," George began. "And you are not ours. It took the walk to this place for me to realize that. This walk and studying this man I portray and studying everything he stood for." George let out a deep breath, the sound like dry leaves tumbling across hard ground. "Our enemy is the Dayles, and together we will fight them. With these primitive muskets and knives, our artillery and our hatchets."

George knew where the Dayles base was on this terra-formed eighteenth century Earth, as that's where he'd been given his orders. He detailed a plan for marching there, again crossing the Delaware, and this time going south. Maybe the Dayles would see us, probably would see us. But maybe they wouldn't consider us a threat with one-shot guns.

Maybe they wouldn't think an army of skeletons—half-dressed, half-starved, a handful of us still leaving bloody footprints in the snow—could best them.

And maybe we couldn't.

"But we will try," George said. "Too soon we quit rising up against the Dayles on our home world."

I saw several of the lizards nod after the words had been translated.

"Too soon we gave up and gave in."

More nods, followed by low-pitched hisses that sounded almost musical.

"The man I portray never gave up and never gave in, and it is past time we follow his example."

We didn't rest in Trenton more than another hour, George fearing that the Dayles might swoop down in one of their carriers and cart off our "prisoners." He intended to lead us to the Dayles' base, where he dreamed we would be victorious, and where he planned to capture a carrier and take our war back home.

So we set off again, this day after Christmas, lizards and humans, retracing our steps . . . easy to follow the traces of pink snow.

Easy to follow George all the way to hell.

I thought about my wife and the twins, probably play-ing with their toys under the tree, maybe thinking about me. I thought that I would probably never see them again. And I thought it bad of me that I was having no regrets.

Because some small part of my mind said that maybe our little act of defiance here might inspire others; word would get out, I knew. This Revolutionary War of ours could turn into something inspiring.

My wife and the twins had never lived in the freedom our ancestors enjoyed. But if George and I had our way, they and the rest of the planet someday would.

A GIFT OF WAR

Josepha Sherman

THE glory of war, Gerhardt thought. Wasn't that what the nobles called it?

Maybe it was like that, glorious, for the dukes of either side up there on their hills watching the battle in their spotless, shining armor as if it were some damned game. Chess. A polite game where you didn't get your hands soiled.

Down here on the field, there were only men crowded in together at the front line, us against them as the day wore on, and barely enough room to swing his sword, barely a chance to tell us from them because by now everyone was equally coated in mud.

They'd all lost any sense of "for God and country" two days back. By now, there was nothing but the struggle to stay upright in the cursed slick footing of mud and blood and he didn't want to think about what else, and to stay alive. Somewhere near this was the border over which they were fighting, but damned if he knew where it was in all the mess. Their orders had been simple: just go forward and keep going forward.

Right, but unfortunately the other side had plainly been given the same orders, which meant no one was going anywhere. The archers had exhausted their arrows after the first day, and none of them were going

112

to risk their lives down here looking for replacements. The knights weren't going to risk their valuable horses in this muck. So it was pretty much up to the foot soldiers. They'd been fighting and dying over this same cursed piece of mire for four days now. He stank, Gerhardt thought, they all stank, of sweat and other men's blood, huh, if they were lucky, other men's blood. He felt his sword grate against someone's mail, heard a grunt, but knew from the feel it hadn't drawn blood. Before Gerhardt could try again, someone else's sword struck a glancing blow to his helmet, knocking it askew, staggering him and making his ears ring. He fell back, frantically fighting to get the helm twisted about to shield head and neck again, sure someone was going to cut him down before he could—

The trumpets. Calls from both sides: Too dark to fight anymore today, so retreat.

Gerhardt risked a glance up. Damn, yes. Twilight, or at least a dimming of the cloud-covered sky. Retreat. Back over the ground they'd just been fighting to take, the all too familiar ground, and the other side drawing back, too, probably feeling the same despair. Nothing gained, nothing lost. Again.

Save for the dead, of course.

Knightly honor and sheer practicality both, leave a no man's land between the two armies. No chance for someone to slip across and maybe poison the rations or stab men in their sleep. The first day, they'd shouted insults back and forth across the empty, torn-up space, them and the enemy, back when they were all still full of energy and hope, but that had grown old pretty quickly. Now each side pretty much ignored the other.

Gerhardt spat. His head still pounded from the blow he'd received, his whole body was one big ache, and as far as he was concerned, knightly honor was nothing but a stinking piece of—

Hell, never mind. He'd signed on to this, head filled with dreams of taking some noble ransom, finally earning some decent money. He was just as stupid as the rest of them. Luckier than most: He had a complete mail coat and a decent helm and sword.

Tired as everyone else, he found a log to sit on and just flopped down. Other men, too weary to hunt for even that small nicety, dropped where they stood. New faces among them, Gerhardt noted, replacements for those who hadn't been able to retreat. You didn't make friends on the front line, not for longer than a day, anyhow.

Welcome to hell, Gerhardt thought dourly.

Not much to burn by now, but after a day like that, you needed the comfort of a fire, and soon a few little flickers of flame shot up, burning God knew what. Men slowly started gathering around the tiny fires, sharing dried meat and flasks of warm, stale-tasting water or equally stale-tasting beer.

"Think we gained any ground?"

That was one of the new men, so young it hurt Gerhardt to look at him. Instead, Gerhardt washed out his dry mouth with a sip of water, spat it out, then took a deeper swallow. "Hell, no," he said. "See that rock, the one with the notch? Same rock as yesterday, and we're seeing it from the same angle as yesterday. Haven't gained a thing."

Out there on the battlefield, the dead were being dragged off by those who always seemed to take on that job. Not much to scavenge from common soldiers, but whatever they got out of it, whatever their motives, at least they got the bodies out of the way.

There wasn't much talking. No one wanted to waste time that could be better spent in sleep. You were here on the front lines, you slept wherever you could find dry ground, wrapped in your cloak, if you were lucky enough to still have one. Gerhardt had reached the point where he could have slept in the middle of a rainstorm or the battle itself. He simply curled up with a sigh and gladly escaped for a time.

* * *

Gerhardt woke with a gasp, staring into the night, one hand closing about sword hilt before he even knew what had alarmed him.

"You can see me."

That, Gerhardt thought, had been a woman's voice. And *that* just wasn't possible. No women here, Gerhardt's mind insisted; not even the whores who followed every battle made it out here to the front line. There were no women here, even as he scrambled to his feet and saw . . . her. So pale she was nearly pure white, with long waves of pale hair and flowing white robes, spotless, all of her, spotless. And she . . . floated just above the ground and glowed with a clear blue radiance.

Gerhardt dropped to his knees. "Holy Mother . . ."

A gentle smile formed on her lips. "That is not my name."

"A saint, then, you have to be . . ."

Damn, no, he had to be dreaming. Or maybe that blow on the head had addled his brains. Or . . . had it given him a gift . . . ?

The figure laughed softly. "You do see me. I really am here." Her voice was sweet as gentle music.

"Why me? I mean, why appear to me? I'm just a soldier . . ." He glanced back at the others, but they were all asleep with the fierceness of the truly exhausted. "They—"

"I have been here all along. It would seem that only you can see me."

"But why?"

"That is a question for those mightier than either of us."

"No, I mean, why are you here? Lady, this isn't exactly a place for a saint!"

"Where better than where men suffer and die?"

"Well, uh, yes, I guess there is that, but you're a woman, I mean you were a woman—"

"Don't doubt, man. Believe. Fight gallantly."

"Then we're, uh, heaven's on our side?"

She laughed musically. "What do you think?"

"Lady, your pardon, but that isn't an answer—"

But as suddenly as a heartbeat's time, she was gone, and the night seemed all the darker.

It could have been a dream. It had to have been a dream. Saints simply did not appear to ordinary foot soldiers.

It would have been nice if she'd given him a clearer message, too. Something to show that, well, heaven really was on their side. If he'd actually seen her, of course. Which he probably hadn't.

But just the same, Gerhardt fought with new fervor, almost daring to hope, almost sure that this time, this day, things would be different. The enemy would give way and they would take this field, they would finally take this field and move on into the hills, and maybe their duke would force the other duke to surrender, and it would be over and they would all be able to just go home.

But the clouds that had been hanging over them all this while finally broke, and rain poured down in steady sheets. And a field that had been muddy before became a swamp in which men struggled and slid and fell, and the goal became not that of moving forward but of just keeping upright and not drowning in the newly liquid mud. Anyone who fell and was trampled was suffocated in the mess. Gerhardt saw the youngster he'd spoken to that night go down and caught him with his free arm, all but hurling the boy back on his feet, ignoring his stammered thanks.

Where is she? Gerhardt thought. *Where is the saint? Where is our help?*

If she was watching over them, she wasn't visible to him. Gerhardt abandoned any hope of divine aid and turned all his efforts to simply surviving. Damn her, damn this weather, damn those dukes safely up on their hills out of this mess . . .

He glanced up, into the rain, then glanced again. Yes, all at once he did see her, hovering over the field, and

Gerhardt nearly cried out in horror. He'd been wrong. Dear sweet Jesu, he'd been wrong, because what he had taken for a saint was smiling with joy at the carnage, and those lovely eyes were hot with a lust that would have put a whore to shame. Not a saint, oh, no, never anything holy—that was a demon as surely as ever the priests had preached, and she was enjoying their war, drinking up their despair, feeding off the agony of their deaths.

No wonder we're not getting anywhere! She wouldn't want the battle to end.

But gawking up like a fool was going to get him killed. Gerhardt returned to the battle with desperate ferocity, fighting with the frenzy of a man who has lost everything but a single fierce determination: He would live long enough to slay the demon.

The day darkened. The rain remained, pouring down in relentless curtains. As the trumpets once again sounded retreat, Gerhardt sat apart from the others, ignoring the boy he'd saved, huddling into himself, trying to ignore the rain, the cold, the aches of his body—the pounding of his heart. Damn it, what was he trying to do? Killing demons—that was a priest's job.

Maybe. But there were no priests on the front lines. Just foot soldiers. And what good would it do to tell anyone else? They'd just think he'd gone crazy. Hell, maybe he had. He was the only one who could see her, after all.

If only she returns to me.

If only she can be slain.

While we're on the subject, if only she leaves a solid body.

At least he wouldn't have any trouble staying awake, not in all this.

And yet, despite the rain, despite the cold, Gerhardt was so weary that even as he was worrying over those thoughts, he did drift off to sleep as he was, huddled in a ball, but with one hand closed about the hilt of his sword.

*   *   *

"Ah, you can still see me."

Gerhardt came awake with a start, staring wildly about. Damn, he hadn't meant to fall asleep!

She was looming over him, smiling at him, looking so pure, so sweet, he could almost believe she really was a saint. Or rather, he might have believed it had he not seen her in that demonic joy over the battlefield.

"Yes," he said, hiding the sword half-under his body.

"You know what I am," she purred. "I saw you on the battlefield."

"I saw you, too, demon."

"Oh, what a narrow word!"

"I'm a soldier. I don't have any prettier ones."

"You amuse me. I thought your death on the battlefield would be more splendid. But you were too stubborn to die."

"Still am," Gerhardt said, and lunged upward. As his sword stabbed through the woman-thing, with his other hand, Gerhardt dragged out the plain crucifix he wore around his neck. The woman-thing screamed like sword edge against sword edge, in agony whether from blade or cross, swirled in on itself in a blaze of blue-white light—and was gone.

Gerhardt sat back in shock, panting, staring. Gone. He'd killed it, or banished it, or did God knew what to it. And it hadn't been mere madness; with the demon gone, there was a new . . . lightness to the air. God, yes, and now that the evil was lifted, there was no reason for this endless battle.

The rain had finally stopped, and the first streaks of dawn were lighting the sky. Heart racing anew, Gerhardt waited with as much patience as he could for full daylight. Before the call to battle could be sounded, he raced out onto the empty strip of land.

"Hear me, all of you!" he shouted. "A demon controlled us, locked us in that endless fight. But the demon is gone! Don't you feel the difference, the new hope and lightness? We are no longer being forced to fight!"

An arrow tore into him, he couldn't tell from which side, staggering him sideways, another brought him to his knees. Damn them, damn them all, he'd been wrong. It hadn't been the demon forcing them to fight, just enjoying the feast. They had *wanted* to fight, those dukes untouched and clean up on the hills, sending the common men off to die and watching the game. The glory of battle was the thing—when you weren't the one doing the dying.

A third arrow cut into him. As the darkness took him, Gerhardt's last thought was *I'm better off out of this.*

Then . . . he was.

HOMO

Donald J. Bingle

SOMETIMES you don't even know when you are on the front lines of a battle.

Although it was early afternoon, Henri nudged the switch to turn on his oversized flashlight and played the beam across the wide crevasse in the north side of the eroding, wooded hillside. "You've got to be kidding me," he murmured over his shoulder at his assistant, Alec.

Alec eased off his backpack of delicate equipment and stepped over to look where Henri had pointed the light. Although the crevasse was in shadow, Alec's face was in full sunlight, so Henri watched as his assistant shaded his eyes and squinted until he stepped forward far enough to be enveloped by the cool shade provided by the intervening bulk of the hillside. After a few moments looking at the opening, Alec simply shrugged his shoulders. "That's why you went to university, isn't it? Med school, laboratory training, DNA analysis, forensic techniques . . . everything. You went through all of it— I'm going through all of it—so when they find a body they call you." He leaned forward to inspect the size of the opening deep in the crevasse, then eased back. "Well, they called. And here we are."

Henri grimaced as he knelt next to the hillside and measured the opening with a retractable tape. "Jesus,

120

how did they even find it? Who would just shimmy through a hole that size?"

"Little ones, of course. It's always children that find caves. Adults don't go poking their heads into holes to see if they open up into something larger. Youngsters haven't had their natural curiosity beaten out of them by life . . . or the bureaucracy. So they explore. And sometimes they find things, and we get called."

Henri gave a curt nod to his rambling assistant as he appraised the scene. Alec was a helpful and technically adept assistant; he just didn't know a rhetorical question when he heard it. Of course it was kids. Henri would have known that even if he hadn't been told on the phone call summoning him here. He could have explained all that to his eager assistant, but instead he just grunted and jerked his head back toward the van. "Fetch the shovel. We're going to need to widen the opening to get ourselves and the equipment in."

"Right away, doctor." The lad was fifty meters away before he turned back. "Don't forget to get some photos before we . . . uh . . . disturb the scene."

Henri simply held up the high-tech camera already in his hands. Alec nodded and scurried away. Henri had more digital pictures than he could imagine ever needing long before his hard-breathing assistant returned with the shovel. Despite the fact that his young counterpart had already gotten plenty of exercise, Henri motioned for him to do the actual digging. Henri didn't get five postgraduate degrees in order to do manual labor. Besides, the lad was fanatical about regulations, and if Henri were digging, Alec would just be fussing over whether the opening was being made too large. The Interior Ministry had strict regulations about altering the geology and climatology of caves, and they wouldn't care that three boys passing by after football practice had discovered a body in this one.

Finally, Alec put down the shovel, and Henri relit his flashlight and got down on his belly to begin the crawl inside. He took only the basics of his equipment with him, things small enough to fit in the many pockets of his coveralls, things like evidence bags, that would not bulge and add to the discomfort of his crawl or hang up as he eased through tight spaces. Alec was a few meters in back of him, dragging a bag of equipment behind himself by looping the handle around his right boot. It would take several such trips to get in the full complement of equipment they might need in their investigation of the scene, but that's what assistants were for.

Most people, especially the tourists that seasonally flooded the region and visited many of the larger caves that dotted the area, had no idea what real caves were like. Tourist destinations had level floors and tastefully hidden electric lighting, with guardrails surrounding open holes or delicate or dangerous formations; the loose gravel and debris that littered the cave floor and often choked any natural entry way was excavated and removed. This, however, was a real cave, Henri noted as he painfully pulled himself over a dense layer of gravel into the darkness, the glare of the flashlight in his right hand careening haphazardly about as he used his hands to pull his way farther in.

The cave widened horizontally fairly quickly as he got through the enlarged opening, but it opened up vertically much more slowly and gradually as he moved forward, typical of caves caused by flowing water in the sedimentary rocks over time. The cave air was stale and dusty and, although cool, did not have the tinge of humidity that would suggest that this was still a hydrologically active system. The flow of the air also indicated that the cave had other openings, perhaps vents at the top of the hillside. Those might explain how a body had gotten into this desolate and secret place. Finally, there was a sharp downturn in the gravel pile, and the cave opened up so that he could stand, hunched at first but eventually upright, so long as he watched his head for low-hanging rocks. A jumble of rocks and stones still littered the uneven floor, but he started making better time, hampered now more by the lack of light than anything else.

He heard a slight whoomp as Alec set the first bag of equipment down along the way Henri had just come.

"It should be just ahead, behind a large rock, according to the kids' statements," Alec shouted, louder than he needed to in the otherwise silent place, his words reverberating in the shadowy darkness. "Hold up a moment and I'll get some of the portable lights set up."

Henri stopped picking his way forward. Alec was right. It wouldn't do to compromise the scene or disturb something by blundering into it because his flashlight was turned the wrong way at the crucial moment. So he stood and played the light about, getting a feel for the contours of the cave—more rounded here than near the entrance. Instead of horizontal cracks narrowing into infinity, there were curved walls, no doubt created by erosion by a higher volume of faster moving water when the cave was still wet.

It didn't take Alec long to set up a couple of lights. He left one by the pile of gravel to demark the entrance and brought another one up, pointing forward from Henri's position, illuminating the path ahead, creating a haphazard mosaic of bright light and dark shadows.

It was good that Henri had waited for the lights. Not twenty meters south of his waiting place, he could see the foot of the victim they had been called in to investigate. With the light from behind and the supplemental beam from his flashlight, he could see the tracks of the footballers who had found the body—the tread patterns of their trendy footwear strikingly out of place in this environment. He shot some photos, just for the record, but was still careful about placing his own, booted, feet so as to not disturb anything. Alec had seen the body in the distance, too, and followed behind tracing Henri's steps, after quickly retrieving the first bag of equipment.

Alec gave a low whistle as they rounded a large, jagged rock and got a view of the full body. "Would you look at that . . ." he mumbled, as his flashlight pierced the rock's shadow to reveal the largely skeletal remains of a young male—the hips were always a quick give-away on gender. The left leg was broken, both the weight-bearing tibia and the fibula. "No wonder he couldn't get out," Alec continued. "Looks like a nasty break."

Alec played his light upward, no doubt seeking out a vent or hole that the male could have fallen through, but Henri didn't even bother to look. "That break's not from a fall. It's crushed, not broken." He shone his light farther up the torso. "And see there? Look at the barrel-shaped ribcage. Broken ribs . . . on both sides. You don't fall on your left side and your right side at the same time. Quick guess, this guy was beaten to death."

Alec quickly lowered his flashlight back to the body and traced farther along it. The arms of the figure were up, the hands behind the obscured skull, the elbows forward, aside the hidden front of the head, which was face-down in the dirt and rocks of the floor.

Henri snorted. "Looks like he was trying to protect his head."

He moved a bit farther into the cave, trying to get a better angle on the scene or at least figure out where to position the next portable light to best assess the situation. Suddenly, his right foot came down on air and he flung himself backward in a desperate attempt to keep from falling forward. He succeeded, wrenching his back in the process and falling backward onto the rock strewn floor. He winced in pain as several stones tore through his coveralls and gouged at his flesh, and he gasped in astonishment as the beam from his flashlight arced upward revealing the ceiling and upper walls of the cave as he fell back. The light tumbled from his hand as he hit, coming to rest between two rocks, angled heavenward.

Alec rushed to his side, but Henri paid no heed to his anxious inquiries as to his well-being. He simply stared at the cave walls. Eventually, Alec turned to look where he was staring.

"Jesus," gulped his assistant. "We've got graffiti." He shone his light on the extensive markings and crude drawings. "Somebody else has been in this cave."

Henri nodded as he gingerly got back up. He held out an arm to keep Alec from blundering forward and targeted his light on the area that had caused his fall. He inhaled sharply as he saw the eight meter drop. His flashlight clattered to the ground as he saw what was at the bottom of the pit. "Yes, they have," he gasped.

As Alec came up to look, Henri retrieved his light and pointed it down into the pit. They both stared down at another male skeleton, this somewhat taller, in the tumble of rocks below. Two bodies. And graffiti.

"What the hell happened here?" Henri asked the silent stone.

Dirk froze in place when he heard their voices on the wind, straining to discern their tone if not their words. Had they seen him? Were they hunting him even now? But their voices were muted, their tone flat—there was no urgency, no anger yet. Still, they were coming this way. He could not afford to be caught by them. He hunched over as he loped toward a deadfall of tree branches upslope and took cover to hide while they passed.

He had feared this ever since he had chanced upon the local watering hole with an overabundance of knotty pine where they obviously hung out. He had quickly fled, without even getting himself a drink first. He knew they didn't like his kind, and it wasn't just from the staring and pointing and rude gestures. He had seen first hand what had happened to Kurt when he had been caught one night by a group of their ilk—he had been tied to a tree and beaten to death. His body had been an almost unrecognizable mass of blood and hair and exposed bone; both legs broken, the face bashed in, the skull cracked and oozing gray matter.

What he didn't understand was why. He and Kurt were different from them—that much was clear. But so what? In his younger days there had been more tolerance, or at least no outright violence. He had met plenty of folk who had not seemed bothered by his presence or even by what they no doubt thought was his outlandish appearance. He certainly didn't see what was wrong with it; his mother had always referred to him as a "pretty boy" when he was young. Why did his appearance now cause such hatred? It had, of course, been years and years since he had seen his mother or the rest of his family, since he had . . . left. He had not changed, but times had changed for some reason. No one, certainly not these brutes on his trail, would call him "pretty boy" with sincerity anymore.

He tried hard to parse it out as he watched the three boys—no doubt they thought of themselves as men, real men—move up the hill, talking and laughing with each other in soft voices. They were taller than he was and rough looking in his estimation, with well-muscled arms and no trace of flab. They were obviously close comrades, used to working and hunting and eating and camping together. He longed for that kind of companionship, but he was denied not only that, but any kind of companionship altogether.

He didn't know why these boys hated him and others like him so. It wasn't as if there were many like him about. It wasn't as if he could reproduce—it had been years and years since he had even thought about a woman other than his mother. He was alone in the world, more alone than he had ever thought possible when he left his family to find another home with others of his kind. He had never seen anyone from his family again.

He slowed his breathing so as not to reveal his presence as the three boys that would be men passed close by to his position, but he must have left some sign. The tallest of the three stopped suddenly and inspected the ground, then turned to glare with obvious malice in Dirk's direction. Dirk gasped when he saw the bone-white handle of a knife in the boy's hand.

That was enough to give him away.

With guttural yells, the three boys leaped toward the deadfall. Dirk jerked himself up and away, moving as quickly as he could to gain distance as the boys detoured around the deadfall and regained his path in pursuit. Dirk was compact and sure-footed, but he had no hope of outrunning the pack behind him for long. They fanned out, as he expected they would, so that one would gain ground no matter which way he turned and no obstacle strewn along the path could slow them all.

As he topped the hill, Dirk veered left hard and, once he was his body's height below the crest, turned sharply back right, hoping to confuse his pursuers into heading the wrong direction as they loped up the slope after him. It should have worked. It would have worked, but for the fact that the way to the right was blocked by a tumble of dirt and boulders from a recent landslide. The sharp rocks and broken tree branches from the landslide slashed at him as he made his way through the detritus littering the hillside, slowing him enough that his right-most pursuer saw him from the top of the hill. Dirk ran on, heedless of the pain from the tree branches and thorny brush, wincing only as he heard a throaty bellow no doubt informing the others of his location.

He could not defeat the three of them. They would do to him what they, or others like them, had done to Kurt. Although he was not a violent sort, his only hope now was to take them out one by one, before they could attack him as a group. So, after squeezing between two broken boulders on the hillside, he secreted himself behind the uphill boulder and waited for the first of those hunting him to catch up. He cast about for a weapon and found a sturdy club, a broken branch from a tree that had fallen in the slide. He was pleased. The green wood was solid and covered with rough bark with deep grooves. The club would not break if he made a solid hit and the bark would scrape the skin of his opponent if he but succeeded in a glancing blow.

He heard his opponent approach, his steps slowing somewhat. Dirk reached down with his left hand and hefted a small rock into the brush where he would have been running if he had not stopped to ambush his hunter. The sound urged his opponent forward at a quicker pace, getting closer and closer.

As the boy burst through the narrow gap between the two broken boulders, Dirk swung his tree limb with both hands parallel to the ground, aiming for the middle of his attacker so as to be sure not to miss entirely. He felt a satisfying thrum as the branch came into contact with soft matter and heard a whoosh as the air in the boy's lungs was expelled and he doubled over. Dirk pulled the branch quickly back to prevent it from being grabbed and to prepare another strike. This one was more vertical, than horizontal, coming down on the base of the skull of the bent-over boy. The head snapped up and back as the club struck the top of the neck, pivoting on the point of impact. There was an audible snap and crunch and the boy fell limp to the ground.

Dirk had hunted. He knew that sound, knew that collapse, for what it was, but he couldn't help himself. He kicked the limp corpse again and again and gave the head another swinging blow from his club. Bash Kurt? Kill Kurt? Kill everyone of his kind? Well, we can bash back.

It was only when he heard a shout from one of the remaining boys that his wits came back to him. The danger was not gone; in fact, it was fast approaching. And he had to be gone if he was not to end up like Kurt or this pitiful, nameless cretin he had just vanquished. He dropped his club and ran. Only after he was meters away, too late to turn back, did he realize his mistake. Fight or flight were not exclusionary choices. Why had he dropped the club? It didn't matter any more. Now he had to flee.

Perhaps if his attackers were more civilized, the beaten and bloody body of their friend would have slowed them more, but it only seemed to spur them to greater speed and anger. Words that he could not understand, but which he knew conveyed concepts that were both obscene and cruel, echoed about him as he cast about for a way to escape.

When he saw the hole in the ground, he dove for it, shoving his body in, praying that it was deep enough that his legs would not be left hanging out, giving him away. He elbowed and clawed his way forward deeper and deeper into the complete darkness of what was, it was now clear, a cavern. He couldn't see his hand in front of his face, but he rejoiced in that. His enemy wouldn't be able to see either. He pressed on and on into the gradually widening crack, unmindful of the scraping stones beneath him. Just as he was about to stop to listen for sounds of pursuit, he found himself sliding down loose rocks and gravel and being tossed onto a rocky floor. He cried out involuntarily in surprise and pain, cursing himself mentally even as he did so. The sound of his cry reverberated in the cavern, the vibrations no doubt amplified through the tiny opening in the hillside outside.

Sure enough, only moments later, he heard voices and scrabbling as his enemy came into the cave after him. He could try another ambush, but there were two of them together now, he had foolishly tossed away his club, and a rock would have neither the speed nor the extended reach of that lost weapon. He moved farther into the cave—perhaps he could exit somehow and leave them wandering in the dark while he made his escape. Maybe he could even double back to the entrance if he got them far enough away from it first.

He moved as quickly as he could, biting his lip to keep from crying out as he stumbled over the uneven stones and barked his shins on sharp rock outcroppings. He steeled himself for the worst—for the battle to come, for the beating he would receive, and for the violent, painful torture and death that was almost sure to come. And for what? Because he was different? He couldn't help being what he was. It wasn't his choice. But it was his destiny.

He didn't know what, in the blackness, alerted him to the danger—perhaps a minute change in the direction of the airflow about him. But he somehow sensed the pit looming before him. He reached out with his right foot and felt nothing below him. He dropped to the ground and inspected the way as best he could with his hands. There was a hole, no telling how deep, stretching across the entire width of the cave, as far as he could determine. There was nowhere to go. He would have to make a stand here. He took cover behind a large boulder and felt about for a hefty rock to use as his final weapon, scooping up a handful of dirt and pebbles with his left hand at the same time. He put his back to the covering rock and stood up to await his fate.

When he heard his enemy close by, he flung the dirt and stones in his left hand deep in to the darkness of the cave past or, for all he knew, into the pit. The stupid brutes following him—how could they possibly be superior to him?—fell for the simple trick, just as their deservedly dead companion had before at the landslide. They quickened their pace.

Suddenly, rather than bashing the lead attacker with the rock, as he had planned, it came to him. He simply stuck out his leg from behind the rock and tripped the first pursuer into a headlong fall. There was a yelp, a sickeningly pleasing thud, and a dying moan.

Dirk didn't wait to hear more and he certainly couldn't see more. He swung the rock overhand toward the space between his covering boulder and the pit, waiting for the soft resistance of a skull or shoulder or the satisfying snap of a femur. But there was no resistance; the rock, still in his grasp, sailed through empty air, his arm and his suddenly overbalanced body following it until they hit the cave floor at the top edge of the pit.

The sound gave him away. The first kick caught him in the ribs on his left side. He heard two ribs snap and felt a shockingly sharp pain pervade his chest. Suddenly he was gasping for breath, too distracted by the pain and the lack of air to think about resisting. Unfortunately, his enemy had no such distractions but instead had vengeance to fuel his hatred for Dirk and those like him. Dirk twisted away, despite the anguish it caused, and tried, instinctively, to crawl away, but a heavy rock crushed his leg. Then the kicks began again, this time on the other side. Not long after, apparently unsatisfied with the damage that could be inflicted with brute force, his foe began to assail him with the bone-handled knife that was not nearly sharp enough to be merciful. In the end, Dirk could do no more than attempt to curl up and throw his arms up to protect his head and the face that his mother had once called pretty, though it was apparently frightening to this boy—this man—that was now killing him.

He prayed for oblivion, but it only came after much pain.

Alec came into Henri's office, his face tired and drawn. "It's the Interior Minister . . . again . . . on line two."

Henri's lip curled into a snarl, but he picked up his phone and stabbed at a button with a beefy hand. "Yes?"

"Why haven't you released the cavern to my department yet?" queried the minister without so much as an insincere greeting.

Henri tried to remain calm, but his right eye was already twitching. The twitching increased in intensity and speed as the conversation progressed. "I keep telling you, Minister, the graffiti is unimportant compared to the rest of the scene."

"And I've told you before. Stop calling ancient cave paintings graffiti. These are important cultural discoveries."

"Pah. You have cave paintings all over caverns in the area. And, by the way, they probably were the equivalent of graffiti to the people that made them. The important things are the bodies. Don't you understand what they represent?"

"Your analysis of the bodies can't possibly be correct. I'm not going to let you embarrass the Ministry with unfounded speculation."

"My analysis is goddamn correct, Minister. Not only is the structural analysis of the bones conclusive and, quite frankly, obvious, but Alec here has had the DNA retrieved from the marrow of the hip bones confirmed by three independent laboratories. Isn't that right, Alec?" Henri held the phone up and pointed the handset toward his somewhat frightened assistant.

"Uh, yes, Minister. The mitochondrial DNA is conclusive and . . . uh . . . verified beyond any doubt."

Henri turned back the phone so he could continue his

tirade. "See? Conclusive. Verified. Much more important than some damn art."

"Don't be dramatic, Henri. It's not like either is a new species or the missing link or something. There are plenty of specimens of these types. They're commonplace all across the Continent."

"Not together, you moron! Not at this date, 29,000 years ago, the same date for both! Not with clear indications that they were battling each other!"

"I'm not an archaeologist or a forensic anthropologist, Henri. What's so important about all that?"

Henri threw his hands up in disbelief, then held the handset at arms length in front of him, so as not to get in the way of his full-scale bellowing. "Because, for all we know, you effete primitive art tour guide, this could be where the *Homo Sapiens* caught and killed the last *Homo Neanderthalensis* on the face of the planet."

THE BATTLE FOR TREHINNICK'S GARDEN

Jody Lynn Nye

"CAN you see anything yet?" Sergeant Lasset asked.

"Sir, no, sir!" announced Picket. The younger pixie's cheeks glowed as red as his hair. He raised his pointed chin and aimed it toward the garden gate. "I can hear 'em, though, so I can."

"So can I." Lasset pushed his basin-shaped tin hat up his forehead over his shining black hair and parted the thistles to peer outward. He wore armor made of living wood over his ordinary knee-length tunic and stone boots on his feet. "And smell the blood on 'em, so." Twilight had softened the autumn day to grays and browns and cast long shadows over the packed gravel pathway leading eastward into the Cornish village of Roos, but the full moon was looming already upon the horizon. They would see the enemies' shapes long before they reached the gate, but would it give him and his small troop enough time to aim and fire? "Stand ye ready, men."

There was some grumbling from the ranks among the female pixies, but that was what you called soldiers. The women didn't bother to argue the small matters when the larger ones had everyone too worried to think beyond the next hour. Only twenty of the house fay were still in any shape to fight, and they feared what would happen if their number shrank any further. Another ill-fought battle could finish them, and the war was not won yet.

They shouldered their weapons: silver knives and forks sharpened to a fare-thee-well, small gardening tools, and a pair of sewing shears poised to snip off a limb. Seven of the pixies held their positions about Lasset's pride and joy, the catapult. This had been loaded with a heavy round stone the size of an apple. The stone, like the other weapons, was covered with silver. It was the only defense they had that was proof against the foe. Lasset had learned the art of war from watching the Big Folk, when they had gone to the defense of their homes on this island sixty years ago, and ninety years ago, and all the times before that, going back over the four and a half millenia to when Lasset had been a sprite. This was *their* home. They were defending not only their lives but also that of Mr. Henry Trehinnick, age 82, the owner of this house and garden. The old man was completely unaware of the war going on underneath his nose, and if the gods were good, he would live out his peaceful days without ever knowing. Lasset was determined to spare him the fret.

The situation in the village had been growing more desperate by the day. Lasset could easily put a date on when the trouble began. Six lunar months ago exactly, it had been.

In a small town everyone knows when new people arrive. The fine house in the extensive, gated grounds out on Trewiss Road had stood empty for a decade. One day, a man with streaks of silver in his black hair had roared through Roos in his fancy roadster, followed by the removal van. It turned out that his furniture wasn't all he had brought with him. He had company, and he had a curse.

That very night, the first night of the full moon, blood-curdling howls had split the air. The pixies were disturbed from their supper of milk and bread that the old man had left out for them. Lasset, always known to have a bit of sense, asked the owl who lived in the ancient tangle of ivy that crept up the cottage wall to go and see what all the fuss had been about. On silent wings, the bird had departed. He returned, his usual composure shaken. A sheep had been slaughtered right in the roadway, he had reported. The local police car was there, trying to pretend it had been an automobile accident, but the animal's throat had been torn out.

"By teeth," the owl had said. "They can't fool my eyes, no matter how dark it is."

Lasset glanced back at the house. The blue glow in the window told him the old man had settled down in front of the telly for the night. It was safe now to prepare their defenses. There was a chance the foe would pass them by, to harass and kill in some other garden. The less attractive they made their patch of ground, the greater the chances that they would be left alone.

He made a handful of witchfire, the green flame that the fair folk control, as a signal to Jelly and Ioreth. Granddaughter and grandfather were as woodswise as they came. They crept down to the threshold of the garden, joined hands, then drew apart. Between them stretched out a length of creeper, dark green in the dimness. It sprouted leaves, then tendrils, then long, sharp thorns. The brambles grew and grew until they were twice as high as the gate. The new hedge thickened once, twice, thrice. A bull couldn't charge through the resultant wall. If only it was a stupid, blundering, mortal bovine they faced. Another sign, and the entire contingent of pixies not manning the catapult clambered up and perched in the trees on either side of the gate.

Lasset heard a noise. Something had stepped on a dry leaf. He drew the silver-plated fruit knife from his belt and held it like a sword. It was longer than his arm. He felt the blade with a thumb. Sharp as death.

"Steady," he whispered. He felt the others grow tense. Long shadows streaked the eerie orange light on the road. The Red Caps were coming here. No hope of avoiding a fight tonight.

With a cry, the enemy charged toward the gate, carrying torches that lit up their ugly faces with red light. They stood twice as tall as pixies and were much broader in the body, with crooked ears and gapped teeth. The leaders called out orders. A handful with axes sprang forward and began to cut away the new made hedge, shouting threats and curses at the pixies within.

Red Caps, also called powries, were unknown in Cornwall until six months before. They had been a Scottish scourge for centuries. Storytellers that had plied the highways since mankind could tell stories sang of greedy elves who killed big folks for the fun of it. The red of their notorious caps was from dipping them in the blood of their victims. A round hundred of them had come down from the Highlands with their cursed leader, who furnished them with plenty of blood. They worshiped death, as the pixies loved life. Until the Red Caps came, they had never killed except for food or to rid the garden of a pest that wouldn't respond to their spells. In the last six months they had had to learn.

Jelly and Ioreth worked their magic on the thick hedge. Lasset heard the crackle and rustle of new tendrils trying to trap the Red Caps forcing their way through. He laid his hands on the spiky vines and closed his eyes. Eight of them wielded long knives or hand axes. Each time they chopped at the growth, he felt the plant's pain. As fast as the pixies created more shoots, the enemy smashed and tore them apart. In moments they would be through the brambles.

"Ware, now," he called.

Jelly looked up at him, her face full of pain. "They're getting past us, sergeant."

"Block all you can, dear," he said.

Grimly, Lasset made another hand of witchfire. He held it up so that all the wee folk in the garden could see it.

The pixies braced themselves. Below him, Lasset could see the edge of the first ax. He threw the fire into the air. At the sign, the pixies charged to meet the enemy.

Brandishing his knife-sword, Lasset leaped down. He landed on the back of a stout Red Cap. Hanging on with his knees, he kicked with his hard stone boots. The elf yelped with pain and swung his ax up, hoping to dislodge his unwanted passenger. Lasset knocked the cap flying with a swipe of the hilt, then plunged the blade down into the nape of the creature's neck. The ruffian let out a hoarse yell. He spun, trying to dislodge Lasset. With determination borne of fear, the pixie held on and stabbed again. The Red Cap leaped into the air and landed on his back. Lasset's reactions were swifter than his. He jumped free before his enemy hit the ground and swiped again as the Scottish haunt tried to get to his feet. Lasset leaped for him. The Red Cap grasped both his hands, trying to make him drop his weapon. He was not above fighting dirty. When Lasset wouldn't let go, the Red Cap bit him.

"Curse you!" Lasset yelped. Blood spurted from his wrist, making the knife turn in his hand. "Spirits of the earth, aid you me!"

Blades of grass shot up around their feet, tangling the much bigger male in their toils. Lasset pulled loose and backed away.

"Ye'll no catch me like tha'!" the Red Cap said, laughing. He tore his legs free one at a time. Raising his ax above his head, he chopped at Lasset's head.

The pixie was not there when the blade fell. He danced behind his enemy, and stabbed twice with the fruit knife. The second struck the Red Cap's vitals. He fell, groaning, and the grass grew over the body, burying it deep. Lasset held his wrist, panting.

Another big Red Cap with long, greasy black hair jumped at him, a stone the size of his torso in his hand.

"I'll smash yer," he said, grinning.

Lasset jabbed at him with the silver knife, then jumped away as the powrie brought his weapon crashing down.

He missed. Lasset nimbly edged out of reach, looking for an opening to attack.

"Sergeant! He's here!"

Lasset looked up. A rough-edged shadow sprang into their midst and blocked out the light of the moon. On all fours, hunched slightly under a hairy spine, the werewolf loomed fierce and deadly. It smelled of death. Its teeth gleamed white in the glint of moonlight that followed it like an obedient candle.

The sight of the terrible beast caught Lasset off guard. The werewolf laughed, a noise between a grunt and a howl, and kicked him into the bushes with a swipe of its paw. Lasset scrambled to free himself and to find his helmet and sword. He wound a strand of grass around his hurt wrist.

"They're making for the house!" Picket yelled.

"Move to intercept!" Lasset shouted back.

They tried to blockade the lycanthrope and his attendants, but they were shockingly outnumbered. The Red Caps threw rocks that knocked the wood-clad pixies over like ninepins and swung axes that lodged momentarily in the hard shells around their bodies. Lasset directed his tiny force of twelve as best he could. Instead of taking on one huge enemy at a time, they formed a phalanx in the center as they had seen the Romans do on this very field two thousand years ago. They fought their way forward, moving inexorably toward the werewolf himself. The Red Caps battered at their outer shields. Ioreth, the eldest, let out a hoarse cry as a Red Cap dropped a stone the size of his body that dented his helmet in. He fell in the scrimmage and was lost to view. Though he felt stricken at his friend's injury, Lasset had no time to look for him. They had to get to the monster himself. He ordered the others to close ranks.

On all fours, the werewolf was twice the height of a pixie, but he outweighed even the stoutest of them over a hundred to one. He leaped over the small troop and lollopped toward the blue light shining through the lounge window.

"Break!" Lasset called. "Get him! No one else matters."

As swiftly as they had formed up, the pixies ran off in all different directions, mostly eluding the disorganized mob that swung at them. In the confusion, they mainly hit one another. Lasset dipped under meaty arms and around thick backs, making toward the werewolf.

Picket and Nonni, his shield-sister, intercepted the beast on the garden walk, ten yards from the door. They brandished silver salad forks. The cutlery had been extracted at great personal risk from Trehinnick's parlor by a foraging party of pixies as soon as they knew the nature of the threat. The old man hadn't touched it since his wife had died, ten years before. He never knew any of the set was missing, but it had been necessary to remove it to make weapons to save his life. Picket stabbed up at the wolf's throat. The tines brushed its cheek. The fur crackled and burned.

Angrily, the werewolf snapped at Picket. While it was distracted, Nonni feinted with her fork. She was quicker than the moon-touched wolf. She actually managed to get the tines tangled in the fur on the back of his paw before he snatched it away. Picket was more successful on his second try. He jabbed the wolf in the shoulder. The wolf howled in pain. Lasset was grimly satisfied. By then, he and six more pixies had caught up.

"Good job, Picket!" he shouted. "Give him another one."

He signed the others to join the attack. Bluebell and Russet rushed to get around the beast's left flank. Lidd and Kett, brothers older than Lasset knew, bided their time while the werewolf spun, then charged. They stabbed at the beast's suddenly exposed right side, jabbing him with butter knives. No mortal steel or iron could penetrate the cursed hide, but sacred silver laid open gaping black wounds in the hairy hide. The wolf howled again. He rose to his hind legs. Unlike a true wolf, he could fight on two legs as readily as on four. The pain inflicted by the silver weapons distracted him.

The Red Caps shouldered in to protect their master. The pixies called on their allies of plant and woodland creature to keep the Scottish elves at bay. Jelly drew waist-thick tendrils of thorns from the ground to block them. With nightfall, Giddy called upon the bats and the owls to swoop down upon the enemy. The Red Caps found themselves too busy defending themselves to fight against the pixies or defend the werewolf. Lasset hoped the distraction would last long enough.

Lasset heard the telltale rumble of the catapult's wheels. Hun captained the homemade carriage until it was in place.

"Steady—aim!" Lasset shouted. The team surrounding the catapult sprang to work. They had drilled and drilled until they were able to shift the carriage in their sleep. The lycanthrope's ears turned sideways as the wheels creaked. He looked down in surprise and let out a howl.

"That's it, sir," Hun called.

"On your mark, fire!"

Lasset heard the twang. The werewolf let out a wild scream. Lasset's own ears perked up. That was a different sound than it had made before. He looked up. The creature clawed at its chest. In the center, the fur had been burned away, leaving a round black mark. In the near darkness, its blood ran in black streaks. It howled again, in pain and fury.

An answering howl came, echoed from the throats of the Red Caps. They tried to fight their way toward the catapult. It took all Jelly's skill to raise a wall of thorns to protect it and the gunners.

"Pixies! Stand ready!" Lasset bellowed. "Reload!"

The team of seven sprang to their tasks. Lasset heard the creak of the throwing arm being cranked back into place.

"Ready, sergeant!" Hun shouted.

"Aim and fire!" Lasset yelled back.

Whing! The second rock went flying. It hit the werewolf square in the forehead. The fell beast toppled over onto a contingent of dark elves. They yelled a protest.

The wolf scrambled onto its belly and rose to all fours. Lasset called for an attack, but the werewolf had had enough. It sprang away from them, galloped across the lawn, and cleared the mangled hedge in one smooth leap.

That left the Red Caps.

"Regroup!" Lasset shouted. "All of you, regroup!"

He brandished his small sword and made toward a couple of the ruffians.

But the Red Caps had no stomach to continue without their bully boy. Jeering, they retreated toward the gate and ran away into the darkness. The neighbor's dog started barking as they ran past his house, which set off the dogs the rest of the way up the street. Lasset waited until he was sure they were all gone. Then he called an all-clear. Miraculously, the battle had not disturbed Old Man Trehinnick. The evening news claimed all his attention, something about sports in Argentina.

The pixies gathered together next to the hedge under the silver light of the moon, now nearly overhead. Giddy thanked the night creatures and sent them on their way. Jelly waved her hands, and the thornbushes shrank back behind the gateposts and under the grass. The others repaired the bottom of the gate where the Red Caps had chopped through.

"We did it, sergeant," Picket said. He looked exhausted. All of them did.

"We only drove them away," Lasset said, glumly. "Rosemary, how bad is it?"

The most herbwise of the women came over. Her hands were stained with blood, and her long, taffy-colored braid was askew. She shook her head.

"Mik and Bank are hurt badly. And Ioreth won't wake up. The werewolf kicked him into a tree. What happened to your hand, so?"

"Only a scratch," Lasset lied, trying to hide his aching wrist behind him, but Rosemary was not fooled. She pulled the arm around and brought a little of her cooling magic to bear upon the wound.

"Not so bad," she said. "A day or two, and you'll be

well enough. But the others need time to heal, if they
will at all.

"So, we're seventeen, now," Isa said, shaking his
silver-maned head. "We just cannot go on for long with
our numbers diminishing so."

"Aye, so," Lasset said. He surveyed his little troop,
looking bedraggled and tired. "We have a month. We
need to win next time, no doubt."

"How?" Picket asked. His youthful face was so for-
lorn that Lasset patted him on the back with his good
hand.

"I do not know," he said. "Best ye think on it. Best
we all do. Our time runs short. We have a month."

A month less three days, in truth, until the next attack gave the pixies time to heal and consider their
options. Lasset helped gather herbs for Rosemary and
the healers. Old Ioreth had died during the night. He
had been born in the year following the retreat of the
ice, the oldest pixie still living in this corner of Cornwall. They were losing their history, Lasset thought,
savagely pulling up shoots of pennyroyal. They must do
something. Something different. They could not defeat
the werewolf as they were. Every month chopped away
at their numbers. Soon, it would be no contest, and
their lovely corner of the world would be lost to the
magic of life.

Pixies had lived in that same spot around the cottage
for thousands of years. Before the gardens were enclosed, this had been a lovely meadow, stretching from
the tors to the moor. The first human huts were erected
near that little pond on the opposite side of the road
over ninety-two hundred years before, when the only
metal was a precious and rare bronze spearhead that
the homeowner/hunter had used to kill prey, but the
primary source of food was the crops planted in the
field. The pixies did not travel far from the spot of their
birth. Once the stone fences began to go up, some hundreds of years later, the pixies of the valley chose their
patch of ground, happy to be well rooted and well cared

for. Some of the fair folk were better treated than others.

Trehinnick took good care of his pixies. He had been taught the old ways by his gran, a tiny woman with bright black eyes like a robin's who had been born in and had died in the cottage. Rain or shine, rheumatism or no, he left a saucer of milk on the step every night, with a crust of bread laid by to show the feast was meant for them. He had never seen them, except for a quick sidelong glance or two, caught by accident. He believed in them, though. He always left them that saucer of milk and that crust of bread, even on the day he went to bury his beloved wife. In exchange, the pixies saw to it that his garden grew like no other. No slug troubled his roses. No flies laid eggs on his apples. No ill-meaning creatures crossed his threshold. There was never a mole undermining his smooth, green lawn. Now, their defense of him had had to become more emphatic.

Lasset shook his head. Funny how warmly he felt toward the humans. Funny that he felt willing to fight and die in their defense. They owed him as much consideration as they had always had from him.

The old man's favorite motto was "Just because something's small doesn't mean it's unimportant." They felt they fell under that adage. So did their defense of one old man in one wee village at the far west end of the great island. If evil conquered here, it could start a chain reaction that would result in the eventual death of the old good ways.

Six months before, after the first killing, there had been a grand meeting of the fair folk of the valley to summon up the defense of the valley. Numbers of the pixies, elves, sprites and all had declined greatly over the years. There was no way to muster an army of any size. All the scattered troops of little folk could do was to protect their own turf. And so they had done, to the best of their ability. The year was winding down, now, and the pixies felt cold standing guard in the muck and the wet of a typical Cornish autumn. Winter was coming, and with it the dark power would grow. They had to defeat or drive away the werewolf before the cold time, or their life-based magic might not be enough to turn him back.

The new werewolf threatened to open up the whole valley to evil influences. Normally they were kept at bay by an ancient agreement, but this werewolf had proved himself different. It just went to show how people no longer embraced civilization, a gift given to them by the earliest efreets in the center of the world. He wouldn't accept the weregild, the traditional sop that would keep them from trying to kill the normal, nonmooned humans. He had laughed at the contingent of the fair folk and kicked them out of his grand house.

It wasn't that the pixies hadn't seen a werewolf before. Mrs. Bentley, the artist who lived next to the grocer's in the middle of town, now she was a werewolf. Most of the month she spent out on the Lizard or one of the other beauty spots of Cornwall, painting harmless watercolors. The three nights of the full moon, and a day on either side for safety, she locked herself up in the root cellar with the telly and her crossword puzzles, until the curse passed. Once a year she killed, as the ancient agreement went, usually an animal that was old or suffering and never one unwilling to be sacrificed. This new werewolf was different. This one *wanted* to kill. He wanted it so badly that the pixies could taste the bloodlust he was feeling. They feared him, for if one of their precious cottagers fell, then the neighborhood would begin to deteriorate, and the magic would leave this place, as it had passed in so many others. It was worth fighting—yes, and, perhaps, dying for.

Old Man Trehinnick came out the next morning and tsk-tsked over the mess in his front garden.

"And I thought I cut that hedge, but look ye at the thorns hangin' over the gate! It's a hazard to navigation, so." He chuckled. The pixies, watching him from the cool of the bamboo copse at the side of the garden, knew how much he enjoyed making references to the sea. He had been in the Royal Navy in his youth, and his military training informed his whole life. He kept himself tidy and upright when so many of the elderly in the town were hunched over with age.

Trehinnick kept up his chatter as he reached for the newspaper stuck in the rails of the gate. He often read it aloud, to hear the sound of a human voice, even if it was his own.

"What's this, what's this? Ach, oh, what a shame. A robbery with force. A shooting, look ye," he said, shaking his head. "But the pollis caught the man, and he had not the gun on him. Threw it away, without a doubt, so. But they will find it."

A gun? Lasset's ears perked up.

"We've got to find it," he told Picket.

"A big folk gun?" Picket asked.

"It's death to us," Jelly said, looking worried. "It's steel. It's dangerous."

"It's set a fire to fight a fire," Lasset said. "It's the answer. We must go out along the road to find it. It can't be far from the pavement."

"Travel?" asked Isa, a look of horror on his face. "Leave the garden?"

"It's the answer," Lasset said. "No matter what it costs us, it's the answer. We have to be the ones who find it. This is for Trehinnick."

Picket looked stricken. "Well, then, travel we must." He blanched, but put up his hand. "I will lead a party."

"And I," others spoke up. "And I."

"Two parties," Lasset said, proud of them all. "I will lead one, and Picket will lead the other. We will each take one side of the road. It cannot be far away or far from the pavement. Ask the birds and the animals. Someone will have seen it."

Hours of searching the long, unfamiliar roads left Lasset and his searchers footsore. It was after moonrise when they slogged back into the garden. Rosemary and her healers met them with restorative herb tea, and sections of bread crust.

"Where's Picket?" he asked. "Did he find it?"

"Not back yet," Rosemary said grimly. "It's night. Should we send out searchers for them?"

"No. They know how to get home again."

Rosemary couldn't look him in the eye. She fussed over his wrist, tying a new bandage over his nearly healed wound. He remembered that Picket was her son. "What if those damned Red Caps find them?"

"They can flee," Lasset said. "Nature herself will protect them. It's Trehinnick who can't run."

The second party did not come home that night, nor for three more days. Lasset was nearly ready to give in to the worried parents and loved ones of the missing when, at half past noon on the fourth day, bedraggled, dirty, and tired, Picket and his team reappeared.

He and Hun were pulling a heavy package wrapped in newspaper by the strings that tied it. He dropped the ropes and came up to Lasset.

"Sergeant," he said, snapping a salute, but unable to keep his young face from beaming like the sun, "we have it."

A Big Folk gun was nothing at all like the pictures they saw in the discarded newspapers in the composting bin, nor in the programs they had spied Trehinnick watching on the telly. It was a huge, cold, dead lump of metal, unwieldy as a snake.

Bank and his team undertook the dangerous task of unloading the thing, then taking it apart to study. According to a Sunday Supplement magazine in the bin, it was called a revolver. The pixies had to wear protective gloves made of frog skin and heavy armor grown out of hazelwood by Jelly to protect them from the steel. With practice they were able to put it back together and reconstruct it with minimum risk of harm to them.

"What about training?" Bank asked. "We must practice firing this horror."

Lasset surveyed the six shells laid out upon a dock leaf. "We can't spare any of these," he said. "Not only can we not make the gun noise without attracting the neighbors and the pollis, we have no extra bullets in case we miss the werewolf. We will have to learn to use the machine without the ammunition."

There was some grumbling, but everyone could see that Lasset was right. They would have to find a substitute.

With three weeks left to go, the pixies had to train hard. All who were still able bodied took it in turn to help maneuver the wheeled cart, pull back the hammer, and draw the trigger. The first was the easiest job, since they had made the cart themselves. The gun itself was very hard for them to use. It was almost as long as Lasset was tall, and heavier than any three pixies. It could not go off by accident. It had to be braced firmly, and ropes tied around the hammer and the trigger pulled hard by at least two pixies apiece to make it fire. The steel of the gun radiated cold at them. Protective clothing or no, they could not stay in its presence for long. Lasset assigned rest periods to all the teams to give them time to heal in between times of contact.

"We have no one to spare," he said.

Since they could not risk firing the bullets, Jelly made them compressed puffs of dandelion silk to test the aim. The team that steered the carriage practiced aiming.

"And the firing team can load the bullets in their dreams," Hun said, proudly, reporting to Lasset on their progress.

"It's not a dream that concerns ye, but a nightmare," Lasset reminded him sternly. "Get it right. We may only have the one shot. It must count. It must *kill*."

In the meanwhile, Lidd and Kett undertook to cover the bullets in silver foil hammered from ancient sixpences and other old silver coins they found in the grass, much as they had done with the catapult stones.

"Can't make them too wide," Kett said. "Else back they will not go."

Humans paid so little attention to metal. The wrong kind could kill the fair folk. The pixies always had to be on guard about bits of ancient barbed wire, or discarded cooking pots that some tenant had buried instead of throwing away. The werewolf could use cold steel. He knew who was ranged against him. Lasset always lived in fear he would make use of their weakness. As if the curse was not enough.

"How will we make sure he comes to us, not one of the other neighbors?" Picket asked, as the moon waxed more full.

"We *don't* want him here," Jelly said. The plantwise woman had changed since her grandfather was killed.

"We do," Lasset said, gently. "We are better prepared than the other gardens, so. If we can rid the world of him, it will save the deaths of who knows how many of our fellows."

"Who cares about them? We rarely see them!"

"But they are there, we know it. We can feel them. This is for the greater good." At the sound of distant footsteps, Lasset looked over his shoulder. In a few moments the old man marched a trifle unsteadily through the gate and carefully latched it behind himself.

"Pixies, ye should have been in t'pub tonight," he said, as he unlocked the front door. "A fine night. T'beer was good. Good night to you, and sleep well."

It closed behind him. Lasset looked at the others.

"We're doing it for Trehinnick."

The next night was the first of the October full moon. All of them could feel the fell magic of the hallowed evening. A protesting Jelly had to be ordered to deliberately leave the protective hedge thin and seedy, a temptation to the Red Caps to choose that house and no other.

As Lasset had thought, they did not resist the temptation. They burst through, not even noticing that the gate had been left open as well.

This time the pixies were more mentally prepared than ever before. They realized that they had not taken advantage of having the fight on their own territory. All their allies were in place. On silent wings, owls came swooping in to harry the Red Caps from above. Bats and night birds flitted among them and squeaked in their ears. The invaders almost forgot about the pixies. They covered their faces and heads with their arms against the owls' tearing talons and the bats' sharp little teeth.

"Hey, ye wretches!" Lasset called, taunting them from the middle of the green expanse of lawn. He, Kett, and Rosemary blew derisive raspberries and lifted two fingers at the invaders. "Ye big fools! Clumsy oafs!" He danced about and waved his sword, which caught the first yellow glintings of the rising moon. "You'll not catch us!"

The Red Caps rose to the bait. They charged at the dancing pixies. Three of them promptly fell through the smooth lawn and disappeared. Giddy had called moles and badgers from the village common that abutted the cottage's rear garden to dig deadfalls and holes. Jelly caused to be covered over by long, thick grasses. A pixie, who weighed less than a pound, could walk across them, but anything heavier would plummet a foot or more.

The other Red Caps immediately became wary of the ground, and poked ahead of them with their axes. The pixies threw silver-tipped spears at the remaining elves, then drew their weapons as the bigger sprites closed in upon them. Lasset heard a defiant yell from Picket. Isa closed with another of the invaders, hammering at him with a silver-coated mallet. The Red Cap knocked it out of his hand with a stone. Lasset leaped back just in time to avoid his opponent's ax, then turned and jabbed Isa's enemy in the shoulder. The Red Cap bellowed in pain and dropped his stone. Isa took advantage to grab his fallen mallet, and smashed upward with it, sending the powrie flying.

A big barn owl flew overhead like a passing cloud and hooted. The pixies immediately braced themselves, and

the gunnery team broke away from the battle to flee into
the rhododendrons. The Red Caps laughed at them and
turned to assault the remaining defenders.

The werewolf leaped into the garden and was in their
midst in two bounds. Kicking aside the pixies that rushed
to intercept him, he stalked toward the door, his eyes
gleaming, his jaws slavering. Lasset knew he could smell
the tender flesh of the old man asleep in front of the
telly just yards away. Lasset made a handful of green
witchfire and sent it soaring into the air.

Under Picket's command, the gunnery team rolled the
gun out onto the front stoop.

The werewolf stopped for a moment at the sight of
the tiny creatures surrounding the gun, which had been
roped to a platform made of an old rollerskate and a tea
tray. He let out a terrifying howl of laughter. The Red
Caps laughed, too.

Lasset didn't wait. He gave the signal. "Fire!"

With a shattering explosion, the gun fired. The kick
back sent the entire contraption, team and all, careening
backward along the stoop. Hun and the others leaped
off and grabbed the ropes, hoping to catch it before it
fell off the other side. It fell over with a crash.

The werewolf laughed again, louder. The bullet had
missed. He acknowledged the cheers of his hangers-on
with a wave of his tail, then rose to his feet to start
pulling at the door handle. The cottage door only opened
by a key on the outside, a latch on the inside, but the
incredible, unearthly strength of the wolf began to pull
the door frame apart. Lasset and all of the pixies leaped
to help right the gun. Heedless of the pain of touching
the steel gun, they got underneath it and pushed upward
until it rocked unsteadily back onto its wheels. Together,
they all pulled down the hammer. As ten of them helped
aim it and held it in place, the gunners leaped to the
trigger.

The werewolf set his foot against the frame and
wrenched again at the door handle. Lasset heard the
wood give out a pained creak.

"Fire," he ordered.

The door frame splintered at the same moment the gun went off. The werewolf looked under his arm at the black hole in the side of his rib cage. He whimpered and sank to his knees. The Red Caps gasped. As they all watched in astonishment, the black-furred beast collapsed on its side. It twitched violently, then lay still.

Inside the house, Old Man Trehinnick came to the window and threw it open.

"What be all this din?" he demanded, peering out into the darkness. "Who is there?"

The Red Caps shrieked with fear. They tried to run, but the pixies had been waiting for them to lose their nerve. They leaped off the gun carriage and ran after the enemy, knives and forks drawn. They stabbed and slashed at the retreating enemy. There'd be no blood for their caps that day.

"Is that children? Get thee from my garden! Go, before I smack thee with my cane! Wait until I get out there. I'll tell your parents."

Jelly, her little face set, threw out handful after handful of green magic until every one of the Scottish elves was bound tightly. She clapped her hands together, and the Red Caps sank into the pitted ground, yelling and struggling.

Trehinnick appeared on the stoop. "Look what's become of my door!" he said, his voice shaking with anger. "I'll get the pollis on yer, so I will." He looked down at the hairy body at his feet. "God in heaven!" He tottered back inside. The pixies heard him shouting.

"Hallo, 999! A thief tried to break into my house! He's collapsed on the step! Come now!"

"Hurry," Lasset said. "The pollis will be here soon. We don't want Trehinnick blamed for this."

At his direction, the pixies hastened to unfasten the gun from the carriage. They hauled it by the strings and shoved it carefully into the right hand of the naked body. In death, the lycanthrope was already beginning to revert to his human shape. It would be a mystery the local constabulary would never solve.

* * *

By dawn, the police and photographers were picking up and clearing out. The pixies watched them from the safety of the bushes to make sure nothing befell Trehinnick. He was interviewed over and over again, but it seemed clear to the investigators that he could not have wrestled such a fit, young man, taken a gun from him, and shot him. The lawn and hedge had been restored hastily by Jelly while they were waiting for the police to arrive.

"Sorry to trouble you, Mr. Trehinnick," the lead investigator said, leaving the old man at the door. He was a stocky young man in a suit, probably thirty years of age. "Thanks for the tea. If you will just step around to the station later for a statement, we would be much obliged."

"Aye, yes, I will, Lieutenant," Henry Trehinnick said. "I shall come after lunch time. Trefusis up the way is to come at thirteen hundred hours to repair my door. Goodbye, now."

"Good morning, then." The young man locked the gate behind him and got into the car with the police constable. They drove away.

"Good job, all," Lasset said. "Heroes we are. At last the scourge is gone."

"Tis a pity we won't have our names in the paper," Picket said, with a grin, clutching his scorched arms. "No rewards neither."

"We don't need them," Rosemary said. "We saved our home, you ungrateful puppy. Here, let me see to your burns. Metal, indeed!"

Trehinnick picked his way down the garden path and took his newspaper out of the fence, where the paper boy always left it.

"Must get meself shipshape," he said, unfolding the paper absently and reading the headlines. He looked up and shook his head. "Ah, and in all the confusion I nearly forgot!"

He disappeared into the house, then returned with a saucer of milk and a crust of bread. Bending down very carefully, he set them down at the left side of the stoop.

"Enjoy it, then, pixies," he said. He went inside.

"There's our reward, so," Lasset said, surveying the homey treat with pleasure. "And a finer one I could never hope to have."

WITH OPEN HAND

Meredith Simmons

"Go steady the younglings," Chol said.

A negation sprang into Karz' head, but the words died unsaid. Who else did Chol have to send? But Karz hated the job, hated the need to supply courage and common sense. His commander correctly read his reluctance.

"You're the best at this," Chol said. "Go."

Karz went, unconsciously staying in the shadows, his gait smooth despite a stiffened right leg.

The two younglings crouched in a depression near the pit the squad had labored to dig during the daylight hours. Too near. Karz dropped in behind them.

"We need to move back to the rocks," he said. "When the pod falls into the pit, it will thrash about like any injured animal." He didn't add that the pod might not fall. The things had an uncanny ability to detect pits, even though the sand covering the thin, fabric top looked no different than the surrounding area.

"I've never seen a pod," said the smaller of the two younglings, his voice tight with awe or fear. Fear, more likely. At least if he had good sense.

"You'll be able to see it better from behind the rocks." Karz put his hands on bony shoulders and turned his charges around, pushing them out of the depression and toward greater safety. The shoulders felt so fragile. The

154

younglings had reached adult height, but hadn't developed adult bulk. The light of the setting sun brought their faces into stark relief, angles rounded as if there were still something unfinished about them. He remembered that they had dug and hauled sand with diligence, however. Soldiers, for all their lack of years.

Karz got them situated. The rocks themselves still baked with the heat of the day, hot to the touch. In contrast, the long shadows behind the rocks were welcoming and cool. Their view down the defile was unimpeded. The pit was within easy striking distance.

"I'm Brin," the smaller one said, raising his hand and spreading wide his three fingers.

"I'm Tarn," said the other, echoing the gesture.

There was no help for it. Karz raised his hand. "And I'm Karz."

He watched his name register, saw the unwarranted wonder in their faces. He could nearly read their thoughts. Karz, hero of the evacuation of Hantelow. Karz, survivor of a hundred battles. Oh, they had heard of Karz. He completed the formula, the two younglings speaking with him. "Together we three form a Hand, and we will make this Hand a fist."

The three stood in the deep shadows of the rocks, now with fists raised. Karz wondered if the younglings knew the words they spoke so solemnly were intended to start a game of Malqua, a game they had probably never seen. Just as they had never seen Hantelow of the Springs. Lush, green Hantelow would seem a myth to them. The tall trees, the flowing canals, the building burnished golden in the sun—all this just a story told in a land of sand and rock.

But the Hand was indeed now a fist, a bloody fist that beat against the power of the invaders, doing itself as much harm as it did the enemy.

The sun was nearly down, throwing the entire shallow canyon into shadow. The pods would soon come. The younglings nervously shifted from foot to foot.

"Waiting is the hardest part." Karz said. A lie, but one kindly meant. There was no way to prepare younglings for the gut-churning fear that preceded an actual attack, the lightning flashes from the pod that froze muscles and paralyzed will. There was no way to forewarn them of the tantalizing odor of cooking meat that drifted from the downed carcasses of friends, or of the self-disgust that came when stomachs cramped in hunger and mouths watered. And the screams, screams that echoed forever in the mind, haunting sleep. It was best to focus younglings on the waiting, which was something they could understand.

"You were in Hantelow when the pods first came, weren't you?" Tarn asked, eyes filled with hero worship.

"Yes," said Karz, and he told the story as he had a hundred times, told of the objects appearing in the sky, at first so tiny, black cylinders with white, silky filaments above them, looking like Shapotta pods shed from celestial trees. "On the ground, they were huge and frightening, but we could only think that they had been sent by the gods, and so we met them with the open hand of friendship."

Karz had recounted these events so many times that he was no longer sure whether what he said was true. He really didn't remember exactly what had happened that day. But his account of the attacks by the hard-shelled creatures that tumbled from the pods had been polished with retelling and left his audience breathless.

"And this is when you led all the citizens to safety," Brin declared, the youngling having heard the tale many times.

Karz was saved from the embellished version of the frantic flight from Hantelow by a rumble from down the defile. "A pod comes," he said.

The younglings crouched down, as if they could be seen in the darkness. Karz could hear their breathing reduced to quick pants. Pods were terrifying as they hissed and grumbled across the sand. Lights flashed around then, illuminating the paths the soul-destroying lightning could take.

He placed his hands on his charges' shoulders, feeling

the quivers of anticipation or dread. "Hold, hold," he said. "We must stay hidden until the trap is sprung."

He had confidence that Brin and Tarn would know what to do when the time came. The village elders only sent younglings who had been fully prepared and had honed their skills. While Karz had grown old during this war, the younglings had never known anything else.

The ground trembled with the passing of the pod. Lights flashed among the rocks, blinding the eyes. Karz held his breath as the pod approached the area of the pit; tension coiled around his muscles as he waited for the thing to suddenly veer away from the trap. But it rolled inexorably on.

Perhaps at the last moment one of the creatures inside realized the danger. The pod slowed; the pitch of its horrible rumbling changed. But it was too late. Too late! The sand-covered fabric gave way. The pod tilted, throwing sand in a fountain at its rear as it fought for purchase.

Lightning flashed in all directions, crackling against the rocks that protected the three of them. The younglings gathered themselves. To flee? To attack? The direction a youngling might run was never a sure thing at a moment like this, although Karz would bet on the movement being one of attack. Younglings arrived at the front filled with the green wonder of lost Hantelow, brimming with hate for the things that had driven them away.

"Not yet," Karz said, tightening his grip.

The pod lost its battle against gravity and tumbled into the pit. Its lightning now only shot straight up, harmlessly puncturing the night sky. A ragged cry of victory and defiance echoed in the canyon. Brin and Tarn raised their cudgels above their heads and screamed, dragging a cry from Karz in unconscious response.

"Wait for the creatures to climb out," he said. "Wait for the nets."

This last maneuver was tricky. If the creatures were not netted, the four Hands that made up the squad could easily be wiped out. But the netters were veterans. They knew what to do.

One of the creatures crawled out of the pit. Backlit by the pod's useless lightning, it appeared as a brooding shadow. It fired its own lightning bolts, but they were smaller and couldn't reach where any were hidden. A second creature appeared. Then a third.

Let that be all, Karz prayed. Let there only be three. A Hand. There was luck when your opponent also approached as a Hand.

The three creatures clumped near one another. Foolish, but the creatures never seemed to learn that they made the job of netting easier by staying close together.

A Hand of netters appeared as if they had sprung from the ground. Fleet-footed netters who darted forward oblivious to the creatures' lightning, nets unfurled behind them like spider webs blown in the breeze. Karz willed them onward, prayed for luck.

One of the netters went down in a flash. Karz felt again the searing pain in his leg, remembered agony. The other two swung their nets. Karz watched the nets fall. Yes! One of the creatures ensnared. Then the other two, captured in one throw.

The creatures were not harmless, no more than a wasp held in the hand was harmless, but they were contained.

"Now!" Karz yelled at the younglings.

They shot forward like rocks from a sling. The smaller paused briefly, looking back, his eyes wide, reflecting the flashes of impotent lightning. "I'll see you in Hantelow," he called and smiled. Dear gods, he smiled.

The younglings ran to the first ensnared creature, cudgels raised. They brought them down. Sharp, loud blows that echoed among the rocks. The two creatures that had been entangled together struggled against their bonds. One managed to get his weapon free. Lightning flared.

One of the younglings went down. No scream, just a silent crumpling, his demise somehow made more poignant by the lack of sound. The other youngling turned toward the other two creatures, toward the lethal flash.

And Karz found himself running across the sand. There had been no thought, only a bone-deep need to unite with his Hand. Karz picked up the cudgel from the fallen youngling, the smaller, Brin. I-will-see-you-in-Hantelow Brin. A wild keening of fury issued from Karz' mouth.

The remaining youngling pounded on the more ensnared of the two uninjured creatures. He too suddenly collapsed. Karz was close enough that he could smell the odor of cooking meat, a stench now disgusting, no longer with appeal.

Karz raised the retrieved cudgel and brought it down on the creature's flailing arm, the arm that held the lightning maker. There was a satisfying crunch. Then Karz attacked where a face should be. The hard exterior skeleton of the creature cracked and broke, but Karz pounded on and on until the outer layer broke, revealing the soft thing that lay beneath.

Karz stopped his attack and leaned on the cudgel, panting, drained of all energy. The face of the creature looked up at him, a face not so different from his own. Oh, it was strangely hairless and had no true muzzle, but the eyes, the nose, the mouth, were very similar. The mouth was open in a gasp.

"Why do you come here?" he whispered to the corpse of the creature. "Why do you come here when our air is poison to you?" It made no sense. It had never made sense.

Then Chol was grasping his arm and swinging him around. "What are you doing?" Chol yelled at him. "This is not your job. This is not the position you play. You're to inspire, to steady, not, not, this." Chol threw out his hand to encompass the trapped pod, the dead or dying creatures.

Chol was angry, perhaps afraid. He and Chol had grown old in this war. He and Chol had been in the original Hand, when the field had been green and Malqua a game.

"I . . ." Karz started, but could think of nothing to say. I responded to the need of my Hand was what he wanted to say, but Karz knew that the younglings were never truly his Hand. That part was strategy, a strategy that he'd used many times.

"Do you remember exactly what happened the day the pods came?" Karz asked softly, his change of topic smothering Chol's anger.

Chol looked confused. "No, I really don't remember," he said.

"Did we approach them with open hand?" Karz asked.

"We must have. That is what is told, what has been told, since that time." Chol put his arm around Karz' shoulders and led him back toward the rocks. The pod still hummed and shot its lightning into the sky, but it would die when it was baked in the morning sun. "These are not the thoughts for a battlefield," Chol said.

Chol reached out and removed the cudgel from Karz' clenched fist. "Do not do this again," Chol said. "If we are to win this war, there must be both heroes and martyrs. You, Karz, are the hero, and we cannot lose you."

Karz leaned against the rock. The heat of it had been leeched out by the darkness. Was he a hero? Had he been? Or was it all a legend that he had somehow taken as his own? He felt so tired, boneless. He laid his head back against the rock.

"I need the names," Chol said, businesslike, the cool voice of a commander.

Ah, yes, the names. The names for the list of martyrs. "Brin and Tarn," Karz said.

"Brin and Tarn," Chol repeated. Then he reached down and pulled up Karz' hand where it hung by his side. Karz hadn't realized that his hand was tightly fisted until Chol smoothed his fingers out. "Brin and Tarn and all the others yet to come."

POTTINGER'S STROLL

Jim Fiscus

Y URI Pottinger woke in darkness. He spun from his
bunk, reaching for his autoshot as his bare feet
slapped to the floor. Distant voices echoed his cry of
"Mortars!" Explosions ripped the night.

Pottinger grabbed his magazine vest and ran. He
jumped from the hut's doorway, landing on packed sand
and using his momentum to vault a low wall of sandbags.
Rockets whistled overhead as the explosions of mortar
rounds shattered the night. A voice screamed in pain
from a shattered body. The rockets slammed into Lewis
Station. Pottinger shoved his back against sandbags and
glanced up into a night sky filled with stars. "Jackers
couldn't let me get a night's sleep my first day in town,"
Pottinger mumbled, "It was supposed to be a nice easy
supply run to Xin Dag, then three months of leave on
Earth."

The square pit of sandbags was about two meters
across and a meter high. Pottinger checked his shotgun,
freeing the round magazine and then clicking it back in
place to make sure it was seated. Two traders crouched
together in the far corner of the pit. One sat holding a
square hat tight to his head, his other hand grasping a
blast rifle like a lifeline. The second squatted naked in
the sand, clutching a white pillow to his chest.

A figure slipped around the inside wall and dropped

beside Pottinger. The man held a pistol belt and a heavy handblaster. He wore an aspirant's nova on his collar, silver representing a Company officer. Fancy blaster, Pottinger thought, but I'll keep something that doesn't break when you look at it. Pottinger nodded, "Asprint Sudor, I assume. You were on patrol when I landed."

"Just got back. What I heard is that you crashed our supply ship," Sudor said, nearly sneering.

"Shot out of orbit is more like it," Pottinger said, angry he'd been taken down so easily. "Too much work for you jackers to tell us the Musca had you blockaded?"

"With them holding the hyper relay? Hell, yes," Sudor snapped. The mortar explosions marched through the darkness, each closer than the one before.

"Okay, no link makes it hard to talk to folks." Which will slow down a rescue fleet from Earth, Pottinger thought. Could be here for months. I'm tired of being shot at. He realized that his fatigue was mental more than physical, two years of constant combat pulling on his mind and body, but the League had driven the Musca from a dozen planets.

Sudor reeked of sour sweat. He glanced up at the sky. "Jacking pile of sand's supposed to protect us. Feels like the bottom of a funnel."

"With luck, any hit will dig into the sand before it goes off and you'll only lose a leg or two. Where's our counterfire?"

"No rounds left. The Jikky have slammed us for a month." Sudor's voice cracked slightly, his tension showing. "They'd drop rounds on our heads. We'd smother the hills with counterfire. A few minutes later, they'd fire again. We'd fire back. If we were lucky, our patrols would find a spot of blood on a rock. We burned though our shells in a week."

"With boulders covering the hills you'd need a direct hit to do much damage. Who ordered heavy fire?"

A rocket slashed overhead. Sudor gasped and shrank back against the sandbags. "Director Choy."

Leave it to the jacking civilians, Pottinger thought. The

rocket exploded, followed a heartbeat later by a series of larger explosions and a bloom of light. Pottinger watched flames leap into the sky. "Relax and enjoy the show, Asprint. You won't live any longer, but you'll have more fun," he said, thinking, *that sounds more casual than I jacking feel.*

"You're League Commando, right?"

"Eleven years," Pottinger answered, thinking, *and it's past time to get out.* Hearing a loud curse, Pottinger raised the autoshot.

A tall man loomed out of the darkness and fell against the sandbags. "Come on, you cowards!"

Pottinger smelled the harsh local whiskey on the man's breath. "What went up?" Pottinger asked. The man half turned, and in a flare of light Pottinger recognized Station Director Choy.

Choy ignored Pottinger's question. "Out, you peggers." He stumbled and caught himself on the sandbags.

Pottinger listened for firing from the perimeter. He heard only the screams of the wounded.

Sudor started to stand.

Pottinger put his hand on the younger man's shoulder, forcing him down. "Keep your butt in here. No one's attacking the wall."

"I'll have you shot," the director called, staggering away. "We've . . ." They heard him fall, his rant breaking off in midcry.

"Director?" Sudor called.

"Fell on his ass," Pottinger growled.

Across from Pottinger, the trader clutching the rifle stood up. "We have to defend the compound."

"Get down!" Pottinger yelled, an instant before a mortar smashed into the ground outside the rampart. Fragments of burning metal whistled into the darkness. The trader's head shattered, showering Pottinger with blood and brains.

Light cast upward from a holomap made Station Director Choy look older than his ninety-five years. Choy was berating a technician, demanding that the holomap be sharpened. Pottinger leaned toward Sudor. "Dark in here."

"Adds drama to Choy's show," Sudor whispered.

Bastard killed a man with his drunken panic last night, Pottinger thought. He doesn't care who's next on his butcher's bill.

"Sudor, take a company and give the Jikky a lesson in manners." Alexan Choy leaned toward the holomap. His finger hovered over the valley holding the low-walled containment of Lewis Station. He traced a track into the rocky hills, the map shifting as he followed the route, and stabbed at a cluster of huts. "We've not hit this village before." Choy's short black hair made his pale skin look nearly transparent. He rubbed a scrape on his forehead, a memento of his drunken fall.

"We have three lifters, Director," Sudor said.

"Hogenberg Base doesn't have enough troops to force the passes if the Jikky resist, and if we lose a lifter going into the hills, we won't have the capacity to get us to Hogenberg if we have to pull out."

"Then you walk to the target!" Choy snapped.

Pottinger studied the holomap. "That's half a day's hike, with a dozen places for an ambush."

"You League bastards think you're gods, but you don't have the guts to take a stroll in the hills?" Choy met Pottinger's gaze, shivered, and turned away. "When I reopened this planet for the Company, I roamed the mountains for a year. I had no trouble with the Jikky."

Pottinger's temper flared. "It just took them a while to get to know you. Don't forget, Director, the Company may have trading rights on Xin Dag, but you operate under a League mandate. You cause a rebellion, and that mandate will be withdrawn." When the fleet gets around to breaking the jacking blockade, he thought—only one Musca ship and a few patrol craft in orbit, but that's all it takes to trap me on this rock.

"The Jikky were damned happy to've been found by

civilization after a few centuries on their own," Choy said.

"Jikky?" Pottinger asked.

"Jikky. Dirt eaters. Colonists," Choy snapped. "Whatever you call the scum we planted on Xin Dag."

Ignoring the rant, Pottinger said, "Jikky works, but if those villagers aren't your enemies now, they will be after you raze the place."

Pottinger turned as a man stepped slowly into the light. He was a handspan shorter than Pottinger's two meters, with the look of an athlete who was going to fat as he crept into middle age. He wore a dark blue robe belted with a silver band. His high black boots clicked on the wooden floor as he walked. Two bodyguards stood behind him.

Choy turned, nodded to the man and turned to Pottinger. "Bobo Rygmas, kraj of the Quanjaq clan. He rules Balak City and is the Company's friend."

Ah, Choy's pet Jikky, Pottinger thought.

"Kraj, this man, Pottinger, is from the League. He's one of their commandos. Very tough." Choy spoke as if Pottinger were not in the room. "But all he's managed to do so far is crash a spaceship."

Pottinger shook his head, thinking, I was a fool. Never should have agreed to make a supply drop on the way home.

"Director Choy is right." Bobo Rygmas' voice was high pitched and grating, like the scrape of metal on metal. "The Paolojaq rule the hills. Attack them." Rygmas moved to Choy's side. "But the people of that village are Quanjaq. The Paolo are the ones attacking you."

"That's been your excuse for not stopping the attacks," Sudor said.

"You do not understand the balance of power between the jaq." Rygmas' stomach rumbled. "I rule the Quan, but I only influence the other jaq. I can't strike at the Paolo. You can."

"Not without . . ." Sudor started.

Director Choy's voice rose. "Asprint! Enough." He turned back to Rygmas. "Kraj, who should we punish?"

"Strike the Paolojaq." Rygmas pointed kilometers further into the mountains at a larger village. "Here. Their main town. The clan leaders have gathered to honor their dead and plan further attacks on the Company. One attack can eliminate the leadership."

"Excellent," Choy said, "To ensure that we kill them, we will destroy the village."

"Many have gathered for the Remembrance who are not leaders," Rygmas said.

"We only have the Company's local troops, the gunzis, and cannot be subtle in the attack," Choy said.

"As you will," Rygmas answered, lowering his head slightly.

"That village is another half-day's walk from the first," Pottinger said. "An ambush is certain without eyes up. You can't use drones for the same jacking reason Hogenberg can't send us air support or more troops. If you send anything up, the Musca will shoot it down from orbit."

"I don't tolerate cowardice, Pottinger," Choy snapped.

"You don't tolerate good sense," Pottinger said, his voice harsh as adrenaline drove fatigue from his mind.

Choy ignored the jibe. "Asprint Sudor, take the troops out in an hour. Pottinger, I'm sure Sudor will welcome your help—as an advisor."

"The last thing I want is command this mess," Pottinger said. Stepping from the darkness of the map room into a lighted office, Pottinger asked Sudor, "So Bobo Rygmas wants us to kill his enemies for him?"

"We use each other. Our money helps him stay in power, and he helps us control the Jikky," Sudor said. "He usually gives sound advice."

"And he recommended a tight attack, not random terror."

"I trust the Director's judgement," Sudor said.

A stone dug into Pottinger's knee as he lay just below the crest of a steep hill that overlooked a valley and the village it held. Sudor lay beside him. Half the valley was still in early morning shadow. Despite a chill in the air, he was sweating heavily from a final forced march. A hundred and fifty gunzis lay in a line to either side of the two men. Dressed in black and tan coveralls, most held long-barreled bolt-action rifles that were easy to manufacture—local and reliable. A few men held short, shoulder-fired missile launchers. Their officers, all Company warrants, carried blast rifles.

"We drill them hard. They'll fight well," Sudor said.

They'll fight like the peggers they are, Pottinger thought, but said, "Jikky fighting Jikky. They'll do fine."

The column had marched cross country through the night, losing two men who tumbled over cliffs and four left along the route with broken ankles. They had finally stopped long after midnight, starting again as predawn lit the sky.

"You really think this will end their attacks?" Pottinger asked. "The Company abandoned the colonists on this rock five hundred years ago, and you expect them to love you when you come back to see how they're doing?"

"It was a good plan," Sudor said. "The Jikky would mine khyberium to shield the Company's jump engines and be paid in the supplies they needed to stay alive." Five hundred meters away, the village's mud-brick buildings climbed the hillside. Smoke curled upward from open firepits. A stream flowed through the valley after spilling over a dam at the valley's far end.

A patchwork of fields divided by irrigation ditches covered the valley floor, sections of dark green trellised vines alternating with bright yellow grain. Above the lake formed by the dam, a handful of mine shafts opened into the cliff. "Turned out we just didn't need the planet—till the Company ran out of khyberium on the other mining colonies. When we came back to Xin Dag, we found happy farmers in the lowlands and these semibarbarians clinging to the mountains where the ore is. Nobody was mining ore."

Pottinger studied the valley. He smiled as one of Xin

Dag's flying lizards soared over the fields. Wingspan over two meters, the lizard's iridescent blue and yellow feathers sparkled in the early morning light. All I want to do, he thought, is go home to Earth and sit by a stream fishing.

"Our job is to make them mine the ore we need," Sudor said.

"Who'd the Company hire to run the operation? King Leopold's ghost? Every pegger here hates you."

"You don't know the Jikky. They respect power," Sudor said. He shifted, looking down his line of troops. "Director Choy wants us to destroy them. Bobo Rygmas gave us a good target. We level the village. We go home."

"It won't stop the attacks." Pottinger engaged his visor and was shocked into momentary silence. "Pull back. Now! There's food cooking over the fires, but no one's around. They know we're here."

"Not likely," Sudor said. He stood up and waved down the hill.

The line of troops rose with Sudor and moved toward the distant village, rifles ready. Sudor jerked back, falling over a rock. A heartbeat later, the sound of the shot reached them. Puffs of white smoke blossomed atop the distant cliff, and gunfire echoed across the valley, the shots accurate and deadly.

A man grabbed his stomach and doubled into a fetal ball. Another clutched a shattered leg. Pottinger slipped to Sudor's side. The young officer gasped for breath as Pottinger examined his chest. "Your armat stopped the round." He pulled Sudor behind a bolder. At least thirty men were down, writhing in pain or lying with the stillness of death. "You cheap jackers didn't give your own men armat," Pottinger said. He grabbed a rifle dropped by a fallen gunzi.

"It's in next year's budget," Sudor gasped.

Pottinger shook his head in disgust.

The Company warrants pulled back, the troops rallying about them. A few men fled uphill. Sudor raised his blast rifle and fired. A white bolt vanished against the hillside. "Damned shipboard blasters don't have the range."

Pottinger stuck the rifle out, tripping a running soldier. He grabbed the gunzi's missile launcher. He tapped Sudor's arm to get his attention. "You any good with this antique?" He raised the launcher to his shoulder.

"Not the snipers. Give it to me." Sudor grabbed the rocket launcher. "The Director wants the Jikky to suffer." He aimed the weapon toward the distant dam.

"If you take out the dam, you'll scour the valley, and you won't stop the snipers. How many do you want to kill?"

"We'll kill as many as it takes to crush them."

"You'll only make more enemies," Pottinger said, but his words were lost as the rocket fired.

The missile arced across the valley. It struck low on the dam and vanished. For an instant, nothing happened; then a flash of light and shower of dirt erupted from the earthen face. Seconds passed, and the front of the dam crumbled, releasing a three-meter high wall of water.

The fire from across the valley stopped. "Move. Let's get these poor bastards out of here." Pottinger called to two warrants. "Move!" The officers drove their troops toward the crest of the hill, keeping them from stopping and watching the flood.

The deluge swept across the fields, scouring them of crops and topsoil. The slurry of mud and water slammed into the hill beneath Pottinger and rebounded across the valley into the village. A mass of women and children ran toward higher ground from buildings on the valley floor. Pottinger knew they would not make it, and he turned away.

Gasping for breath as he climbed through the boulders, he thought, been fighting in cities too long. He slung the rifle and held his autoshot ready. Sudor followed twenty meters downhill, driving stragglers before him.

*   *   *

The station medic closed a gash on the back of Pottinger's right hand. As she worked, he thought back over the long retreat from the valley and the dead village. Despite efforts by flankers to drive them off, the Jikky had dogged every step the gunzis took, firing into the straggling column. Two thirds of the men died in the long march back to Lewis Station.

"You were lucky." She had dark brown hair and stunningly blue eyes. "We couldn't have rebuilt your hand at Lewis if you'd taken a direct hit."

Pottinger turned as Sudor pushed open the door, glanced at the medic and said, "Thank you," and joined the younger man.

"Any more die?" Sudor asked.

"Three."

Sudor's anguish showed on his face. "I lost over a hundred men!"

"The key is to not make the same mistake again. And give some credit to Choy. He ordered the attack."

"I followed the orders."

Fatigue settled on Pottinger again. He forced himself to ask, "What's happening outside?"

"We sent out scouts. They report Jikky pouring into the hills overlooking the station. They estimate a thousand already, with more coming, but we need eyes up to really know. Do we just wait for them to kill us?" Sudor asked. "How do you stop a rebellion?"

"You start by doing what the Karj suggested. Find the leaders and kill them. Treat the rest humanely. But Choy can't be bothered to identify the leaders. When you attack, you kill everyone. And you're surprised they hate you?"

"The Director believes strong measures keep the Jikky under control."

"Do you believe that?"

"I used to," Sudor answered. The young officer looked crushed by the failure of Choy's policy. "No. Choy's orders were wrong." He straightened. "The Director is

waiting." He almost fled the room through an outside
door.

The station's square central parade ground stretched a
hundred meters across. Fine rake marks ordered pebbles
into waves. The heat of late summer rippled into the air.
Two ripcannons sat near the center of the field inside sand-
bag walls, both useless, their ammunition long expended.

Two rows of buildings ringed the field, all standard
Company construction—plastacrete sprayed on an inflatable framework. Only large red numbers distin-
guished one white building from another. Their walls
curved upward to form half-pipes. Sandbags ringed some
buildings. Above-ground mortar holes sat beside each
doorway. Most buildings displayed gaping holes or the
light gray of recent patches. The station medic stood in
the sun a few meters away, the afternoon light burnishing
her brown hair. Pottinger smiled as he watched her.
There is still beauty, he thought.

Earlier doubts seemingly gone, Sudor started toward
Choy's hut across the field. Explosions ripped the compound. Both men dropped flat, the medic's scream in
their ears.

Ignoring the explosions, Pottinger ran to the woman.
She lay on her back, a gaping wound in her chest. Her
blue eyes stared lifeless at the sky.

Director Choy was centimeters taller than Pottinger,
but he appeared far shorter as he shrank back against
the holomap table. "We leave today." Pottinger's harsh
whisper reverberated through the room.

Choy sidestepped. "We must stand firm. The Company
does not retreat from scum."

"There are over a thousand Jikky in the hills with
free fire into the compound. We only have two hundred
gunzis who've not stripped off their uniforms and
slicked home. We must move to a more defensible
position."

"You're not even an officer." Choy stiffened, facing
Pottinger. "You don't command me!"

"In this place, at this time, I am the League," Pottinger said, thinking, they might cashier me for exceeding my authority, but I can't let this clown kill more people. "You will do as I order. The containment is surrounded. Our people can't walk in the open without being shot. We have no heavy weapons. No counterfire," he continued, speaking as much for the benefit of Sudor and several warrants who stood beside him as for Choy. "Bobo Rygmas offers us sanctuary, and we must accept it. Cross country, we're two k from the city. The ore lifters can easily make it, as can the troops. Once inside Balak Rygmas, we'll be able to hold out till the fleet lifts the blockade of Xin Dag."

Sudor stepped further into the light. "Pottinger is correct, Director. He is senior League official present. He showed restraint in not taking control sooner. Follow his orders, or I relieve you of command."

Choy slumped against the table. "You don't know what you're doing, but you League bastards always have the authority."

The ore lifter edged along the main street of Balak City. Pottinger sat beside a driver forward of the ore box. He held his autoshot, watching the angry faces of the city's people. A flat pallet six meters long by two, with solid meter-high side walls, the lifter forced everything off the street ahead of it. Station Director Choy sat on a bench seat mounted in the lifter's center, flanked by Company warrants holding blast rifles. Two more warrants sat in a rear seat watching the street behind them. Supplies covered the deck. A dozen gunzis lined the sides of the lifter, their rifles gripped by white-knuckled hands. Two other lifters followed, crammed with supplies, traders, and the wounded. Sudor rode in the rear vehicle. Lines of gunzis on foot paralleled the lifters.

Balak City sat astride the road to the lowlands and the spaceport at Hogenberg. Three- and four-story mud-brick and stone buildings filled with shops flanked the street, making it feel like a canyon. City residents wear-

ing pants, shirts, and jumpsuits shipped from the lowlands bumped and pushed each other out of the way of
the lifter. Jikky from the hills, standing out in their heavy
coats and boots, refused to move until the lifter pushed
them aside. The smells of roasting meat and alien spices
filled the air. Pottinger wished he had time to grab a
kabob, but he kept scanning the angry faces that flowed
around the procession.

"Way too many Jikky from the hills," Pottinger said.
"How far to Balak Rygmas?"

"Streets twist. I don't know," the driver said, and
pointed across a square packed with people.

A column of men in dark blue uniform pants and tu-
nics jogged into the plaza and forced their way through
the crowd. "Two hundred or so troops," Pottinger called
over his shoulder. "Blue uniforms."

"Bobo Rygmas' guards," Choy answered. "As I said,
he is reliable."

The guards split into two lines facing outward, and
forced the crowd to open a corridor for the lifters. A
man whose uniform glistened with gold braid called to
Pottinger in a heavy accent that resembled a lisp, "The
Karj invites you to Balak Rygmas."

The streets narrowed as the lifters turned from the
plaza. Bobo Rygmas' guards cleared the way. Without
room to walk beside the lifters, the gunzis bunched before and after each craft. Pottinger felt the invisible target in the center of his back that always came when he
expected attack. The air grew warmer as they moved
deeper into the city, further from even a hint of breeze.
He called to the warrants behind him, "Keep your men
watching the buildings." A dark stone cliff loomed
above the houses. "Damn," Pottinger muttered, "it's
a castle."

Balak Rygmas rose above the city. The building
seemed an organic part of the cliff against which it sat,
stone walls streaked with lichen and stained by three
hundred years of weather. Towers grew from the cliff
face, rising to larger fortifications atop the bluff.

They broke from the winding street into another wide

plaza, bordered on one side by one of the fort's walls and on the others by houses and shops. Statues portraying the First Landing dominated the center of the plaza, showing a tall lander surrounded by the heroic figures of the Jikkys' ancestors. Lampposts circled the statues.

The lifters stopped before the balak's gate. The Karj's men lined the plaza, facing the city and a growing crowd.

Sudor jogged to Pottinger's side as gunzis jumped from the lifters. "I'm putting our men between the lifters and the local peggers, with the walls at our back."

"Good. But put a file on each lifter. That'll give thirty men with good firing platforms," Pottinger said, thinking, they'll hold the mob about five minutes if we don't get into the fort. He glanced at the massive stone castle. "Impressive place. As long as you don't have artillery or blasters."

"You can't see it, but the walls are sheathed in khyberium. They'll hold."

Rygmas' troop commander stepped to the lifter. "Director, you and two men may enter."

"Our honor. Sudor, you and Pottinger with me," Choy said, sounding as if he was choking on Pottinger's name.

The guard commander bowed and moved to talk with several of his subcommanders.

"No, we need Sudor with the troops." Pottinger pointed to a gunzi he remembered from the retreat. "You, Murshhko, with us." He added softly to the Choy, "We need a local man who'll understand what's happening."

"I understand Bobo Rygmas and the local situation."

"Your successful policy has proven that, Director," Pottinger said. "Murshhko comes." Pottinger edged Choy into the lead and followed with the gunzi.

The commander joined them at a heavy metal-clad door set beside the main gate. Pointing to Pottinger's autoshot, he ordered, "That must stay outside."

Pottinger handed Sudor his autoshot. "If we don't get out, good luck."

Sudor stared at Choy, who was clearly impatient to

enter Balak Rygmas. "Don't risk yourself for that clown."

Pottinger smiled. "We have to know what the Karj wants."

Pottinger shivered in the cool entry hall. He had expected the old fort to be dark, but it was brightly lit. The commander led them through a narrow hall to a room that was part office and part lounge. Rygmas rose from a heavy wooden chair. Intricate carvings of space ships and landers covered the chair's back.

"Director, welcome." The Karj embraced Choy. "I am surprised by your visit. You seldom leave your compound these days."

Bobo Rygmas' high voice dug at Pottinger's nerves.

"The Paolojaq would have had us trapped soon. We are here to accept your offer of refuge. Once the blockade of Xin Dag is lifted, the Company will show its gratitude."

"Yes. Once the blockade is lifted," Bobo Rygmas said, his stomach growling as if he'd not eaten in a day. "But will it be lifted? Might not the Musca win their war with your League?"

"No," Pottinger said. "The League has been pushing them back across the sector. The ship that shot me down is a raider. It has enough patrol craft with to keep us blockaded, but they'll run as soon as our fleet shows up."

"So you believe. In any event, the Paolojaq are now my allies, my people."

"Allies!" Choy swallowed, then stood with his mouth moving soundlessly.

Oh, shit, Pottinger thought. He dropped the handle of his sleeve-knife into his left hand, keeping it tight against his leg, and shouldered Choy aside. "Do you withdraw refuge?"

Rygmas nodded. "Politics require it, I fear. My cousin who was karj of the Paolojaq died in your attack. I have been elected to succeed him, uniting our people." He backed away, turning to his guard commander. "My cousin's death, and the deaths of his deputies, would have been good, but you killed over two hundred people in that valley. The Director ordered their deaths. The rebellion will grow and will sweep me away as you are destroyed if the Director does not face my judgment.''

"You told us to attack him," Choy said, his voice rising.

Doors swung open around the room, admitting a dozen soldiers who entered silently. The commander raised a blast pistol. Pottinger flipped his knife to his right hand and whipped it across the commander's face, feeling it slice into bone. The man fell back, his hands trying to staunch the gush of blood. Pottinger's left hand grabbed Bobo Rygmas and jerked him forward, holding him as a shield. Pottinger's blade, gleaming with the commander's blood, caressed the Karj's double chins, drawing a drop of blood. The guards shifted, clearly uncertain what to do without orders from their commander.

"Director, to me. Murshhko, take rear." Pottinger shoved the Karj toward the exit, followed by Choy and the gunzi. He called to the guards. "You jackers can try to kill us later if you want, but move now and this scum dies."

"Kill him, kill him now," Rygmas yelled.

The commander waved one hand back, and the guards lowered their rifles. He grabbed a cloth from the table and pressed it to his face. "Go."

Another change of command? Pottinger frowned as he pushed Rygmas into the entry hall. "Let's hope the commander is reluctant to kill his old boss."

"The man is loyal," Rygmas said. "He will kill you if you injure me."

"A loyal praetorian. There's a new idea." Pottinger used the Karj's body to push the outer door open.

Staggering ahead of Pottinger into the plaza, Rygmas gasped, "He's my younger brother." He added, his voice uncertain, "I trust him."

"Always trust brotherly love." Pottinger shoved Rygmas against the nearest lifter, said, "Hold him," to a gunzi, and took his autoshot from Sudor. "Bobo here wanted to execute the Director. I demurred. But I think we have a palace coup. Not sure how good a hostage Rygmas is." Under his pumping adrenaline, Pottinger's anger swung from the Karj, to Choy, to Sudor, and finally to himself for not taking command and stopping the slaugher.

"Jacking well better be a good one. We have a mob pressing into the square. The Karj's guards are holding them off."

Pottinger jumped onto a lifter. The gunzis knelt or stood around the lifters, using them for protection. Fifty yards away, a double line of blue-clad guards faced a crowd that grew as Pottinger watched, fed by people pouring in from the streets entering the plaza. The front line of troops held shields and heavy swords. The second line held rifles and a few blast rifles.

A horn sounded from Balak Rygmas. The troops raised their rifles and fired into the air. The front row of the crowd fell back, and the entire organism recoiled. A horn sounded again, and the troops wheeled and jogged back toward the fort. They flowed around the statues.

"Hold firm," Sudor called to the Company men.

Rygmas twisted and snapped a punch into the face of the gunzi holding him. "To me. To your Karj!" He called to his passing guards.

A subcommander and two soldiers turned aside and grabbed him before Pottinger could jump from the lifter. Instead of hurrying Rygmas toward the fort, the officer drove a fist into his stomach. Rygmas doubled over. The guards flung him toward the mob. The subcommander shouted, "For the Paolojaq!"

Bobo Rygmas sprawled on his face. He rose to his knees, glancing up as the mob engulfed him, dragging him toward the statues. A rope looped over a lamp post. Feet kicking, the Karj swung into the air.

"We have to get the hell out of here," Pottinger yelled. "The fun won't keep them busy long."

Murshhko, the gunzi who had escorted Pottinger and

Choy, pointed away from the heart of the city, "The spire. That's the Cathedral of the Landing. Even the mob would respect its sanctuary."

"Move," Sudor called to the lifter drivers.

"Don't fire on the crowd! Let them forget us a moment," Pottinger bellowed over the mob's cheers. The gunzi on the ground jogged beside the lifters as they sped across the smooth stones of the plaza. "Form between the lifters," Pottinger ordered. Sudor and the warrants urged the troops into tight blocks of men running between the three craft.

The street leading to the cathedral was less crowded than those entering from the city center. The lifters sped toward it, not slowing. The mob parted, flowing around them into the plaza.

Pottinger glanced back at the body kicking feebly at the air. "At least the pegger's of some use."

Two blocks toward the cathedral, a warrant rocked back, grabbing at his throat above his armat. "Snipers!" Sudor called as two gunzi fell, the Jikky's heavy rifle slugs tearing gaping holes in their flesh. "Where are they?" Sudor and the other men looked wildly around the windows.

Pottinger caught movement in a second-story window, thumbed his mag to explosive slugs, and cycled two rounds into the building. The window exploded outward, showering the troops with wood and glass shards. Pain slashed through Pottinger's cheek. He reached up, touched wet and saw blood on his hand. Too close, he thought. Hope that was a shooter and not some kid.

The blast failed to slow the other snipers, and more men fell. "How far to the cathedral?" Sudor asked Murshhko.

"Right at the next corner and two blocks." Murshhko crouched behind the driver of the lead lifter, jerking back as a bullet smashed into his chest.

Choy huddled between sandbags. "The station. Back to the station. We'll be safe there."

"Politely ask the Jikky to give it back?" Pottinger said.

"You had to start a war." He swung the autoshot into Choy's face. "Too much splatter." The lifter spun in a tight right turn.

"Pottinger! Barricade!" Sudor's voice cracked with fear.

A large freight wagon lay across the next intersection. White smoke from rifle fire slowly obscured the barricade. More guns blasted from the buildings lining the street. The last warrant fell, so many rounds hitting his armat that his organs turned to jelly from the shock. Most of the gunzis were gone, dead on the streets behind them, trying desperately to stop the flow of blood from wounds, or cowering into doorways, waiting for a chance throw off their uniforms so they could blend into the city.

"Back up!" Pottinger yelled, an instant before an explosion sent a shock wave that drove him to his knees. He looked up, saw Sudor's mouth moving, but heard nothing. Pottinger picked up his autoshot and turned. A bomb had broken the third lifter in half. The debris blocked the street. Slowly, his hearing returned, and he thought, This is too well organized. It's not a spontaneous mob. It's part of the coup.

A ragged crowd of Jikky charged from the barricaded intersection. Pottinger leveled his autoshot, saying, "What it was made for." He swept the weapon across the advancing Jikky, who seemed to dissolve in a spray of flesh. Pottinger felt a bump on his arm, glanced up, and saw Sudor pitch out of the lifter. He whipped the autoshot forward again and fired at a second wave of Jikky. No one else fired from the overturned wagon.

"It's time, Director." Pottinger stood, grabbed the man's coat, and lifted him to his feet. "Time to talk to the Jikky." He kicked the man out of the lifter, watching as he stumbled a few steps and fell to his knees staring at the Jikky who ran toward him.

"All I wanted was a bit of leave," Pottinger said, but no one was alive to hear him. He glanced behind the lifter. Small groups of Jikky ran toward him, sheltering behind the middle lifter. The nearest broke into the open. Pottinger raised the autoshot, paused, and thought, No point. There was never a reason. Smoke spouted from the Jikkys' rifles. Pottinger waited for the bullets' impact.

DINNER ON A FLYIN' SAUCER

Dean Wesley Smith

ETHEL was lookin' at me like a skunk done crawled up my ass and was making a nest. I suppose I couldn't really be blamin' her. I figure that havin' dinner on a flyin' saucer would be a hard lump to swallow whole, especially when I smelled of whiskey and had lipstick-lookin' red marks all over my coveralls.

And, to boot, it was three in the mornin'.

Ethel stood there in the front door of the double-wide that I had bought and paid for with the sweat and hard work from my own bare hands like she owned the thing, leavin' me stuck like a dog after he rolled in the mud on the second step halfway up to the porch. She was makin' sure I didn't have a thought of goin' inside past her, even though it was cold and kinda real damp out.

Behind her the light from the kitchen was showin' through her bathrobe and nightgown, outlinin' things that Ethel should *never* let be seen.

Now no disrespect to my wife, but Ethel is a big woman, taller by a pretty fine lick than my five-foot height. She never was much of a sight to see at three in the morning, and this morning was no great exception to the rule. She had them there big curlers in her hair that jabbed me every darned time I rolled over in bed. She had on her flannel robe over her nightgown, and her favorite slippers with the pink furballs on the toes. Right at that moment her face was all screwed up like she was about to spit, and she had my shotgun cradled under her tits just like she carried it when she hunted.

At the moment I figured out real quick I was the game, and if I didn't do a little scamperin', tellin' her what happened, I was going to end up with an ass full of buckshot. Or worse yet, dead on my own front steps.

I held up my hands like I'd seen them criminals do on *Cops*. "Give me a chance to tell ya the story at least."

"Tell," she said, gesturing with the barrel of my gun.

"Can't we go inside so I can sit?" I didn't want to say nothin' about how the whiskey was makin' me feel right about then.

"Tell."

That time the gun gesture she made got her point out *real* clear like. She didn't care about no fog or cold or dark night. She just wanted to know where the hell I'd been and what the hell I'd been doin'.

I took a deep breath of the thick air and figured the best place to start my tellin' was at Benny's, a bar down on Owl Creek Road, right near the Miller place. Benny owned Benny's, ran it like every drop of booze was the most important drop of booze on the planet, never givin' no man a free drink for no reason. Cheap bastard, but a hard worker, and I liked him for that.

Benny had one of my elk head, a seven pointer, on the wall over the pool table. I was damn proud of that head, and I spent many an evenin' in there drinkin' and starin' at it and makin' sure no one hit it with a pool cue.

"I was at Benny's," I told her.

Ethel snorted, clearly not surprised.

"Two Buds and then I left, I swear. I was aheadin' home for dinner by half past six."

"Dinner got ate at seven," she said, the anger in her voice so strong that behind me I imagined I could feel the trees startin' to shake with fear. I know I was, but I couldn't be showin' her any weakness, and I couldn't be upchuckin' no cookies from being sick on the whiskey. I had to keep on talkin' and talkin' fast.

"Tossed your dinner out at nine," Ethel said. "I let the dog eat it."

I wanted to ask her if the dog liked it, or if the dog was even still alive, but I figured real quick like to just not be saying anythin' real stupid with her still holdin' my shotgun. So I just nodded like I understood and kept on tellin'.

"I was walkin' down Owl Creek, headin' home after only two Buds, when this bright light comes at me from over the trees like a big bird diving for a rabbit. That there light just sort of hovered right smack over the road above me. I tell ya Ethel, that there light was so bright I had to go and cover my eyes."

She grunted.

I was sure she wasn't believin' me, but the story had to be as I started it, since changin' the tellin' now would cause me even more problems, and more problems at three in the morning, facin' an angry woman with a shotgun, is not somethin' any man wants.

So I just went right on, makin' the details real thick like, cause I heard once that details make a story sound more right.

"And there was this wind," I told her, swingin' my arms up and around as if I was a warmin' up to throw something, "like that storm we had last winter that knocked down the chicken coup. I tell you, that there wind was real strong like, blowing dust into my face."

"No wind here," she said.

"The wind was a comin' right out of the light."

"Oh," she said.

"Then suddenly the light just sort of grabbed me and picked me up and sucked me through this big hole and into this really big room that was real dark considering it was inside the bright light."

She grunted, and I didn't much blame her, since this was soundin' a mite stupid to me. What on God's green earth had made me think tellin' her the truth about gettin' taken by aliens would stop her from shootin' me? But I was committed to the tellin', and I figured right then and there that the only way to get this out was to just tell her fast, before she decided I was too stupid to live and just shot me. Dyin' from a blast with my own shotgun just wasn't my idea of how to leave this life.

Takin' another deep breath to push back the whiskey dizzies, I went on.

"I was frozen like a deer in a truck's headlights, standin' there starin' at three little gray guys, little fella's no taller than my belt, skinny, big long fingers, just like they had on the tee vee in that movie we saw last year. You know the one with all them aliens?"

She stared at me and just said nothin' and when Ethel says nothin' I knew buckshot and a quick burial was a comin' next. You didn't go messin' with Ethel, and I doubted if Sheriff Bob would even bother to arrest her for killin' me once he heard why she had done it.

It was three in the mornin' and I was whiskey stupid and didn't have a lick of sense to begin with anyway, so I kept on tellin' her about the aliens.

"One of these little guys with only three long fingers took my hand and walked me across the room to a table and then pointed to a chair. I remember readin' in the *Enquirer* that they usually did things no man wants done, but they didn't seem to have read the same issue I read, which pleased me a mite I can tell you. I sat right down, let me tell you, since I was scared plain out of my wits and about ready to dump a big one in my pants."

Ethel just grunted and shook her head.

"The three little guys went around the table, each a sittin' on one of the other sides. They must have had booster chairs under them because they could see over the edge of the table and look me right in the face with their big, slanted eyes. The one closest to me pointed at the plate in front of him and then at me."

Ethel hadn't moved, even to shift her bulk from one swollen foot to the other, which for Ethel was some special thing. I knew that if I managed to get out of this alive, I'd be rubbin' her feet for a week.

She made that gesture that said I should go on, so I did. "Right then I noticed that the table was set like for a special Sunday dinner, with white plates, silverware, and food, lots of food, and it smelled real nice as well, like that wonderful turkey you made us last Thanksgivin'.''

Figured a compliment or two couldn't hurt any, but it didn't even get her to blink, so I kept on with my tellin' real fast like.

"It seemed they wanted me to try some of that there food in front of me, since the little fella next to me kept pointin' at the plate and then at me. The plates in front of them didn't have no food on them, but it seemed they wanted me to eat anyway. Now let me tell you, Ethel, I wasn't real pleased with the idea of eatin' no dinner fixed by little gray guys with three fingers who traveled in some beam of light. And I didn't hanker much to eatin' alone while they watched, but I figured I had no choice right about that point."

"You tellin' me you had dinner on an alien space ship?" Ethel asked, my gun moving more than I wanted it to move.

I ignored her question because that was what I was about to tell her that I'd gone and done.

"When I picked up the fork on the outside like I had seen in that movie, they all clicked like a bunch of crickets, only louder, so I put the fork back down, and they stopped clickin' and just stared instead."

Ethel just shook her head.

"It's gettin' cold out here," I said, easing my way up completely on the second step. "How's about I finish this at the table?"

"Keep on goin'," she said. "I don't want no blood in my house if I have ta go on and shoot ya."

I wanted to say it wasn't her damned double-wide, it was mine, since I had bought and paid two thousand good, hard-earned money for it long before we had gone and gotten married, but contradictin' a woman with a shotgun had never been good thinkin'.

"Well, Ethel, let me tell you this," I said, going back to what had happened up there in that there spaceship, "I picked that fork back up and they went to clickin'

again, stopped when I put it down, started when I picked
it up, like there was somethin' really important about
that there fork.''

I took a deep breath and kept right on, not even lookin' at Ethel.

"Finally I got tired of playin' with 'em, so I just dug
the fork into what looked like mashed potatoes with
brown gravy and shoved a bite into my mouth like I
hadn't eaten in days. Clickin'? You ain't never heard so
much alien clickin', but I didn't much care because them
there mash potatoes were the best damned potatoes I
had ever tasted, even better then the ones your Aunt
Sarah used to make with that real butter that she took
down to the church socials.''

"You tellin' me you ate some alien's *food*?'' Ethel
asked.

"Every bite on the plate, turkey drumstick, dressin',
potatoes and gravy, roll, wanted to lick the plate it was
all so good.''

"You're eatin' while the perfectly good food I had
worked hard to fix up for you sat gettin' cold on the
table?''

"I couldn't help it,'' I said. "It weren't my idea to get
sucked up into that light and sat down at that table and
clicked at. I just did as them there little fellas wanted
me to do.''

"And them there lipstick marks on your overalls?'' she
asked, swingin my shotgun around to point at my chest
that was covered in red marks that looked like a woman's
lipstick. "Them from the little fellas as well?''

"They are at that,'' I said. "After I finished eatin' that
there food they had given me, all three of them got up
and came over and started puttin' their three fingers on
me all over and clickin' like mad. It was their fingers
that left these here marks.''

I pulled my coveralls away from my body and sort of
held the chest part out for her to look at. "See, these
here ain't no woman's lips. You can see for yourself
they're alien fingerprints. Just look nice and close.''

Again Ethel snorted and didn't move.

It was them there alien fingerprints that I was a hopin' would prove to her that my story was true and all. Alien fingerprints are damned hard to ignore I figure.

"So why did they want some fella like you?" Ethel asked.

"Directions," I said. "Them little guys were flat lost."

"The only place you know directions to is Benny's."

"Not true," I said. "Remember when we was lost two years ago, up in the hills, and I got us out."

"Luck," she said, disgusted and waving the shotgun for me to go on tellin'."

"Well, it seemed that all their touching was a way of talkin'." I held out a section of my overalls to make sure she could still see the little red marks. "Ya see, them there little guys was warriors, soldiers, fighting in this big ol' war goin' on between them and these real ugly sticklike slug-creatures. I could see it all because it was like they was a runnin' a movie in my head."

I shuddered rememberin' it all, but kept on. "I could see the fightin' and killin' so clear, and let me tell you, them stick slugs were ugly and really tall. Hell, I wanted to jump in right there and offer to help them there little gray fellas fight them ugly slugs. So I did."

"You did *what*?"

I took a deep breath and just kept on tellin' her the truth. "I up and said I'd help em in their war."

Ethel just shook her head, and the shotgun swung around at me again. I wasn't going to get a chance to die for them gray guys. Ethel was going to kill me first. And I bet they didn't give out no ribbons for gettin' killed tellin' your wife the truth.

"Let me just finish, will ya?"

She shrugged, so I went on.

"Like I said, them little fellas was really lost, so that's all they wanted, but let me tell you, they was touched I offered to fight with them."

"You're the one who's touched," Ethel said.

"You just go and wait until them there big tall slug

fellas start marchin' up the driveway. They fire light beams that can cook ya faster than Uncle Ben's barbecue pit."

She snorted. Not a good sign when Ethel starts snortin'.

"Look, I am knowin' you don't believe any of this, but what I saw when them there little gray guys touched me really opened my eyes, let me tell ya. This here is the battlefield. This country, this planet. All around us, right here, only not really here where we can see it, but yet right here. You know, like when a dog can hear a whistle and we can't?"

Ethel didn't say anythin', which was a degree worse than snortin'.

I pointed at a tree. "One of them there tall skinny slugs could just come right out of that trunk right there and we'd both be dead. Them little gray guys called it somethin' like multidimension or somethin' Twilight Zoneish."

Ethel glanced at the tree.

"But the little gray guys seem ta know when the tall stick slugs are a comin' and where, and they keep em from doin' that, which is why I up and offered ta help."

"How can an idiot like you help them?" Ethel asked, disgusted.

"Guide," I said. "They showed me a map of the area and somehow, with all the clickin' and touchin', got me to understand they was a lookin' for a dock at Steven's lake. I pointed right on one of their maps where it was at and we got there in a flash of white light, and let me tell you, just in time to stop them there slug sticks from comin' out. Slug sticks blow up like popcorn under the little gray guys weapons, which would be just horrible for huntin' but great for killing enemy slug sticks. After they was all done fightin', I was a hero and they offered me more food, but I told e'm I had to be gettin' on home."

"So, how come you're not still fighten' with them if you're such a hero?"

. "I said I'd try to get more help and then be here when they needed me."

"Help?" Ethel asked. "You're gonna' tell other folks this story?"

"Sure," I said. "Told them there little gray guys I would, get more guides, get a few folks like me workin' for 'em. So they let me go, right back through the white light and on the road where they'd taken me. I sort of staggered back to Benny's, and since it was right before two in the mornin', I caught Benny before he closed up and had a couple of whiskeys to calm my nerves. And then I came straight on home, I swear."

I put up my right hand like I was on one of them tee vee court shows where people argue and yell and have all sorts of fun.

Ethel just shook her head and stepped toward me, grabbing my overall and lookin' at the red marks. Then finally she said, "You're sleepin' with the dog."

"Now hold on there," I said, but she swung the shotgun around to point directly at me.

"It's three in da mornin'," she said, "and you been drinkin' and playin' pool and missed my dinner because you're a damn fool drunk. And if that there raspberry rubbin' don't come out of your overalls, I'm goin' ta make ya wear them anyway."

She turned, and before I could get another word out of my mouth, she went inside and slammed the door on me. Can't say as I blamed her for not believin' my story.

I turned and whiskey-stumbled down off the two steps and headed for the doghouse, which I had built when we got the mutt a few years back. It weren't really no doghouse, just a lean-to against the chicken coup, but the dog liked it, and who was I to argue with a dog. I was a goin' to be covered in fleas by mornin', but I suppose that's not as bad as an ass full of buckshot.

I had made it halfway to the doghouse when a bright light hit me from overhead, a wind whipped up dust and dirt, and then the next damn thing I knew, I was back in the alien ship with the three little fella's clickin' at me. I was swayin' dizzy like from the whiskey and the ride on the light.

I can't say I was happy to be seein' them again so fast, but after facin' Ethel and that shotgun, they looked pretty darned harmless.

This time they wanted me to try some really nice-tastin' ice cream. Strawberry, with swirls right in there of some sort a chocolate. Ethel would end up even bigger if she ever laid her hands on the fixin' for that there stuff. They studied every move my spoon made like I was an artist at the ice-cream-eatin' event in the alien Olympics.

And I can tell ya, my spoon did some real fancy dancin'. After three full dishes of the stuff, I waved off a fourth, then with them gettin' more red marks on my coveralls, I told them where Deacon Creek Falls were. They let me lay down and catch a few winks while they went and killed the slug sticks, since ice cream and whiskey don't match if you do much movin' around after, and I couldn't see how I'd be much use in a fight throwin' up and all.

They finally woke me up with a bunch of loud clickin' and shot me through the light back by the doghouse.

It was a comin' up on dawn and Ethel was already up and cookin' breakfast, so I just went on inside. She pointed at the table just like them aliens had, only without clickin', and served me my favorite breakfast, buttermilk pancakes smothered in maple. She never mixed up a batch of buttermilks unless something was wrong, or she really needed somethin' from me. And after the tellin' of my story, I had no idea what that might be.

I ate as much them as I could, and let me tell ya that wasn't no easy chore after a night of doin' nothin' but eatin'.

I kept waitin' for her to say whatever she wanted, because with Ethel I could always tell when something was runnin' around on her mind, but she just watched me eat in silence, no talkin' no clickin' and didn't say nothin' about my story, and I didn't go tellin' her about my ice cream visit to the little fellas and hours of sleep on the alien ship. I figured she wouldn't have believed me no how.

Besides, there was just no point in gettin' in even more trouble for not sleepin' in the dog house.

Finally, after I just couldn't eat another bite, she finally spoke her mind. "You go back, get me them recipes."

I stared at her like she had gone and lost her grip on reality.

"Recipes?" I asked. "There's a war on, woman."

"I don't care about no war," she said. "You can help them or not, make me no mind. But I want them alien mash potatoes recipe, and the dressing one if you can get it too. Monthly social is a comin' up and . . ."

She stopped like she knew I knew what she was a sayin'. I couldn't believe my luck. She had just up and gave me a free ticket to husband heaven. She needed me to get her somethin', and from the looks of the buttermilk pancakes, she was a willin' to pay. I was goin' ta be eatin' good for a week. And havin' my beer toted to me in my chair in front of the tee vee. And no more doghouse for stoppin' at Benny's every night. Any darned time I wanted somethin' all I had to say was I was a tryin' to get her them there alien recipes.

"Next time them little fellas come and get me for some eatin', and guidin'," I said, nodding to her real serious and all, "I'll ask them. How does that sound ta ya?"

She gave me her sad smile and shook her head, which puzzled me for a moment. Then she stood, moved over to the stove and pulled out my shotgun from a spot she'd hidden it.

"You were supposed to be a sleepin' in the doghouse," she said, pointing the gun right into my face, "so where was ya? And don't go tellin' me ya went back to them aliens for dessert. There ain't no aliens, no recipes, just you, an old drunk lyin' to his wife. So no lyin'. Where was ya? Widow Matti?"

I should have known Ethel wouldn't have gone and believed me, since she never read *The National Enquirer*.

She didn't know them there gray guys got folks from all over the country ta help them in their big fight with the tall stick slugs.

The visions of my husband heaven left me like a cat being chased by a dog. Now she thought I was a cheatin' on her with the widow Matti.

But I had to tell her the truth. I just couldn't think of anythin' else while lookin' down the barrel of my shotgun.

"I'm not a cheatin' on ya. Them there little fella's took me in the light again, gave me ice cream, asked directions to Deacon Creek Falls, and let me sleep on the floor. I swear!"

The red in her face sort of crawled up from her thick neck like a burner on the stove gettin' hot.

I held up my hands as the business end of that shotgun sort of got bigger. "Okay, wait, wait, I stumbled into the woods to toss my cookies and passed out near the woodpile."

"Checked there," she said, her face gettin' redder and startin' ta look like a ripe tomato.

I was about as desperate as a man could get, and my brain was a workin' on too little sleep and too much food and didn't seem ta be helpin' like it was supposed ta be in a husband crisis. So, without really doing much thinkin' I shouted out what she wanted ta hear.

"Okay, okay I was at widow Matti's cabin, and she rode me like a cowboy rides a bull, and I can even show you her spur marks in my side if ya want."

Ethel's face was about as red as I had ever seen it.

I glanced around at the door, figurin' that if I made the outside and ducked right, she might miss me enough with the shot for me to live. But if Ethel was anythin', she was a fine shot, and I just wasn't that fast.

I was just about to make my break when suddenly the build up exploded, but not like I had spected. She burst out laughin' and lowered the shotgun.

I stared at her, more stunned than I had remembered feelin' starin' at them there three little gray men inside the light. She was laughin' and shakin' her head, and the flesh on her arms was a movin' in all sorts of directions like waves on a beach. It was like Jay Leno had just told a joke right there in the kitchen.

"What's so danged funny?" I asked after she managed to catch a breath.

"Your story," she said, startin' to laugh all over again. After a moment she just shook her head. "You and the widow Matti. Now *that's* funny."

"Why is *that* so danged funny?" I asked.

The widow Matti had given me a few looks, but I sure hadn't told Ethel that, and I wasn't a bad-lookin' man, even if I didn't shave much and wore the same shirt for a few days in a row.

"Stick with them aliens servin' ya food story," Ethel said, shaking her head and startin' to clean up the kitchen. "And when I tell ya ta sleep in the doghouse, you better get your ass in there real pronto-like."

I opened my mouth to say somethin' real smart back in return, then decided that anythin' I might say wasn't real smart at that point, which is a good rule to follow just about any time with Ethel, but especially now after I had lied to her about bein' ridden by another woman, so instead I just sat right there at the kitchen table and nodded like a toy dog in the back window of a pick-up truck.

Still, it hurt that she didn't believe her own husband would be somethin' the widow Matti might ride some night. The widow had taken on old Chester from the service station, or at least Chester claimed she had every time he had a few too many drinks.

I believed Chester, yet my own damned wife didn't believe me about the widow Matti or about them there aliens either. Or the war with the tall stick slugs. Maybe next time them little guys took me up into the light for dinner and directions, I *would* ask them for the recipe for them there mashed potatoes.

Then I'd give that there recipe to the widow Matti.

I bet the widow Matti would be real grateful like, and

maybe give me a ride like she'd done to Chester. Especially when she found out I was a real war hero and all, keepin' the world safe from them stick slug invasions.

The widow Mattie would go and believe me. And then that would show Ethel.

SHADES

M. Turville Heitz

LATE-night silence overtook the inn as the infant gazed from Leefa Ka's knapsack with more wisdom than he should. Leefa ignored the warmth of the inn's banked fire and the soft snores of travelers.

She must not sleep.

Her vision blurred for only a moment.

She forced herself to focus on the now sleeping infant. Had she slept? Her heart began to pound, but no shades raced from the night to steal them back to death.

She inched her sword closer. The blade emitted an unworldly glint, the cold milky light from a land never touched by sun or a slice of moon from a place moonlight couldn't penetrate.

How had she survived so long without sunrise? This morning, she thought she'd burst with joy on the first sight of it, or breathe too deeply of autumn and battle-bruised turf. For one hundred years only shadows: she would not go back.

It had been autumn, like this, barely a month after she'd won a place among the King's Watchers. Her gray danced beneath her that day, his neck an impatient arch and tail flailing in a cool wind full of leaves and puffs of seed as they crept toward Leefa's first battle. Each valley opened upon a brighter rank of trees. Golden fields stood stark against pasture green. Creak of leather, jangle of harness, clank of sword, and that heady breath of autumn set her blood to coursing as she contemplated proving her mettle to Old Ka, her father. She gripped the hilt of the sword he'd taught her to wield, impatient to test its edge.

A scout, chased by a trail of dust, galloped down the rutted road toward them, the corps halting as one on Old Ka's signal. From the hill's crest, The Wood gave off a golden haze, girdled by pastures that thickened to forest in the valley beside the road. Leefa pictured herself galloping beneath a golden arbor of falling leaves kicked skyward by her mount as she pursued her foes.

"Five, six if they have a scout," the Watcher called out as he reached the dozen soldiers surrounding Ka. "They made camp just up the road."

Ka frowned. "Daglad couldn't hope to hold the road with but a handful. He knows we have three corps this side of the Wood."

"We can cut through them before they know it!" Leefa said, raising her sword.

"Certainly we'll have the advantage," Ka said with a barely indulgent restraint. "But there's something odd about this. Are they a scouting party? A van for a larger contingent? Bait?" He grinned at his daughter's battle stance, then ordered his corps into two wings. One he sent to flank an enemy wearing the gray livery of the wizard Daglad, servant of King Atri of Eastland. The other wing, Leefa among them, raced along the road to engage the enemy, their blue cloaks whipping behind them.

Leefa's wing bowled into their foes before they could rise from their smoking cookfire. Leefa's sword slammed hard against a firm defense, ineffective. Her mount danced aside on cue, taking her beyond the warrior's reach. She again brought her sword around, only to meet air. Her blood pounded in her ears, tense gasps pulling from her every movement. The clank of weaponry chased birds skyward. Hooves beat the sod to punctuate the warriors' appeals to the battle gods. Leefa's weapon glanced off a shield. The flanking wing thundered through the wood to them, leaves falling around it with abandon. Slivers of mud flew up from hooves. The skirmish ended in moments.

Leefa gasped, every sensation attuned to the moment, her heart pounding with the thrill of the challenge, though her blade remained free of first blood. Instead of praise for the success of the assault, Old Ka frowned at the dead as if reading prophecy in their sprawled bodies. Ka swept up a bloodied strip of cloth marked with charcoal that had been removed from a body.

"They have King Andran and his guard pinned at Mark's Edge," he stated when he looked up from markings that remained cryptic nonsense to Leefa's eyes. "This was a feint."

"Then we must ride to Mark's Edge," a Watcher said.

"I doubt we can 'round the Wood inside of two days, more if we wait for reinforcements," Ka said. "Daglad can march five times our number there in hours."

"We could go through the Wood," Leefa said. "It might be slower without roads, but we'd be there this afternoon."

"Foolish words, Leefa." Ka brushed away her suggestion like stable flies.

"Daglad's dead haunt the Wood," another muttered under his breath.

"Fireside tales," Leefa scoffed. "The king's in danger! We can't let harvest ghosts frighten us. Certainly King Andran's wizard would have destroyed such creatures if they existed. I've heard Ferhid claim Daglad's spells were made powerful by our willingness to believe them. We can't just yield king and country after eighty years of war because the King's Watchers fear a haunted wood!"

"Not harvest ghosts," another Watcher muttered. "Daglad calls them from the ground."

"You would not speak so lightly of them if you had met a shade in battle," Ka said in his lowest tone, the one of warning. "And we've said nothing of yielding."

The gray pranced beneath her. She imagined autumn as a flurry of color in her wake, like pennants raised on a vast battlefield.

"Look at the Wood!" She threw her arm broadly at the golden haze on the hillside above. "That's no place of shadows! If shades exist, would they live among gold-leafed silverbarks and sunny glades?"

Ka's forehead crinkled a little, and other Watchers glanced nervously up the slope.

"I'm not afraid of Daglad's magic. I'll go through and return to show the way," Leefa told them, sitting straighter on her mount. She gazed up the hillside at the Wood.

"It's more death than magic that worries me," Ka said.

"I'm not afraid," Leefa stated. Then, to feed her strength, she laughed, setting loose again that thrill in her blood. Ignoring her father's shouted protest, she goaded her horse to a labored gallop straight up the hillside and into the Wood. She didn't look back.

She laughed again as she rode beneath the eaves of the wood. The trees arched overhead, sending a soft rain of gold leaf upon her as she crested a small hill and raced down animal trails that led her to a fast brook. The horse plunged through the stream, kicking up a brilliant spray.

Her laughter died suddenly. Reining in, she found the sunlight dimmed, not penetrating a canopy grown brown with great oaks instead of silverbarks. The animal trails ceased, and thickets barred her way.

In no time she lost her bearings as each tree loomed larger and taller than the last, its branches entwined in witches' brooms. The oaks gave way to some tree with bark dark and damp, as if clothed in a mist. Many rotted where they stood, crowding so close no way could be won among them. No leaf touched the ground here. All clung somewhere above her in the thicket of branches. Echoes of the elders' warnings and her defiance bedeviled her thoughts, but Leefa dismissed them. Certainly, if trees such as these existed, superstitious warriors would claim this to be the heart of Daglad's terrors.

Beneath her the gray grew restive, sidling over loamy soil that quickly grew packed and slick. Certainly the beast only sensed her doubt.

The Wood fell still. The light went dim, and the deeper black of tree trunks gathered around her, indistinct, as if they formed a hedge. She gripped the hilt of her sword, white knuckled as she studied each shadow in a host of shadows. She heard nothing but the rip of her quick breaths and the horse's occasional snort and grumble of fear. It couldn't be far before she should crest a ridge and see the land fall away toward Mark's Edge and the other side of the Wood.

A stench of something putrid and charnel-sweet grew. Suddenly, darkness raced at her like a storm boiling across the southern plains or a black fog, thick and noisome. The horse squealed and shied, unseating her. It bolted, leaving Leefa sitting on the cold floor of the dark wood. Stunned, she could do nothing but stare at the dark that coiled about her like morning smoke over a lake. Vinelike tendrils of black groped from the deepest shadows as if the tree branches now reached for her.

In an instant icy fingers gripped her, coarse and twining as roots long-buried. Something watched her. She fought to raise her sword and strike at a dark glitter, like eyes in a night so complete she couldn't see her own flailing limbs. The hold on her arms tightened. The stench of decay made her gag. The silence closed, deafening but for her own heart and breaths. This, she decided, was death.

And at last she gave in to it.

Leefa opened her eyes to night so deep that she knew she was *somewhere* only because she could smell, taste, feel: the repulsive odor of a *presence* around her, the coarse, soillike sensation of something in her mouth that must be food, the icy touch of unseen creatures gripping her. Absolute silence reigned. She stumbled trying to rise, falling to her knees.

Those first moments—discovering the darkness, her eyes slowly adjusting to a dim world where darker shadows emerged from an overall night—stayed with her while all else faded. Time passed her, each moment an eternity. And in the timeless dark she knew spindly shades surrounded her. Their eyes glittered in the twilight of "day," when starlight stood overhead and a dim glow limned the horizon, never enough to give warmth or denote color. She didn't need to *see* them; the stench of death clung to them, and the cold damp of underearth was in their touch.

In this early time, of hours or days, she wasn't sure, she felt as one who cannot wake herself from a tedious dream. The shades led her to a niche formed by fallen trunks of moldering trees where, if she slept, she awakened to find food awaiting her. If she wandered away from the niche, invariably she would find herself returned to it. At first she sought to escape the dark forest—stumbling into tree and root, or slipping in muddy ditches, then learning her way through the dark until she'd worn paths. After a lengthy hike, just when she was tiring, she'd stumble across her niche to find food, a washbasin, and her bed awaiting. As she wandered ever farther afield to test this circular wood, she somehow acquired a knapsack that held an endless supply of food and water.

At some point, she couldn't say when in the lethargic world of the shades, she concluded she abided among the dead. Clearly she was a dead fool. Had her fellow Watchers followed her to their own deaths, unable to warn anyone of the king's straits? What became of King Andran?

Pining over the living world served nothing. The afterlife selected for her was one of waking, a mockery of nourishment, and sleep. She explored the confines of the circular wood, learning to sense objects, even seeing their outlines in twilight; she knew where the ground was slick or where a rotting branch threatened to trip. In time, her eyes no longer watered in the presence of the shades. She studied their fleeting images, concentrating on the way they watched her, how the smoky sense of them almost mimicked the human shapes they might once have worn, or how their icy touch made her cringe. She hadn't become like them, yet. Her warm flesh didn't leak the water of decay.

It might have been many days, or weeks—she often
had trouble remembering the moment before—when one
waking she found a cluster of shades hovering beside
her. They made no sound, never implied thought or
want, only stared. She looked around; beside her knapsack lay a sword scabbard. She drew the weapon. A slice
of the moon glittered, so bright it blinded her. Around
her, the shades' eyes blazed fiercely as she held it up to
view. Like no sword she'd known before, it curved
slightly and wore a wafer-thin edge, so balanced it
seemed an extension of her arm. And real! So often in
this place she couldn't even recall the texture of a thing
moments after she'd touched it—wood, stone or mud.
The sword felt solid, cold and sharp and already part of
her. A memory she'd buried erupted, sending the blood
coursing in her. She wanted to throw her head back and
laugh, but she couldn't seem to utter such a sound here.
Find battle, the sword called to her. She followed, ea-
gerly. She strapped the scabbard to her waist and strode
from her niche.

Like so many things that happened in the Wood, without knowing what path she trod, she found herself on
the edge of an open plain she'd never encountered in
the Wood. The shades crowded behind her like a cold
blast from a deep cellar. A dim light fell on a battlefield
where many gray shadows fought. The openness of the
place as twilight hovered on the horizon revealed the
figures of helmed warriors in silhouette, serpents coiling
upward from the helms' crests like the very scourge the
gods had driven from the world. The shades willed her
to join the battle against the serpent-headed enemy; she
could not hesitate to fight such demons as tormented the
People in the dawn of the world!

Leefa drew her sliver of moonlight, a spark in the
shades' eyes. Was that a war cry she heard erupt from
the shades? Did they wear ancient armor, a ragtag assem-
blage of hundreds of years of warfare? Shadowy pennants unfurled, and at their head she raced onto the field.
The demons fled before her, the serpents on their helms
writhing as she laid about her, the war cry of the shades

in her throat. She never felt the sword strike, but first blood she drew. She threw back her head to laugh, only to hear a snarl erupt from her. Storming the demons' camp, she slew those directing the battle, the remainder racing from the shades' fury and the sense of dread and fear they drove before them.

Strangely, mere moments after she thought she recalled standing victorious beside the fallen leader of the demons, she awoke in her niche to find the same bland food she tasted each day, and all that was the same in this world was the same again. *Had* she fought a battle? Had she stood on a field victorious? Was it all a dream? No. For now she carried with her the slice of moonlight at her side. Instead of aimless wandering, she went to battle with imaginary creatures, stabbing dummies of vine-bound leaves, running through the Wood, leaping stone and ditch, log and stream until her heart felt as if it would burst as she honed herself for the next skirmish. As waking passed to waking, in reward for her diligence in finding the right paths through the Wood, she fought many battles at the head of an army of shades. Yet with each victory she woke as if from a dream.

One waking she again found the shades watching her. Another call to battle? She'd dreamed dozens of battles in her few days in the Wood. On reaching for her sword, she discovered an infant boy in her arms, blinking at her, clinging to her, rooting at her breast and seeking her warmth. He didn't come from her womb, but instinctively she clung to him. Warm. The child was warm, not cold and dead like her. A child? He couldn't be more than a few seasons old, a creature of flesh. And here in her arms! When she looked up from the child, she found herself alone. How long had she studied his tiny digits and limbs, or the bright birthmark beside his ear that darkened when he grew fitful and faded when content. She tested words on him, her voice hoarse, the sound falling loud on the silent land.

His curious arrival drove her again to seek any edge

of the Wood. She carried the infant with her, the knap-sack oddly accommodating. Again, her farthest treks still brought her back to her niche. Yet she still might be led to battle in places unseen before, the infant remaining in the niche where he suffered no want. Leefa again gave up wondering at the oddity of this place. It was the world of the dead, and, like her, the boy had come to it too soon. One day, Leefa imagined, she, too, would be cold and dark and give off the stench of the shades. Would the child push her away then? Would the darkness seem less dark?

Perhaps shortly after the infant arrived, a fitful sleep gave way to the icy touch of the shades gathered about her. Their eyes glittered urgency. They stood between her and the infant. To battle, then. She took up her sword and let them lead her at a run into the forest. Unlike the dreamy battles of the past, no battlefield loomed suddenly before her, nor did demons raise their swords against her or run in terror from her wrath. She knew the grip of her sword in her hand, felt its weight, as if she might truly remember this encounter and not awaken in her niche. The cold anxiety of the shades fol-lowed her as she sped over slick and moldering turf she knew as intimately as the touch of the infant's cheek.

At last, on a path she'd worn through the Wood, she saw ahead the hint of something ghostly white, gathering the twilight into itself and reflecting back a brilliance that competed with her sword. She crept nearer. A man sat upon a blinding white horse whose eyes glowed a misty gray. So bright was the apparition that it forced her to cover her eyes. She squinted through her fingers to dis-cern the dark tendrils and smoke of the shades hovering among the boles of the trees, then turned her study to the man astride the white horse. The warrior's gear mim-icked the bright blue livery of the King's Watchers, though muted, without true light to give it substance. Astride a living horse was a man of living flesh, his dark beard combed smooth. Some magic had come into this world, and it smelled rich and loamy.

"What are you!" the man demanded as Leefa stepped from the cover of The Wood and raised her sword in challenge. "Yield!"

"*You* are the stranger here," Leefa replied, blinking.

"I come on behalf of the king to reclaim his son!"

Leefa relaxed a little, resting the tip of her sword on the floor of the Wood. "I think you may have taken a wrong turn, good sir," Leefa replied, with what felt to her lips like a smile, the expression alien and unnatural. "This is a place of the dead."

The man stared at her, startled, a mere stone's throw distant. "She doesn't know," he muttered at the horse, his voice carrying. The horse cocked an ear at him.

"Leave this place. You don't belong here," Leefa ordered. The shades agitated in their hiding places. She could feel them willing her to fight. The light, or perhaps the magical horse itself, clearly frightened them, their gazes lidded. What threat did he pose to them?

"I am Erdrick of the King's Watch. I will not leave without the king's son." Erdrick urged the white horse closer.

Leefa straightened and raised her sword, thinking of the infant waiting for her. Could he be the child they sought? She would not part with her only warmth! The boy existed among the dead now. They couldn't take him back. "I have seen no king's son here. Besides, the king has only daughters and the queen likely too old to have gotten herself another child."

Erdrick's forehead scrunched up. "The king indeed has two sons, no daughters, and I think thirty none too old for the queen to mother more."

"You must be thinking of a different king." Leefa shrugged. "Are you an Eastlander done in the livery of the Westland? Perhaps it's an Eastland prince you seek. He isn't here."

"I must pass, mistress," Erdrick said more softly. "I've sought the prince for ten years, and I'll not be turned aside when I'm at last this close. We've paid too dear in wizard's magic to let anyone stop us." The horse beneath Erdrick leaped forward, in two strides abreast of her.

Leefa brought her sword up to meet his and stood her ground. Their blades met. She pressed Erdrick's aside, swung around and struck him so hard he lost his balance defending himself. He fell on the muddy forest floor. The horse stopped instantly, staring back at Erdrick as if ordering the warrior to mount again. Leefa moved between them. She faced a King's Watcher; she could see it clearly in his garb now. The pin at his shoulder marked him a Captain of the Watch. She faced one who ranked her with a bared sword? Battle blood raced in her veins.

"Captain Erdrick," she nodded, letting him regain his feet. He studied her with a dubious expression, his eyes squinting as if he could barely discern her in the fullness of twilight. What did he see? Did she appear a shade? "You call me a liar, captain, and I think that unworthy of a man of your rank."

Erdrick inclined his head and resettled himself in a battle stance. "I think perhaps you don't know the truth," he said. Leefa brought her sword around to meet his. She struck again and again, moving in on him with comfort in the dark. Erdrick parried each blow as if uncertain from where it might come. She pushed him back toward the place he had entered the darkness, the white horse following, its glance sending the shades back like wind against a fog. Would she glimpse the world of light beyond when she thrust him from her wood? Could she pass beyond, leave the boy— She couldn't entertain such thoughts in the midst of battle. She forced Erdrick toward a rotting branch on the forest floor, feeling a rare glimmer of satisfaction when he stumbled backward.

"You are accomplished," Erdrick gasped as he recovered. "Worthy of the King's Watch."

"I *am* a King's Watcher!" She wanted to hate him for bringing a memory of life into this dead world. She struck harder, deftly twisting her weapon to loosen her opponent's grip, then swiftly bringing her blade back around to force him to change his grip and again lose balance, slipping on the moldering tree branch. He dropped to one knee. She could finish him this moment; yet he smelled so much of life! She could see it in him:

how he had flushed with exertion, the sound of his breaths bursting from his lungs, his musky odor reminding her of the training halls that had been her home. He raised his sword defensively.

"King Andran the Fourth had *no* sons," she returned, bringing the sword around for the final blow.

"Leefa Ka?"

She hesitated, her weapon quivering like the moon above her. Had a warrior come to rescue her? But this man sought a prince.

"Legend tells of the Watcher who faced the Wood in defense of King Andran the Fourth, only to be taken by the shades."

"Legend?"

"The young prince I seek is Andran the Fifth, first son of King Mergreth. Your King Andran died one hundred years ago at the battle of Mark's Edge, in the fortieth year of his reign—"

"You'd have me believe you're losing a battle against a woman one hundred and twenty-five years old?" Leefa gripped her sword, ready to let it fall. "Why would shades want an infant prince?" she asked, mostly of herself.

The horse tossed its head. Erdrick studied her with a mix of pity and awe. She wished she could just bring her sword down into it, this so-human of faces that reminded her of a life lost.

"Andran's marriage was to form an alliance between Eastland and Westland, to end centuries of war. Here the child is a tool and trophy for which one might barter—"

"You don't understand the Wood at all, Captain," Leefa protested. She lowered her blade, but didn't sheath it. "Such politics is outside our existence. Shades battle only demons, and as a shade I fight beside them to defend the living—"

"Leefa Ka," he said softly. "This place is the making of Daglad's spells. It was known even in your time that Daglad sent shades to battle against Westland. Daglad found in you a great warrior spirit to drive his foes from the field."

"I would know Daglad's forces on a battlefield—"

"He has the power to conceal his hand. So great is Daglad's power that he raised the spirits of dead warriors of both sides, even King's Watchers, to fight for him. With shades as his warriors, fear drives the living from the battle."

If possible, Erdrick's words came even softer. "The most fell of our enemy's warriors is a woman with a sword like a slice of the moon." He gestured at her weapon. "Like no other spirit of the dead, her will fells our soldiers. Among the shades, only she carries a weapon that draws blood. I myself fought on a field this apparition touched foot upon, and drew back in terror."

"A fear you clearly overcame." Had she fought her own people? Demons, she'd battled . . . she barely remembered the dream battles, sweeping her enemies before her. She glanced at the shades among the trees, the dark wisps reaching out tentatively, darting back from the white horse in what might be fear.

"You are not now that apparition. That creature wore the grisly face of the dead, an illusion Daglad wished upon you, perhaps even as he wished us to appear to you as demons. You are more than half alive here. This wood, it is merely a gathering place of the spirits of dead warriors from our past, where they await the next call to respond to Daglad's spells."

"Then I *am* dead," Leefa stated. "This is where I dwell. And if truly here, your prince is dead as well."

Erdrick's beard twitched; he might have smiled, but he didn't. The white horse stomped its foot, and the shades retreated deeper into the shadows. "If I'm to believe Ferhid, you aren't dead, but under Daglad's spell. A spell to hide Andran from his people sent him here, into this same half-life as you."

"How can I believe this? How do you know this?" She allowed him to regain his feet and sheath his sword.

"The kings want peace. Daglad won't yield, and he's held Andran enchanted these ten years. Ferhid," he jerked his head at the white horse that perhaps did bear some resemblance to the ancient wizard, "is certain we'll find the prince here. We must hurry! Soon Daglad will realize we slipped through his spells—"

"An infant?"

"Of only two seasons when stolen from us. If time works on him as it has on you . . ." He must have seen the stunned look on her face. "A small birthmark, by his ear—"

She spun away, staring back toward the niche she had lived in only a few days. No! *One hundred years!* She sensed Erdrick behind her, expected the icy touch of death on her arm or even a dagger against her throat. Instead a scent of life, earthy, flooded her, his grip warm on her arm.

"Leefa, help us. You are still a King's Watcher and owe him that." Words, soft, fell in ears that had lived with silence for almost forever. "And you will come with us. Beyond, autumn passes. Legend names you the dervish spirit of autumn—"

She ripped from his grasp. The things this stranger knew of her! Escape. To what? If Erdrick spoke true, she'd face blame for the deaths of her own people, everyone she'd known already dead. Yet, how could she deny Andran hope?

She ran for her niche, the shades trailing her. "Andran," she whispered to the child. She tucked him into her knapsack. Ten years, yet an infant. She slung the sack at her back, too stunned to think, emerging from the niche to find Erdrick astride the white horse, the beast so bright she could barely look at him. A shade's touch, icy and penetrating, delved into her living flesh. Her head throbbed. She moved closer to the horse and noted how the shades retreated, not daring to reach into the circle of Ferhid's influence.

"That's the child?" Erdrick asked, his words taut with the kind of victory that follows so long a search. She merely nodded as he pulled her up behind him on the white horse. The power in the flesh of wizard-turned-beast beneath her, the life in the man whose middle she grasped, their presence felt stronger even than the child

to which she'd clung. Like her, Andran's life spirit lost
to Daglad, he'd been an infant among the dead.

The white horse leaped away, the ground sucking at
pounding hooves. Branches slapped them. The Wood's
silence drummed Leefa's ears like hoofbeats and Erdrick's pulse beneath her grip. Around them, the flitting
shades awaited the call to battle.

"We're discovered," Erdrick gasped. As he said it,
Leefa heard the distant war cry of the shades' charge.
Ahead, through a tatter of dark, a gray-blue twilight
emerged on a path she'd never found. The light strength-
ened as they neared. Silhouettes of horsed soldiers stood
on a ridge against the sky, blurred as if behind a curtain
of falling water. Weapons drawn, they faced the charge
of other riders in the helms of the King's Watch.

An icy grip took her arm. A shade's eyes glowed out
in the growing twilight, inches from hers. They dared,
now, with war cries erupting from their dead throats, to
reach toward the brightness and pull her from the horse.
She wrenched her arm free. More reached out, black
smoke dimming Ferhid's white aura. The putrid stench
forced Erdrick to cover his nose and mouth as he shrank
beneath their gazes as she had once cowered and fallen
prey to the fear, the stench, the cold, the dark.

Leefa twisted around and swung the sword of the
shades' own twilight. The weapon sliced into the slips of
darkness, the cold of each clinging to the blade a moment
before it was gone. Cold crept up into Leefa's arm and
shoulder, a weariness that made her want to slip from
the wizard's back and return to the dark wood. But twilight grew around them.

Erdrick leaned lower over the horse. Leefa left bones
in her wake. Those who had sheltered her, she cast free.
Each blow released some warrior summoned from the
grave back to the dirt, bleaching bones clattering to the
ground in her wake, the shadowy smoke dissolving in
a gasp.

As they neared the blurred silhouettes, Erdrick turned
to look at her and the infant bobbing at her back. "Take

Andran on ahead to safety. We must kill Daglad to undo his spells. You and Andran aren't free until then. This place will cease, as will all within it." He didn't need to explain to her the consequences should Daglad's spells return them to a place that would cease to exist. "In sleep you're closest to their world and can be made to do Daglad's bidding. Don't close your eyes!"

As they raced toward light, Ferhid gave off an ever greater glow, forcing Leefa to again cover her eyes. The shades retreated, leaving the cold of their passing in her sword arm.

Ferhid raced for that part of the curtain most blurry and uncertain. Leefa twisted the knapsack around so that Andran bounced in front of her, where she could see him. He watched her with the knowing eyes of more than an infant.

"We pass from the dead to the living, Leefa Ka," Erdrick said. "Protect the prince! We will find you when Daglad falls."

They burst into the light in the midst of battle. A shout rose up around her as dozens of horsemen fought in the bright predawn of true day. Stunned, Leefa found herself abruptly on her feet, the silvery sword of the dead raised in defense. Her eyes watered in the glare. Her mind reeled. The white horse became a naked wizard with a long white beard braided with silver, silvery-white hair streaming behind him. He chanted some spell as he drew a sword from Erdrick's pack. It all came at her in an instant, more real than any she could remember.

Her sword grip strong, solid she faced foes with defined features, their shouts loud in this cacophonous world. She breathed deep the scent of bruised undergrowth. Her ghostly sword drove through a warrior's armor. Another tumbled from his horse into the trampled turf, to look up into a sliver of the moon falling upon him. Her foes fell back. Like the shades, the living now collapsed at the touch of an icy weapon forged for the dead. A small whimper from Andran reminded her of her purpose.

To her enemies this bright predawn remained night. Soon full morning would be upon them, Leefa revealed and vulnerable. She ripped reins from the hands of an enemy, stabbed the man before he could gasp out his surprise, and leaped onto the man's horse. She goaded the beast to gallop down into the open of fields, sky, pasture, light.

Leefa rode all day before reaching a landmark that oriented her to her homeland. At first, she fled west to keep the blazing dawn behind her. Autumn glowed on the land. The din of lowing livestock, bird chatter, insect buzz roared in her ears; she wept long after the sun had stopped burning her eyes.

They weren't free yet. Even as evening closed, she smelled pursuit, sensed the cold, icy grasp within reach. Long silent, Andran whimpered. She gripped her sword, knowing the eyes of the night watched her. Daglad yet lived. Erdrick and Ferhid must have failed.

While the stench again raised a chilling memory of decay, it beat against her senses less strongly than it once had as she held her fear in control. She swung the cold sword at the darkness. Her weapon clattered against the night. The limbs of shades crumbled to bone in her wake as if she swept debris from her path. She might not fear them at all were it not for Andran gazing up at her, depending on her to keep him among the living.

At last she found an inn. She hesitated after stabling the horse, thinking to hide in the mow. But safety came in numbers and Andran needed the warmth of a fire and food, now that her knapsack no longer yielded its tasteless sustenance. She listened beside the inn door as half a dozen travelers shared news of the wars and talk of politics, often in words she didn't understand.

Then an older voice speaking of the fall campaign muttered, "They say the autumn is Leefa Ka's," to murmured agreement.

Her breath caught in her throat. Night huddled around the lamplight leaking from the inn as Andran watched her. How could the legend of Leefa Ka name herself? What if someone guessed she was the tool of terror in battles past? Andran whimpered.

At last, she had to venture in, her silence about herself unchallenged as long as she wore the moon at her side. To earn a share of the pot for her and milk for Andran, Leefa swept the inn and plucked chickens for the next day's meal. The infant prince dangled in the knapsack, silent and watchful as she studied the corners and shadows for a hint of shades.

Now, as the last patron stumbled to his room, Leefa and Andran were again alone, the shades flitting out of the corners to taunt her. Had Erdrick failed? How would he know where to find her? She might go a few days without sleep—but all the way to King's Home? How would she feed Andran? Could they welcome back a King's Watcher who had fought and killed her own people?

Leefa opened her eyes with a start. She had closed them! She should have risen, paced, splashed cold water in her face, not merely settled beside the fire and let the sleep take her. She swiftly sat up and held Andran up to view. He smiled at her.

"Are we alive?" Something seemed so different about him. His legs kicked out in a wild joy she'd never seen in the child.

"Yes," said a voice from the shadows beside her. Leefa reached for her sword. Gone!

Erdrick moved into the fire's light and crouched beside them. He touched the small mark beside Andran's ear. Leefa smelled blood on the warrior, the sweat and grime of battle, and noted a rent in one sleeve, a bandage there, among many small marks of engagement. His dark hair had tangled and broken free from its tie. A crust of blood had matted in his beard. He smelled alive. "Light has entered the dark wood."

"I failed, Captain," she said. "I slept."

"Yet I followed a trail of bones to you. They are swept into the corners of this very room. How do you think you failed?"

Leefa shrugged. It didn't take much to kill the dead. "What is there for me now?" she asked.

"Life." Erdrick helped her up. As she hung the knapsack and Andran from her shoulders, she smelled infant, felt the bond of living things. The slightest hint of *otherness* remained, a taint she even sensed in Erdrick. They had crossed into the world of the dead. They hadn't retreated unscathed, but perhaps unafraid.

"We must return Andran to his family. And you have a deal of experience to share with the King's Watch." He grinned then, a thing lively and bright in that dark beard. "I'll warrant even I can learn a thing or two from such an old master."

"My sword—" Leefa began.

"It was made of wizard magic, and that wizard's gone."

Leefa stared at the door. Something vibrant lurked beyond the plank and stone of the inn walls.

"Legend names you the autumn spirit," Erdrick said in that soft voice of his. "We speak of a day Leefa Ka blessed for battle when the sun rises on an autumn campaign. The tales say you ever sought the dawn in places none had seen before. Will you now venture into my world and look upon an autumn Leefa blessed?"

"I think I'll race a bit slower this time, old as I am," she said, testing a smile. She yanked open the door. The golden glow of morning struck her, all the shades of darkness driven away, save a slender, white trail of bones, leading back to the Wood from which she had fled.

TWILIGHT AT THE SPEAKEASY

Lisa Silverthorne

Raw fire raked down his leg, the laser blast finding its mark. Lieutenant Conner Davis fought down a scream and dragged himself out of the line of fire that cut down trees and blasted dirt into smoking sludge. Aldebaran, neutral ground, was halfway between home system and Earth's distant colonies. The perfect place for a civil war.

His breaths came in heaving gasps, his platoon massacred around him, obliterated by colony fire. Wang lay beside him, empty black eyes staring up into the green-gray sky. Deluga lay face down in front of him, the red circle of blood spreading across his khaki uniform. The metallic stench was cloying.

Conner squeezed his eyes closed, the pain in his chest sharp, knowing his buddies were already dead. The steady red wink of his rifle told him the charges were nearly exhausted.

No more ammo. And still the colonists kept coming.

He drew in a painful breath, holding it as he dragged himself deepering into brush. Even with his shielder still jamming his position, he knew he probably had minutes to live.

Beyond the brush edging the field was the trail leading to the sprawling Aldebaran town of Altisa. But he'd get no help from the Altisans. Neutral to a point of shunning,

214

they hid themselves and their establishments from violent cultures. Whole towns appeared locked and empty to warring races. And that included all Earthers.

He'd heard about a famous little bar on the main square, a place his people called the Speakeasy because it had been impossible to find. And impossible to enter, shielded from everyone except those the Altisans deemed safe. Maybe if he laid down his weapons and approached the town unarmed, he'd find refuge there? And help?

With the colonists closing in, it was his last hope.

Footsteps skittered past. Conner froze and held his breath, pressing his broken body deeper into the thick gray brush that smelled like mildew against his face. His fingers locked around his assault rifle, the minutes ticking by, his blood staining the ground as voices whispered through the undergrowth.

A branch snapped. Another whisper. Steady sweep of red laser light drawing closer as it panned the brush, tracking movement. He drew in a long slow breath, the fear cold in the pit of his stomach. Or body heat.

His heart was a piston pumping against his rib cage, his mouth dry, the sour smell of sweat in the air, but he held still as the colony force swept past.

Conner's gaze flicked toward the path leading into Altisa. To even reach the town, he'd have to open himself up to attack.

And that included turning off his jammer.

"Where's the homeworlder?" someone demanded.

"Over here," a voice replied, sounding near and Conner held his breath, trying not to give away his location.

"This way! He went this way!"

His jammer/shielder kept the colonists' instruments from detecting him, but even it was badly damaged. He couldn't keep his location shielded much longer. He'd have to make a break for Altisa. Only the Speakeasy could save him now.

Conner slid his pistol out of its holster and laid it in the dirt. His hands shook as he unfastened his ammo belt, laying it in the brush beside his assault rifle. He had nothing left, not even the hatred, as he half-dragged himself to the edge of the trail. It snaked in wide turns, three in all, and disappeared behind a distant copperstone building.

It would be a miracle if he even got to that first bend.

"A bonus to the man who gets the last homeworlder!" one of the colonists shouted from somewhere behind him.

Conner pulled in a breath, balancing himself on his good leg, as he reached down to the little jammer box clipped inside his torn jacket. And turned it off.

Every step was a knife blade in his belly as he staggered forward. He concentrated on the copperstone building ahead, ignoring the curves of the trail.

"There! Up ahead!"

Adrenaline spiked as a laser blast burned the grass in front of him. He staggered left then right, zigzagging his way toward the building. Past the first turn. Two more.

Another bolt tore across his shoulder, and he swallowed the scream, falling into the dirt. He clawed at a spindly stand of trees until he was on his feet again. But the pounding of boots was closer now. In his ears.

He lurched forward, into the second turn, moving into another stand of trees. Another laser blast went wide as he gasped for breath, struggling into the third turn.

A red lasersight fluttered across him, and he threw himself to the ground as the blast exploded above him, burning his face. Momentarily blinded, Conner reached toward a tree trunk to pull himself up, but the rasp of copperstone touched his palm.

He'd reached Altisa.

He rose up on his knees, both hands against the building wall as he struggled to his feet.

Get around the corner, his brain screamed. Into the square!

He was halfway around the building when he felt the burn of a lasersight against his chest. Right over his heart.

"See ya soon, Wang," he whispered through dry lips and closed his eyes, pressing his cheek against the rough stone. He hoped the marksman wouldn't miss and make his last moments worse.

A warm blast of heat rolled over him, and he opened his eyes. Staring at a paper napkin, wet and sticking to the ruddy, burled wood . . . of a bar. The thick slab of varnished wood gleamed in the pale gold flicker of lanterns hanging in clusters overhead. He lifted his head from the bar, surprised not to find a gaping hole in his chest.

"What will you have, Earther?" asked a lithe Altisan woman behind the bar. Her pearlescent skin had a pale blue cast, the thick, braided strands of teal hair in an elaborate sweep off her face. Her eyes were ocean blue, lips a pale blush of mint as she smiled at him, a towel in her hand. Silky fabrics in yellow and frosted teal hugged the gentle curves of her waifish body.

The Speakeasy! He laughed despite the stabs of pain in his shoulder and leg. He'd found the Speakeasy.

"Am I in?" he asked, glancing around at the copper firepit crackling in the corner.

Three Altisans, all males with that same pearlescent skin, huddled by the firepit, sipping pale liquid from tiny cups nestled in their palms. They ignored Conner, not even casting a curious look at him. Like typical Altisans. To them, humans were little more than animals, and they were content to sit back and watch them kill each other from the safe shielding of their cities.

Curved benches wrapped around the firepit, made from this warm, burled wood like the bar. Along all three walls of the cozy little bar were dark wood booths that stretched floor to ceiling, the thick grain shimmery in the firelight. Little places to curl up and escape the world and a decade of civil war.

The bartender nodded, tilting her head down in an almost shy expression. "You are in. What will you have?" she asked again.

They deemed him worthy to at least stand in their presence. He didn't feel honored; he felt disgusted.

The air smelled spicy with cloves and something he

didn't recognize—like a fragrant wood oil that infused the air with calm. He let go of his viselike grip on the bar's edge and sank back in the padded black chair, his body burning with pain. His eyes were closing. He just needed to rest a while and wait out the colony forces.

"Something warm," he replied, feeling a chill wash over him. "Cognac maybe."

"I'll see what I have," said the woman as she turned away, toward the racks of bottles behind her. Rich fabrics in golds, rusts, and reds draped across the ceiling to pool against the hardwood floor on both sides of the bar.

His hand slid into a side pocket on his pants, and he found his blood-spattered wallet. He opened it, removing his deducter card and a few folded credit vouchers. Behind the vouchers, a picture smiled back at him, the video paper looping through the group shot of his twelve-member platoon. That was taken two months before they'd shipped out for Aldebaran.

Wang brushing a hand across his close-cropped black hair as he stood to Conner's left. Deluga on the right, poking Conner in the shoulder before throwing his arm around his and Wang's shoulder. Parker, Kaczinski, Strauss, Richards, Tsing rough-housing behind them—all of them dead now. His eyes stung, and he rubbed them with thumb and forefinger.

The bartender set a square glass bowl in front of him, tinted yellow. Inside, amber liquid steamed, the faint hint of apricots rising as he leaned over it.

"Run a tab?" she asked and he nodded.

Conner picked up the drink in both shaking hands and pressed it to his lips. The warm alcohol trailed down his throat and into his stomach, leaving a wake of calm and numbness as he settled back against the chair. Sip after sip brought him farther from the gnawing pain at his shoulder and leg. And his duty. And he was grateful. He'd wait here until twilight, until the pain was softer and he was stronger.

He wasn't sure how long he'd rested his eyes, but when he opened them, he was in a corner booth, a second glass of the Altisan cognac (or whatever it was) half full beside him. Deluga grinned at him from across the booth.

"Danny?" Conner said with gasp, staring at his dead friend.

"Conner, how you doin'?" Danny asked, popping him on the shoulder, a bottle of beer in one hand. "We got our butts kicked out there, didn't we?"

Wang set his empty whiskey shot on the table beside Conner as he leaned back, crossing his legs.

"How'd it happen?" Wang asked. "Anybody know?"

"It was Parker," said blond-haired Will Strauss from the table beside the booth. He turned toward Conner, his always-serious hazel eyes studying him.

"Parker?" Conner demanded, glancing back at Deluga and Wang who were nodding. He fixed Strauss with his gaze. "What do you mean, Parker?"

Kaczinski walked past the table, a beer in his hand. "Had his jammer turned off. They knew we were there from the start. No wonder it was a bloodbath."

"Damn you, Parker!" Wang shouted at the room then rose from the booth. "I need another shot."

Conner stared at Deluga then Strauss. They were both dead. He'd seen their battered bodies in the aftermath of the colonist's barrage. They'd lain beside him in the brush, burned and bloodied. How were they here in the flesh?

He reached across the booth to touch Deluga's arm—solid—and Danny fixed him with those dark brown eyes, sad now.

"Danny," said Conner, shaking his head. "I saw you die out there."

He nodded. "Helluva end. But you still have a chance. You can still make it out. For the platoon, Conner. You gotta avenge us." He gritted his teeth into almost a growl. "Make them pay."

Make them pay. Conner balled his hands into fists. More than anything, he wanted to make them pay, to avenge his platoon, to win this war, to . . . He slid out of the booth, feeling confused. To what? For ten years, this civil war had raged. Against his own kind. Against people so distant from him and the homeworld they'd come from . . . and a futile attempt to control such far-away shores. Maybe it was time to just let them go? Would that be so horrible?

"Kick their butts, Conner!" Wang shouted, patting him on the shoulder as he walked toward the booth and sat down across from Deluga. Two dead men sharing a drink.

How many times had this cycle played out within these walls? He tasted the bitterness of revenge against his tongue, not even the cognac smoothing it away. Kill and keep killing until both sides lost everything. While the Altisans sat and watched the carnage. No, it wasn't their problem, but with their intellect and advances (and neutrality), maybe they had the power to negotiate an end?

Conner craved the higher ground, but he just couldn't find the path. Either way, he knew that whatever path he took, neither one would change the war's outcome. It only mattered to him now. Unless he could convince the Altisans otherwise.

He glanced out a smoky window near burled double doors that led out into Altisan streets. Where the colonists waited to finish what they'd started. Twilight was already darkening the landscape.

The bartender moved toward him from behind the bar, carrying a paper ticket. The tab. It was time to pay up.

"Your bill," she said and extended the paper toward him.

He reached for the bill, but he stopped when he noticed Eric Parker hunched on a bench beside the firepit. His right leg was gone, his uniform torn and frayed, face bone-white despite the warm lick of flames from the firepit. Across from him sat the three Altisans.

Conner limped back from her, holding up his hands. "Just a moment," he said and struggled against the pain starting a slow burn over the alcohol again as he limped to the firepit.

"Parker?" he said and dropped down with a groan onto the curved bench.

Parker sat with hands folded in his lap, staring into the firelight with an emptiness that made Conner's chest ache. The moody young man had never been well liked in the platoon, but Conner had always tried to look out for him. He laid a hand on the young man's shoulder.

"Lieutenant," he said with a sigh, flicking his gaze at Conner for only a moment.

"Why'd you turn off your jammer?" he asked.

Tears welled in Parker's eyes, and he bit his lip, his body beginning to shake.

"I thought I was helping," he said, a quiver in his voice now as he turned toward Conner. "Thought if we laid down our weapons and tried to end it without exchanging fire . . ."

His voice trailed off as his gaze fell to the one remaining chukka boot on his left foot.

"Was it this place you were trying to find?" Conner asked, motioning around the hushed quiet in the bar. He hadn't noticed how deathly quiet the place was until now.

Parker shook his head. "No, someplace farther away."

"Where?"

"A truce. An end to this stupid war. I've killed three of my own cousins on this planet, Lieutenant. And I don't even know why they had to die. I just thought that if laying down my weapons got past Altisa's shielding, then maybe they would see us as worthy of effort."

Conner sighed as tears funneled down the young man's face. He reached out and slid his arm around Parker's shoulders, patting him on the back. Then he rose from the bench, hobbling toward the bartender, his bill still in her outstretched hand.

He took the paper from her and noticed sadness in her eyes. Like she might offer some dumb animal with its leg caught in a trap.

"How much do I owe you?" he asked.

"Up to you," she said as she stepped back toward the bar.

Up to you. Her words sounded hollow.

"Is it?" he asked, turning toward her. "Is it really up to me?"

She cocked her head to stare at him a moment in that same stoic silence as the others. "The payment?"

"No, the war. Ending the war."

"That is an Earth problem, not ours," she said, picking up a towel and wiping down the bar.

Conner glared at her. "And when someone's drowning, do you turn a blind eye to that, too? When all you'd have to do is reach out and pull them up? Risk that simple gesture to save a life. Thousands."

The three Altisans rose from the bench to stand beside the bar, staring with unblinking gazes at him.

"We're backward and violent by your standards," Conner said, holding out his hands, the bill fluttering. "But we're worth saving." He pointed at Parker who had covered his face with his hands, shoulders shaking. "He laid down his weapons in the futile hope of drawing your attention, knowing he'd die. But you ignored his sacrifice. Like you ignore everything."

"It's not our fight," said one of the Altisan men, a hand against his braided beard. "None of our concern."

Conner bowed his head. "Even if you have the power to stop it? The ability to negotiate a peace that could save thousands? I'm asking for your help."

For only a brief moment the bartender smiled, but the emotion was quickly lost in that Altisan neutrality.

"What will you do now?" the bartender asked, watching him with interest.

"Nothing," said Conner. "I've laid down my weapons. I won't fight anymore. But others will, over and over as you've already seen for a decade."

He turned toward the door and gripped the brass doorknob that turned slowly against his fingers.

And the rough copperstone was scraping his palms again, the raw fire in his leg burning up through his groin and into his shoulder as a colonist in an olive drab uniform crouched in front of him. And the red lasersight was searing against his chest. Above his heart.

Had he ever set foot in Altisa's Speakeasy? Had it ever existed at all?

His mouth was dry and tasted like dust as the colonist

rose to his feet, dark hair plastered against his face, looking like just another guy in Conner's platoon. Conner held up his hands in surrender.

"I won't fight you anymore," he said, staring the dark haired man in the eye.

For a moment, he saw indecision in the man's eyes as he recognized some hint of kindred there. A flash of regret. Never strong enough to last, Conner knew. He'd seen it staring back at him from the mirror too many times, so he understood the reluctance. Conner caught the man's gaze again and held it, trying one last time to get through, to find that path to higher ground.

"Last one," a voice smirked behind him and Conner turned.

The man behind him, blond, reminding him a little of Strauss, lifted the laser rifle, and the sight danced over Conner's heart.

He'd wanted an end to this war, but not by annihilation. He'd wanted a chance to change it, but the man was right. Parker was already dead. And he was the last one.

"Set up a beer for me, Wang," Conner whispered into the twilight.

He winced against the flash of red as the laser sight found its mark. But in that red strobe fading to dark, he caught a glimpse of Altisans in the street.

IN THOUGHT

Peter Orullian

JOHN Smith stared into the dawn from the glassed-in breakfast nook . . . and trembled. In the warm light of the sun through the window, with a hot cup of coffee cradled in his palms, the shivers caught his lips and cascaded down his back. Even in the comfort and soft chatter of his wife and daughter as they took their morning toast (a family favorite), the anticipation of another day *in thought* stole the safety and pleasance of family.

In thought. John smiled wanly over the euphemism. *War, they mean.*

He looked over his left shoulder, down the hall toward what he deliberately called his "war room." Bile rose at the sight of the closed door. He sipped again at his coffee to wash the sour taste from his tongue.

From far away, he heard his little girl, Katy, talking to him, but he could tell nothing of her words (the war room in his head). Then came Cathryn's soothing voice with soft, remonstrating tones for their daughter—ever keeping things on an even keel.

Especially during times of *thought.*

But for the third time, Katy poked John's arm with some craft or assignment she meant him to look at. "See, Daddy. See!"

As flashes of yesterday's hours spent in his war room coursed behind his eyes, the cocoon of anxiety and cold broke, and the warm chatter of morning sizzled hot on his reserve. Without thinking, John seized the item Katy brandished and twisted it in his angry fist. "Not now! I don't have time for this!"

A horrible silence stole over the sunny nook. Something was broken.

Probably me.

With the ache of dismissal hanging still on the air, John stood, his chair's legs loud in the hushed morning sun. His eyes had not left the door down the hall.

Soon, his body followed. Another day *in thought* . . .

He paused at the door, taking a deep, steadying breath. No use. Filling his lungs with air only made the thrum of his heart more noticeable in his chest.

I can't keep doing this.

And with that thought, he pushed the door open and went to war.

The room beyond lay mostly bare. No windows. No art upon the walls. Certainly no entertainment devices of any kind. Few distractions. There was a small table just inside the door with a pitcher of water and a glass.

John gave his wan smile again. The space was remarkable for only two things: deep, plush carpet with the thickest pad underneath that could be bought; and the chair.

Closing the door behind him, John eyed the device. Simple in form, elegant maybe, the chair appeared essentially as a sleek, stylish recliner. Rather, it was the weapon of a new age of warmongers.

I'm the new weapon, the chair just enables me.

He was splitting hairs.

And stalling.

But that was part of the routine. He had need to trace the evolution of it all (every morning) to try to make sense of his place in the machine, the device.

John had chosen the military early, age ten actually. To be more accurate, it had chosen him. Career soldiers for Earth's Confederation were identified young and for one reason: a genetic predisposition for resistance to the side effects of the chair.

Stepping toward the instrument, John's foot sank into the soft carpeting. He circled the simple object as a combatant might his opponent, when in truth they were dangerous only when partnered against the enemy.

He reached out and touched the head rest, another part of his ritual preparation. The padded semicircular extension where John's head would rest appeared little more than a comfortable place to lay back his head. *Ingenious bastards.* The headrest was really an amplifier and conduit.

Science had shown late in the 21st century that space didn't really exist. That what they'd believed to be dark matter was really the connective tissue of the universe. And more importantly, *thought* was the universal mechanism for communication that could move along the pathways of *all* matter. But like the radio or any other communication vehicle, it needed a transmitter.

The chair.

John climbed in, not yet reclining, not yet ready to fight.

Initially intended as a communication device, the technology that allowed thought projection was coopted by the military. Good thing, too. In those first years of off-world exploration, Earth's Confederation woke a slumbering neighbor that brought the first intergalactic conflict in Earth history.

Conventional weapons were useless.

Intrusion into the mind, the wounds of memory, were not.

And once that enemy lay in mental ruin, expansion had begun.

But by then, John had sewn his career too deeply . . . no other useful skills. A family to support.

He rested his head, and the almost imperceptible hum of the chair began. With his eyes still open, John watched as orders flared across his vision. There was little need to read them; the commands entered his consciousness regardless.

He felt himself offer another wan smile toward the ceiling.

The new military. No uniforms. No salutes. Even orders were offered in conversational language. All to cloak the stultifying effects of their business, their trade, their assault upon the minds of an enemy so far away that starships wouldn't reach the defeated world for thirty years.

Clean. Efficient. *Thought*.

And so he went.

A black vortex opened up in his mind's eye, swirling, crackling with energy. John gave himself to it and hardened his mind. The blackness rushed past him at dizzying speeds. He passed waves of light as he rushed headlong mentally toward a battlefield that existed only in the subconscious of his foe.

The travel across space and time always left him exhilarated, despite his purpose. He reveled in it briefly, being one of those who could use the chair without losing themselves (losing their minds) completely in its use.

That was his genetic fortune.

For him, the effect of thought transfer was to cleanse the mind, filter out the noise and superfluous information. It was like a cleansing diet that left his psyche trim and fit and more vigorous. Where for others, it was cerebral death. And he couldn't deny that it filled him with a sense of power—moving at will across a wide expanse, outstretching colonization.

He felt a touch of immortality in those moments, omnipotence, omnipresence.

And often he saw in the memories of his enemies a beautiful world he would have liked to have known better.

But only as a traveler, not a warrior.

And that's how it always ended—in some construct of mind where he sought to tear down a stranger from the inside.

Like now.

The black vortex fell back as John cascaded down toward a remote planet called Gellania. That was the name the Confederation had given it. Human language couldn't simulate the indigent name.

Like a rush of dark wind, John swept through clouds, seeking the surface. His orders took him automatically to the place and person. Terrain blurred past like trees through wet, steamy glass.

Then came the shrieking.

The pitch rose as he narrowed in, drawn to a set of memories and a persona. The sound of entry into the enemy's mind changed with each new race they fought. Today, and for weeks now on this world, the entry came with a fading whistle, like a train disappearing up a stretch of tracks.

John caught a glimpse of the individual's face as he entered *in thought*—a handsome, proud face.

Then, inside that mind, millions of miles from his chair, John felt new panic. Something was different this time: awareness, preparation.

As he occupied the space of memory and cognition, John suddenly found himself standing on a broad, darkened plain. Overhead, heavy clouds moved fast, threatening storm. Shale covered the land beneath.

And standing opposite him, twenty yards distant, was a figure whose loose clothes furled in the wind sweeping across them both.

It reminded him of any number of baneful scenes told by fantasists in the books he liked to read for escape when he wasn't *in thought*.

Oh my God. He knows—

Before John could finish his thought, he felt the probing of his own subconscious begin. It came like the pressure of being deep underwater, completely enveloping him, finding his soft spots, compressing his ability to breathe (think).

He stared across the barren plain at the figure watching him and pushed back. With a brightness of hope sprung from his own memories—holding Katy as a newborn, passionate love with Cathryn—he erected a bulwark to stave off discovery of memory wounds his enemy might exploit.

Even as he did so, he shot a communication back to the Leadership about what he'd encountered. If this world was as well informed as it now seemed, their objectives would be difficult to acheive.

Worse. If they had counterintelligence . . .

Light years away, John felt his face smile at the term— *counterintelligence*—nothing could have been more apt given the circumstances.

With his slight distraction came another surge from the mind who'd created this scene to define their battle. He knew John all right. But now it was time for John to do what he'd been trained for.

Like the taking of a great inward breath, John set himself mentally and focused on the individual *consciousness*—not simply the ominous figure standing in a field of badlands. He reached out, seeking the blind spots in an infinite matrix so expansive that it often folded on itself to make connections. It was the world of a life's experience held private in the mind of its owner.

And the universal truth the new military banked on with each new conflict and race was the sublimation of personal tragedy.

A soldier's task was to root out those moments and expose them in awful cruelty.

If enough of these were brought to light, the individual consciousness could not suffer it . . . and would die.

Or be rendered inoperable.

Either way set the stage for adoption into the Confederation, or perhaps colonization. It all depended on the world and its population. Really, it amounted to the old adage: The best defense is a good offense.

Earth would not be conquered, so they chose to conquer.

John was at the front of that.

And at its core were moments like this, when he sought the hidden griefs of another in the hope that enough of them would collapse the matrix.

Probing, John identified one of those blind spots, a patch of experience somehow muted in the collection of conscious moments. Immediately, he channeled himself into it, drawing out the scene from behind repression.

A great shock of darkness erupted, followed by a wail of regret that filled John's mind.

And the memory began.

Jental strode quickly toward the hospital. Under a pair of bright suns, one more red than white, he noted thick foliage encircling the place in sprays of yellow and orange and green. About him, others moved more slowly, recuperating, lost in worry, enjoying the warmth on the courtyard. Jental hurried past them all toward a set of doors.

John felt the reluctance to follow this memory but easily forced its continuation.

Inside, Jental bore right, passing the areas for disease and convalescence. Today his visit held a happier aim: the maternity center.

A comfortable feeling settled over him as he rushed through soft lighting and familial décor. *Welcoming.* This place gave the sense of deep familiarity and casualness, as though birth were such a part of life that it might happen anyplace.

A powerful tug threatened to distort or change the scene. A mind willing the memory down.

John tightened his grip.

Jental didn't stop when he asked directions to his wife's room, giving Honna's name as he but slowed his step toward the delivery rooms. After a mild remonstration to be careful not to rush, a young birth assistant offered Honna's room number and pointed. Jental turned and ran, his heart pounding not from exertion but sheer excitement.

A host of images coursed though his mind—all the things he meant to do with his child, the things he wanted to share, to teach. The sight of new parents here and there gently stroking the small features of their babies got inside him.

It had finally happened for them.

He could think of nothing else but holding his child, perhaps offering the soft songs of his ancestors to the infant, telling her the stories he'd grown fond of in his own youth.

And Jental wished to kiss his wife. Thank her. Share the knowing smiles that would fill the room after the long wait.

At the door, John felt hatred and sadness scream for him to release this memory.

Jental pushed open the door and stopped. The anticipation compressed suddenly into a painful look. On the bed lay Honna cradling a bundle with small, delicate hands. She sobbed low, shaking her head in denial.

He went in, noting a hard fall of light in perfect squares on the floor underfoot from windows opposite him. On the other side of the bed stood a biology attendant gently reassuring Honna as he measured her wellness with a small handheld device.

"What's the matter?"

When his love looked up, her face showed utter despair.

Jental stopped short. Could he know this? Bear it? Was the child ill? Was Honna?

His body tightened, but he finally forced himself to her side and sat on the edge of the bed. He could not help the leap in his heart as he looked down at his . . . daughter. "I'm a daddy," he said.

Looking back at the face of the child, Honna whispered, "No."

"But . . ." And it hit him. Slowly Jental inclined, the sorrow descending upon him as each moment passed and his little girl had not yet taken a breath.

Her small, perfect features sat still, tranquil. But forever quieted. When he touched her soft cheek, he thought he might die. The great hope and love in his chest battled with the swell of mourning and regret.

And hatred. John felt fury from his enemy for the vivid remembrance of this moment.

"She lived only a few hours." Honna's words trembled from her lips. "If you could only have been here to see her, Jental. She was so sweet. Is so sweet . . ."

The violence of his grief sought release, but he did not want to remove his fingers from the fresh, clean skin of his little girl. Some moments later, he crawled onto Honna's bed and gently took the child into his arms. They would come soon to remove the dead, any moment perhaps, and he wanted to know the feel of cradling her against his chest.

The hardest thing he ever did in his life was release his little girl when an attendant reached to take her from his arms.

The memory snapped back, complete.

For an instant, he stood again on the endless, blackened plain where forever winds coursed around the figure wearing loose, tattered garments. The clouds had bruised further. The shale tinkled occasionally as light pieces were being lifted by gusts.

And the figure—Jental now stood closer to John.

Then blackness took all. Streaks of light. A vortex of sound and emotion and clouds.

And John fell from the chair to the soft carpeting in his war room.

He lay there, breathing hard, his skin slicked with sweat. He felt shame, as he always did, for shining a light on the dark places of another's heart. He pounded a fist into the plush padding. "Damn!"

The worst part for him was that calling these things to mind meant he had to experience them himself. Sharing the cognitive space of another man's psyche literally meant *being* that person when the memories came back.

No, the worst part is retrieving these memories at all. No one should have to relive them.

When his breathing had normalized, he pushed himself to his knees beside the chair. He didn't yet trust his legs, so he crawled to the table beside the door and carefully poured himself a drink of water. He slopped most of it onto himself trying to take it in, but that wasn't so bad either.

Then he collapsed against the rear wall of his war room and tried to forget what he'd seen. All of it.

When he felt he'd come fully back to his own mind and life, he struggled to his feet and went out, shutting and locking the door.

The Chief Director of Military Leadership welcomed John with a firm handshake. "Have a seat, John. May I call you John?"

"Of course, sir." John pumped the man's hand once.

"No *sirs* here. Just Sherman." He motioned for John to sit. "What we do is a long way from boot camp and regimentation."

"I guess."

The Director then pulled up a second chair, and they both sat.

This "war room" stood in sharp contrast to John's. The walls had been pained a subtle shade of brown, beige maybe. Narrow lamps on finely carved bases glowed in the corners. Reproductions of master paintings hung museum style on every wall—Bosche, Dali, Klimt, Rubens. Bookshelves teemed with books that appeared to have actually been read. And dark wood furniture, elegant but not ornate, set an informal, studious air to the place.

This was a room mean for *thought* John imagined. Each man had his own way.

After a long, thoughtful pause, the Director began in a soothing tone. "We got your communication, John. To say the least, we're concerned. What else can you tell us?"

John related the scene with his enemy on the endless darkened plain. "I usually drop directly into their minds. We don't go to a place like that. We don't go *anywhere*. We fall to consciousness and feel for the *undisclosed*. When I saw the figure with ragged clothes fluttering in the wind, I knew he knew me."

"Knew you?" The Director focused his stare on John.

"I was taken into the military because of my aptitude to resist the chair, but the side effects . . . I read to escape."

The Director nodded. "And you read about the kind of place and person you saw *in thought* today."

"It's escapism. Stories with relatively clear lines of right and wrong."

"And material weapons," the Director finished in a knowing tone.

John said nothing.

"An age ago, they said the second fatality of war was fidelity. Today it may well be sanity." He offered John a shallow, reassuring smile. "What I mean is, I understand an escape where there is less moral ambiguity and the weapons are something you have to aim."

Having heard little, John nevertheless nodded and cut to the point. "If he knew me well enough to construct that scenario, then he has an advantage I can't risk."

"You think he's got advanced intel on who you are, is that it?" The Director sat back, steepling his fingers beneath his chin.

"Yes. And I may not be so fortunate next time I go *in thought* to him."

The man named Sherman stared for several moments. "How old is your daughter, John?"

"She's eight, why?"

"It's natural for a soldier to have doubts when he's a family man. To be honest, I'd be scared if you didn't—"

"It's not just about this one man," John interrupted.

They sat a few moments before the Director answered. "We know, John. The nature of today's mode of engagement itself allows us to monitor our men and women and how they're holding up."

"Then you know I can't keep doing this."

The look of concern and ready explanation rose on the man's cheeks and brow. "You can, John. And you must. I understand it's difficult. But the truth is, that your empathy and reluctance are precisely why you're so insightful when you go *in thought*."

John opened his mouth to refute.

The Director held up a hand. "I know. Dark irony. Unfair. Exploitive. And a thousand more colorful ways to describe it. But it is war, after all, John. Cleaner in some ways. But more painful in many others.

"You can question our moral authority and expansion-

istic plans, but I'll tell you what I've seen, hand to God."
The Director lifted his right arm, palm up, in imitation
of the old sign—a token of honesty before the All
Mighty. "Since finding the ability to reach beyond our
own cluster of planets, the races we've encountered in
deep reconnaissance make me fear for our future, the
future of our *eight-year-olds*, and that's no lie. We've
woken the sleeping dragon with our galactic mobility. All
we're trying to do now is secure our future before it's
taken from us."

John laughed. "I'd expect you to say the same thing
even if our moral ground were unstable."

"I know. And our people at the front are right to
question. But . . ."

"You're sending me back."

"First thing tomorrow. Same mind."

"And if he gets the better of me?"

Ignoring the question, the Director went on, "For the
very reason you came here, it's imperative you confront
him. We think he's an isolated empath, in which case we
need to eliminate him as soon as possible. If he's not the
only one, then we need to escalate our offensive, remove
the broader threat. And you, John, are one of our best."

"Then you'll personally explain it to my eight-year-old
if her dad dies in the chair."

It was Sherman's turn to say nothing.

John got up and crossed to the door without so much
as a wave goodbye, let alone a salute. Reaching for the
door handle, he paused, caught by something the Director had said: *We think he's an isolated empath.*

John turned.

"You *knew* Jental possessed foreknowledge about
me." And saying it out loud brought a cascading recollec-
tion of other assignments, in the minds of other combatants worlds over, where the contest of *thought* with
another proved damaging for John.

*So that I sit in the sun with hot coffee in my hands
and shiver.*

"Come sit down, John. There's much we should discuss." The Director's face showed equal parts reassur-

ance and (something new) authority—flexing his military muscle.

Not that he'd have accepted Sherman's invitation anyway, but John felt suddenly powerless with the revelation: In stage after stage of conflict and expansion, he was being targeted at those whose natural gift wasn't simply resistance to a device (like John's immunity to the chair) but rather the ability to connect with the *one great matrix*.

John thought he might be sick.

The unifying theory of dark matter had given rise to a new age of thought on the topics of both the paranormal and the divine. For instance, the understanding of dark matter proved the interconnectedness of all things— one great matrix; it made possible thought transfer for war (among other things). Imagine, then, a being with the capacity to tap that matrix: omniscience, omnipresence . . . God.

Not unlike the reconnaissance the new military did to draft assignments for John and all the others *in thought*, except on a different scale and with different intentions than a creator.

An alternate theory held that the aggregate thought of intuitives shared across the great matrix *was* God. Whatever the case, John began to sense a dark purpose in the plans of the new military.

They were waging war on heaven.

One mind at a time.

The Director shattered the silence. "Remember, John, that your family is a courtesy we allow. Your career takes its toll on you, but it also makes your family possible in the first place. Don't jeopardize it. Do your job." He gave a smile to relax the tension. "Come. Sit down. Let's clear the air a bit."

John gave Sherman a last look and pulled the door closed on his way out.

Without the lights, his clothes still on, John crept into bed.

He lay down beside Cathryn, the gentle musk of body-warmed sheets a familiar, welcome smell. In the dark, his breathing slowed, but sleep wouldn't come.

And listening to the shallow rhythm of his wife's respiration, he knew neither was she asleep.

"You okay?" she asked. Her voice carried low in the dark.

"No. How about you?"

"I'll be fine. It's your daughter you should think about, John. You're so distant lately. Even when you're in the room, you're not with us. Some ways, that's worse." Cathryn rolled over to face him, though they couldn't really see each other—she liked it pitch black to sleep.

"These *thoughts* lately. They're . . . I don't know. Heavy. It's always been hard. But now . . ."

"What can I do?" Her hand stole out to find his.

John made no reply. Had none.

But in the next moments they touched, caressed, kissed. And found each other's love again in a sweet, slow union where neither of them could see but knew each other more completely for that.

Later, when the silence of the night came loudest, Cathryn's breathing fell to long, restful pulls, and John got up, still unable to sleep.

He wandered the house, stood in front of windows looking out on vistas he only imagined beneath the dark of night. Distant lights flickered miles out over the bluff and lake—someone moving to some intention in the wee hours.

Like John.

Who ambled, but knew he meant to go back *in thought* while his heart felt calm.

He passed Katy's door on his way and paused, thinking he might check in on her the way he had when her bed had been a crib. Worried he might wake her, he chose not to go in. He might not be at the top of her invitation list, in any case.

At his war room, John went in without hesitation, leaving the lights off. Not seeing the chair helped him ease toward *thought*. From great familiarity, he poured a glass of room-temperature water and drank deeply. Then he walked a circle in the windowless room, sensing the presence of the chair, more aware now that it not only pushed his mind out to battle but also carried information back to the Leadership.

Nothing for that now.

He put out a hand in the dark, touched the headrest, took hold, drew himself in.

Sat down.

Lay back.

Humming. Louder in the small hours of night.

And the black vortex opened, less noticeable.

And the rushing began. Streaks of dark and bright. Exhileration.

Clouds. Shrieking.

And a fading whistle, like a train moving on to some distant, unknown stop. Perhaps an endless, darkened plain . . . where John again stood, looking at the figure whose tattered garments fluttered in a desolate wind charged with the immanence of storm. John thought of his fantasy books, of moral certainty, of wood and steel used to make war.

Then he pushed his consciousness forward. Because he knew the Director's threat to his family was real. Because he needed to know what it meant for this *intuitive* to have foreknowledge of John's appearance.

As he occupied the figure's same space of mind, the question came: *Do you know where this leads?*

At first, John imagined he hadn't heard the query at all.

Then it came again.

John did not attempt a reply.

A powerful mental shove from his enemy rocked John's soundness, instilling a flood of doubt and fear behind which a wall of his own hidden memories waited to break free. With the simple thought of his and Cathryn's tenderness in the night, he framed a defense. *God, what would I do without her love for me? Or mine for her?*

Before another question could weaken his resolve, John laid hold of the matrix. This time, Jental's mind came more readily, and he scoured quickly to a memory buried deeper than the first. Collapsing the fold of two disparate points of time, John opened another window onto Jental's past.

A flash of darkness.

Jental cursed mildly. He was late.

His son Malus' theater performance—if it was on time—had already started. And Jental hadn't even had time to go home and change into proper attire.

But he wasn't missing this for anything. It was part of the reason he worked a second shift in maintenance. And Honna would be saving him a seat.

He pushed his rover madly through the thick evening congestion and came quickly to his son's school. White chiseled marble rose skyward in straight lines, spires crowning several points across the face; each glowed in a cone of light shining up from the school rooftop, giving the place a majestic appearance.

Theater night.

Ducking inside the auditorium, Jental met the expectant quiet of the crowd, which focused on the stage, where a single voice spoke with gentle authority into the hush.

It was Malus.

Pride rushed up through Jental's body, that warmth and sweet adoration only a father feels for a son he hopes will know fewer pains and greater joy. He then scanned the rows for Honna, finding her near the front on the left. It was only then, standing still in the rear of the hall, that Jental realized he carried the scent of his day's labor.

Others would have to pardon him this one time.

John felt a pull—Jental trying to shut down the memory. But he handled it, kept the wound in place.

That's when John wondered: Am I controlling this too easily, especially if he's an empath?

Bent over, Jental crept down the far left aisle to the third row, then excused himself as he cut across to the empty seat beside his mate. She patted his leg and pointed to Malus, as if Jental hadn't already noticed their son on stage.

Jental nodded and folded his fingers in her hand. He heard her sniff once. "I know," he whispered. "Still in my one-suit. I had to get leniency to get here this fast."

She smiled without looking over, and they settled in to watch the performance.

Each line, each movement, felt like success to Jental— Malus' and his own.

And the night swept by sweetly.

When it ended, the crowd stood and bowed their heads in deference and congratulation. It was a unanimous and compelling ovation that brought emotion thick into Jental's face and shoulders. He grinned pleasantly through it all, wanting now nothing more than to find his boy and take him in his arms.

Not long after, the crowd began to dissipate and Jental gave Honna a squeeze before shooting to the side door of the auditorium. He burst into the hall and wove through those filing out into the mild evening air. Not far ahead he turned right into the anterooms, where performers prepared and retreated.

The area teemed with parents and children congratulating one another, laughing, comparing notes, and making late evening plans.

And there was Malus, among them all, taking his adulation in stride and thanking each kind word.

The crowd prevented Jental from getting closer. "Malus. Son. Son!"

Some few looked up at Jental, who tried to pry his way forward to his boy.

He called again, "Malus. Malus!" His voice resounded over the masses, perhaps the one physical gift he'd bestowed on his child. And Malus' eyes darted his direction . . . then quickly away. Perhaps Malus hadn't really seen him.

A painful wave hit John's psyche—something he could only describe as profound regret. It pressed heavily upon him as if to say: 'You may know this, but it comes with a price.'

As if Jental weren't going to resist the exposure of this dark, hidden secret, after all.

"Malus!" Jental shouted. "I'm here! I made it!"

At that, a fellow dressed in resplendent robes turned. "Who, Malus, is this—in the uniform of maintenance, no less—that is making such a nuisance of himself to get your attention?"

A few near Jental backed away, eyeing him up and down critically, one woman covering her nose.

Finally, Malus' attention could not be easily diverted, and the rear staging area grew quiet as the night's lead character was given a second stage and audience.

Jental became acutely aware how out of place he looked in the cramped quarters where parents wore the clothing of tier-one accreditation. He was out of his class, here at all simply because he'd been willing to go over-time to make the costs for Malus to attend. His one-suit seemed to reek in his own nose as he looked to his son for acknowledgment.

Malus stared back, unspeaking, his eyes uncertain.

And Jental's heart broke.

The child who had come and lived after his daughter had died in her mother's arms. The child whom he'd cradled and hefted and tickled. Who'd laughed in his ears and cuddled close when frightened. Who had once stood on his feet when he wanted some bit of advice, and they'd walk and talk and end up on the long grasses beyond their home to stare nightward and talk about things.

His son, with his silence, denied knowing him.

The embarrassment Jental must have been on the verge of causing his boy . . . He, a menial worker in the ranks of the martial forces, come to this eminent affair in his one-suit and claiming the time of the evening's celebrity.

Jental looked down at the hands he used to make Malus' schooling possible and saw his fingers rimmed with soot and soil.

When he looked back at his son, it was through eyes glazed with tears that he managed to say: "Sorry to have bothered you. I don't really know the boy. I'm just looking for the maintenance office."

As laughter erupted around them at the fool interrupting their celebration to find a mop, Jental showed his son a sad smile. He'd saved his boy from the embarrassment of his father. And in doing so, he'd lost some part of their relationship that he would never reclaim.

He nodded once and shuffled back through the crowd toward he knew not what.

Darkness flared again, dropping John back on the plain of shale, where now the figure stood just inches away.

Again the question came in his mind: *Do you know where this leads?*

In the shadows, he could not see the face in the cowl until he reached and pushed the hood back.

It was not Jental's face he saw, but his father's.

The shrieking of minds converging.

A whistle.

And two points of time previously collapsed together unfolding to show a memory wound John had not imagined . . . his own.

The knock on the door filled John with dread. His father strode past him where he sat in the bay window, his bag at his feet. He thought he could still smell cake on the air from the celebration of his tenth birthday the day before.

As the front door opened, bright light spilled in around the tall, lean figure of a man dressed not in a uniform but in shorts and a shirt with no collar. This was the military recruiter?

Panic set in, and John desperately looked about the room. He wasn't searching for an escape route. He was gathering memories, recalling the instances of his life that had taken place in this very spot—rainy days caught inside, standing on the bay window seat and reciting pirate poetry by Robert Burns and Robert Louis Stevenson, holding his big sister when she was sad about having to go away to school two years before.

Like John now.

Except *he* had somehow qualified for military training. Still, being identified didn't mean he *had* to go.

I can't do this again! Stop! Please. I don't want to remember . . .

But Jental, or whoever it was, wasn't listening. Turnabout, it seemed, was fair play.

He turned to make his last plea to his dad—he'd worked it all out ahead of time—when Mom came to the entryway from the kitchen. His little sister, Anoria, stood clutching Mom's leg.

"Dad?"

His father rounded and brought up his hands on his hips the way he always did. "Yes, John?"

"I know you think this is the best thing for me. But please let me stay. I promise to keep my room clean and help out around the yard. You don't have to worry about school either, because I'll study all the time."

"John, we've already—"

"No, Dad, I mean it." He stopped, choking back the emotion. He needed to show his dad he could be grown up. "You can ask Mom, I told her, too. No more fighting with Anoria. No more sneaking downstairs at night for extra cake."

His father's eyebrows went up. And he looked over to Mom.

John looked at the man in the door, who seemed to be measuring his father's reaction to all this.

Then his dad brought his heavy glare back to rest on John. "It's not about your behavior, John. You're a good boy. But this is an honor, son. Do you know how many even get this chance?"

John said nothing.

"Less than one thousandth of one percent. You've got an opportunity here, John. I can't let you waste it. You'll thank me one day, even if it's hard for you to understand now." He held out a hand for John to come forward and get going.

And John began to weep. Not cry. He kept it quiet so that it would be dignified if nothing else (just the way dad had taught him). But there was no help for it. The decision had been made. No appeal would help. So he wept.

On the endless plain of shale, John pleaded: I'm sorry! Stop it! Please! Don't make me relive this! I can't!

But the face of his father remained implacable in the watery light.

John picked up his bag and stepped slowly to his father's feet. Mom came up beside them and hunkered down. She kissed his cheek and hugged him tight. Anoria did the same. John felt Mom's own tears when they embraced. Anoria sniffled the whole time.

His dad stood tall, sharing a look with the man in the doorway. John looked up. "Dad?"

"Yes, John."

"Please . . . let me stay." He had to ask one last time. He said it with all the hope left in him. "I love you. I don't want to go." The tears ran freely to his chin and dropped.

His father simply patted his shoulder. "We better get that bag into the truck, huh?" And he walked out with the military recruiter, leaving John to follow behind.

Leaving the only home he would ever really know, until he had a family of his own . . .

The darkness descended again, brilliant, complete. All John felt was the rushing of wind. All he heard was the tinkling of shale and the whip of loose, tattered fabric—the shadowed, ominous figure (his father) stood a breath away, but the clouds had finally occluded all light from the sky on this astral plain.

Out of the darkness—maybe in his mind, perhaps from the mouth of the figure resembling his father—came the simple phrase: *It is thought that no man may know the mind of God . . .*

The wind stopped.

The silence suddenly as ominous as the dark.

And connections formed in John's mind: To lose a

child; to be denied, considered a shame; and, from John's own life, to have a plea go unanswered. These were wounds of memory; these were tales of holy writ since time immemorial.

My God . . . is this what it feels like to be in the mind of . . . Have I found the ultimate target in the plans of the new military . . .

Was Jental . . .

But all that crumbled suddenly beneath the onslaught of the memory returned to him of the day his father pushed him away for good and sent him far from home.

All the way to the minds of beings a universe away, where he surfaced their own private hells to torment and destroy them.

John began to tremble in the isolation of the far away plain and consciousness and turned the pain of it all to a great, loud yawp that broke the darkness and sent him spiraling back through the vortex to his chair.

He tumbled to the carpet, burying his face in the softness, the roar from his own lips muffled in the deep fibers.

He lay a long time before his strength returned enough to kneel. The fever in his body continued to burn, his hair and shirt drenched. But the heat cleansed him. And when he crawled to the door and pulled it back, he delighted in the draft of cool air that hit his chest, chilling his nipples. Delighted more in the small craft tucked just under the door and now visible in the light of dusk—he must have been *in thought* all day.

He cupped and raised it up with tremulous fingers: a snowflake cut from white paper.

Katy's craft.

John smiled. Stood. And found his daughter's door—late a second night in a row. But this time, the hour wouldn't deter him from going in.

He sat at her bedside and gently stroked her hair until she woke. "Hi, sweetie."

"Hi, Daddy."

He held up her snowflake. "Thank you. It's the best present I ever got."

She smiled, proud.

"And I'm sorry I've been grumpy lately. But that's over." Because he knew now where it all led—the memory wounds, the stranger on the darkened plain—back home, to his family, to his daughter, where he needed to be *present*.

"Good, I'm glad. Let's get mom and go make some toast."

Nothing in the world sounded better.

BREATHING STONES

M.M. Hall

T HE rocks still stand.
Underneath the tallest one is buried the only one
who died at the last battle, my father, Big Hands.

Today on the Full Moon Day of Rebirth we honor the
memory of the victory. All of the village children who
have not yet come of age are led to the site where We
kept the Others from destroying our lives. It is a sacred
site and during the Ritual's reenactment, especially
thrilling.

The story of what happened there is a lesson in courage that must never be forgotten. How brave our defenders were!

I am Big Hands' daughter, Clear Eyes, and I tell this
story so that others will share in our joy of remembering.
It is for all people, all lands to know that fear can be
vanquished when a unified power is unleashed and the
ritual of the standing stones begins.

My father was seventeen. I was a baby nursing at the
breast of my young mother, Crow Flying.

We live in a valley next to Open Lake that many of
my people call Two Forks, and the Others covet it. They
do not look like us. They run on all fours, like beasts,
but their shiny, noisy devil companions are even more
confusing. These things act like they are alive, but our
wise man told us that they are dark magic creations that

do not serve Spirit, just the Others' lust for Power. I also think they liked to eat our flesh. But I am not certain. All I know is that since Time began, they have been our enemy.

Nothing they say makes sense—they make no effort to learn our language. All they do is take and destroy. The first time they came, according to legend, half of our tribe was murdered. The second time, more than half. But a bad sickness made their assaults on our Valley end many moons ago, and they went away, tricking us to believe they had decided to leave us in peace. And it is true, for a long time, the Others left us alone. We became careless, trusting in good fortune. We thought we had won. Then they came back. And they can come back again, and if we are not prepared, we will die.

I am now the Wise Woman, and it is time to share the lesson Breathing Stone taught my father and the children of our tribe before me. How to defend, protect, and to defy infidels who would take what is not theirs to take.

My mother told me the day of the Thrilling Last Battle and Victorious Ritual of Rebirth dawned sunny and warm. The leaves had begun changing, but sunny yellow flowers still bloomed in lush Near Meadow. Even in Far Meadow, where our horses grazed, the tall grass still sighed with the green of full summer.

The sound of the Others came first. A screeching thunder. The grumble of their foreign tongue, the scrunching voices of their demon servants horrified all in their path.

"They are come!"

The boy who spied them from the Woods by Near Meadow breathlessly pounded on the Warning drum. My father quickly made him stop.

Everyone came out of their huts, abandoned their work, and gathered in the Place of Instruction. Breathing Stone, our teacher, our Guide, motioned for silence. He was the only one who did not seem surprised.

"What does it mean?" A girl with wide eyes whimpered. A few children had already begun weeping. An old grandmother tore at her silver hair and sighed.

My mother held me tightly she said, whispering to me

that I was strong and protected. She said I did not cry. Her heart, however, shivered inside her breast like a dove in a cold rain. She knew then her heart might never be free again because my father's face had already begun turning chalk white with fear. And fear is always our worst enemy.

"The Others want our village. The Others want our home."

"But they are not our people," a boy said, eyes flashing.

"They are not people. They are Others."

"They come from the sky." A girl pointed to a hawk chasing a crow.

"They come from the devil," another said, crying.

"They come." Breathing Stone nodded.

The monsters' approach could be felt under the ground, closer, closer, closer.

"Who can help us?"

"Who will save us?" My mother sighed.

"We have to save ourselves."

The children turned in unison to face Breathing Stone, who held one hand up. "It is time," he said.

My father looked scared, my mother said, "Are you sure this is wise? They are so young. They should not be forced to do magic."

"There is no other way, and no one can be forced to do magic."

My mother said she went back to her hut. She said clouds and high North winds made her tremble, but the tears came from the fear of losing her husband. She started to hide me under a bearskin although she knew I was not old enough to join the children in the Ritual. For awhile she just sat there, and then she got up, grabbed me, and ran to the Near Meadow. She loved Big Hands too much to let go. Not yet.

The Others always like to do battle in Near Meadow. Mother said everyone except for a few followed our defenders to where the last battle would banish all fear and save our people.

The children, led by Breathing Stone and Big Hands,

lined up like a strong fence, waiting for the Others to come. They sat down quietly, but a few of the older children frowned. "I don't want to play this game," one child said, pulling the petals off a sunflower.

"We must. And it is not a game," Breathing Stone said.

My mother gathered with the rest of the village behind the children.

Breathing Stone walked down the line of brave children, chanting the Ritual Song:

"No fear is greater than the fear of hope.
No hope is smaller than the pain of hate
No hate is larger than the love of anger
No anger is sharper than the love of peace.
No peace is kinder than the grace of Spirit
No Spirit is greater than Life
I persist; I prevail; I am You.
We live.
We die.
We live.
We die.
Community:
We live.
Is, was, and will be.
Forever is eternity."

Breathing stone nodded, and the children linked arms, making a living fence across Near Meadow, facing the direction of the Other's Army.

When their warriors came, their Beast leader stepped forward and made a rude gesture, indicating that their weapons be pointed at the living barricade. The children stood tall and became stone. My father yelled as the firing began and started to turn to run back to my mother and fell, struck down by the Other's fire.

The largest rock, Breathing Stone, grew taller, and the children became wider. The attackers fell away, trembling, their companion whirling about aimlessly, unable to function. Slowly, slowly, the Others moved away from Near Meadow. The villagers gathered behind the rocks, crying and touching the smooth hard surfaces of their defenders.

The tallest rock standing, Breathing Stone, did not move.

"Are they dead? Did they die defending us?" One elder asked.

"No," a deep voice said from within the tallest stone.

The stones rippled. The stones laughed, shifted, sighed. The children erupted like ghosts from the rocks, and Breathing Stone appeared last, stretching his arms like an eagle's. The children were alive! Everyone cheered except my mother, who held my father as his life left his bleeding body, her tears like rain on dry ground that had come too late to revive dead grass.

"Return to me," she cried.

"I will," he said. "You can not kill stone."

Breathing Stone knelt beside my father after taking me into his arms. He touched my forehead and put a tiny pebble into my fist.

"I charge you, Clear Eyes, daughter of Big Hands, to stare down fear with the strength of your father. Stone breathes."

And that is the lesson I share with you today as we walk among the stones of Rebirth in Near Meadow and wait for my father's return.

You can't kill stone, and the battle will never end until fear does. Now gather around and hold hands and repeat after me:

"You cannot kill stone." Take a deep breath and feel our bodies changing.

Now repeat after me: "Rebirth."

Can you feel the power of stone?

After the Ritual and our bodies leave the stones, I still cannot find him.

That is the other lesson I share with you today. To be brave when faced with the unknown.

EYE OF THE FALCON

Janet Berliner

(Inspired by and including excerpts from *The Horde*, an unpublished novel by my friend, the late, great Jack Kirby)

Mrs. Roseann Jackman picked up the TV Guide and fanned her face. Lord, it was hot in Harlem. Why was it always so godamned hot in godamned Harlem?

She walked over to the window, opened it wide, and stared at the children playing on the street below. Unmindful of the heat, or of the crisis that threatened their world, they leaped about in the broken glass and splintered wood of the spaces left by wrecking crews.

One boy, standing off to one side, away from the others, drew her attention. He was always there, always alone, like her Hardy, who was not quite a loner but not a joiner either until he enlisted. She wiped the sweat off her face. Wherever her son was now, she hoped it was cool. And green.

She flipped on the television, as much to distract herself from thoughts of her MIA offspring as to hear the latest hype about the Horde. It was all a hoax, of course. Pure crap, designed to sell newspapers, to get people panicked enough to rush out for gas masks and extra food supplies. As if an army could—or would, even if it could—mole its way under the world in some under-

252

ground tunnel that stretched from Outer Mongolia . . . Mongolia, f'Chrissake . . . to Paris. Except that she had researched "Paris tunnel" and "Rome tunnel" on the computer Hardy had acquired for her before he was given his marching orders. Tunnels were nothing new. Rome was riddled with catacombs. Three tunnels, each close to 1000 meters long, had been excavated in Napoli. Two of them could still be used. She remembered, too, having read about a terrorist plot, way back when, to set off explosives in the PATH railway tunnels beneath the Hudson.

It was all nuts, especially since the kinds of tunnels they were talking about now—all those miles of them and the equipment to build them and shore them up, not to speak of housing and feeding the workers and providing transportation for them in and out and in and out, would take billions of dollars. CNN talked about countries that couldn't even feed their own people, that's how she thought of places like North Korea and Mongolia, funding the war tunnels. If they couldn't buy food or medicines, how could they possibly pay for this craziness?

The answer was something she preferred not to face.

It was like what had happened fifty years ago, when George Bush invaded Iraq. The troops found hunger and palaces, disease and despair, side by side with caches of millions in cash and piles of gold bricks underground. The same thing had happened in Gaza and the West Bank. The people there lived on the world's charity. Yet they bought rifles and rockets with it instead of Ruffles with ridges, she thought, returning to fiddling with the remote control until a flash of the Eiffel Tower told her that she had found CNN.

Some things just made no sense.

Straddling the kitchen chair nearest the television set, she popped her beer can and checked beneath the tag to see if she had won anything in the company's latest promotion. "Yeah. Right," she said, "I'm a winner for sure." She tossed the aluminum ring into an ashtray and turned up the volume to drown the recurring reminder

that she was living the way she was out of choice. She'd
had plenty of chances to move out of Harlem, but no,
she'd wanted to change the world and figured Harlem
was a pretty good place to start. So she'd stayed here
and passed that need for something better on to Hardy.
Now he was God only knew where, trying to prove to
her and himself that he was something.

"Larry Whitfield, reporting to you live, by satellite,
from Paris. We are the entrance to the Metro Denfert-
Rochereau." The camera moved away from his face and
stopped at a sign written in French. "That sign you see
reads 'Stop! This is the empire of death.'" He paused
for affect. Roseann saluted the screen with beer.

"Twenty-five meters underground there are tunnels,
catacombs reinforced by secondary walls of dry stone.
They have been there since around the end of the fif-
teenth century." Again he paused. "People live down
there. And creatures without names that guard millions
of bodies transferred there when there was no more
room left in the graveyards of Paree."

The camera panned the sky, a gloomy, gray blend of
soot and rain cloud. Then it panned the crowds, filling
the screen with a mass of pushing, frantic, agitated, people, bathing the screen in colors of stress and anxiety and
fear. Roseann shivered. She wasn't hot any more, but
she sure was sweating.

"My grandfather stood here once, taping a broadcast
before the Nazis showed up. He described empty streets,
tense silence, a city waiting for the stamp of jackboots.
This is a different kind of war. The city is jammed with
people—"

The television crackled as a series of tremors shook
the picture, splitting it into multiple images. Larry Whitfield's out-of-focus features were marred by waves and
streaks. The picture blanched, dulled, tilted, returned to
a semblance of clarity. In the background, behind him,
a flurry of activity drew his attention. The crowd jostled,
pushing against him. He strained to retain his balance.
"Look out for that equipment!"

People rushed by the camera, blocking Roseann's view. She inched closer to the set.

"Oh, my God!" Larry Whitfield's voice had lost all semblance of modulation. "The Horde! They're really here. They—"

The camera focused on a widening crack in the street. A helmet appeared. Roseann recognized it as G.I. issue.

"*Hardy.*"

She didn't realize she'd said his name aloud until the camera panned in, and the man in the helmet looked up.

"Hey, Roseann," he hollered, as if he could see her. "It's me. I'm takin' the long way home."

Two Years Earlier

Outside Tegujai Batir's tent, camp noises had taken over. Tegujai, his destiny—predicted by shamans and devils alike—was soon to be fulfilled. Satisfied, he relaxed on his mound of skins and made rapport with the sound around him. His fur-booted feet were drawn up to support the overhang of his arms. A cigar rolled lazily like cud in the slow rotation of his jaw.

"*Shacquebai! Shacquebai!*"

The cries of the Reader rocked Tegujai from where he squatted. He tore at his holster and rose quickly to his feet. Only a shred of reason kept him from firing into the old man who burst summarily into the tent.

"Dung eater! You were formed for birth in a camel's behind."

He returned his gun to its holster. Pulling at the slash of black mustache that hung over each side of his upper lip and the small chin beard of fine, soft hairs that lent him the air of chief of demons, he faced the Reader.

"*. . . and it is written that when he with the sword in his mouth has been cast into the fires, when the false prophet, his ally, has been quartered and strung up to the wind, when the dragon has been thrown back into the pit . . .*"

Tegujai stood close to the old man and looked down into the wild, staring eyes, forcing himself to listen yet one more time.

"Yet another shall rise, speaking no language but understanding all. And he shall see the worm, and rouse the worm, and say to it, 'I shall be your will and bid you to grow one mighty arm for striking and another with which to feed yourself.' . . ."

The old man's lumpy face raised itself heavenward, toward distances beyond Tegujai, and he spoke the rest of the words that had put the stigmata on Tegujai at the age of fifteen and cast him from the tribe.

"'I shall bid you to grow feet. And when you have grown the Striking Arm and the Feeding Arm and the Mighty Feet, I shall shout down through the length of your body. And you shall move forward and eat the world.'"

The Jinn had entered him that day. No Moslem prayer had been found that could drive it out. No superstition. No shaman or spokesman of Allah. Nothing could close the mystic door through which the Jinn devils had lunged, for they were spirits created by God out of fire. They were not usually visible to the human eye, but he could see them, for he had been given the eye of a Falcon. He had seen them bowing before Adam in great numbers in caves and in graveyards and above the ground, where they harassed the tribes, tempting them to walk away from Allah, who had given them permission to do as they pleased.

A loud moan escaped Tegujai Batir. Then the frightful cry of the damned shook the yurt as he seized the Reader.

"Robber! Fraud!" he shouted. "You took my manhood from me! You took it!" Tegujai's mouth was drawn back like the wolf he had been since the Jinn had reshaped him to their own design, first as a wolf and then as a Falcon with the vision to select a site for the tunnel and to pluck the Feathers that would make the Falcon fly.

Now, finally, the brain of the Falcon rested and waited for the signal to be given. The worm was an army in readiness, and the tunnel was at the edge of completion. Only one thing remained to be done before the worm could curve its way through the tunnel, ready to emerge in victory and devour the white man's world.

One more Feather must be added to the Falcon . . . one more, so that the march could begin . . .

Hardy Jackman was in the Afghan tunnel. The fact left his spirit unchanged. Since he thought of himself as a loser, a shift in environment was nothing more or less than an expected transition to further misfortune and a new set of fears. As a small child in the streets of Harlem, he'd worried about being beaten up by the bigger kids; at school, he'd expected his teachers to pick on him. In each case, when his fears were realized, it came as no surprise; when they weren't, he wondered why not. In high school, he'd refused to go out for football in case he didn't make it. Later, he'd refused to apply for work any more demanding than rolling a cart through the garment district or driving a delivery truck—jobs he felt he could manage without too much mishap.

Here, in the tunnel, his oversized, yellow, motherfucking jailors didn't seem to care whether he lived or died. They kept him alive and left him to his own devices.

Their attitude, all too familiar to Hardy, put him at his ease.

His only moment of genuine fright had come from the North Koreans. When they ramjammed his supply outfit and dumped him in that refrigerator of a prison camp, they put the eye on him and subjected him to a crude process of reorientation.

Thinking about it now, Hardy grinned. They'd scared the shit out of him for sure. His natural truculence had made them savage and derisive. Some screamed at him in frustration, others jabbed him angrily with gun butts. They couldn't understand that he just didn't like them, that all he wanted after his miserable Korean experience was to wait things out and be sent home.

Hell, the law of averages owed him at least one break.

Hardy rolled over, glanced at Big Tully, whose rag pallet lay next to his, and wondered if he smelled as bad as his neighbor, who generated a heady odor from his vanishing fat.

Not that he had anything to complain about, Hardy thought, settling back down. At least not compared with what the North Koreans had put them through. Things were looking pretty grim when the Mongols came. He was a taut and nervous animal then, cold, hungry, bedeviled by the jungle-psycho ethic of his captors. The Afghan tunnel put an end to all that.

Hardy was anything but a religious man, yet from his very first contact with this new experience, he'd sensed that there was something about it that transcended the physical. He'd felt overwhelmed—as if somehow the great jaws of a whale had opened up and swallowed him. Forever at the mercy of others, Hardy knew he was confrontating something really big.

But what?

Scattered religious images flashed *POW, POW, POW,* in his mind, providing cryptic answers to whatever his eyes beheld. The feeling had washed over him when he arrived; it remained with him now, in the dark of the night.

Leaning against the fence, the guard, Quali Beg, lit a cigarette. Though he could not see the smoke in the darkness, Hardy imagined it swirling toward him and inhaled. He wondered what would happen if he asked for a smoke, but he wasn't about to find out. Better to maintain a healthy respect for an efficient guard with a well-cleaned machine gun than to end up dead.

Like the others, Hardy was prodded to work and prodded to rest. The Mongols were big guys, young as Hardy, competent with their weapons, and always alert. Most of them weren't shy with words, but to Hardy it all came out Fu Manchu. The particular young Mongol who guarded his immediate area said nothing and did nothing to interfere with this imposed existence. Work, eat, crap, and sleep, that was the routine, the simple life. Maybe there was more they could do—maybe they could stretch their boundaries, Hardy thought. The North Koreans had offered Red orientation classes in exchange for better treatment. Little bastards. These people here offered nothing at all, not even a frigging smoke, which right now he wanted more than almost anything else.

In an attempt to distract himself, he reprised the image of Colonel Anstreiker being hauled off in a blanket, blood pouring from his nose and mouth. Hardy and his buddies—the remains of what had once been an integrated battalion—had been here a month or so before the man who'd called himself Colonel Anstreiker assembled them all in the prisoner's section. Including the scattering of men, also black, who had already been there when they'd arrived and lived in a segregated, sectioned-off area of the tunnel they were helping to build, they numbered around thirty. As to where the tunnel was leading or why they were building it, that they'd not been told.

From what Hardy could gather from Anstreiker's broken English, he and a total of several hundred men, Australians and Greeks included, had been flown by air transport across the face of China to an undisclosed location on its western borders. Anstreiker identified their captors as Mongols of the Sinkiang area. The project absorbing their efforts was, he said, a tunnel with serious military implications. He promised to contact the proper people in charge and initiate a procedure to open channels with the Red Cross in Geneva. Then he left.

Anstreiker's appearance sparked the formation of what could, at best, be called a loose military structure—loose enough that it neither impressed nor disturbed the Mongol guards, who remained impassive. Indifferent. When they spoke at all, it was to each other—of seemingly unrelated matters. At any rate, they didn't interfere.

Hardy saw Anstreiker twice after that. The first time, the colonel was part of a work gang, sweating behind a large metal cart, unloading its quota of rock and soil into a waiting truck. There was mechanical aid in the setup, but it was crude enough to make the job a back-buster and to raise doubts about the colonel's influence with those in charge of this gigantic hole.

Shortly after, the colonel was carried past Hardy's very nose by two Mongol guards and taken to parts unknown. There was no way to tell whether or not he was alive.

This kind of thing was not exactly a morale booster, but to someone like Hardy, used to being at the bottom of the pecking order, it meant nothing as long as it was happening to the other guy. As far as he was concerned, his real job—his obligation to himself and to his mother—was pumping juice and waiting for what was owed him. He could not conceive of a fate so cruel that it lacked even one element of fairness; therefore, some-where along the line, whatever was playing footsie with his life was bound to drop its guard, and Hardy would ram through. He was angry, tired, and above all, ever patient.

"When those Chinks gonna bury you, Tully?"

Alabama's pallet was on the other side of Tully. He was awake and bored

"I hope it's soon, man." Detroit clasped his nose and rolled his eyes. "You're rotten outta sight."

Tully's ass exploded twice. "This ain't rottin', man," he said. "This is reducin'."

"Fuckin' gasbag! Kill that shithole gasbag!"

"Weeeeeooooh! Will somebody plug up his ass!"

"We gonna dip you in cement, Tully. You gonna be a block o' cement."

"That's no good. He's gonna fart his way out of it."

"Stuff it," Tully shouted. "Reducin' and fartin' ain't hurtin' me none. It ain't hurtin' you none."

Hardy joined in at this point. "Wanna run for Con-gress on that ticket, y'fat bastard?" His knee jammed into Tully's pliant back. "Move over."

Tully turned to him. "Don't do that, man. Y'ever see cattle doin' that to each other? Even they be polite to each other. They just lay around lookin' nice 'ntil they butchered." He looked over at the guard. "Ain't that right, Fong Shit?"

"You can bet your ass on that, Tully," Quali Beg called out, his words enunciated in excellent English. "You're going to be a choice rump steak."

"Holy . . . !" Hardy sat bolt upright. This was going to mean trouble—big trouble. In the month that they'd been there, the guard had not so much as opened his mouth. He waited for the sound of bullets.

But Qauli Beg clearly had no intention of shooting them. Instead, he laughed. Gently. With a wholesome, youthful quality.

Hardy Jackman did not laugh with him. Instead, he lay down on his pallet and started to think.

The Falcon's bias against the white man ran deep and steadfast. And deadly. How much of the color had seeped into the black skins of these captives was an ever-present question for the Falcon. So, in this area, the rigid rules of Tegujai—the head of the Falcon—became more permissive. Thus Quali Beg, a Falcon Feather, had been left to make his own decisions when it came to dealing with the black ones, his special charges.

Quali Beg was a product of the Falcon. He was eighteen years old, a puritan in principle, a dilettante by nature. Secure and self-assured, he was well aware that the harvest of the friendship seed took careful reaping. Even after the incident with the black ones, he maintained his distance from them. If a Feather were to emerge from their ranks—as Tegujai predicted—it could not be a man of Quali Beg's choice. Only the Falcon could choose.

Bert Wilson scored first. The cocky, thin, string of a black from Kentucky slipped in his sly request for alcohol during an early, cautious effort at intercourse with the Mongol guard. Wilson was visibly staggered when he got the bottle of rye.

"It's the real stuff," he boasted to the others. "No piss, I'm not jivin' yuh." He took another pull at the bottle before he handed it to the man closest to him.

There was a concerted flurry of movement from the others, and Wilson had to risk his neck to get the bottle back. "Fuckers," he moaned. "Stinkin' bastards. I got the booze. It's my booze." He looked mournfully into the bottleneck and saw what was left. "Thievin' jerks," he cried.

Purvey Madison was the second to try. He was a big man who liked to lie on his stomach. His large head rested on crossed arms, but his gaze found Quali Beg. "Any more of this in stock, Mongrel?"

"Sure. I'd do anything for you sacks of shit," Quali Beg said.

A storm of catcalls broke upon him, flavored with laughter and obscene gestures. One man rose to his knees and shambled toward him, wringing clasped hands in mock despair.

"Please, Massa," he cried, "My ass's on d'cold, cold groun'n ah kin sure use some mo'a dat good booze."

"Yeah, Yeah," came the chorus. "Come on, Mongrel. No drinkee, no workee."

"I'm not your houseboy." Quali Beg stood casually, half propped against a gnarled table. "If you want something, go get it." He scanned the groups of prone men, studying each section of the compound without fixing his attention on any one person. Then he lit a cigarette and waited.

If his judgment was half as good as he thought, all hell was about to break loose.

"Hey—you mean that?"

"You mean we kin just get up and walk out o' here?"

"Siddown, man, it's that old Communist shit again."

"Hey, y'know, daddy, if these commies throw in some cigarettes we can smoke in class."

"Uh, uh. Crap on it. I ain't listenin' like a monkey, repeatin' like a monkey."

For a moment, Hardy imagined his mother mourning him in the heat of a Harlem summer. Propelling himself to his feet, he alone, in that surly group, he looked hard at Quali Beg and, without word or hesitation, walked past the Mongol guard.

The Jinn hissed like serpents in grand approval. High above the compound, electric lamps swayed on slender cables. Small grains of dust fell from the concrete ceiling as, basic, powerful, mystic as the very essence of the invisible, the Jinn energized the cells of Hardy Jackman—

making a thing of him undreamed of in the crap-coated tenements in which doting mothers raised his kind.

Hardy Jackman couldn't hear the hiss of the Jinn, but from that moment on, he began to see the tunnel. He no longer simply sensed it as a source of noise, movement, sweaty exertions, fire in his lungs. He *saw* it—as if it were some kind of enchanted construction opera—and somehow he knew that, in time, the great artery would stand whole in his inner eye. It would expand, pulsate—a large mass converted to a large movement.

The hugeness of the tunnel implanted itself in his consciousness, growing, breathing with winds that swept in from undiscovered passages, and he felt good. More alive than most men. More alive than he'd ever been, popping sparks, spoiling for a fight, and, he suddenly realized, hungrier than a hound in heat. Stepping into the path of a Falcon officer flanked by two men, he saluted, gave his name, rank, and serial number, and said, "I sure could use some chow, sir. How do I get some without going back to the POW compound?"

The three men faced him down. The officer, a handsome Mongol in his early thirties with a pale, sharp mask for a face, talked straight at Hardy. "You walk away from your compound, asshole? Your guards see you go?"

Hardy was still riding the momentum of his wild move. "That's what all this shit's about, ain't it, sir? You may be puttin' me down, but you're not shootin' me down. And if you're not going to shoot me, I sure as hell don't see why you'd want to starve me."

"So you'd like some chow . . ."

"Sure would, sir."

"But not at the compound?"

"I—I just don't feel that I have to go back, sir. Not if I don't want to. Am I right?"

The officer grew rigid and somewhat menacing. "Don't push it," he snapped coldly. "Move your nigger ass back two."

Hardy tightened up and sucked in air. The possibility of a bullet was not a moot issue. Taking two steps back was a move that made sense. He didn't like being called a nigger. Didn't like it one bit. Maybe he needed the distance to keep his cool.

"Still hungry?" asked the officer.

"Yes, sir."

The officer motioned to Hardy. "Fall in behind us," he said, his attitude showing signs of defrosting.

They merged with battalions of humanity, in disciplined squads and small, isolated knots with assigned tasks. No one took any notice of Hardy. Another roll, another score, he thought. A boot in the ass for gloom and doom, and another big cigar for guessing right. He got it now. Winning was regenerative.

Hardy's military escort led him to the biggest damn mess hall he'd ever seen. Long lines of tunnel personnel shuffled slowly toward steaming food counters and dispersed to forage for space in a vast, adjoining dining area. The atmosphere was oriental, but the image in any form was army. Unlike the prisoner's compound, the sounds here were healthy. The lonely, knocking echoes one heard in the semisilence of deterioration in the POW pens didn't exist in this place.

He seized a wooden tray and steel utensils and stood in one of the chow lines. He was on his own, wedged in a moving belt of passive, indifferent strangers, his senses engaged with the food-rich air. If the Mongols were playing the same game with him as the North Koreans—

He didn't think so.

A maverick principle was at work here: a man either did this thing, or didn't. There was no push or penalty. The option to explore was open to him and people like him. Intriguingly, it seemed that such choices were closed to the whites. At least, he'd never seen a white man in a position of power in all his time here. Rumor was, they died in this place as victims of bigotry. Why this was so was not apparent to him for the moment, but Hardy no more questioned it than he did his own existence. Bigotry was a hard and dirty truth, like shit spread on a wall.

He'd seen his share of it, and more, growing up back in the good ole U. S. of A.

He ate his food in studied thought, chewed it slowly,

absorbed it along with the options that arose in his brain. The future began to look different, like the food on his wooden tray, the warm drink in his cup. What he was ate now was basically clots of meat, fish, rice, a fruit, and this milk called kumis. It was neither prisoner's slop nor home cookin'. It was simply different, the shadow of a new lifestyle.

A lifestyle that he was claiming for his own.

He made visual forays among his fellow diners at the long table they shared. His glances were brief but incisive. Intuitively, he began to distinguish between the Chinese and the Mongols. The large bones and the wider shoulders—a more flamboyant manner—identified the Mongols. To a man, they all drank kumis.

He made slow circles with his spoon in the depths of his drink, sipping it slowly and rolling the cup between both palms. These cats seemed to make the most of identity exchange with their prisoners. There was a give and take, learning and teaching.

They treated Hardy and his gang back in the compound fairly, like men. Unlike the North Koreans, who became horrible caricatures of regional America in their efforts to patronize and deceive, these Mongols cast images familiar to Hardy as his own.

Like a blind man running sensitive fingers along the living hide of an unseen creature, he began to trace his first, faint view of the thing that drove them, the Falcon. One day he would know it from eye to claw.

Liyu Quan sat to the right of Hardy, engaged in light conversation with several other girls while she waited for the black man to make the first move.

"You chicks kicking me around the track?" he asked.

"Eat shit," the woman across the table said.

"Buzz off, boy," another added.

Jackman's teeth set in a fierce, defiant smile. He stood up, reaching for every inch of height he could muster, his smile still fixed and rigid, his strong palms slowly fitting themselves to the edge of the table.

Liyu Quan placed her hand upon his, cool and soft,

pressing with gentle firmness. "Don't do it," she said. "To die now would be foolish."

He looked at her, and she saw herself with his eyes: tall, plump, serene, a sensual roundness transforming her simple dress.

Hardy began to relax. Her hand was on his wrist now, communicating her calm self-assuredness. Hardy's smile uncoiled. He looked somehow off-balance. Vulnerable. Unexpectedly, he patted her hand and turned to leave the table.

"I'm Liyu Quan," she said. "Do you know what you're going to do?"

"What do you mean?"

"What are you going to do? There's no end to the tunnel. It's very big. You keep wandering about, and you'll either drop or run into serious trouble."

"Is that right?"

"I saw what happened to one of the others. He tried to get liquor from the wrong parties, and they shot him."

"Hold it, hold it," said Hardy. "What others?"

Liyu Quan paused uncomfortably, then said the words as if they had to be said. "The other—the people like you. The black ones. They're wandering around, just like you."

"I'll be goddamned. All of them?"

"That's a stupid question," she laughed. "How would I know? I'm not assigned to counting the walkabouts."

Her eyes sought his, her full lips rubbed against each other. "You were the first," she said. "You were the first to get up and leave the prisoner's compound, weren't you?"

Hardy's face was a tough block of dark tektite. "How did you know?"

"Just a guess," she said. "You're alone, shifting for yourself. Looking for a purpose. The rest of them are just running loose in yapping packs. Looking for what they can get."

"They need more than that." Hardy's expression changed. "I could use some help," he said.

Liyu was the only one listening now. "Okay," she said. "Let's see what you've got in mind."

What Hardy had in mind seemed to her as nebulous as galactic gas. Still, she led him where he wanted to go. The longer she was around him, the more impressed she became.

He tracked down the remainder of his fellows. The casualties among his cellmates now added up to four. Three dead, another one in the infirmary, but slipping fast. Some were back in the prisoner's compound, and others were still heading for trouble somewhere in the vastness of the tunnel.

"Don't give me any horseshit, now," he railed at Quali Beg. "If we have rights in this big hole, I demand to use them." He pointed at the sorry lot in the compound. "These guys have bottomed out, but they're not prisoners. They don't belong here, right?"

"They don't belong anywhere else," the young guard answered. "Come on, don't give me a hard time. Let it hang and take off. It's not your ass, is it?" The soldier looked at Liyu Quan and said in Chinese, "You've chosen well. The teaching of Tegujai holds true. The Falcon is universal, it can even drop a Feather among pigs."

Unable to understand a word but fearing the worst, Hardy broke in before the girl could answer. "Leave her out of this, Ching Chow. She's just a friend, so don't step out of line. Talk to me. Now, what do I have to do to spring these guys? Does it take paperwork, or can they just walk out now, in my custody?"

It took an interview with Hussain Taiji, the section commander and—so it was rumored—as close a thing to a friend as Tegujai had. He was a pipe smoker, small and thin.

Hardy strode up to him in his foreign uniform, saluted, and with cold assurance told Hussain what he needed.

Apparently the commander was impressed, because things began to change. Hardy and the rest of his gang were assigned to another section of the great tunnel, an isolated barracks area, gray and ghostlike in the artificial light, with graded drilling turf and free of echoes.

A week later, there were many black men there. They had bunks of their own, cooks of their own, and drivers of their own. They elected their own noncoms, and they took their orders from Hardy Jackman. If there was Mongol scrutiny of any kind, it was low profile and with a minimum of intrusion. They seemed to be free to choose their own destiny. It was an odd arrangement, neither prison camp nor garrison but a place for men to live in military fashion, learning bit by tiny bit about what governed the new patterns of their lives. It was still dark, dreary, and far from where he wanted to be. Still, in the complex skein of it, there was a glimmer of hope.

Hardy could see it.

He communicated it as best he could to the rest. "It's the long way home," he said, when they assembled on the drill ground at dawn. "It's the long way home," he told them, night after night when the day was done. He began to believe it, to live for it, and the others chanted the phrase till it became their survival code. It restored their pride and confidence.

The whites in the prison compound weakened and died. When their numbers thinned, a new batch of replacements appeared to fill the empty pallets. If there were blacks among the newcomers, they were soon hustled off to Hardy, who knew now how badly he'd underrated his true capacities for his whole life.

He was a leader.

He was good at what he was doing. Very good—and growing better all the time.

While his mind chewed on things entirely unrelated to his early dreams, if in fact they had been dreams at all, he structured the lifestyle of a group, which had begun with his small band of unruly stragglers and eventually filled out to company size. He wasn't aping the officers in charge of his original outfit, either, he thought proudly. He was putting their methods into new and innovative context. Better yet, he did nothing that didn't make sense to each individual under his command. The motivation he handed them was simple: comfort and provisions.

And the path home.

Somehow, conditions improved as the men took on

the semblance of *snap-shit* soldiers. In time, they even began to take themselves seriously. On their own in this tunnel, each man was able to grow in value, to pull his weight. There were those dissidents who clung to despair—a few of them, and fewer as time passed. They never lasted long before they vanished into the dark jaws of the endless underground.

In eight months, this once deserted corner of the tunnel was alive with activity. The barracks blazed with light, and human shadows sped across each window in animated succession. The men had acquired a mini motor pool, and they serviced and ran their own vehicles. They drilled, they exercised, they rejected dry rot, and they found reward in their own toughness. They laughed without cynicism and didn't give a damn why they felt better. They had unlimited freedom of movement and a social life, of sorts. The female personnel, involved in paperwork and heavier duties, were certainly not off limits, and whatever it took to stock a reasonable PX was accumulated for their use.

Things just weren't too bad, that was all. Fear of the tunnel had been drawn out of them like a bad tooth, and they experienced a consistency of life and of purpose that was palatable on all levels.

Although no section of the tunnel was denied to them, Hardy's men as a group showed no interest in exploring the length of it. As for the few intrepid souls who toyed with delusions of possible escape, Hardy took no notice of them. He knew they would come back after discovering the sheer impossibility of making it home alone, which was nothing if not helpful to his cause of solidarity. Nor did the Mongols make any effort to stop these adventurous dreamers. If they reached the tunnel's mouth, there was still the endless land, the world's broad curve, the pockets of hostility that waited like a hidden army of sharpened *punji* sticks for the unwary step of the stranger.

The only way they would make it home was together.

It took desperation to seek solitary freedom. Hardy's

men just didn't have it What they would be leaving seemed far safer and saner than a mad break into the dark alone.

Sometimes, Hardy tried to analyze what had happened to him and his men. It seemed that the Mongol rulebook denoted the blacks as creatures for contempt, but not for suffering. When suffering, though not mandatory, did take place, it was a condition they had to modify on their own. In his new mode, with the Falcon in his mind and soul, this made total sense to him. To share with the Mongols was not enough. To match them on their ground became a must. He drove his men to the task. His noncoms barked, and the men stepped. His mechanics made objects of art of their vehicles, and his cooks outclassed any man's mother in the kitchen.

Two years passed, during which time Hardy acquired a Mongol wife, a year-old son, and a destiny that made him pump inside like an engine churning with hot fuel. His past in the projects, then as a bottom feeder in the army, had been forgotten—a distant echo, without meaning. He liked that a lot. He began to make an effort to get his men to cut down on insulting the Koreans and Vietnamese, whether about their size or color. To be honest, he didn't get too far, but at least he tried. He felt good about that. Then the time came that he learned that the tunnel had reached completion. For a day, he told no one. He thought about new lives, new visions, fulfillment in ways never imagined; he thought about old hatreds. At last, he shared the news with the others.

They weren't quite sure what this meant to them. They had taken part in the work. One man named Hollister had even managed to assume responsibility in the capacity of engineer. Another, Arlo Shandy, had devised a speed-up method to reach a score of men who were strangling on gas during a cave-in. A third, Bud Bascom, was shot for killing two Chinese truck drivers in an argument over tailgating. One man—Isaac Huber—had been nothing more than a common field medic with a history of cleansing wounds with penicillin powder and taking smears for V.D. detection. Here he had taken a crack at complex surgery and succeeded before the astonished eyes of the tunnel medical staff.

Some black men had scored, others had funked out. The bright ones had found exhilarating channels for their abilities, unmindful of reward or morality, but most of them had simply rolled along on wheels that shimmied but carried the load.

Hardy Jackman had done his job; they had done theirs. Now the Falcon was ready, and it was time to go home.

Without fear, he watched Tegujai Batir—the head of the Falcon—emerge from his tent and descend to the mouth of the tunnel.

"Son-of-a-bitch, really," Hardy said. All of these years, and he had never once seen the man whose dream he'd been fulfilling. "This is it."

He gathered together his men. The women, knowing what they must do, put together their few belongings and took hold of their small children. They would form the rear, trailing the worm until it burrowed to the surface in Paris. They watched, pressed against the walls of the tunnel, as the Feathers gathered and the Falcon marched before his commanders and administrators, who turned their faces to Tegujai.

Hardy Jackman did not wait to be asked. He led his men into formation with a natural snap, which they matched with a majesty they'd never known before. This was no longer a unit identifiable with any other, he thought with pride. These were polished, hair-trigger sharp foot soldiers, the future alive in their hearts. Sure, their uniforms were still courtesy of Uncle Sam, repaired and patched. But that did not matter a damn now that he knew the road that stretched before them did not end at the tunnel's mouth. They fought for the Falcon. And justice.

The Jinn demons watched Tegujai throw back his shoulders and march to the front of the ranks. They saw that he was tired and growing old. It was in his physical body that they had made their leap to reality. The Word, interpreted by Tegujai Batir, had encompassed the lives of all who knew him. He was the head of the Falcon, but it was from their minds and flesh that the Word was feeding and evolving, gulping space with the appetite of a giant.

Tegujai had lived by it and was fulfilled. His time was done.

Knowing this, the Jinn looked around for his successor, and they remembered Hardy. Once before, they had hissed their approval of him and rewarded him by opening his eyes to the tunnel; this time, when they entered him, they also opened his soul to the Word.

Though he did not recognize what it was, Hardy felt the overwhelming evidence of the Jinn's power growing inside him. He had never felt better, stronger, in his life. Feeling no fatigue, no thirst or hunger beyond what could be easily satisfied, he pushed his men past the head of the worm. As he looked down the long, wide road, his mind's eye was able to conjure up the image of the Falcon, its striking arm leading the worm in its endless phalanxes. The vision was staggering and fearful to behold: two million men, stepping with ease within the walls of a tunnel constructed by man. A hundred men abreast in awesome and silent ranks, moving like phantoms toward the mouth of the tunnel, with him at their head.

He did not know what was driving him, even when he came abreast with Tegujai.

But Tegujai did.

When Hardy and his men came into view, Tegujai showed no surprise. Their appearance, after all, was part of the Word. They had merged as one massive body of pigment, stamped with the agonies of the past and the hope for the future. He stood aside and let them pass, acknowledging Hardy Jackman as the Jinn's choice. "I have become old," he told the black man. "You will become the Eye of the Falcon and lead in my place."

An hour later, Hardy faced the end of the tunnel. He held up his hand, knowing the worm would take heed and come to a halt. He thought briefly of Liyu and his son. Even the Jinn fell silent. In silence, they opened his inner eye and showed him a ladder of his soldiers, standing foot upon shoulder against the wall of the tunnel. Above them, through a gaping hole, loomed the gray Parisian sky.

Seeing that, Hardy did what was needed. "Watch out, world," he yelled. "The Falcon's coming through."

The Jinn carried the echo of Hardy's voice through the maze of tunnels and arteries so that even Liyu, trailing with the tail of the worm, could hear her husband's voice.

Listening to himself, Hardy drew from the Jinn's elemental forces. "I am the Eye of the Falcon," he said.

Above him, the earth blistered and broke open

"Let's go!" Hardy yelled.

Tully was the first to respond. "Yessir!" Grinning, he flattened himself against the tunnel wall.

Alabama was next, then Detroit.

The Eye of the Falcon watched the human ladder grow to within five feet of the hole.

"That's high enough!" he called out. He adjusted the strap of his G.I. helmet. They were probably waiting up there with guns and tanks, he thought. Well, shit. He wasn't scared of dying, but they sure as hell were going to know whose head they were blowing off.

Hoisting himself up, Hardy began to climb. When he stood on Detroit's shoulders, he straightened up and poked his head through the hole.

"Hey, Ma," he hollered. "It's me. I'm takin' the long way home—"

—Roseann Jackman's hand splayed across the television. Her son's face grew huge beneath her fingers. Eyes blazing, mouth twisted into a wry grin, it filled the screen. Shaking, she dropped to her knees. "Hardy!"

The picture tilted. She thought she heard the word *Falcon*. Then, with a slight pop, the screen went blank beneath her fingers as it emitted a steady, electronic drone—the single measure left of reality in a room and a world grown dark . . .

IN DEMETER'S GARDENS

Nancy Jane Moore

"So our job is to stop this riot, preferably without kill-ing anybody." Caty Sanjuro looked at her troops to gauge their reaction.

Sgt. Russell Begay cleared his throat.

"Did you have something to add, Sergeant?"

"Why us, Captain?"

Short and to the point, but pretty much the same question she'd asked the colonel ten minutes earlier. The war on Ceres was supposed to be over. The rebel leadership had surrendered a month earlier. The mop-up work remaining belonged to peacekeepers and MPs, not combat Marines, and an army peacekeeping division with a significant MP component was now deployed across Ceres and the smaller asteroids of the Belt.

About half the Marines who'd fought here were already gone. The next orders for Sanjuro's company were supposed to be for home and some down time, not putting down food riots in Demeter.

When her com had sounded, Caty had been sitting in her quarters, working out a strategic plan to get the Marine Corps to send her to graduate school. She was rereading the letter from Prof. Andrea Bogdosian accepting her into the xenology program at Berkeley, and she didn't pick up until the second beep.

The colonel said, "Sanjuro, we've got a riot in progress

in Demeter. I need your company in the city fifteen minutes ago."

"Excuse me, sir," Caty said. "But isn't that an MP assignment?" Before Ceres, she'd have simply said, "Yes, sir," and hit all call to get her people together. Combat always affects people—killing does not leave most human beings unscathed, despite the violence that permeates history—but before this operation she'd always been able to put her job in context. Sometimes there were no good choices; sometimes war, ugly as it was, beat the alternatives. She'd never questioned that before Ceres.

The colonel was probably glaring, but Caty hadn't hit visual on her com. She waited for his response.

He said, "You're reinforcements. There's only a small force of MPs in Demeter, and they're still struggling with the low grav. The whole thing's veering out of control. They need backup. I'm sending details now."

That wasn't as much information as she wanted, but the tone of the colonel's voice made it clear that the Q&A period had expired. "Yes, sir," she said, and hit all call.

Her company was packed in the briefing room. Like most buildings on Ceres, the ones on the Marine base were made from local dirt and rock. They might have been nice if they'd had windows and been painted something other than utilitarian gray, but those in charge had deemed artificial light more practical, given the short lengths of Ceresian days and nights. It added to the feeling of depression that had settled over her troops— seasoned fighters all, but sick of this war. No professional soldier likes fighting amateurs, particularly amateurs who believe in their mission. More than one of her people struggled with the same conflicted emotions she felt. She knew these people, knew the last thing they wanted was to deal with was a riot.

Caty shoved her own doubts aside and went for the kind of words that always worked well with Marines, "The army can't hack it."

"So what's new?" someone yelled out, and someone

else said something Caty couldn't quite catch, which drew loud laughs. She didn't have to hear it to know that it was at the army's expense.

"The MPs they put in Demeter don't even know how to handle a riot."

More laughter.

"They need Marines."

That drew a few cheers.

"We're the closest backup, and they know we can do the job."

"You bet we can," somebody said, and there were more cheers.

"Anybody else got a question? No? Get your armor on. I want you on the transport in five minutes."

"Good job," Lt. Gloria Elizando said as she and Sanjuro left the troops to their sergeants and moved into a private room to suit up. "You almost got me to cheering, too. But then I remembered we were going out to deal with a fucking riot, which is not supposed to be our job." She grabbed her hands behind her back and leaned forward to stretch. "Kuso! I'd hoped we'd seen the last of battle armor for awhile."

The armor was a metal-cloth alloy, flexible but a lot heavier than the heat-regulating body skels they usually wore. It was worth the extra weight—it would block most projectile weapons, diminish the effect of explosives, and, when the headgear was in use, filter out gas, but everyone bitched about it anyway.

"Me, too." Until the captain had been shot, she and Glory Elizando had each run a platoon, but now Caty was technically in charge of the whole company. Six months worth of seniority had given her the nod, but Glory hadn't resented it. They got along okay.

Even in uniform they didn't look alike: Glory exceptionally tall, with dark brown skin and bright gold hair, Caty short only by comparison, with thick black hair, light tan skin, and just enough of a fold along her eyes to justify the name Sanjuro. Her father had always insisted she use her late mother's name. Sgt. Becca Sanjuro had died winning the Medal of Honor on Europa, and the cash award given to her heirs provided the money for Caty's gene enhancements. Without those tweaks, she'd never have made it through the academy, would have ended up career enlisted, like her parents.

"Guess this is why they left us down here on Ceres instead of moving us up to the station," Caty said.

"Too bad they didn't leave one of the other companies down here." Actually, they both preferred being on the surface. Being on the station that moved in geosynchronous orbit around Ceres meant making polite with the brass, and both of them had the line officer's contempt for those who made battle decisions from afar.

The transports ran on mag-lev lines between the base and Demeter. Utilitarian, like everything else, but at least they had windows. Through the mild distortion of the arched cover that encased the transport line, Caty could see sunshine filtering through the mass of treelike plants that covered all parts of the asteroid that weren't under a dome. The exobiologists said those gene-modded plants would give Ceres a breathable atmosphere so that people wouldn't have to live in sealed domes forever. There would be room for more settlements, and eventually the workers who'd completely adapted would be able to make real lives here. Another fifty years, the biologists said—soon, but not soon enough for the people taking part in the riot.

Caty knew the history, but until she'd arrived in the asteroid belt, it had only been dry facts. The war on Ceres started as a miners' strike, and workers in the Asteroid Belt's other main industry—tourism—soon joined in. No one expected two such wildly diverse groups to get together. The miners were people who couldn't pass exams for most types of work, while the tourist workers included thrill seekers who liked to lead extreme expeditions and aspiring actors who flocked to the Belt's low-grav theme parks. But, as it turned out, they had several things in common—poor pay, safety issues, and atrophied muscles that kept them in stuck in the Belt.

Most long-term workers sooner or later stopped doing the exercises that kept their muscles in shape for higher gravity. Their hours were long, the exercises took lots of time, and most found their work easier to do if they adapted completely to low gravity. Unlike the Marine brass, who simply ordered their people to the do the exercises, most company execs weren't really displeased if their workers didn't bother. It meant they had no place else to go.

The strike was illegal—the contracts that got workers the fare to the Belt prohibited unions as well as requiring people to work for the company for a set number of years. The Ceres government, at the request of the corporations, sent local soldiers out to break it. Some of the local troops were retired members of the systemwide Combined Forces run by the Solar System Union, but most were soldier wannabes who couldn't pass the exams for enlistment in the interplanetary forces. A small troop, they had only one advantage over the strikers: weapons. They broke the picket lines.

The strike ended, but the leaders quietly began to organize something more deadly. Two years later they announced their resurgence with a bomb attack at the adventure park on Vesta. Killing tourists got them labeled as terrorists and allowed the Ceresian government to ask for SSU military help. Combined Forces sent in Marines—Caty and her people had come in with the first division. One division hadn't been enough, and more people soon joined them.

The outcome had never been in doubt—the rebels couldn't get their hands on enough money or weapons to win—but nothing about it had been easy. A year of effort had brought the war more or less to a halt, but the cost in lives and injuries had exceeded projections by over a hundred percent. Every time Caty looked at her troops, she remembered the ones who weren't there.

Caty's father, Jake Horner, had died on one of the small outlying asteroids. He shouldn't have even been out there. He was in his early sixties and the highest ranking enlisted Marine on Ceres. But the colonel in charge wanted to be a general, and when he got intel that some of the rebels were holed up on that rock, he'd led a raid, bringing along Horner and some other experienced troops as a squad. It had been a trap—a mine buried deep inside had taken all of them out, as well as the tiny asteroid itself.

Jake's death made Caty realize how far things had gone in her own mind. As angry as she was, she couldn't hate the rebels for it. They were undisciplined, violent—the antithesis of everything her father had raised her to be—but even a Marine could see the conditions working people lived in on Ceres. It left her with an uncomfortable jumble of emotions, one she hoped to make sense of once she was off this godforsaken rock.

Confusion greeted them as the company poured into the former corporate office that served as military headquarters in the city. Like the buildings on the base, the structure was a series of interconnected domes made from local dirt and rock. But the walls were painted bright yellow. It might have even looked cheerful if the windows hadn't been occluded and the room rearranged to serve as a command center.

"Dios, I'm glad you're here," said the captain who appeared to be in charge. He was staring at a holographic projection of the city outside. A line of words flashing in red drew Caty's eye to the key in the upper left hand corner of the holo: "True Visibility at Five Percent." The image itself was crystal clear, and showed a mass of rioters running in all directions, with soldiers bouncing around trying to keep order. A couple of soldiers were hunched over workstations, probably running the holo.

"We got a bomb threat at the high school about fifteen minutes ago," the captain said. "I sent our bomb squad over to check it out, and now I can't raise them on com or get a scan reading. I'm desperate to know what's happening there, but meanwhile we've got one hell of a situation out in Governor's Circle, and I can't pull any people out of there." The captain's headgear was open, and his right eye kept twitching.

"What's going on in the Circle?"

"Rioters everywhere. We used gas, but they must have been expecting it, because they just keep coming." He waved his hand at the projection, which did, indeed, show people constantly materializing. Or rather, a simulation of that—it was running a comp program based on scan data, Caty realized. The captain saw the look she gave it and said, "Vid's not working. The gas made it bad enough, but then the rioters set off some smoke bombs. You can't see a thing out there except by using scan. And since everything doesn't register on scan, we thought we'd better get the comp to run some projections."

Great, Caty thought. Made up data.

"I've got three squads out there, trying to round people up, plus one in the council building protecting the politicos. But the baka Ceresians just move too fast."

Four squads should be enough, Caty thought. "How many rioters are there?"

The incredulity in Caty's voice must have been obvious, because the captain's reply sounded defensive. "Probably about a thousand." He waved at the projection again. "We're real short staffed. Everyone figured any trouble would hit the mines, not downtown Demeter. We've just got a company of MPs down here, plus the bomb squad."

Caty looked at Glory. The bomb threat at the high school was probably a hoax, but nothing was certain in this kind of chaos. Adult rioters probably wouldn't target the school, but kids might.

"We better check out the school," Caty said to Glory. "Take one squad over there—leave me the rest."

"Right." Glory gave an order, and a dozen people headed for the doors. Caty hit com. "And Glory, stay in touch, okay?"

"Yes, ma'am." It wasn't quite sarcastic.

"Who's in charge out there?" Caty asked the captain.

"I'm trying to run things from here," he said. "Usually it's better when I can see the big picture."

"Well, tell your people we're on our way. And make sure you let us know what you see."

The rest of the company moved out at the lope that

was standard fast pace on Ceres, making them look like
a troupe of oversized ballet dancers doing a series of
grand jetes. Most people picked up the lope fairly
quickly; it took longer to figure out how to turn or stop.
Caty's company had spent close to a year on Ceres; they
knew how to move.

Demeter—like most domed cities—had been laid out
in circles rather than right angles. Governor's Circle was
the only real park—open space came at a premium. The
council chambers, another series of interconnected
domes, were the main buildings on the circle. Other government buildings took up about half the circle's circum-
ference, with the rest of the space given over to high-
end retail and upscale offices. Even an outpost like Ceres
has an upper class.

Caty wondered why the army hadn't called in the
troops at the mines. They weren't as close as the Marine
base, but they could still get here fast. She let the thought
slip away; right now her attention had to be on her job.
By her reading of the scan, there were considerably
fewer than a thousand rioters out there; the army captain's comp projection had distorted the situation, even
if some rioters weren't registering. The readout showed
MPs foundering around, trying to catch Ceresians and
falling as they turned too fast or reached out too far.
They bounced back up just as fast, but by then the
Ceresians were gone. There didn't seem to be any rhyme
or reason to the MPs' actions.

Even her people couldn't move as fast as the
Ceresians—the only way to develop perfect movement
on a low-grav world was to give up high-grav muscle
definition. "Circle your people around in the passways
one block off the park," she told her sergeants. "Once
we control the perimeter, we'll trap the protesters in
front of the Council building. I'm going to check in with
the army people holed up in there, see if I can get their
people organized so that they're helping rather than hin-
dering. Keep your weapons on disable. Doesn't seem to
be anything more vicious than rocks out there." Though

a few people probably had something more lethal. They always did. "And no more gas. There's way too much of it now."

She ducked into the Council building the back way, reassured the sentry who blocked her path that the Marines had come to save his ass, and found a full squad in the front part of the building, where a barricade with gun turrets had been erected during the war. This wasn't the first battle in Governor's Circle. A lieutenant paced around behind them, alternately checking scan and com.

"Lieutenant, you've got more people than you need in here," Caty said, not bothering with the niceties of introduction. "Two sharpshooters can keep the front steps clear. We need to put all the troops we can out on the streets to round these people up."

"Who . . . oh, you're the Marine the captain said was on her way. I don't know if we can . . ."

"I do. Put your two best shooters there, and there"— she pointed—"and get the rest of them out on the streets. We'll hook 'em up with my sergeants out there; they'll know how to position them. Hell, you'd think you people never dealt with a riot before."

"We haven't," the lieutenant said. "Most everybody in this company is fresh out of training. All the experienced troops are over at the mines. Nobody expected . . ."

"Anything to happen at Demeter. So I've heard. Well, let's try to fix this mess so that your first riot won't be your last one."

The lieutenant stared at her. She didn't have her headgear on, so Caty could see the tension in her face. She hesitated for a few seconds and then hit her com. "Captain, the Marines say we can hold this building with a small force, so I'm sending most of my people out to help with the roundup." A pause. "Yes, sir." She turned to Caty again, "He says we might as well follow your directions, because nothing else is working."

"A real vote of confidence," Caty said, without bothering to hide her sarcasm. "Let's get moving." She headed out the back door, into the block behind the chambers.

It was slow going. The borrowed soldiers stumbled as they moved. Caty wondered what all these inexperienced troops were doing here. Surely the Combined Forces brass had known they'd need peacekeepers and MPs once the war was won. With all the hot spots on Earth, the army had to have plenty of people with substantial postwar mop-up experience. They could have sent some of the pros for low-grav training six months ago and had the right people here.

And relying on scan was becoming a real pain in the ass, especially since it didn't seem to be registering an accurate number of rioters. Even granted that Ceresians moved fast, the constant up and down of the numbers couldn't be right. But as near as Caty could guess, given the state of her data, most of the rioters were actually in the Circle, not on the side streets.

Caty sent the soldiers around to the blocks outside the park to mix in with her Marines and pulled the MPs who were roaming around inside the Circle back out to the edges. It took longer than she wanted, but after fifteen minutes she had the perimeter, with troops spaced evenly around. Now all they had to do was walk in, herding protesters as they went. It ought to work. They moved toward the Circle.

Com beeped. Glory. "Hey, Sanjuro, we're at the high school. Looks copacetic. Bomb squad found nothing. Hardly anybody here anyway—looks like the kids are all out your way. Teachers, too, probably."

"Great. Come on back. We could use the help."

Glory didn't answer.

"Glory? Elizando, stay online." No response. "Come on, Glory, talk to me." She tried their private channel. Still no response. "Oh, kuso." She hit all call. "I've lost Elizando on com. Is everyone else here?"

The reassuring sound of voices reporting in was interrupted by a thundering explosion. It momentarily deafened her. She switched from local to wide area scan and saw red alert alarms about where the high school ought to be. Double kuso. Without com there was no way to know if Glory's squad was outside the damage area—

and therefore able to bring it under control—or blown to Pluto with the building.

The army captain's voice was hysterical as it came over com. "The school blew up."

"I know, Captain. It was hard to miss. Stay calm," Caty told him. Her own mind was racing. Should she pull everyone out of here and head for the high school? It didn't feel like the right choice, but she couldn't figure out why. Go on your instinct, Sanjuro, she told herself. She spoke to the captain. "Send someone over to the school area and find out what's going on."

"I don't have anyone to send."

"Pull one of those people off your sims. They're not doing us any good. Or go yourself. We have to know what's up, and I need to get this situation under control."

She continued leading her troops in. Rioters screamed and cursed, and threw rocks and worse at them. The smoke began to clear in spots, showing her angry people waving signs, nothing more. Their faces were contorted and they were screaming and throwing things, but they were moving forward under the pressure of the armed soldiers. Caty's people could get this under control, assuming that whatever had happened at the school didn't ignite more trouble.

A fresh wave of gas blew across the protesters. "Goddamn it," Caty said, "whoever set that off is looking at a court martial." Now she couldn't see anything again. She called up scan, and the number of enemies doubled before her eyes. Damn it, scan had to be malfunctioning. Otherwise, where had those people come from?

Begay's voice came through com in a shout. "The new ones got live weapons, Captain." She heard shots ring out, saw flashes register on scan. Somebody screamed through com, and the sound almost pierced her eardrum. If the sound came through com, the screamer had to be one of hers.

It didn't make sense. Another scream. More explosions nearby. She knew they'd never caught all the rebel leaders, had never rounded up all their weaponry. If her people were screaming, somebody had to be firing armor-piercing rounds. Something still felt wrong, felt off, and she still didn't trust scan, but she'd run out of time. She hit all call. "Reset your weapons for kill. Fire on any target firing at you." That last point was a brief curtsy in the direction of standard operating procedures; she knew damn well that once they started firing live rounds, people would be shot regardless of whether they were holding rifles, rocks, or babies. But she couldn't let her people die without fighting back.

Caty reset her own weapon and began firing along with the others. Eighty-odd troops let loose a barrage. She began to hear lots of screaming from the people in front of her. She realized she wasn't hearing any more screams through com.

Begay's voice again boomed through all call. "Stop the firing. Tell them to stop, Captain, tell them to stop." His voice cracked. "Scan's wrong. They aren't armed. Stop the firing. Please stop it."

Her scan was still registering enemy fire, but she had been in too many battles with him to distrust Begay. "Cease fire," she said, repeating the words as she moved toward Begay's location until she heard the shooting taper off, stop. "Sergeant, what's happening?" She stumbled on something, recovered, leaped over it, and then turned back. On the ground lay a teenager. His eyes were wide open, but he stared at nothing. The gaping hole in his chest told her all she needed to know.

Begay said in her ear, "Scan lied." He was crying.

Caty left the boy's body, thankful to get away, and met Begay. He knelt in the street, cradling the head of a dead man. The deceased had the same kind of broad, brown face as the sergeant. She put a hand on Begay's shoulder.

"Dios, we killed civilians." The sergeant wasn't even trying to stop his tears.

Caty knew how he felt. Com buzzed in her ear. "Captain, Lt. Elizando sent me over to tell you that things are fine at the school. We've got some kind of com glitch." Another voice cut in, "Captain, I got to the school and everything's fine there. Nothing blew. I don't know what the explosion was but nothing blew. Just some kind of com problem. I had to come back halfway to get through."

The explosion. She hadn't felt it; just heard it. Probably through com, now that she thought about it. It had been so loud she'd assumed it was an outside noise, but something that big should have shook the ground. She called up the Army captain back at the Combined Forces headquarters. "Captain, get medical out here on the double."

"But scan's still showing . . ."

"Scan's fucked, Captain. Along with everything else. We don't have anything out here except dead and dying civilians. Get medical here now."

Caty was surprised that the colonel suggested they meet in his quarters. She'd been there once before for one of those parties that people went to for career, rather than personal, reasons. The accommodations were spacious, particularly for a space station; they had clearly been designed with the assumption that an officer might bring a spouse and children to a posting, though the colonel had neither. He took her past the formal room meant for social occasions back into a small den. It was the room where he really lived. One corner held a desk messy enough to show that someone worked there. A couple of comfortable chairs were set up in another corner, and the colonel had set out a bottle of wine and a couple of glasses on the table between them. The walls were covered with masks from a variety of Earth cultures. Caty recognized the ones from Noh theatre and some others that appeared African in origin.

The colonel noticed her looking. "I collect," he said, in a slightly apologetic tone, as if hobbies were a weakness. "Please, sit over here. I've got some Europan wine. Their grapes aren't quite up to Earth standard yet, but they'll do. They'll do."

Caty sat, took a sip of the wine. It was certainly better than that offered in the officers' mess.

"I thought we'd be more comfortable here," the colonel said. "No recording devices. And the place is swept regularly to make sure no one else is listening."

Caty nodded. Even if he were telling the truth, it didn't matter. She wasn't dumb enough to say anything to a superior officer that she wasn't willing to have on the record.

"It was a terrible thing, that riot in Demeter. We've done some digging into it. Scan was hacked, of course. And the com glitches turned out to be a nasty little worm. The explosion and gunfire were just playback devices built into com after the worm opened the door. You probably heard about all that."

"Yes, sir," she said. "Though I haven't heard who did the hacking."

"Neither have I. If Intel has figured it out, they aren't telling me."

Caty assumed he was lying.

"I've read your report. The second one. The one addressed to the Marine Commandant."

Caty stiffened. Her wine glass wobbled, but she managed not to spill anything.

"It's all right, Captain. I understand why you tried to go around me. You must have assumed that I knew the facts and was doing nothing. No hard feelings."

She didn't really believe that either, but it sounded sincere. "I should have copied you on that, sir." She set her glass on the table between them.

"Well, it would have made things a little easier when the Commandant asked me about it, but no harm done. He sent it back to me."

Caty looked at him. He hadn't said "sent me a copy;" he'd said "sent it back to me."

"The brass want to keep this whole thing on Ceres, Captain."

She'd never heard a colonel refer to "the brass" before. "I guess that's why I haven't seen anything about it on any of the newservs."

He nodded. "And you won't. Unless you're planning to send your report to them."

Caty was glad her wine was sitting on the table. She

was pretty sure she'd have spilled it if she'd been holding the glass. "And why would I do that, sir?" The calmness of her voice amazed her.

"Because you're not going to be happy with what I'm going to do with it."

"Which is?"

"Nothing."

There was a hint of disgust in his voice that surprised Caty. She looked at him. He was grimacing.

"Someone set this up, Sanjuro. Someone who wanted to make very sure that not only did the rebellion fail but also that no one would start another one for a hundred years. And they succeeded. A massacre . . ."

Caty winced at the word.

"A massacre like that early in the war would have given the rebels more to fight for. At this point, though, it just drives a stake through their hearts."

She nodded.

"I don't know who set it up. I wasn't party to it. You may not believe that, but it's true. I'd like to think no one military was, that it was an outside deal, but the fact that the army set inexperienced people down in a situation that called for real pros makes me think someone was bought off somewhere. I'm pretty sure there were even plants among the Ceresians to set off the riots." He finished his glass of wine, poured another. "But I have nothing resembling proof of anything, and the resources that should be able to give me proof aren't cooperating."

This time he refilled Caty's glass to cover his pause.

"Your report's been purged from the system, Captain. Not just deleted—purged. Except for the copy that I'm sure you've kept. And you'd be wise to purge that one, too."

"Why, sir?"

"Because all you've got are allegations. You can't prove any of what happened."

"I can prove that people died, sir."

"Yes, but you can't show who set them up. Maybe you can stir up trouble and be seen as a hero. Or maybe they'll just hang the whole thing on you and shut you down. Never think they can't do that, Sanjuro. They might even use your father's death to argue that you were out to get the Ceresians."

"What?" Though it shouldn't have surprised her. So obvious—her father's death gave her a reason to hate Ceresians. The fact that the person she hated was the bakatare colonel who gave her father stupid orders wouldn't make sense to anyone except a few sergeants. And no one would understand the sympathy her father had with the rebels. It hadn't kept him from doing his job—from dying because he was doing his job—but a man like Jake Horner who knew how many opportunities he'd missed in life because his genes weren't quite good enough couldn't help feeling sorry for the workers who were stuck on Ceres. And that was just all too complicated for most people.

"Whatever happens, odds are the real guilty parties will never be found."

"Are you ordering me not to talk to the newservs, sir?"

He smiled. "No. If I did, you'd probably call them up just to spite me. I'm trying to explain to you that it won't make any difference. It might just be news for awhile and then blow over. Worst case, they'll need a scapegoat. And that scapegoat will be me, or you, or, just possibly, the army captain who was running those incompetent MPs. But it won't be whoever actually pulled this off."

Caty nodded. She got up to leave.

He held out his hand and she shook it.

Prof. Andrea Bogdosian replied promptly to Caty's message.

"Captain Sanjuro: I am sorry to hear that the Marine Corps refuses to allow you to attend graduate school as part of your military duty. However, we are very impressed with your credentials and would still like to have you in the program. So long as you are leaving the military on good terms, I am sure we can find a fellowship to support you during your studies."

She looked at the words: "So long as you are leaving the military on good terms." She wondered what Bogdosian had heard. The professor was reputed to have major connections throughout the System. Or maybe she was just guessing, based on Caty's sudden request for a fellowship following close on the heels of a messy war.

Caty hadn't actually asked the Corps about graduate school. She'd decided to resign to give herself the option of blowing the whistle. The hell of it was, the Marine Corps would probably be willing to send her to school at this point; she was pretty sure the colonel would recommend it if she asked. He'd know it meant she wasn't going to tell the newservs anything. But she obviously couldn't tell them anything if she wanted Bogdosian's fellowship, either.

And what good would it do to tell the newservs? They probably wouldn't have any more luck at digging out the whole truth than she had. She'd tried—she knew people in Intel, had friends who were better hackers than she. Everything had come up empty. The colonel was probably right: If she did go public, someone would be made a scapegoat. But the truth would stay hidden.

She wrote Bogdosian back, assuring her that she was leaving the Marines on good terms, with a recent promotion. Then she carefully composed her letter of resignation. Her reenlistment date was coming up; she doubted they'd hold her to the absolute minute of it. If she wasn't talking, she didn't have to leave, of course. But maybe if she put some distance between herself and the military, she'd be able to forget about all those dead people lying on the ground in Governor's Circle.

As soon as she finished she went next door and woke up Elizando. "Hey, Glory. Let's hop the elevator down to Demeter and get drunk."

THE LAST BACKYARD DEFENDER

J. Steven York

A cold wind whistled across the big, backyard, and Backyard Joe huddled in the trench, feeling every year of his age, feeling every popped rivet and stress crack in his tired, plastic body. The enemy was out there somewhere, waiting to finish them off. He just knew it.

He tried to tighten the broken chinstrap on his helmet, and popped his head over the top of the berm like a prairie dog looking for coyotes. He ducked back down and reviewed the scene, burned into his mind like a Polaroid picture. It was the same scene as always: tall grass, old snow tires, the empty doghouse, paint peeling, an overturned lawn chair, the rusted swing set, older than he was and even more neglected. Nobody came to the backyard any more. Nobody here but Joe and memories.

Still, the enemy was out there, even if he couldn't see them. He tugged nervously at his own dog tags. "We need reinforcements," he said to the wind.

"There aren't any coming," said the Limey. "We're all that's left."

His eyes moved to see the Limey, sitting in the bottom of the trench next to him. *That's right,* he silently corrected himself. *Nobody here but me, and memories, and the Limey.*

The Limey was a relative newcomer, though he was a seasoned soldier too. He and Joe were distant relatives.

Joe had seen pictures of the Limey in his younger days, and they could have been brothers, but the Limey looked different now, his hair spikier, his chin more pronounced.

"I've changed with the times," he'd once told Joe. "You should too."

To hell with change. The others in his platoon had changed, for all the good it had done them. They were long gone now. Only Joe remained. He'd defended this backyard through generations of children, and he wasn't about to stop now that they were gone.

The Limey looked at him, his eyes dead. "Why do you do this? The kids have stopped coming. You're all that's left. There's nothing left to defend."

"You," said Joe. "You're here."

"If you say so," said the Limey, his voice skeptical.

"Besides," said Joe, "what else would I do? I'm a soldier, through and through." He clutched his M-1 rifle, one end of the sling detached, the barrel missing, and shouldered it defiantly. "The enemy may take this yard, but I'll make them pay for every blade of grass."

"You could Go On," said the Limey.

"That's sissy-talk! There's no paradise waiting when we Go On, soldier! All that talk of museums, glass shelves and track lighting is just superstitious mumbo-jumbo! All that's waiting for us on the other side are thrift stores and landfills. I'm not ready for oblivion, soldier, are you?"

The Limey said nothing. He just sat there, and something about it made the elastic bands deep in Joe's stomach tie themselves into knots.

He snorted in disgust and limped down the length of the trench, hobbled by his long-missing right boot. He mentally inventoried his meager gear: the green ammo box with the missing lid, sleeping bag with the busted zipper, the frayed ammo belt, the machine gun with the broken tripod, the canteen with no cover, the tent without pegs or poles.

It wasn't much, but it would have to do. There was a time when he could count on a resupply drop every

Christmas and birthday, but that was long ago. "What happened?" It was a rhetorical question.

"You know what happened," said the Limey, bitterly. "They don't need our kind any more."

Joe angrily slammed his hand against the packed earth of the trench wall. "Shut up! That's not true! They need us! They need us more than they ever did, even if they don't know it!"

"Maybe," said the Limey, "the world has passed us by. They say we were warmongers."

"We keep the peace. Can't they see that? We're here to keep the peace."

"Peace through strength, Joe?"

"That's right."

"If you say so."

The Limey could be a bastard sometimes.

Night fell fast and hard, crushed-ice stars floating in a black-coffee sky. The wind cut through the broken zipper of Joe's sleeping bag, and his exposed foot was numb from the cold. As he huddled there, he could feel his rivets rusting in the damp air. If was hard to tell waking from sleep. They were both dark, cold, and painful.

"They aren't coming," said the Limey's voice, coming somewhere out of the shadows.

Why wouldn't the damned Limey sleep? Joe knew he was jealous of the sleeping bag, but he shouldn't have lost his, along with the rest of his gear, that last summer of play.

"Shut up. I don't care about reinforcements. I don't care about supply. We don't need them. We'll hold the yard with what we've got."

"I'm not talking about reinforcements," said the Limey, his voice cold as death. "I'm talking about the enemy."

"Bull!"

"They've won already. They don't need the yard, Joe. They never needed the yard. They don't care, and they aren't coming."

"Bull and double bull! Shut up and sleep."

Maybe the Limey did finally fall asleep, or maybe Joe did. All Joe knew was that he found himself transported back to the golden light of that first, glorious, year, so long ago.

He hadn't been alone then. There were whole platoons of troops, uniforms clean and crisp from the box, standing proud, dogtags gleaming in the sun. There had been the home team, of course, but allies came to the big backyard from all across the neighborhood, to pitch their tents, dig their foxholes, and set up their camouflage nets.

There had been no shortage of equipment or supplies back in those days. Jeeps and armored cars patrolled the sandbox, helicopters kept watch on the perimeter fence, and jet airplanes taxied the patio runway, ever vigilant for attack. He even remembered that summer, not long after, when he'd patrolled the depths of the inflatable pool in his midget submarine! Great days!

But there had been darkness too. Life in the yard was hard and dangerous. There were wounded. There were casualties. It didn't matter. They lived for the danger, because they knew that some of their number would always live to fight another day.

Then there were the hardest times of all. In those days, the backyard patrol really knew only three great enemies: firecrackers, pellet guns, and puberty. There had been many losses, all the more painful considering the source of attack. "They're growing up," Joe had once said as they sat mourning their fellow soldiers. "They're moving on."

As for Joe, he had always escaped those dark days. Oh, yes, many times he had been redeployed to the basement, or the garage, or the closet, but every time, sooner or later, the dusty box would open, and he would return to the big backyard, to serve another commander.

Never again would his uniform be as crisp, his joints as tight, his plastic as shiny, his painted hair as unscratched, as that first, golden day. But as he emerged from the box and returned to the backyard, it was like being reborn, like rolling off the assembly line a new soldier.

Then the day had come when the yard fell quiet, and Joe was left behind to fend for himself. Alone . . .

The golden light was gone. The warmth was gone. He shivered in the darkness. "Why me?" His voice scratched and gurgled in his chest like an old record. "Why wasn't I taken?" Better to be blown apart by your own than to go on like this.

He rolled over and looked out of the trench at the dim swath of sky. Fog had rolled in, and even the stars were gone, replaced by a glow perceptible against the wall of the trench, mainly as a lighter shade of black.

Then, suddenly, there was a flash of light, of color, so brief, that he wondered if he'd just imagined it. He waited.

"What was that?"

The Limey had seen it too!

"The enemy," he said, his voice stronger now. "I told you, they're out there."

Another flash, red and blue and green, and there was a sound this time, a garbled crackle that turned into a crack, like the report of a rifle, followed by garbled fragments of recorded voices.

"I told you, damn it! They're out there!"

Things moved in the darkness: a rustling in the grass, the slick slide of plastic against plastic, the slithering of wires against wires. More crackling and flashing of lights beyond the high grass. "They're massing out there," Joe said grimly. "They're finally going to show themselves. They're going to attack."

The Limey didn't respond. In the occasional flashes of light, Joe could see his silhouette as he sat with his back against the trench wall.

He put on his helmet, grabbed his gun, and peered over the edge of the trench. He could hear garbled bits of voices, the sounds of strange and unimaginable weapons cocking, loading, and charging to fire. He shuddered. These were the things that had taken their backyard companions away. Things from another age. Things with wires and circuits and chips, machines, designed by machines, built by machines. They didn't play. They simulated. They interfaced. They interacted. But they didn't play.

Joe had been built on an assembly line by countless skilled workers, his face and hair painted by hand. "There's more to me," he whispered, "than plastic and metal." He was certain of it now.

He thought again about the others, the talk of "Going On." Deep in his knotted gut, part of him hoped it was true. He might find out very soon. He looked down at the Limey. "I've got a bad feeling about this."

The Limey was silent for a time. Finally he said, "maybe they'll wait, attack at dawn."

Joe shook his head. "I don't think so. I think I understand now. The enemy doesn't like the light. It lives inside, with the heating and the air conditioning and a roof to keep it dry. That's our advantage. We've lived out here a long time. We're toughened by it. If we can hold them off to dawn, we might have a chance." He looked to the east and thought he could detect just the slightest brightness in the sky there. Or perhaps, like hope, it could just be a figment of his imagination.

"We've got to face this thing, Limey."

"Stop calling me that. I hate it."

"You're British."

"We're practically brothers."

Joe nodded. "You're right. You're right. We're not British or American or made-in-China. We're citizens of the Big Backyard, both of us."

"Remember that," he said, "that we were brothers. All of us in the Big Backyard were brothers."

Joe thought his companion sounded morose. Then he remembered something.

"I know what will make you feel better. I know just what you need!" He took off up the trench and pulled out the old tent, removing something hidden rolled up inside. It was the Limey's rifle. It was dirty, the barrel was broken off like his, and the trigger guard and sling were missing, but it was still there. He brought it back and held it out.

The Limey—the Brit—his *friend,* did not take it. Joe knelt down next to him.

"Look, I know you're afraid. I'm afraid too." He paused, trying to find the words, trying to untangle the knots in his belly. "I know you think I'm the old veteran. I've been in the Big Backyard longer than anybody. But the truth—the truth is—I've never seen combat. Never. People say we were violent. People say we were war toys. Maybe some of the later recruits were. But back in the days, the golden days, there was no fighting.

"We pitched our tents, dug our foxholes, went on patrols, practiced our marching and maintained our vigilance. But we never saw the enemy. Never even knew for sure that there was one. Never fired a shot in anger." He looked up at the edge of the trench. The lights seemed closer, brighter, now. "So I'm afraid, yeah. But I know what we stand for, and I'm not about to give up without a fight. So take this gun, and give me a hand."

"I can't." It was a simple statement of fact, his voice sad. "I can't."

"Yes, you *can.* Get on your feet, soldier!"

"What's the point?"

"The point is—" He struggled for the words. Dawn was a long way away. Too far. "The point is to go out with honor." He looked down. "I can't do this without you."

"Yes, you can, Joe. You know you can. You know you *have* to."

He could hear them now. Moving closer. He held out the gun with more urgency. "Come on, soldier."

Silence but for the cold sounds of the approaching machines.

"Pal. Come on. This isn't funny."

"Goodbye, Joe." The voice seemed to come from far away, and long ago.

The light grew brighter, seemed to fill the trench like rainwater. He looked down at the Limey, saw the cracked BB holes in his chest, the burn marks across his face, the scorched powder burns across his belly where his legs and torso had been blown away. He remembered now. The Limey had been gone a very, very long time.

He had to do this alone. He was the last defender of the Big Backyard. He had to, and he would. Yet he wasn't alone. All of them were there now, all the citizens of the Big Backyard—his brothers. They were there, in spirit if not in body. He had never truly been alone.

He picked up a rifle in each hand, and with a final battle cry, he charged over the edge of the trench.

They outnumbered him a thousand to one, stone-cold killers all, made of pixels and bits, armed with their rocket launchers and their BFGs, their lasers and their needlers. But Joe had a pair of broken, plastic M-1 rifles and the remembered dreams and aspirations of a thousand little boys on his side.

He waded into them, sending digital bodies flying left and right. On and on he fought, new opponents spawning just as fast as he could take them down. But on he fought against the sterile darkness that seemed never to end. His time might be over, but this day, this last day, would be his.

And the light came, the sun creeping toward the horizon, and for a moment, a precious moment, he thought he might prevail.

Then he felt the pain as something old and worn snapped inside, and his tired body went limp. No enemy had felled him though.

No enemy but time.

He lay there, and it seemed only a moment, but the enemy was gone, and the sun was high in the sky, and the wind was blowing clouds of dust across the Big Backyard.

Somehow he knew they were coming for him.

Evac needed! Dust off! Dust off!

And a small boy's hand lifted him up toward the waiting sky.

AUTHOR NOTES

Kristine Kathryn Rusch is a bestselling, award-winning writer. Her work has won awards in a variety of languages. Most recently, her novella, "Diving into the Wreck" (*Asimov's*, December 2005) won the prestigious UPC award given in Spain. Her latest novel is *Paloma: A Retrieval Artist Novel*.

Dave Freer spent two years as a conscripted soldier, long ago and far away. He trained as a fisheries scientist and, among other things managed several fish farms. Now he is a full-time writer, author or coauthor of ten novels, including *Rats Bats & Vats* (no. 7 on the Locus ranking) and *Pyramid Scheme* (no. 3 on Locus), both with Eric Flint, and the successful *Heirs Of Alexandra* series with Mercedes Lackey and Eric Flint. His last solo novel, *A Mankind Witch*, was star rated (meaning they considered it a book of outstanding quality). Freer has written a growing body of shorter fiction, too, all of which is designed to avoid him wasting time rock climbing or diving for spiny lobsters. He lives near Mooi River, South Africa, with his wife, sons, and various dogs and cats somewhere close to middle of nowhere. He likes it there.

Christina F. York is either a romance writer who does science fiction or a science fiction writer who does romance, depending on who you talk to. Either way, she finds it difficult to color within the lines. Her first work was self-published at ten. Finding she wasn't a publisher, she retired to complete grammar school. After college, marriage, two kids, divorce, and another marriage, she returned to writing, with the encouragement of her husband, writer J. Steven York. Since then she has sold nonfiction, short stories, and novels and has worked as a technical writer. Her latest novel, *Alias: A Touch Of Death* was released in late 2006. A native of Oregon, Chris has always lived on the West Coast. The Yorks now live on the Oregon Coast, where Chris has a view of the ocean from her office window. She and her husband split their time between solo and collaborative work and serving their two feline masters.

K.D. Wentworth has sold more than seventy pieces of short fiction to such markets as *FASF, Hitchcock's, Realms of Fantasy, Weird Tales,* and *Return to the Twilight Zone.* A three-time Nebula Finalist for Short Fiction, she has seven novels in print, the most recent being *Stars/Over/Stars* and *The Course of Empire,* both from Baen. She lives in Tulsa with her husband and a combined total of one hundred sixty pounds of dog (Akita + Siberian Husky) and is working on several new novels with Eric Flint. She also serves as Coordinating Judge for the L. Ron Hubbard Writers of the Future Contest. Her website is at: www.kdwentworth.com

Diane A.S. Stuckart is a member of that proud breed, the native Texan. Born in the West Texas town of Lubbock and raised in Dallas, she crossed the Red River just long enough to obtain her degree in Journalism from the University of Oklahoma before returning home to the Lone Star State. She's the author of several pieces of fantasy and mystery short fiction written under her own name. Writing as Alexa Smart and Anna Gerard, she also has published five critically acclaimed historical romance novels, the first of which was a Romance Writers of America Golden Heart award finalist. Though she will never forget her western roots, Diane recently moved to the West Palm Beach area of Florida, where she is finding new sources of inspiration among the alligators and palm trees.

Laura Resnick is the author of such fantasy novels as *Disappearing Nightly*, *In Legend Born*, *The Destroyer Goddess*, and *The White Dragon*, which made the "Year's Best" lists of *Publishers Weekly* and *Voya*. Winner of the 1993 Campbell Award for best new science fiction and fantasy writer, she has published more than fifty short stories. You can find her on the Web at www.LauraResnick.com.

Cynthia Ward was born in Oklahoma and lived in Maine, Spain, Germany, and the San Francisco Bay Area before moving to Seattle. She has published stories in *Asimov's SF Magazine*, *Bending the Landscape*, and other anthologies and magazines and has written articles and reviews for *Amazon.com*, *Locus Online*, and other webzines and magazines. Her market news columns appear in *Speculations: The Magazine for Writers Who Want to Be Read* (*http://www.speculations.com*) and *The SFWA Bulletin* (*http:/ww.sfwa.org/bulletin/*). With Nisi Shawl, she has written the nonfiction guidebook *Writing the Other: A Practical Approach*, which is the companion volume to their critically acclaimed fiction workshop, *Writing the Other: Bridging Cultural Differences for Successful Fiction*. Cynthia is completing her first novel, a romantic SF mystery tentatively titled *The Killing Moon*. Her website is at *www.cynthiaward.com*.

Jean Rabe is the author of eighteen fantasy novels and more than three dozen short stories. An avid, but truly lousy gardener, she tends lots of tomato plants so her dogs can graze in the late summer months. In her spare time (which she seems to have less of each week), she enjoys role-playing, board, and war games; visiting museums; and riding in the convertible with the top down and the stereo cranked up. Visit her web site at www.jeanrabe.com

Josepha Sherman is a fantasy novelist and folklorist, whose latest titles include *Son of Darkness* (Roc Books), *The Captive Soul* (Warner Aspect), *Xena: All I Need to Know I Learned from the Warrior Princess, by Gabrielle*, as Translated by Josepha Sherman (Pocket Books), the folklore title *Merlin's Kin* (August House), and, together with Susan Shwartz, two Star Trek novels, *Vulcan's Forge* and *Vulcan's Heart*. She is the owner of Sherman Editorial Services, www.shermaneditorial.biz. She is also a fan of the New York Mets, horses, aviation, and space science. Visit her at www.sff.net/people/Josepha.Sherman.

Donald J. Bingle is an oft-published writer in the science fiction, fantasy, horror, and comedy genres. His battle-action oriented works include his novel *Forced Conversion* (a science fiction tale about a military force whose task it is to locate and convert the last humans remaining on a largely depopulated earth) and stories in the anthologies *Civil War Fantastic*, *The Search for Magic* (a Dragonlance anthology), *Transformer's Legends*, and *Fantasy Gone Wrong*, as well as a story about battling mechs published in *MechForce Quarterly* and the definitive history of the *Battle of the Bones* (in the Forgotten Realms). His latest novel, *Greensword* (January 2009) is a darkly comedic eco-thriller. He can be reached through his website at www.orphyte.com/donaldjbingle.

Jody Lynn Nye lists her main career activity as "spoiling cats." She lives northwest of Chicago with two of the above and her husband, author and packager Bill Fawcett. She has published thirty books, including six contemporary fantasies, four SF novels, four novels in collaboration with Anne McCaffrey, including *The Ship Who Won*; edited a humorous anthology about mothers, *Don't Forget Your Spacesuit, Dear!;* and written more than eighty short stories. Her latest books are *The Lady and The Tiger*, third in her Taylor's Ark series, *Strong Arm Tactics*, first in the Wolfe Pack series (Meisha Merlin Publishing), and *Class Dis-Mythed*, cowritten with Robert Asprin.

Meredith Simmons is an escaped English teacher who now sells real estate to support her ink-cartridge-and-paper habit. She long ago discovered that it was easier to sell houses than grammar. Her stories have appeared in such diverse venues as *Asimov's Science Fiction*, *Paradox*, and *The Rocking Chair Reader*. Meredith's first published story was the grand prize winner for *Writers of the Future XVII*. She's now attempting to write novels and has discovered they're very different from long short stories. She lives in North Carolina with her husband Bob. They have one terrific son and two fantastic grandsons.

Jim Fiscus is a Portland, Oregon, writer and historian. His first fiction sale was a story using SF to explain the theological basis of the present regime in Iran. That story let him make practical use of his master's degree in Middle East and Asian History and his experience teaching military history. He has also used history when writing alternate history, science fiction and fantasy stories, and this story. He spent a numbers of years as a medical writer and has recently returned to writing nonfiction history. He has written books for high school and middle school students on the 1956 Suez Crisis, war in Afghanistan, America's war in Iraq, and—for a change of pace—the movie monster King Kong. He also edited a nonfiction anthology of readings about World War II.

Dean Wesley Smith is the bestselling author of over eighty novels under various names. He has published more than a hundred short stories and has been nominated for just about every award in science fiction and fantasy and horror, and he even won a few of them. He is the former editor and publisher of Pulphouse Publishing. His most recent novel in science fiction is *All Eve's Hallows*. He is currently writing thrillers under another name.

M. Turville Heitz is a freelance writer and editor, organic farmer and apparently perpetual college student. Her short fiction has received regional recognition and has appeared in a variety of venues including *Interzone, Pan Gaia,* and in the anthologies *Blood Muse and Wizard Fantastic.* She lives in Wisconsin with her son and an ever-expanding collection of pets and farm animals.

Lisa Silverthorne has published over fifty short stories. She dreams of becoming a novelist and writes to discover the magic in ordinary things. Her first short fiction collection, *The Sound of Angels*, is available from Wildside Press. You can visit Lisa's website at: www.drewes.org/

Peter Orullian has recently been published in other fine DAW anthologies as well as in *Orson Scott Card's Intergalactic Medicine Show.* For grocery money, he works at Microsoft in the Xbox division. And while he desperately hopes to make a living writing, his abiding passion is music; Peter recently returned from a European tour with a successful hard rock band. He has a New York agent currently shopping one of his novels, which he hopes will allow him to retire from Microsoft and sing and write until everything bleeds.

M. M. Hall frequently contributes to *Publisher's Weekly*, and her critical essays are included in the *World Encyclopedia of Supernatural Literature* edited by S.T. Joshi and Stefan Dziemianowicz (Greenwood) and *Icons of Horror & the Supernatural* edited by S.T. Joshi (Greenwood). She's published numerous short stories in various anthologies, most recently in *Retro Pulp Tales*, edited by Joe. R. Lansdale (Subterranean Press), and *Cross Plains Universe*, edited by Scott Cupp and Joe R. Lansdale (monkeybrain books), and in other print and online magazines such as *Realms of Fantasy*. She edited and contributed to *Wild Women* and just completed a new dark fantasy novel.

Janet Berliner is the author of six novels, including the Bram Stoker award-winning *Children of the Dusk* and the four-way collaboration *Artifact* (with Kevin J. Anderson, Matthew J. Costello and F. Paul Wilson), as well as over a hundred short stories. She has also edited six anthologies, including two with illusionist David Copperfield and one with Joyce Carol Oates. She is a former president of the Horror Writers Association and a member of the Council of the National Writers Association. For further information, please visit www.janetberliner.com/

Jack Kirby is one of the giants of the comic book industry. He is credited with illustrating over 24,000 pages of comics. He created and/or drew Captain America, The Green Arrow, Skymasters, The Fantastic Four, Spider-Man, Thor, the Hulk, Ant-Man, Nick Fury, Iron man, the X-Men, Silver Surfer, and the Avengers, as well as the villains who fought them.

Nancy Jane Moore's novella *Changeling* is one of the volumes in the Conversation Pieces series from Aqueduct Press. Much of her work can be found in anthologies, including *Talking Back, Polyphony 5, Future Washington, Imaginings,* and *Imagination Fully Dilated: Science Fiction.* Her short fiction has also appeared in magazines ranging from the *National Law Journal* to *Lady Churchill's Rosebud Wristlet* to *Andromeda Spaceways Inflight Magazine.* In January 2006, she spoke at the Library of Congress on "The Resurgence of Feminist Science Fiction." In addition to writing, Moore trains in and teaches the martial art of Aikido. She blogs on In This Moment (hopeandpolitics.blogspot.com). Her website is home.earthlink.net/~nancyjane.

J. Steven York is the author of roughly a dozen novels and many short-stories that have appeared in various anthologies and magazines. An avid collector of toys, he and his wife, fellow author Christina F. York. each year fill their VW Beetle to the roof with toys and donate them to launch their local holiday toy drive. He also produces a weekly web comic called "Minions at Work," photo-illustrated using action figures. He and Chris live on the Oregon coast and maintain a shared web site at www.yorkwriters.com.

Tanya Huff

The Confederation Novels

Tanya Huff

Tony Foster—familiar to Tanya Huff fans from her
Blood series—has relocated to Vancouver with Henry
Fitzroy, vampire son of Henry VIII. Tony landed a
job as a production assistant at CB Productions, iron-
ically working on a syndicated TV series, "Darkest
Night," about a vampire detective. Tony was pretty
content with his new life—until wizards, demons, and
haunted houses became more than just episodes on
his TV series...

"An exciting, creepy adventure"—*Booklist*

SMOKE AND SHADOWS
0-7564-0263-8 $6.99
SMOKE AND MIRRORS
0-7564-0348-0 $7.99
SMOKE AND ASHES
0-7564-0415-4 $7.99

To Order Call: 1-800-788-6262
www.dawbooks.com

S.L. Farrell

The Cloudmages

"Besides great, fast-paced fun, full of politicking and betrayal, Farrell's tale is a tragic love story with a surprisingly satisfying ending."
—*Booklist*

"Richly imagined fantasy... Intriguing, fully developed characters abound. This entry can only enhance Farrell's reputation as one of the rising stars of Celtic fantasy."
—*Publishers Weekly*

HOLDER OF LIGHTNING
0-7564-0152-6

MAGE OF CLOUDS
0-7564-0255-7

HEIR OF STONE
0-7564-0321-9

To Order Call: 1-800-788-6262
www.dawboks.com

DAW 71

CJ Cherryh
The Foreigner Novels

FOREIGNER	*0-88677-637-6*
INVADER	*0-88677-687-2*
INHERITOR	*0-88677-728-3*
PRECURSOR	*0-88677-910-3*
DEFENDER	*0-7564-0020-1*
EXPLORER	*0-7564-0165-8*
DESTROYER	*0-7564-0333-2*
PRETENDER	*0-7564-0408-6*
DELIVERER	*0-7564-0414-7*

To Order Call: 1-800-788-6262

www.dawbooks.com

DAW 8

The Novels of
Tad Williams

To Order Call: 1-800-788-6262
www.dawbooks.com

DAW 102